SHADOW MAN

MARGARET KIRK

First published in Great Britain in 2017
by Orion Books,
an imprint of The Orion Publishing Group Ltd
Carmelite House, 50 Victoria Embankment,
London EC4Y 0DZ

An Hachette UK company

1 3 5 7 9 10 8 6 4 2

A CIP catalogue record for this book
is available from the British Library.

ISBN (Trade Paperback) 978 1 4091 6550 7

Typeset by Input Data Services Ltd, Somerset

Printed and bound by CPI Group (UK) Ltd, Croydon, CR0 4YY

www.orionbooks.co.uk

To Martin, who believed

1994

By midnight, there are bodies everywhere. Her tiny flat is crammed to bursting, but people are still stumbling through the door, waving packs of Stella or Strongbow and wrapping her in cheerful beery hugs.

She doesn't remember inviting them all – doesn't recognise half of them, when she stops to think about it – but so what? For the last four years, she's been juggling coursework with her shifts at the all-night garage, slogging away at her degree while it felt like the rest of the world was out getting laid, or legless. Or both.

Doing it her way, she'd told her parents. Standing on her own two feet, and they couldn't argue with that, could they? Even if Mum had thrown a massive wobbly at the thought of her baby girl rejecting St Andrews and choosing to study at Glasgow.

But with her finals out of the way, she's officially an ex-student. So tonight, it's party time – shedloads of booze, the flat decked out with tea lights and a joke seventies glitter-ball, and all her mates from uni, ready to make a night of it.

Not all of them, though, a snide little voice reminds her. *Things*

1

didn't exactly go to plan there, did they? She shakes her head, swallowing the tightness in her throat . . . and suddenly he's there, watching her from the doorway.

The room's too dark, too smoky for her to see more than his outline, but she knows it's him. Who else could it be? She starts to wave him over, and he steps into the light . . . and it isn't him after all, just some boy she vaguely knows from class.

She drags her hand down, but he's already seen her. He breaks into a grin and starts to push his way towards her – Christ, surely he can't think she'd been waiting for *him*? She spots some girls she knows over to his right and heads straight for them, as though that's what she'd been going to do all along. When she looks back over her shoulder, he's gone.

She squeezes past a nest of couples snogging by the kitchen door and grabs a random can from the table. *Gary,* that was his name, she remembers. He'd given her and Morven a lift to uni when the buses were on strike, walked to the library with them a couple of times – God, but he was a twat. Still, she's ashamed of blanking him like that. But seeing him standing there, just for a moment she'd thought . . .

Someone's messing with the music. Morrissey's cut off, dispatched by the Proclaimers, and then everyone's joining in, even the close-to-comatose, doing the whole 500-mile-walking, arm-swinging thing until she feels the floor bouncing under her feet.

She shoulders her way through the sweating, heat-sticky bodies until she reaches the balcony and pulls the curtains closed, muting the sounds from inside.

Movement behind her. The curtains lifted by the breeze, she thinks at first, their extravagant lengths belling out and pooling at her feet. But no, it's more than that . . . the curtains parting and the music blaring briefly as someone slips through to stand behind her, just beyond the edges of her vision. Calling her name, but quietly, so that she has to strain to hear them.

She spins round, and her heel catches in the curtains. Her right foot slips and she stumbles sideways. Her arms flail, reaching out for something to hold on to, but the curtain is wrapping itself around her, covering her eyes and the railing is right behind her, she can feel it cold against her back – Jesus, if she falls, if she goes over . . .

Arms round her waist, peeling away the curtain, scooping her up and out of danger. Holding her gently, as though she's made of glass.

She looks up at her rescuer, and her eyes widen. Of all the people . . . she starts to ask him what the hell he's doing there, but he puts his finger to her lips, smiling as though he knows a really cool joke, one he can't wait to share with her.

He raises her higher, holding her away from his body. She shakes her head and starts to struggle – why's he mucking about like this? Can't he see how dangerous this is, how close they are to the edge . . .

He turns, still holding her, leans over the railing.

And lets her go.

1

Gatwick North Terminal

Thump.
Thump.
Thump.

Detective Inspector Lukas Mahler looks down at the object battering his left shin.

A chunky boy with a brutal haircut and the hint of a brow-ridge smirks up at him from astride a yellow and black striped suitcase with stubby feeler-like handles projecting from its front and stuck-on features. Some kids' TV character, Mahler thinks, that's what it's supposed to be. Only the eyes are peeling off and half its mouth is missing, giving the face a lopsided look that's either sad or psychopathic, depending on your point of view. Today, Mahler inclines towards the latter.

The boy is reversing, gearing up for another assault. Before he reaches ramming speed, Mahler swings his cabin bag across and dodges to the right, as far as the taped barrier will allow. He glances at the child's mother, but her eyes are glued to her mobile, pudgy thumbs flying as she carries on a life-or-death discussion by text. Consulting a child-rearing expert, he decides, fielding a further assault. That, or a pest control service.

Boarding for the Inverness flight is only thirty minutes late, but the queue has been funnelled into a narrow, glass-walled walkway and left to swelter in the midday sun like ants under a magnifying glass. Sweating gently in his dark suit, Mahler tries to ignore the twist of pain circling the base of his neck. And wonders why Dante had imagined there were only nine circles of Hell.

By the time boarding finally starts, he's wielded the cabin bag three times and his shirt is sticking to him. As soon as he's seated, he strips off his jacket and loosens his tie. He takes out his book, lets it fall open at one of his favourite passages, but the migraine is settling in now, a steady, white-hot pulse that had stalked him through the service and its aftermath. He dry-swallows a pill and leans back, waiting for the plane door to close.

Only it isn't happening. The buzz of chatter rises and falls, punctuated by the inevitable wailing baby, as the minutes pass. Then, as the flight attendant starts a rambling explanation, a woman appears in the doorway.

Head lowered, she hurries along the aisle. She isn't limping, not exactly, but there's a stiffness to her walk that marks her out as different. Mahler, who knows all about different, watches her progress.

She reaches the row opposite his and slides over to the window. He glimpses pale, sharp features, catches a muttered curse as her hands fumble with the seat belt . . . thin, jittery hands, making a pig's ear of the simple task. A nervous flyer, apparently. Perfect.

Mahler sighs, more audibly than he'd intended, and the woman turns to glare at him. At which point he abandons the book and reaches for another painkiller. He weighs the consequences of taking it now or later. He looks back at the woman and goes with now.

When the engines start up, he glances at her again. Pre-take-off weeper or belligerent, in-flight screamer? After the look she'd given him, Mahler can't quite see her as a weeper. But not a vomiter, please God, he thinks. Not today.

He wills the meds to do their stuff and closes his eyes. When he opens them again, the plane is taxiing down Inverness Airport's one and only runway. Mahler straightens his tie and watches as the passengers begin their restless, end-of-flight manoeuvring. As usual, those in the aisle seats hold all the cards – they're up and in position within seconds of the 'fasten seatbelt' signs going off, building little fortresses of luggage to guard their place in the queue. The window-seat baggers and the mid-rowers are trapped, unable to see over the wall of bodies, but tensed, like runners on starting blocks, ready to surge forward the moment the doors are open. All except the woman.

He'd expected her to scramble to her feet, ready to bolt with the herd, but she hasn't moved. Even when the exodus begins, the woman stays in her seat, pale hands clenched on her thighs, her jawline . . . oh, that jawline has nothing to do with nerves, he's suddenly sure of it. There's something driven in the sharp, travel-weary features and cool grey eyes, something that catches him in spite of himself.

He leans forward to take a closer look, and an expanse of sweatshirt-clad belly rears up in front of him, blocking his vision. By the time the man has wrestled a padded jacket the size of a small duvet from the locker above Mahler's head, the woman's seat is empty.

Mahler hoists his bag onto his shoulder and leaves by the rear steps, joining the crocodile of passengers filing into the tiny terminal. The woman is a little way in front, heading for the airport's only baggage-reclaim carousel. An ordinary woman, he decides, that's all. No reason to keep her in his eyeline. No reason her thin, pale face shouldn't blend into the sea of unmemorable others . . . no reason until the conveyor belt shudders into life, and she darts in to pick up a bag. And backs *away* from the exit that leads to the main concourse.

And there it is. Copper's gut, Raj used to call the odd, half-formed imperative he's following, and Mahler supposes it's as good a name as any. Not a thing that will let itself be named, this raw, unfocused thing, not yet. But a discoverable thing, Mahler thinks. A thing to be probed. To be *known*.

He watches her tie up her hair and stuff it under a sludge-coloured baseball cap. She's deliberately standing to one side, letting the other passengers flow towards their waiting friends and family. And then she's moving, merging with a group of earnest German tourists as they head out into the concourse.

Looking for someone? No, Mahler thinks, she's hiding. Hiding in plain sight. But why? And who from?

He ducks past the queue for the parking machines . . . and collides with Suitcase Boy's mother, who's lumbering across the concourse like a juggernaut in flowered leggings to embrace an older woman. A relative, he assumes, judging by their shared fashion sense.

By the time he's extricated himself, the woman has gone. He body-swerves Suitcase Boy, who looks to be planning another ram raid, and runs to the exit. Just in time to see the airport shuttle disappearing through the car park barrier.

'No need to rush, boss – I've got ten minutes left on the ticket.'

The words are punctuated by a crunching sound. Mahler turns to see Detective Sergeant Iain 'Fergie' Ferguson ambling towards him, clutching a family-sized bag of crisps.

'What are you doing here? I thought you were jetting off to the flesh-pots of Marbella on Tuesday?'

'Me too.' Fergie upends the bag and funnels the last pieces into his mouth. 'But Zofia and me had a wee domestic at the weekend, and there was bugger all point going on my own, so I turned in for a few extra shifts. And got told to go and get you as soon as you'd landed. Didn't you check your phone?'

'Not yet. There was a woman on the flight—'

'Oh, aye?' Fergie manages to wink and grin at the same time, giving him the look of a leering potato. 'Fit, was she?'

Mahler rolls his eyes. 'Could you get your mind out of your boxers for one second? She was . . .'

He glances at Fergie and shakes his head. Trying to avoid someone? Behaving strangely in a public place? Undoubtedly. But half the travelling public could probably put their hands up to that one. And on the spectrum of measurable oddness, Mahler knows perfectly well where most of his colleagues would place him. So he's got nothing he can offer Fergie, no rationale for her continuing presence in the forefront of his brain, unless he holds his hands up to a hunch. And he doesn't do hunches.

Oh, Raj would have gone for it, no doubt about that. Raj had believed in the whole copper's intuition, weird-feeling-in-my-water thing – he'd clung to it like an access-all-areas pass, no matter what. And look where that had got him.

'Forget it.' He switches on his mobile and scrolls through the alerts. No surprise about the first three. But the fourth? 'Any idea why I'm being summoned?'

Fergie shrugs. 'Braveheart wants you in asap, that's all I know. I was at a house-breaking in Ardersier when I got told to play taxi driver. But if you wanted to drop in on your mam first—'

Mahler shakes his head. His mother has only called three times, which means she's basically okay and her support worker has his number if anything changes. And for DCI June Wallace to call him in fresh from the airport . . . well, whatever's up, it can't be good.

'I'll look in on her after I've been to Burnett Road. Better not keep the DCI waiting.'

Fergie's ancient Audi is parked between two sleek black 4×4s, looking more like a dustbin on wheels than ever.

'Hold on a minute.' Fergie heaves open the passenger door and slides a slag heap of fast-food debris off the seat and into the footwell. 'There you go. What?'

'Nothing.' Mahler sits down, trying to ignore the sludge-like stickiness under his left thigh. He takes a couple of shallow breaths, inhaling the fags and fish supper fug that constitutes the Audi's atmosphere. And something else, something eye-wateringly ammoniac . . .

'What is making that godawful smell?'

'Weird, isn't it?' Fergie fishes out a Homer Simpson air-freshener and hangs it from the mirror. 'There, that'll sort it till I've time for a wee tidy-up.' A sideways glance at Mahler. 'Boss, I meant to say . . . I'm sorry about your pal. That was an awful thing. Awful.'

'Yes. Thank you.'

'Aye.' Fergie clears his throat. 'Aye, well. Better no' keep herself waiting, eh?' He does something unspeakable to the Audi's gears and the car lurches towards the exit.

Mahler grits his teeth as a series of clunking noises chart their progress over the speed bumps. 'Not a good idea, no. But let's see if we can make it back without being pulled over by our friends in traffic this time, shall we? And for pity's sake keep that window open.'

2

It's only eight miles from Inverness Airport to the city centre – eight deceptively rural-seeming miles, past sheep-dotted fields and dense dark woodland, thick with birch and fir. But the good weather has brought out the tourists and the A96 is at its snarled-up, caravan-congested worst. By the time Fergie pulls in to Burnett Road, it's after 3.30 p.m. and traffic is piling onto the Harbour Road round-about, the main entrance and exit to the city.

Mahler leaves Fergie mucking out the Audi and goes upstairs to find June Wallace. By rights, of course, she shouldn't still be based here. In the dying days of Northern Constabulary, before the unveiling of Police Scotland, Mahler had assumed, along with everyone else, that she would join the exodus to Perth Road's divisional HQ.

But June had never been one for living up to other people's expectations. While half the former CID were wandering round with boxes under their arms and bemused expressions, waiting to be called to the promised land, she'd quietly set up camp at Burnett Road. And made it perfectly clear she'd no intention of going anywhere.

'I like to know what's going on,' she'd told Mahler once. 'See the good folk of Inverness going about their business. And keep an eye on the others – the rapists, the wife-beaters, all the wee chancers that think they're too smart to get lifted by us, until they find out different. How could I do that stuck in an office next to bloody Tesco?'

Though a police station next to a patch of waste ground and a grey sixties college building is hardly in the thick of things, Mahler reflects. Inverness is growing away from its beginnings by the Ness, the fledgling city spreading out towards Culloden and the new university and creeping up towards the hills. Still, he knows what she means.

And even if the place sometimes reminds him of a low-rent office block, all blond sandstone and tinted glass, Burnett Road is home to the MIT, the Major Incident Team. *His* MIT, for better or worse. For now.

June is in her office. She looks up from her mobile and waves him in, but carries on talking.

'For Christ's sake, Pat, it's not rocket science. Bring the little toerag in and – what? Aye, all right. Fine.' She ends the call and screws up the note she'd been scribbling. 'Bloody waste of space.' She looks him up and down. 'Fergie got you back in one piece, then. What was the road like?'

'The usual.'

'Uh-huh.' She pushes her hair off her forehead, flashes of grey visible here and there through the faded blonde. 'Kevin Ramsay. Ring any bells?'

Mahler sorts through his mental rogues' gallery. Kevin Ramsay. Five foot nothing of attitude and breath that could fell a charging rhino. Lifted regularly for petty pilfering, drunk and disorderly and the odd common assault. So what's he done to get June's attention?

'Pretty minor league, surely? Unless he's gone upmarket.'

'Not exactly.' June opens her desk drawer, stares down at an unopened packet of Lambert & Butler, and closes it with a sigh. 'You know Andy Black used him from time to time?'

'As a CHIS?' Mahler tries and fails to imagine Kevin Ramsay as a covert human intelligence source. 'Interesting choice. Is he any good?'

'He was absolute rubbish. But on Sunday night, wee Kevin was out drinking with his pals at the Fluke. He left around eleven, saying he had run out of money, and was last seen near Fraser Park by a mannie out walking his dog.'

Mahler mentally retraces the route. 'Bit of a detour if he was going back into town, surely?'

June shrugs. 'His girlfriend lives in Hilton, so he may have been heading up to see her. Only he never got there. A lassie out for a run found him on the corner of Damfield Road around six o'clock yesterday morning. What was left of him, anyway.'

'Hit-and-run?'

'With half a dozen tyre tracks on his bum?' June shakes her head. 'He wasn't just hit once, Lukas – whoever did it went back and reversed over him. It was a bloody execution! And I want you to get the bastard responsible.'

'Me? Surely Andy Black—'

'Andy Black's off sick after doing his back in at a ceilidh.'

'An unwise "Strip the Willow"?'

June shakes her head. 'Argument with the fiddle player. His pal took offence and clouted Andy with his accordion – you'd think he'd have more sense, a man his age. Anyway, it'll only be for a few weeks. You can handle that, can't you?'

On top of the Black Isle stabbing and the half-dozen other cases she's breathing down his neck about? 'Of course. But I'll need a DS, and Fergie's pretty stretched already.'

'Karen Gilchrist's already on the case.' She gives him the kind of guileless smile Hannibal Lecter probably liked to practise in the mirror. Only with June, he suspects it comes naturally. 'Not going to have any . . . fallout . . . there, am I? After last summer?'

'Of course not, ma'am.'

'Well, then. All she needs is a good SIO to keep on top of things until Andy's back – and you're the best I have, Lukas.'

And the big boys are landing on you from a great height, he thinks. Quarterly figures due soon, big partnership meetings . . . and until Andy gets back, I'm *all* you have.

'If that's everything, ma'am?'

'Enough to be going on with, I'd have said.' Her smile fades. 'Look, I'm sorry about hauling you in straight after . . . how did it go, anyway? He was a good pal, wasn't he?'

The squat, utilitarian lines of the crematorium. The brass, conspicuous by their absence. And Claire shrunk to nothing, as though something was consuming her from within. Raj was my age, he thinks. With a two-year-old. Take a bloody guess.

'Fine,' Mahler tells her. 'It went fine.'

3

'Ms Murray?'

Anna opens an eye. The barman – bar *boy*, she amends, considering he looks about twelve – is hovering by her elbow with a bowl of soup and plate of oatcakes. She doesn't remember ordering anything apart from a glass of wine, but now that it's in front of her she realises she hasn't eaten since leaving San Diego. She sits up straighter in the high-backed leather armchair, hopes to God she hasn't actually been drooling, and finds a smile from somewhere. 'Thanks.'

He blushes, turns away, and turns back. 'I was wondering . . . you're Morven Murray's sister, right?'

She manages to hold the smile. Just. 'If it's an autograph you're after—'

The blush spreads. He stammers through an explanation about how much his mother loved Morven, how meeting her idol would really make her day. Anna keeps the smile in place as she scribbles

15

down his contact details and promises to see what she can do.

She's given up trying to warn people that what they see on screen isn't quite the real Morven. The blonde earth-goddess persona her sister has created is just too convincing for that to be believable. Before they meet her, at least.

As if on cue, her phone vibrates – Morven, checking to see she hasn't fled the country, no doubt, after their not-so-fond reunion at their parents' house. Anna switches it to silent, but it's still vibrating, so she stuffs it into her holdall. And, not for the first time, wonders what on earth she's doing here.

Going back for Morven's wedding, she'd told her friends, as though it was no big deal. As though she hadn't invested years in keeping her past and present five thousand miles apart. And it had worked, hadn't it? She's proud of the career she's built in UCSD's European history department, proud of the way she's adapted to the city's easy-going, small-town lifestyle. After ten years, she can't imagine living anywhere else.

She sticks the spoon into her soup and swirls it round a couple of times. Leek and potato, she decides, examining the floating lumps . . . Christ, she must be jet-lagged. She pushes it away untouched and angles her chair round to look out of the window.

The weather is doing its usual Highland trick of changing two or three times in the course of a few hours. The sun has disappeared now and grey rain-clouds are scudding across the darkening sky. But she certainly can't fault the choice of venue. Bunchrew House is small but startlingly pretty, like a French chateau in miniature, right on the southern shore of the Beauly Firth. Perfect for the wedding pictures, that view. Whoever Morven's sold them to.

She thinks about another glass of wine – after this morning's slanging match with Morven, more wine sounds like an excellent way to pass the time until her hotel room's ready – but lack of food and sleep are starting to catch up with her and there's a man standing on the terrace, looking out at the firth. His collar is turned up against the wind and she can't see his face clearly, but he looks a

16

hell of a lot like Morven's tame journo, the one she'd evaded at the airport.

She pushes back her chair and stands up, as the man turns to come inside. And his mouth falls in a wide, cartoonish 'O'.

'Anna?' The look of shock morphing into a disbelieving grin as he walks towards her. 'My God, is that you?'

A tall man, powerfully built but not in-your-face musclebound. Dark hair curling over his collar, and a slightly crooked nose – an old break, maybe? Something familiar about him, definitely.

She's still trying to place him when the espresso machine behind her gives a sudden hiss. He half-turns at the unexpected noise. And she can't believe she didn't recognise him at once.

'Jamie?' He's lost weight since their time at university, at least a couple of stones, and ditched the heavy glasses that made him look like a fifties newsreader. But it *is* him, she's sure of it. 'Jamie Gordon! What are you doing here?'

'Same as you, guest at the wedding of the year.' He produces an envelope from his pocket. 'Came to drop this off for Morven, but looks like she's not around.'

'I didn't know you'd kept in touch.'

He shakes his head. 'I hadn't. When she emailed out of the blue, I was in two minds at first. But I was going to be up here anyway, so I thought, why not? Wasn't expecting you to come over, though.'

'She's my sister.' Ice touching her spine and sharpening her voice. She picks up the wine she'd ordered earlier and drains it.

'I know. It's just . . . you weren't exactly close at uni, were you?'

'Uni was ages ago, Jamie. All water under the bridge.'

'If you say so.' He flicks through the drinks menu. 'Anyone else from back in the day get an invite, do you think?'

'Only the "A" list ones, like you.'

He rolls his eyes. 'A couple of moderately successful historical novels doth not a celeb make. Have you seen Morven yet?'

'We spoke at Mam and Dad's. Briefly.'

Dad a little thinner, a little frailer than before. Mam fussing with the tea things, casting brief bitter glances at Anna's now-ringless left hand – it's over a year since the break-up, but her mother's still mourning the charismatic, successful son-in-law she'd so nearly acquired. Then there was Morven, spilling out of an airport minicab, wearing her Homicidal Barbie look.

'Though she'd ditched the stylist and photographer by then, thank God. I sneaked out the back and legged it into town.'

Jamie raises an eyebrow. 'That good, huh? You could just have stayed away, you know.'

'Not that simple. I don't come back often enough as it is. And when I do—'

Her holdall is buzzing like an angry wasp. She pulls out her phone and glances at the text.

'I'm guessing that was her?'

'On her way over.' Anna covers it with her napkin. 'You think I've got time to make it back to the airport, if I leave now?'

'I've got a better idea. How about we go AWOL and buy you some breathing space, before the Queen of Daytime TV gets here and sets her pet paparazzo on us?'

'Tempting. But I suppose I should try and straighten things out with her, for Mam and Dad's sake. The wedding's only two days away, and it'll take her at least twenty-four hours to calm down.'

Jamie pulls a face. 'It'll keep, surely? Why don't we head into town and check out the Gellions, see if it's as disreputable as ever . . . unless you're too jet-lagged?'

Half an hour ago, she'd have said yes, she really was. The sensible thing would be to go back to her room and grab an hour's sleep before Morven appears for round two. But running into Jamie like this . . . she'd despised most of Morven's university friends, hated the way they'd looked at her – looked *through* her, most of the time, taking their lead from Morven.

But Jamie had been different. He'd made her feel she was bright and funny and interesting, not just Morven's geeky little sister, and she'd missed him when he'd moved away. She shakes her head.

18

'Too jet-lagged for the Gellions, I think. But I could probably cope with the Heathmount?'

'Good enough. But you need to switch that' – he gestures towards her phone – 'to silent, or she'll be hassling you all evening.'

'No, she won't.' Anna powers off her mobile and drops it in her bag. 'I'll deal with her tomorrow, once my brain decides what time zone it belongs in. Tonight . . . tonight Morven can go to hell.'

4

Mahler's new team are on the first floor, in one of the old admin offices. He watches them through the window for a moment, assessing. A table of uniformed PCs are on phone duty, their expressions ranging from weary to get-me-out-of-here as they wade through the lists of checks and counter-checks. Donna's sucking on a can of Irn-Bru, shaking her head at 'Skivey Pete', whose IT skills are matched only by his near-legendary ability to avoid hard work. Donna looks mildly amused, so Mahler assumes he's not telling her one of his jokes.

And at the far end of the room, a tall woman in an electric blue jacket is adding CCTV stills to a whiteboard. Her hair is dark, almost burgundy, and she's wearing it shorter and spikier than he remembers ... though the last time he'd worked with Karen Gilchrist, her appearance had been the last thing on his mind.

'Evening, all.' He nods at the uniforms, raises a hand in acknowledgement to Pete and Donna and walks over to her. 'Karen, how's it going?'

She gives him an arctic smile and passes him a file from her desk. 'I think you'll find everything's in hand, sir.'

'PM been done?'

'Yesterday morning. I attended with Pete. Dr Galbraith's handling it.'

Mahler shakes his head. The senior pathologist at Raigmore Hospital is precise, methodical and close to infallible, at least by his own assessment. He's also agonisingly slow. 'We'll need to press him. Forensics too. Who's been leading on the house-to-house?'

'Pete and Donna. But we've got bugger all so far. It was pissing down, and most folk were indoors with the curtains closed and the telly on.'

Mahler nods. 'What about the dog-walker, the one who saw him last? Anything useful there?'

'Only that he seemed to be in a hurry to get somewhere.'

'Uh-huh.' He glances at the grainy CCTV stills on the whiteboard. 'Those the best we've got?'

Karen shrugs. 'We're lucky we got those. Landlord said he'd been having trouble with the cameras all week.'

'That's a little . . . convenient, don't you think, given what happened to Kevin Ramsay?'

She shakes her head. 'I talked to the landlord myself. He only had them installed because he'd had a bit of bother after a couple of Caley matches. And it's a wee Inverness pub we're talking about here, not a gangland boozer in the East End of London. Sir.'

He drops the file back on her desk. 'Point taken. But that's no reason to cut corners, is it? Talk to him again.'

'We didn't—'

He holds up his hand. 'Let's make sure, shall we? Find out if he's taken on any new staff recently, noticed any new punters that don't fit his usual clientele – anything that's struck him as out of the ordinary. And I want statements from anyone who as much as rubbed shoulders with Kevin Ramsay that night. Understood?'

'Sir.' Karen gives the clock a pointed glance. 'Did you want a full briefing now, or can I send everyone home?'

Mahler looks round at the team. They look shattered, and he isn't going to fight with June for an overtime budget, not until he's got a clear sense of where this is heading. He sets up a case conference for the following morning and watches everyone file out. Uniforms, Donna, Pete . . . and Karen, pausing at the door to give him a caustic, 'Night, sir.'

Alone, Mahler looks through the file again. June's pulled a good team together for this one, though Skivey Pete will need to be kept on a tight rein to ensure he doesn't live up to his nickname. And Karen's presence is a complication he could have done without. Transferring in from the Met last year, he'd anticipated a certain wariness from the team at Burnett Road. He hadn't anticipated taking over an investigation that had led back through various twists and turns, to one of their own. Warren Jackson had been well-liked – 'one of the good guys,' had been the prevailing view. The revelation that Jackson had sticky fingers and was responsible for leaking information to the press on at least three occasions had caused widespread disgust. But it had made Mahler look like June's personal Rottweiler, and it's a reputation he's still trying to live down.

It's not too late to fix things, he knows that. A witty comeback or a jokey comment with the team tonight would have gone down well with everyone but Karen, but he knows his accent and his manner have always counted against him. And jokes . . . jokes are not exactly his forte.

He abandons the file and walks over to examine the CCTV stills. Close up, they're worse than he'd realised. The rain and the misconfigured cameras have captured a few grainy images of hoodie-swathed figures stumbling across the car park or out onto the road. Maybe they can be tidied up a little, but he isn't hopeful – crime labs on shows like *CSI* might be able to conjure something workable from the kind of impressionist soup he's peering at, but the reality is, these are probably as good as he's going to get.

By contrast, the images of Kevin Ramsay's mangled remains are brutally clear. His legs are crushed, bent at impossible angles, the flesh of his back shredded to a raw, bloody mess and his head

. . . Mahler recoils, bile rising in the back of his throat. Ramsay's hair has been ripped away, the shattered bones of his skull glinting through the mass of blood and tissue. It's only when Mahler takes another look at the shredded scarlet rag lying in the gutter a couple of feet away that he understands exactly what he's seeing. Scalped. Dear Christ, what a way to die.

He studies the image, examining every detail until the raw sourness in his throat subsides. An execution, June had called it, and he can understand why. Whoever had attacked Kevin Ramsay had done it with a brutal determination that reminds Mahler of the Eastern European gangs he'd encountered during his time in the Met.

Had the killers wanted to silence him? It certainly looks like it. But Ramsay's criminal career had been a joke – he'd once tried to rob an off-licence in Castle Street and had ended up with suspected concussion after tripping over his trainer laces and crashing into a chiller cabinet as he went to make his escape. And his brief career as a covert intelligence source had been a non-starter, due to his complete inability to recall any information within half an hour of receiving it. So what could a nonentity like Kevin Ramsay have stumbled into that had been dangerous enough to get him killed?

He makes a mental note to have Karen review everything they have on Ramsay since his release from prison six months ago – new friends, new places of business, the works. The key to what happened to Kevin Ramsay lies somewhere in his recent past, and Mahler knows they've got to find it quickly. It's been thirty-six hours since he was killed, and so far they've got no leads. And Mahler's betting June's got the press office and the ACC breathing down her neck. Which makes him . . . the best she has? Maybe. But unless he turns up something quickly, it also makes him a potential blood sacrifice to the gods of higher up the command chain. *So who screwed up, DCI Wallace? Not your ex-Met Wonder Boy, surely?*

He rubs the base of his neck, conscious of the creeping stiffness between his shoulder blades, and glances at his watch . . . later than he'd intended, too late to call his mother. Too late to eat, even if the sight of Kevin Ramsay's mangled remains hadn't robbed him of anything approaching an appetite.

He thinks about calling it a day. Thinks about going back to his flat and grabbing a few hours' sleep. Then he thinks about waking, sweat-damp and shuddering, the memory of that day at Raj's flat sharp and clear and terrible in his mind. Thinks about the way Claire's screams had mingled with the sound of sirens as he'd raced up the stairs. Thinks about the overturned chair, the dark, slumped shape painted against the light . . .

It might not be that memory which wakes him, of course. The life he's lived has gifted him a storehouse full of bad dreams, all primed and ready to roll when he closes his eyes.

Mahler picks up the file again. And starts to read.

5

WEDNESDAY, 28 MAY

Bunchrew House Hotel

She wakes in darkness, pinned under a soft, heavy mass while the quake plays out around her. Big one, Anna thinks, listening to the rhythmic booming – the sound is exquisitely painful, as though it's feeding through her eardrums directly into her brain. She's out of bed and on the floor in seconds, the mantra of 'drop, duck, cover' ingrained after ten years on the West Coast. Only this isn't her floor. Or her bedroom. And she'd apparently gone to bed fully dressed.

Anna looks round at what's definitely not her North Park condo as the booming sound starts up again. Not a 'quake, either – the noise is too regular, too directional. The door? Yes, the door. Wincing, she gets to her feet. And tries to remember where the hell she is. Inverness? No, the hotel at Bunchrew. She'd met Jamie here, gone out for a drink . . . and after that?

After that, her memory's a series of odd, disconnected images, like stills from an old silent film. Walking somewhere. Trees. A hand on her arm, guiding her. Had she stumbled? There's a patch of mud on her jeans, so maybe she had. Other than that . . . she tries to put the images in order, make them into some kind of sense, but it's hopeless. Not that it should come as much of a surprise, she supposes – drinking on top of jet-lag and an empty stomach? Way to go, Anna. And given how she'd left things with Morven, she's got a pretty good idea that whoever's banging on her door right now, it isn't room service.

She crosses to the door and yanks it open.

The man standing there, his fist raised for another round of hammering, looks like the textbook definition of burly. His Barbour-clad shoulders are broad enough to block out most of the early-morning sunlight, but in spite of his size, there's nothing intimidating about him, not at first glance; his face is pink and plumply good-humoured, like the patriarch in that period drama with Maggie Smith bitching aristocratically over the teacups. But he's breathing heavily, as though he's been running, and there's a faint sheen of sweat across his forehead.

She takes an instinctive step back, and he lowers his fist.

'Sorry.' He looks her up and down, frowning. 'You're Anna? Morven said—'

'That's me.' And it's not hard to work out who this is, even if he doesn't exactly fit the profile of sporting legend turned high-flying entrepreneur that Morven's emails had described. 'You must be Ross?'

An impatient nod. 'Have you seen her this morning? Or spoken to her?'

'I've been asleep. Why?'

'We were supposed to have breakfast together, but she isn't answering her door. Or her phone.'

'So maybe she's slept in? It's only . . .' she glances at her watch, 'half past seven.' Half-past seven. *Jesus.* 'Why don't you give her until eight, and call her again?'

He shakes his head. 'Morven doesn't sleep in. And we . . . we had words yesterday. Nothing big,' he assures her, his cheeks red-dening. 'Nothing major. Wedding nerves, that's all, you know? But I thought maybe you could try?'

'Me?' She begins to tell him just how well that little scene would play, but the look on his face stops her. Wedding nerves . . . yeah, right. It had been a Morven special, hadn't it? More fireworks than Bonfire Night, and at least part of it had been her fault.

'Give me a minute.'

Anna closes the door and pulls on a pair of sneakers. There are painkillers in one of her bags but she has no idea where, so she downs a tumbler of water and hopes it'll be enough to ease the thumping in her head.

Some hope. As soon as she steps into the light, her eyeballs feel as though they're about to burst into flame.

Ross gives her a shamefaced grin. 'Jet lag, huh? Sorry about this. Bit of a wimp, aren't I, getting you to do my dirty work?'

Jet lag. If only. 'It's fine. Really.'

She follows him round to Morven's suite. It's at the rear of the building, in what looks like a former dairy, looking out over the firth.

'Nice, isn't it?' Ross waves at the view. 'I wanted us to go for Skibo, or at least Culloden House, but Morven said this would be more intimate. More special.'

'It's lovely.' A rose-pink seventeenth-century castle by the shore, early-morning sunlight painting the water with silver . . . even nursing the worst hangover in the known world, she can see what a perfect setting Morven's chosen. Skibo Castle might have bewitched Madonna, but Bunchrew House has its own brand of magic. Even if the fairy-tale comes complete with wicked witch.

'Here we are.' He stops in front of a studded oak door that looks as though it leads to Narnia or Neverland, and stands aside. 'You're welcome to join us, you know. For breakfast, I mean.'

Wrong, she thinks. Wrong on so many levels. She knocks on the door and calls Morven's name. 'Have you tried ringing her again?'

27

'Still not answering.' Ross stuffs his phone back in his pocket. 'But she's got to be there – look, the curtains are still drawn.'

Anna shrugs. 'So she's asleep. Maybe she took a pill or something?' She calls Morven's name again and gives the door a push. 'Look, I don't think—'

The door swings inwards. Just a little, but it's enough for her to see the crumpled figure lying by the high-backed leather armchair.

'Morven!' She pushes the door wide, and the smell hits her at once. High and sweet, with a darkly bitter base note. Oh Christ, she thinks, oh *Christ*. Her stomach clenches, and she takes a couple of steps into the room. 'Ross, call an ambulance. Hurry!'

'Why? What's wrong?'

'Just bloody do it!'

Anna makes herself walk forward, makes herself kneel down and touch Morven's outstretched hand. It's cold in spite of the room's warmth . . . cold, and oddly tacky, streaked with the same dark stickiness that's pooling out from under her, soaking the oatmeal-coloured rug she's lying on.

'Morven.' Not moving. Christ, why isn't she moving? 'Morv, you need to wake up. Come on, now!'

Anna lets go of Morven's hand, pushes back the matted blonde hair that's covering her sister's face. And then she's looking down at Morven, looking but not seeing, not *seeing*. Footsteps behind her, running to the window. A burst of sunlight flooding the room. And showing her. *Showing her* . . .

The world turns scarlet, and then grey. Then finally to black.

Surprise, that had been the thing – the look on her face when she'd opened the door. Surprise and that little touch of arrogance poisoning her smile. How little the golden girl had changed in all these years. Always ready to seize an opportunity, no matter what the cost. Ready to batten on the pain of others and turn it to her own advantage.

Small talk at first, about the tacky faux-romantic setting she'd chosen for her tacky, faux-romantic nuptials. Smugness seeping from every pore as she fluffed up her hair, rummaged in her bag and painted on a crimson smile, as though her made-up face could somehow help her cause. Then the testing, the probing, the shock of sudden understanding . . . oh, but she'd understood too little, even then. Had she really thought a bargain could be struck, after so long? Had she really believed herself worthy of such trust – she, the ultimate betrayer?

Morven turning away to pour another glass of champagne, still playing the perfect host. Playing for time, maybe, as though she'd known on some level this final scene could only have one ending. But not watching, not listening, even then. Not seeing.

The sudden snap of the nitrile gloves cutting through the silence when her words had finally run out. Her eyes in the mirror widening in terror, her mouth open . . . to scream? To plead? And then the second mouth, opening swift and straight and scarlet as she's silenced at last.

So much blood. Blood everywhere, its dark tinfoil tang filling the room . . . and worse, the sudden voiding of bladder and bowels, the unexpected stink of death. Morven's final ugliness revealed. And wasn't there a kind of justice in that?

Reaction setting in. Hands shaking, knees threatening to

give way, but staying strong enough to finish what needed to be done. An end to it all, at last ... and maybe, just maybe, a beginning.

6

WEDNESDAY, 28 MAY, 10.30 A.M.

'Bit of a dull day now, eh?' Fergie noses the Audi over the hump-back bridge at Clachnaharry, out onto the old A9. 'Still, it'll maybe clear up again soon.'

Mahler shakes his head. Fergie's daily weather bulletins are a standing joke at Burnett Road, but not even Fergie can put a positive spin on the chill grey rain that's lashing against the wind-screen, cutting their visibility to a few hundred metres. There are days when this drive along the Beauly Firth feels like the opener to a 'Visit Scotland' video, cameras panning over glass-smooth water to the soft, snow-dusted curves of Ben Wyvis in the distance. This is not one of those days.

'I admire your optimism, even if it's totally misguided. Let's hope the SOCOs have come prepared for all eventualities.' Crime scenes are unstable, transient things, their integrity degrading with each hour that passes, and exterior locations are worst of all. If there's any forensic evidence to be found in the hotel grounds, Mahler's guessing the team will have to pull off a minor miracle to locate and preserve it.

'Here we are.' Fergie indicates, slowing to a crawl until he spots the hotel's stone-pillared entrance. 'It's a posh place, this. You can't see much in this weather, but my cousin Mal got married here, and—'

'Look out!'

Mahler grabs the wheel, but it's too late. What looks like a billboard on wheels looms out of the greyness at them and the Audi clips one solid, unforgiving corner.

Fergie groans. 'What the fuck?'

'My thoughts exactly.' Mahler gets out and inspects the bumper. Despite a distinct metallic crunching at the moment of impact, there's no visible damage. Nothing recent, at least.

He starts to beckon Fergie out of the car, and a young PC in a high-vis jacket emerges from the gloom, clutching a clipboard in one hand and holding up the other to bar their way. 'Sorry, the hotel's—'

'Closed.' Mahler indicates the two-metre-high sign blocking the drive. 'So I see. Interesting method of securing the locus, Constable. Very innovative.'

A dull magenta tide floods the PC's round features. 'It was here already, sir. So I thought if folk see it, they'll just think everything's . . . normal. I mean, not—'

'Not a crime scene.' Mahler nods. 'Got it. Except in this weather, they're not going to see it, are they? And if they try to turn into the hotel, they'll do what my sergeant's just done. At which point—'

Somewhere behind the sign, a radio squawks into life. Mahler turns to see the crime scene manager clumping up the drive towards them, her broad shoulders hunched against the rain. 'Not giving the wee fella a hard time, are you, sir? It's his first week out in the big wide world, and he's still finding his feet.'

She glances at the clipboard and shakes her head. 'Every visitor to the scene gets logged in, son, remember? Every one. Now go and tell Eck I said it's his turn to freeze his bits off out here. The nice sergeant here is going to help me horse this thing out of the way . . . aren't you, Fergie?'

'He'd be delighted,' Mahler assures her. 'So what have we got, Cath?'

He's had the preliminary reports, but he wants to hear what she has to say. Beneath her breezy manner, Cath is sharp and efficient, with the kind of mildly obsessive eye for detail that makes her a near-perfect crime scene manager.

The grin leaves her face. 'It's a nasty one, sir. Victim was found by the fiancé and her sister around seven forty-five this morning, emergency services called about . . .' she checks her pocketbook, 'ten to, radioed us at eight-fifteen.'

'Any signs of forced entry?'

'None. Whoever it was, looks like she let them in.'

'So someone she knew, or was expecting, at least. PF still here?'

Cath shakes her head. 'Fiscal's been and gone, sir. Took one look and . . . well, it wasn't hard to work out it wasn't natural causes.'

Fergie joins them as Cath leads the way to the hotel. They're only a few hundred yards from the road, but the drive curves through ancient woodland, tall pines and dense firs lining their route and muffling the sounds of the traffic on the A9.

Billed as a romantic hideaway, Mahler supposes, as the building's round-turreted roofline comes into view. And on a summer's day, with the sun shining on the firth, he can see how the sentimentally-inclined might fall for Bunchrew House's pink-tinged walls and get-away-from-it-all location. Only someone had seen the hotel's isolation as an ideal setting for something more bloody than a lovers' tryst.

'The sister and the fiancé were together when they found her?'

'Fiancé was going to meet up with the victim for breakfast, but she wasn't answering her phone so he went to see if her sister had heard from her. She hadn't, so they went round to the victim's suite. And they found . . .' her mouth pulls into a tight line. 'Aye well, you'll see.'

Mahler nods. 'Keep them on ice for us, will you, Cath? We'll see them when we're finished here.'

She leads them past the hotel's twin-pillared front entrance and round to the rear, where a cordon of incident tape signals the start of the restricted area.

'She wasn't killed in the hotel?'

Cath shakes her head, points to a doorway just beyond the cordon. 'The suite's got a separate entrance.'

Mahler nods. Of course it does. Right at the rear of the building, with woodland on one side and the shore on the other, and no one to observe any comings and goings. Perfect.

He suits up and glances at Fergie. 'Let's see what we've got, shall we?'

He breathes in, slowly, and exhales. Drizzle and haar, a hint of ozone from the firth. Compared to what they'll be breathing in inside the murder room, it tastes like heaven.

He crosses the tape and goes through the doorway, his ID in hand. An access-all-areas pass to the worst shows on earth, according to Raj, and looking at the scene in front of him, Mahler doesn't feel inclined to disagree. White-suited figures everywhere he turns; grim, purposeful ghosts, moving through the room. Cameras flashing, recording the minutiae of sudden, violent death; a tall rococo mirror, its surface spattered with rust-coloured splashes. An ice bucket lying on its side, next to an upturned coffee table. And next to it . . .

'Ah, God.' Fergie's voice is rough-edged with shock. 'Jesus, look at her, man.'

As though there were any sort of alternative. The sights and smells of death are everywhere he looks. Everywhere he breathes. Mahler summons the memory of drizzle and haar and the bite of ozone. And drops to a crouch beside the woman's body.

She's sprawled on her back, an arm stretched out to one side and her eyes half-closed. Calm, he thinks. Even peaceful . . . if it weren't for the bloodied gash that's been ripped across her throat. Deep

34

enough to sever tendons, deep enough to end her life in moments. He hopes. Because below her breasts, the flesh has been torn apart from sternum to groin, the slippery, glistening contents spilling out like an obscene parody of birth. *Eviscerated.* Mahler shakes his head, trying to dislodge the word and its accompanying images from his mind. Knowing he's just added to his store of nightmares for the foreseeable future.

'Nice, isn't it?' The white-clad figure nearest the body pushes back his hood, revealing greying, close-cropped hair and what looks like three days' worth of five o'clock shadow. 'Not the greatest start to my day, I can tell you.'

'Nor hers, I imagine. I thought you weren't back till next week?'

Marco McVinish gets to his feet, peeling off the blue nitrile gloves. 'Sad old workaholic, that's me. Anyway, when this story breaks, there will be mucho pressure landing on us from a great height, and . . .' he glances at Mahler and breaks off. 'Bloody hell, Lukas – don't you recognise her? It's Morven Murray.'

'From *Elevenses*, boss.' Fergie stands back as the photographer moves in for a closer shot. 'And she did that *Schooldays* thing for STV. Don't you remember the roads round the Academy were closed off while they filmed?'

Mahler doesn't. But he vaguely recalls his mother's fascination with a TV chat show, hosted by a saccharine-voiced blonde billed as 'Inverness's own'. Morven Murray – had that been her name? And there had been something on the evening news, something that had caught his eye . . .

'Fiancé's local, yes?'

'Ross Campbell, aye. The footballer?' Fergie glances at him, sighs. 'Aye well, it was a while ago, I suppose. These days he's one half of "Eilean Dubh Brothers" – you know, the gin distillery near Beauly? His sister was on *North Tonight* just the other week, talking about the wedding.' Fergie shakes his head. 'Morven Murray's a star, boss. A real star.'

Mahler looks round at the scene. A pleasant enough place, under

35

other circumstances, the décor comfortable country house rather than cutting-edge luxury. A peaceful place, he thinks. But what had been done here . . .

'She's a victim, Fergie. Right now, that's the most important thing about her.' He points to the ice bucket lying next to two shattered glasses. 'And she either had, or was expecting, company. A good starting point, don't you think? Marco, anything you can tell me right now—'

'Would be guesswork, you know that.' The pathologist waves a photographer over and sighs. 'Death somewhere between last known contact and discovery of the body. A brutal attack carried out by some evil bugger with a very nasty attitude. And that's it until the PM.'

It's hardly a revelation, but Mahler knows it's as much as he's going to get. He nods to Fergie, and leaves the pathologist to his work.

When they get back to the hotel's main entrance, Cath is waiting for them, a look of disgust on her face. 'Afraid we've got company, sir. The pond scum are out already.'

Mahler follows the line of her pointing finger to the logoed white vans parked in the lay-by. Only the local press at the moment, but as soon as word gets out, the big boys from Glasgow and Edinburgh will be haring up the A9 to get in on the action. Looking for answers . . . and right now, he's got nothing to give anyone.

He shrugs. 'It was always going to happen. So where are we with the fiancé and sister? Forensics taken everything they need?'

'Just finishing off the fiancé. He's in a bit of a state – doc's had to give him a wee something, so I'm thinking we'll not get much out of him for a while. But the sister's already been asking to speak to you.'

'She's up to it?'

'Waiting for you in the lounge right now. She's quite insistent.'

Fergie gives Cath an incredulous look. 'After finding *that*? Morven was her sister, for God's sake. You'd think—'

Mahler holds up his hand. He understands where Fergie's thoughts are heading, and of course the suspicion is there right away. It has to be – despite the occasional rantings of the more re-actionary tabloids, death by homicidal stranger is statistically the least likely scenario. A partner, a lover, or a family member, those are the murderers most people ought to fear. But a . . . *butchering* . . . like this means starting from the ground up. And taking noth-ing – absolutely nothing – for granted.

'It's . . . interesting,' he tells Fergie. 'But at this stage, that's all it is. So let's hear what she's got to say, shall we?'

7

The lounge is at the front of the building, in the oldest part of the hotel. Seventeenth century, Mahler guesses, judging by the dark wood panelling throughout. Built for comfort rather than defence, he estimates, though those metre-thick walls would have seen off all but the most determined assailants . . . or those who came by invitation, of course.

The dead woman's sister is standing by the window, staring out at the rain. A small woman, smaller than he'd expected, swathed in forensic whites with one of Cath's uniformed twelve-year-olds lurking awkwardly by her side. Her arms are tightly folded across her chest in classic defensive mode, but there's a suppressed impatience there too, that ties in with Cath's assessment. And something else, something oddly familiar . . .

'Ms Murray?'

At the sound of his voice she jerks round, and her foot catches in the too-large jumpsuit flapping round her ankles. Losing her balance, she pitches forward but Mahler reaches out and grabs her arm. And stares into a face he'd last seen less than twenty-four hours ago.

'I startled you, I'm sorry. Are you all right?'

'I'm fine.' She shrugs off his arm, moves away from him. 'My own stupid fault.'

The hint of a transatlantic accent overlaying her local one. Thin, nervous fingers pushing back the jumpsuit sleeves as she stares at him. Wary grey eyes and a pale, intense face that had grabbed his attention across the aisle of an Inverness-bound flight. Anna Murray, the murdered woman's sister, is the woman from the plane.

If he hadn't lost sight of her at the airport, if June hadn't called him in . . . *Copper's gut, Lukas. What's it saying to you now?*

'Even so, perhaps we should sit down.' He pulls out a chair for her, waits until she's seated and runs through the introductions. 'I'm told you wanted to talk to me?'

A nod. 'I need to get back to Inverness. I . . . I have to tell my parents about Morven.'

'That won't be necessary. We've sent one of our family liaison officers to talk to them. She's a highly experienced professional, and—'

'She's a stranger! And my father has a heart condition. Please, I have to go to them.'

She looks across at Fergie, who shakes his head. 'Best leave it to us, lass. And right now, we need your help to clear up a few things here, if you feel up to it.'

'Surely Ross told you what happened?'

'Mr Campbell isn't well enough to talk to us at the moment, un-fortunately.' If the man can string more than two words together for the rest of the day, Mahler thinks, it'll be a bloody miracle. 'I realise how distressing this must be for you—'

'How? How the hell can you possibly know—' she shakes her head, sighs. 'Look, I'm sorry. But there's not much I can tell you. Ross came to my door because he'd arranged to meet Morven for breakfast, but she wasn't answering her cell.'

'And rather than go straight to see her, he came to you first?'

'He said they'd had a fight. Nothing big, just wedding stuff, but

39

he didn't want to face her on his own in case she was still mad at him.'

'That didn't strike you as odd?'

'Not at all. My sister has a hell of a temper, and frankly, I didn't blame him. We went round to her suite, and we . . . we found her.'

A moment's unevenness in her voice – hardly surprising, given what she'd stumbled into. But only a moment. Mahler glances at Fergie, who's waiting for his cue.

'I'm sorry, this must seem very insensitive. But anything you can remember will be extremely helpful.'

He lets Fergie take her through most of it – at this stage they don't need a formal statement, but it'll help establish a timeline. And Fergie has a way of drawing people out, of interacting with them on a basic human level. Though most people would say that Fergie has the advantage of being human in the first place.

'And when you got back to the hotel you didn't see or hear anything unusual?' Mahler asks once Fergie's finished. 'Anyone hanging around, looking out of place, that sort of thing?'

'No. At least . . .' A momentary hesitation, then she shakes her head. 'I'm sorry. There might have been, but I didn't take much notice.'

'And you didn't look in on Morven on your way back to your room?'

'I really wasn't in the mood for another slanging match.'

'Understandable. So you didn't have any contact with her after you returned from your night out at . . . eleven, I think you said?'

Her jawline tenses. 'No, I didn't. And I told you, it was a couple of drinks and a bite to eat with an old friend, that's all. So if that's everything you need—'

'You're anxious to go to your parents. Of course.' He pushes his chair back, stands aside as she gets up to leave. 'We just need Mr Gordon's number, if you don't mind. Or the name of his hotel.'

A flush of colour rises in her cheeks. 'I . . . I'm not sure I have his number. Isn't he staying here?'

40

Mahler looks at Fergie, who shakes his head. 'Not according to the hotel register. Can you recall where you went last night? With Mr Gordon?'

'The Heathmount first, then somewhere on Academy Street. I don't remember the name.'

'What about where you ate?'

She stares at him. 'What, you want a recommendation? Why the hell does it matter where I ate?'

'It doesn't. But your memory of the entire evening seems a little hazy.' Leaning back and folding his arms. Letting the scepticism colour his voice, ignoring Fergie's *you sure about this, boss?* look. 'Would you say you'd had more than a few drinks, perhaps?'

'No, I . . .' She draws a quick, uneven breath. 'Look, I'd just flown in, I had raging jet lag – what do you want, an itemised bloody bar bill?'

'But you do remember getting back at eleven?'

A shrug. 'I think so, yes. I wasn't checking my watch, for God's sake! And if you've quite finished interrogating me—'

He produces a look of surprise. 'Not my intention, I assure you. But as I'm investigating your sister's murder . . . you hadn't forgotten that, I take it?'

Too much. Fergie's intake of breath behind him, magnifying the silence as Anna Murray's face pales to a shade he doesn't even have a name for.

'I *found* her, you sick bastard! I knelt down beside her and put my hand . . . I *touched* . . .'

Her voice raw-edged, crumbling. She pushes past him and out into the hall in a stumbling half-run, the slam of the cloakroom door cutting off the sound of her retching.

Too much.

Fergie clears his throat. 'Wee bit squeamish for a murderer, boss. Wouldn't you say?'

'Perhaps. But—' Beeping from Mahler's mobile. He glances at the number but doesn't read the texts. After all this time, he doesn't need to. 'Anna Murray had been drinking,' he reminds Fergie. 'It's clear she has a temper, and she admitted arguing with the victim. None of which exactly works in her favour.'

'Maybe not, but to do something like that—'

'Isn't a standard MO for female murderers. Agreed. But it certainly doesn't rule her out, not at this stage. And she's . . .'

'What?'

The woman from the plane. Wintry-eyed and intense, her pale, jittery hands sparking a carillon of warning in his gut. Tension rising from her in jagged static bursts, from the first moment he'd laid eyes on her. And her behaviour at the airport, that hiding in plain sight . . . the actions, the demeanour of someone planning to commit a murder? Not necessarily. But someone with secrets? Yes, he'll buy that . . . and still, he thinks, a discoverable thing. A thing to be *known*. Now more than ever.

'Doesn't matter. Get Cath to check she's okay then I want a proper statement from her as soon as she's ready – i's dotted and t's crossed, everything by the book.'

'Do you want to bring her in?'

He shakes his head. 'Let's hear what Morven's fiancé has to say first – we need to find out what he and Morven were arguing about, and just how serious it was. And get someone to track down this James Gordon, will you? See how much of Ms Murray's story actually checks out.'

'Will do. I'll chase up the rest of the statements here too. You never know, might have been some kitchen staff around having a fag break.' Fergie glances at him. 'You off back to the shop?'

The phone beeps again. Mahler slides it into his pocket and shakes his head. 'In a while. There's something I need to take care of first.'

8

Three texts from June by the time he's reached the Shore Street roundabout, the last one sporting exclamation marks and a scowling emoticon. Mahler sends her a shot of the snarled-up traffic, hoping she won't work out it's the northbound lane, and heads along Academy Street and up into Crown. Twenty minutes, he thinks. Twenty minutes' worth of reassurance, of company. Twenty minutes to avoid making promises he won't be able to keep.

He parks by the dilapidated sandstone shell of the old academy building. Close, but not so close that his car can be seen from his mother's flat. He hasn't met her new support worker yet, but Siobhan sounds eerily like the others did in the beginning – full of determination to do the best they can for his mother, to fight her corner in spite of all the setbacks, in spite of all the potholes along the road that's optimistically termed 'recovery'. He suspects the energy driving Siobhan won't survive for very long, but he's grateful that it's there at all. That *she's* there, doing what she does.

And at least his mother is back in her beloved Crown, even if it's not exactly the way she remembers it. As she never fails to remind him, this was an affluent area when she was growing up. Crown was populated by the doctors, the lawyers, the prosperous middle classes living above the town in solid, stone-built houses, with meticulously maintained gardens and names like 'Mo Dhachaidh' or 'Ceol-na-Mara'. Now the big houses have been turned into flats or B&Bs, and the doctors and lawyers have moved out to the arid identikit modernity of Woodside or Wester Craigs.

He glances up at his mother's window. Was that a curtain moving? He rings the doorbell, waits, and rings again. After an age, the sound of footsteps in the hall. A moment's fumbling with the lock, and his mother appears.

A touch of colour in her face, which means she's been well enough to get out a little while he's been away. So far, so good. She's wearing a pink spotted dress, one he remembers from years ago, and her arms are covered in what looks like a fine white dust.

'You came.'

He moulds his mouth into a smile. 'I always do. Can I come in?'

He follows her down the hall, into the overcrowded living room. Bags scattered around the chairs and on the table, but it's not as bad as he's seen it, and at least the place is warm.

'You're looking well.'

Her mouth twists at the lie. 'You're not. Why didn't you come yesterday? I left messages for you. And I rang the police station.'

Oh, Christ. 'Mum, I've been working. And I went to London, remember?'

'For a funeral. You told me.' She looks down at her arms, frowning, as though she's trying to work out what's different about them, and then her face clears. 'I've been baking. Would you like a scone?'

'That'd be—' he glances at the pack of cigarettes on the table. 'You're smoking again?'

She shakes her head. 'My friend Mina does.' She waves a hand at a pair of grubby bare feet dangling over the arm of her favourite armchair. 'This is Mina.'

Mahler tries to tell himself he's misheard. But even before the woman turns to look at him, he knows who he's going to see.

Banned from half the shops in the Eastgate Centre, two supermarkets and three charity shops, Mina Williamson is an equal opportunities shoplifter with a sideline in mooching off the lonely and the vulnerable. She's a slick operator in her own way, homing in on potential new victims with the precision of a guided missile and battening onto them until a better prospect appears. And Mahler's betting his mother's new support worker has no idea about this latest development.

Mina digs a hand into the front of her T-shirt and hoicks a purple bra-strap onto her shoulder, treating him to a glimpse of mottled blue-grey cleavage. 'You're Grace's boy?' She looks him up and down, nose wrinkling as though she's smelling something unpleasant. 'She didn't say you were a cop.'

He makes his mouth approximate a smile. 'She didn't mention you either. Are you staying long, Mina?'

She shrugs. 'Day or two. Maybe. Gracie and me, we're like that, aren't we?'

His mother darts an irritated glance at him. 'Lukas, don't fuss. Mina's got boyfriend trouble, and I'm helping her out, that's all.'

'You should be taking it easy, Mum. Not getting overtired.'

'I've done enough lying about in hospital.' Faded blue eyes flash with defiance. 'And Mina's taking care of me. She did some shopping for me yesterday, when I . . . I wasn't feeling like going out.'

'How kind.' He wills himself to look away from the dresser with its cache of money.

Mina catches his eye, shrugs. And gives a knowing, too-late smirk.

'Would you like some tea?' His mother looks at Mina and back at him. 'I'll get some tea.'

She disappears into the kitchen. Mina goes to follow her, but Mahler puts out his arm to block her.

'Get off! See your boy, Grace, he's assaulting me here—'

'That's enough.' Mahler nudges the kitchen door closed with his foot, keeping his hands by his sides. 'Not touching, see?' He gestures at the dresser drawer. 'Listen to me. I know how much should be in there and what she spends her money on. So if I come to visit, and something's wrong, I will know. And I visit her a lot.'

'That's not what Gracie says.'

'My mother gets . . . confused.' He glances at the clock on the mantel. He needs to go – if he's not back at Burnett Road in the next thirty minutes, June will have his hide. But he needs to sort this first. 'A couple of days, fine, then you're on your way, understand? And if I ever smell anything stronger than tobacco in this flat—'

'You'll what?'

The door to the kitchen eases open. His mother appears, half-hidden behind a tray piled high with what looks like an afternoon tea for twenty.

'I think I left them in too long.' She looks up at him. 'What do you think?'

Mina grins at him. With two missing teeth next to an overlong canine, it gives her the look of a malnourished vampire. 'Your boy can't stay, Grace. Got somewhere to be, hasn't he?'

Mahler forces a smile. 'I'm afraid so. But maybe I could take one with me?'

His mother sighs. 'And some for Fergie, I suppose. Hold on, I'll find a box.'

'That'd be great. Sorry it's just a flying visit, but I'll be back at the weekend.' He lets the smile die and turns to Mina. 'You can count on it.'

9

When Mahler gets back to Burnett Road, the TV vans are camped outside. The big boys are as close to the entrance as they can get, the rest lurking in B&Q's car park. A holding statement will have gone out to the press already about Morven Murray, but by now they'll be hungry for more and June will be waiting for him to brief her. And to try to collar him for the press conference, he suspects, unless he can find a convincing reason to be elsewhere. But first, he needs an update on the Kevin Ramsay case. Plus the Black Isle stabbing, plus whatever else June has found to pass on to him in the meantime. Against every inclination he possesses, Mahler finds himself wishing Andy Black a speedy return to work.

Down the corridor to the incident room, scanning for June as he passes. As usual, the buzz of chatter fades when he enters. But this time, he's come prepared.

'Any chance of a hand with these?' He holds out the cake boxes he picked up from the baker's opposite his mother's flat. 'I think the cream's starting to—'

'Down here'll be fine, sir.' Pete moves a pile of folders onto a chair and pats a space on his newly cleared desk. 'Those *are* Harry Gow's, aren't they?'

'I think I've been a DI here long enough to know what's expected of me, Pete. There are scones too, if anyone wants them.' Mahler steps back and lets the feeding frenzy unfold while he leafs through the post-mortem results on Kevin Ramsay.

'Massive internal injuries, in all probability as a result of a road traffic accident,' Karen quotes. 'Half a bloody novel to tell us what we already knew. Impressive, eh?'

'Paint flecks recovered from impact wounds sent for analysis,' Mahler points out. 'Which might – I say might – just give us a lead on the vehicle used. Karen, I want you to keep on top of this. And in the meantime, be on the alert for reports of any abandoned or torched vehicles coming through. What have we got on Kevin so far?'

'Not much,' Donna tells him through a mouthful of dream ring. 'All his pals are doing the three wise monkeys thing – heard nothing, saw nothing, said nothing. Though word is, he'd been flashing a bit of cash around the last couple of weeks.'

'Dealing?'

Pete shrugs. 'Wouldn't have said it was his style, but I'll ask around.'

Mahler nods. 'And the girlfriend?'

'Swears he was being a good boy, and told the FLO to do one when she offered support. But we're going back to have another go at her today.'

'Do that. And step up the house-to-house—'

June appears in the doorway. 'So there you are! Christ, Lukas, I was about to send out a bloody search party!'

He starts to apologise, but she waves an impatient hand at him. 'Never mind, you're here now – just in time to get ready for the press briefing about Bunchrew.'

'So it's really Morven Murray?' Pete gives a long, low whistle. 'Man, my ma's going to be in mourning for a week. What's the town coming to?'

Donna rolls her eyes. 'Here we go. All these Romanians and

Bulgarians. Coming over here, committing our murders . . .'

'I never said that!' Pete protests. 'But . . . Morven Murray, man. Killed in her bloody hometown, for God's sake.'

June gives a weary nod. 'Just waiting for the formal ID, but yes, it's her all right. Why do you think that lot are camped outside our sodding door? Her bloody agent's been on the phone already, and Press Liaison are getting all showy-offy at the thought of playing with the big boys for once. So as of now, Pete and Donna, you're drafted onto the enquiry team. Lukas, you're leading on both cases until Andy Black can take over Kevin Ramsay, and Karen, you'll have to double up as needed.' A quick scan of the room. 'No questions, I take it? Fine, then. Lukas, you and Fergie—' she breaks off to peer at the cake boxes lying on the desk. 'Harry Gow's, eh? Nice one. Here, have you bunch of gannets eaten all the dream rings?'

While she's distracted, Mahler gives it one last try. 'Ma'am, about the press briefing. I really think a senior officer—'

'What, and waste that fancy suit you've got on? Not a chance.' June gives him her Hannibal Lecter smile. 'Come on, son. Mustn't keep your public waiting.'

With Karen glowering from her desk, Mahler leaves to meet his fate.

10

THURSDAY, 29 MAY

Something wet. Wet and ice-cold and stinking, hitting his cheek and, fuck, running into his mouth. Donnie opens one eye and rolls onto his side as a gust of wind funnels freezing rainwater through the manky bin bag some eejit had thought would make a fine window for his manky fucking shed.

He sits up slowly, trying to ignore the lurch of protest from his stomach, and looks round. Some mannie's gardening bits and pieces piled in one corner, rusty tools and those black flower-pot tray things, all topped with a thick, cobwebby coating. Like Dracula's fucking castle, he thinks. And his fags? After a minute's slowly mounting panic, he spies them on the bench by the door. No sign of a lighter, though. What good are fags without a bloody lighter?

He hauls himself upright and leans on an upturned wheelbarrow to catch his breath. Better. How long has he been here? He can't remember what bloody day it is. His own phone is nearly out of juice, and the other one . . . there's no way he's touching that, not yet. He scrubs his hand on his trousers at the thought, and his fingers locate a lighter-shaped bulge in his pocket.

A quick smoke, then. Maybe a wee dram to settle his stomach and stop his hands from shaking. And then he needs to decide what he's going to do. He can't go back to work, he knows that, but he can't stay here forever, can he? He needs to eat, for fuck's sake. And . . . and he needs to talk to someone, someone who'll help him think things through.

He takes a step towards the door, his eyes half-closed against the scabby grey light that's bleeding through the cracks. And the world explodes into noise – a thunderous rumbling that's everywhere at once, making the shed walls shudder. His head is banging, worse than it's ever been, as though his brain's being fried inside his skull. He drops to a crouch, whimpering, and waits for the din to stop. When it fades to a background rumble, he nudges the door open, in time to see the tail end of a yellow council lorry disappearing down the track.

Donnie slumps against the door, his heart hammering against his ribs like it's trying to batter its way out, and closes his eyes. The scaffies, for Christ's sake. He'd let a fucking scaffy-wagon put the wind up him. Thank fuck there's no one here to take the piss.

He'd worked on the bins, once, before it got all health and safety. Good lads, good craic. Good times. And now . . . now he's stuck at the arse end of nowhere, scared to go home. Scared to go to work. And oh God, scared of what had come out of the darkness at him, two nights ago.

A shadow, that's what it had looked like. A shadow grinning down at him, the knife in its hand glinting in the moonlight. Eyes watching him through the skull mask. Waiting for him to make a move. *Daring* him, Donnie realises, and he breaks out in a cold, slick sweat at the memory. If he'd done it at that moment, if he'd just turned and run . . .

And then it was too late to do anything. The shadow moved, fast as a dancer, and the knife was under Donnie's ear, shiny-cold and terrible. The voice, firing questions at him – who was he, what was he doing there – then telling him to drop to his knees and strip off his jacket. And he'd done it, of course he had. Knelt there shivering in his rolled-up sleeves, gravel biting into his knees through his thin work trousers. Thinking he knows how this is going to end, and it isn't right, it isn't *fair* . . .

When the money had fluttered onto the path in front of him, he thought he was dreaming. But the voice had talked at him, told him this was his lucky night. Promised him more – *thousands* more, man, like a fucking lottery win! – if he'd just do what he was told and keep his mouth shut.

Dirty money? Christ, yes, he's not an eejit. He knows where that kind of cash comes from, knows the sort of guys who carry wads of it around like it's fucking sweetie money. Donnie had wanted that cash, wanted it so much his mouth had dried up and his breath had come out in weird, whistling gasps. And still, he'd hesitated.

A deal with the devil, that's what it had felt like. Like if he reached out for the notes, the fucking things would burn him. And keep on burning, long after the cash was gone. But he'd done it, hadn't he? Nodded once, and turned away. When he'd turned back, he was alone. His jacket was gone, and the phone and tablet the man had told him about were lying on the path.

He'd stuffed the tablet and phone inside his shirt and scooped up the cash, but when he'd tried to get on his bike to go home, the world had started spinning. He'd crawled into the trees and chucked up, again and again. And all he could think about was going back to his flat and drinking enough to make the whole fucking nightmare go away. But he couldn't even do that, could he? The man from the shadows had told him what would happen if he did. And what if the bastard had lied about the money? What if the next time Donnie met him, the knife would be in his hand again, shiny and eager for his blood?

He's finished his fag, but his hands are still shaking. Donnie looks round and spies the bottle of Bowmore he'd lifted from the kitchens that night, still a quarter-full. Aye, that'll do. A wee something to take the edge off, stop him thinking about . . . fuck, about anything much. His mouth clamps round the neck and he sucks, feeling the burn give way to the warmth spreading through his gut. Calming him.

Fuck food, fuck the job, this'll do for now. Until the pictures in his head go away. Until the devil comes to him again. The devil with the posh, soft voice and the shiny silver knife. Donnie takes another swig and hunkers down to wait.

11

Summer, shouldering its way into the Highland capital after a long, dreich winter and rain-soaked spring. Bedding plants poking nervous heads up on the Millburn roundabout, spelling out their message of one hundred thousand welcomes to the post-Easter tourists making the journey north. And the traffic backed up as far as the Longman, thanks to some idiot in a 4×4 trying to do a U-turn on the dual carriageway.

By the time Mahler gets to the mortuary suite at Raigmore Hospital, he's running an uncharacteristic fifteen minutes late. And however unconventional Marco McVinish may be about some aspects of his calling, having spectators turn up late to one of his post-mortems isn't one of them.

'Good of you to join us, Sherlock.' Marco, green-gowned and masked, gives him an impatient wave as he enters the gleaming white-tiled chill of the morgue. 'Wasn't sure you'd still feel like hobnobbing with riff-raff like us after your TV debut. We're honoured, aren't we, Jack?'

The assisting pathologist shrugs and mutters something

54

incomprehensible behind his mask – which, Mahler concedes, pretty much sums up his own verdict on his performance at the press briefing.

'Glad you found it entertaining.'

'You looked bloody knackered, Lukas.' Marco gives him an assessing glance as his assistant checks the instruments at his side. 'Still do, frankly. You know, you don't actually have to be here—'

'I do.' Mahler looks down at the body on the dissecting table. Morven Murray had been a beautiful woman, no doubt of that. Honey-blonde with classically regular features, if a little heavy around the jawline, and the kind of curves the tabloids like to refer to as luscious. Beyond a certain arrogance in the arch of her brows, it's hard to see any resemblance to her pale, wintry-eyed sister. He wonders if it's purely by chance that the siblings had made their lives on opposite sides of the Atlantic.

'I suppose you do, yes.' Marco looks down at the dead woman. He touches her forehead lightly, a gesture that's half-benediction, half-apology. Then he steps back, flexes his gloved hands, and nods at his assistant. 'Right then, let's do this.'

He bends to his work, a benevolent monster stripping away layers of flesh and muscle. Reducing what had been a human being to its component parts. As always, Mahler leans back and lets his vision go slightly out of focus. There's no official requirement for his presence here, and several DIs he knows would happily send the lowliest PC available, but he's never been able to square that with his conscience. Confronting the young and untried with the reality of their nightmares to toughen them up isn't going to make them better coppers. Harder, maybe, but not necessarily better.

And this is the genuine stuff of nightmares. Not the smell, though the stink of saw on bone has a low-grade horror all of its own. No, the smell is almost bearable, until it combines with the sound of a brain slithering into a receiving dish. He's heard the sound more times than he cares to remember, and it still makes his stomach want to turn itself inside out. *Focus*. Think about the pile of actions from the morning's briefing, the statements to be gone over . . .

'Nasty.' Marco finishes delivering something swollen and purple into a steel receptacle and shakes his head. 'This is a nasty one, Lukas – very single-minded, your man here. Very calm under pressure.'

'Calm? The woman's been butchered.'

The pathologist nods. 'Looks that way at first glance, doesn't it? But the injury to the throat – care has been taken there, no question. One slash, ear to ear . . . from behind, I'd say.' He mimics the action. 'Minimal blood spatter over your murderer, you see? It all travels forwards. Incredibly violent, but very carefully planned. And incredibly, er, well-executed.'

Mahler grimaces. 'How much strength would something like that take?'

'Surprisingly little. I'll get the full report over to you asap, but precision would be the key here, not physical strength. Whereas the other injuries . . .' he pauses to examine a ragged wound on the woman's thigh. 'Yes, carried out post-mortem, fortunately for her. No evidence of bleeding, you see?'

'Your thoughts on the type of weapon used?'

'The throat? Hard to say. But the torso wounds are likely to have been made by a shortish blade with a serrated edge – around five to six inches, I'd say. In fact . . .' Marco bends to take a closer look, frowning. 'Yes, that's odd. The throat injury will have been made by a right-handed person, slashing down like *so* from behind. Whereas the other injuries . . . the angle of the cuts indicate they might have been made using the left hand.' He straightens up, turns to Mahler. 'A couple of options for you. One, this was meant to be relatively straightforward – quick, professional, tidy. But then . . . something changed.'

'Like what?'

'Maybe he started to enjoy himself.' The pathologist steps away from the table, nods at his assistant. 'He decided to take a little time over his work, perhaps. Add a few little finishing touches.'

'Christ Almighty, Marco.'

'I know. But there's another possibility, one you're going to like even less. Two different instruments used, two different methods employed – does that suggest anything to you?'

Put like that, of course it does. Mahler looks at the two sets of wounds, and back at the pathologist. 'Let me get this straight. You think we could be looking at more than one person?'

Marco strips off his gloves and tosses them into a bin before replying. When he turns back to Mahler, the harsh overhead lighting picks out the lines of weariness carved into his face.

'This doesn't happen here, Lukas. Not in Inverness – Christ, you can count the number of murders we've had in the last thirty years on the fingers of one hand! This . . . this isn't us.' Marco looks down at the body on the table. And shakes his head. 'I can hardly believe I'm saying this. But yes – based on what I've seen, it's entirely possible you've got two killers on the loose.'

Mahler has only been away from Burnett Road for a few hours, but his in-tray has exploded while he's been gone, and it looks as though a pack of Post-it notes have been having a party across his computer screen.

He detaches the Post-its, scans the urgent ones and sifts through the pile of folders and reports. Completed statement from the fiancé, the rest of the hotel staff interviews . . . and a note from Fergie to say he's been collared for a diversity awareness refresher course and won't be back for the rest of the day. With Karen doing a follow-up visit to Kevin Ramsay's girlfriend, that leaves him with Skivey Pete and a couple of DCs to draw on if anything urgent comes up. Perfect. He spots Pete heading for the fire escape for one of his thirty-minute fag breaks and moves to intercept him.

'How are we doing with the hotlines – anything I should know about?'

Pete shakes his head. 'Bit of weeping and wailing, couple of ranters wanting to know why we're sitting on our arses while folk get murdered in their beds, the usual stuff. Oh, and Morven's agent, Hadley, rang for you. Wouldn't leave a message, but he's free between two and half-past today if you want to call him back.'

'A whole half-hour? I assume you sounded suitably impressed.' Since news of the murder broke, Glyn Hadley has become the family's self-appointed spokesperson on all Morven-related matters, popping up on everything from *Reporting Scotland* to *The One Show* to voice moist-eyed tributes to her charm and talent.

Mahler can't decide whether the man's cynically milking his fifteen minutes in the spotlight, or whether he was actually as close to the dead woman as his tearful media soundbites suggest. But if Morven had any real friends, so far they've been keeping well under Mahler's radar. Which means talking to Hadley might be his best hope of getting an insight into the woman behind the public persona. Hadley had been her agent since the start of her career – he'll know better than anyone what enemies she's made along the way. And she *will* have made enemies, Mahler's sure of it. The rumours that are beginning to emerge already about her behaviour behind the scenes practically guarantee that.

He moves the Post-it with Hadley's contact details to the top of the pile and scans the list of statements Fergie's left for him. 'This kitchen porter that's gone AWOL—'

'Not the first time, apparently. Likes a dram, according to the sous chef, so he's probably off on a bender somewhere.'

'Any form?'

'Let me check.' Pete goes over to his pc. He hits a couple of keys and scrolls through a list. 'Here we go. Couple of cautions, one minor assault. All drink-related, looks like, but a couple of uniforms are trying to track him down.'

'Good. Keep on top of it, Pete. I want him found.'

Mahler looks at his watch – ten past. Time to fit in a call to Hadley before his next briefing with June. He heads back to his office and punches in the agent's number, half-expecting to have to jump through hoops to talk to the man, but it's Hadley himself who answers after only a couple of rings.

'Inspector.' The agent sounds breezily efficient, as though he's already ticking Mahler's name off a mental to-do list. 'I'm sorry I've been hard to reach, but—'

'I understand. This must be a difficult time for you.'

'Very much so, yes. The death of a client is never easy, and when you've known each other as long as we did . . . Morven was a one-off.'

'You must miss her.' Just a prompt, at this stage. Putting the man at his ease, encouraging him to talk. 'Tell me about her. The real Morven, the one most people didn't get to see.'

'I've already given a statement—'

'I realise that. But we're trying to get as complete a picture of her as possible, and you knew her so well . . . unless you can suggest someone else, of course. A close female friend, perhaps?'

A snort of derision. 'Not Morven's style, the whole BFF thing. You've been talking to that ten-year-old they've wheeled on as a stand-in for her, haven't you? Waste of time, trust me. Barely knew her to say hello to.'

'I didn't realise that.' Not right away, at least. It had taken all of five minutes to work it out. But Hadley's almost preening on the other end of the line, relishing his role as dispenser of vital knowledge to the clueless police, and Mahler's response is enough for him to start talking more freely.

According to Hadley, Morven had been a total professional, an old-school trouper, generous and larger than life. It doesn't exactly tally with the comments from some of her former colleagues, who'd described diva-ish behaviour of carpet-chewing proportions. But Mahler's starting to suspect this is as close as he'll come to a character profile of Morven – two conflicting views, two facets of the same elusive personality. But there's one rumour he needs to find out the truth of.

'She'd been working on *Elevenses* for some time, hadn't she? Was that why she'd been putting out feelers about moving on?'

'Where did you hear that?'

'Is it true?'

A hesitation – only briefly, but it's long enough to tell Mahler he's struck gold. When Hadley answers, the breeziness has gone from his voice.

'Morven was very happy on the programme. Look, she was tough, but she needed to be. And she worked hard to stay ahead of the competition. Bloody hard. But some people didn't like that. And recently, it had started to take a toll on her – we'd grown close over the years, and I knew she was having some issues there.'

'There was competition, then?'

'Every year. Younger, smarter. Hungrier, all snapping at her heels. Morven was . . . she was exploring different options, that's all. She'd been doing *Elevenses* for thirteen years, for God's sake. She was keen to take on more investigative projects.'

Thirteen years of the sort of brain-liquefying tosh Fergie's sent him clips of. No wonder there are rumours that Morven had been less Snow White, more Cruella de Vil when the cameras had stopped running.

'Meaning what, exactly?'

'Well, we were discussing some "fly-on-the-wall" stuff – behind the scenes at an inner-city hospital, inside a women's refuge, that sort of thing. And she toyed with looking into your line of work, too. You know, unsolved murders, unexplained disappearances and so on. I managed to talk her out of that one, of course.'

Morven had been planning to research some cold cases? Mahler adds a line to his briefing notes. 'Why was that?'

'Been done too many times, basically. Trust me, just about everyone's had a go – it's a tired old format, and I told her she could do a lot better.'

'How did she react to that?'

'I'm not sure what you mean.' A tinge of annoyance creeping

60

into the man's voice. 'We'd worked together for thirteen years and she trusted my judgement completely. We were a partnership.'

'I see. Only I gather from your statement that you'd decided not to attend the wedding, and I wondered why that was. If you'd had some sort of disagreement—'

'We didn't.' No mistaking the ice in Hadley's voice this time. 'Morven and I made a great team, and if you'd read my statement properly, you'd have seen I had to cancel because a last-minute conference booking came in that I had to honour. Now I'm sorry, but I have a client waiting. If there's nothing else—'

'I think that's everything for the moment.'

Mahler thanks him for his time and hangs up. Hadley had been holding something back, he's sure of it – from the rumours that are starting to emerge about Morven, Mahler can't see her meekly deferring to the man's judgement, even if they had been as close as Hadley had tried to make out. Whether it's significant . . . Mahler reaches for the painkillers as the pain at the base of his neck bites harder. At the moment, everything looks significant. But nothing seems to fit.

The missing kitchen porter bothers him. Ross Campbell too. On the recording of his 999 call after finding Morven's body, the man had barely managed to string two words together, yet he'd been composed enough to order a double brandy from the hotel bar shortly afterwards. And when he'd spoken to Donna he'd downplayed the argument with Morven that Anna Murray had mentioned. But if it had been that minor, why did he ask Anna to accompany him to Morven's suite that morning?

Then there's Anna Murray herself. Just as many holes in her statement, and she'd also had a vicious shouting match with her sister on the day of Morven's murder. And despite the shock of finding her sister's body, her composure hadn't slipped until he'd pushed her, right at the end. Delayed shock? Maybe. Or maybe not.

Three profiles on his desk. Mahler lifts them up, studies them in turn. The Drunk. The Fiancé. The Ice Maiden. One of the three people he's looking at knows what happened that night at Bunchrew, he's sure of it.

The question is, which one? Or, if he accepts Marco's hypothesis . . . which ones?

12

MONDAY, 2 JUNE

The Murrays live on a quiet street on the cusp of Drummond and Culduthel, not quite as look-at-me prosperous as either but genteel enough to be on nodding terms with both. Though not so quiet any more, Mahler reflects. The TV vans and the lurking journalists have decamped from Burnett Road to set up shop across from the Murrays', and there's no way of getting inside without attracting some attention. Though maybe, he thinks, there's a way to minimise it.

He tells Fergie to drop him at the top of the road, wait for a minute or so and drive down to the Murrays'. 'Nice and easy, so our friends over the road have got time to clock you. And take your time getting out of the car.'

'Boss.' Fergie gives him a sour look. 'Would you like me to paint a target on my back while I'm at it?'

'Whatever works for you.'

He gets out and sets off on foot. A couple of photographers glance in his direction, but as soon as Fergie appears in the pool car, their attention shifts. Mahler quickens his pace and is halfway up the Murrays' drive before they realise what's happening.

Maxine Collins, the family liaison officer, opens the door and waves him in. 'Lively out there today, sir – must be the good weather. Is that Fergie getting chased across the road?'

'The exercise will do him good.' Mahler follows her through to the living room. 'How's it going?'

Maxine runs a hand through her spiky blonde hair. 'They're . . . quiet. Still in shock, and obviously struggling, but keeping it all to themselves. That's always the hardest to deal with.'

He nods. Being a family liaison officer calls for an impressive array of skills, in his view – the ability to connect with the family, to be a supportive presence in their time of need and enough detachment to report back on anything that might assist the police investigation. Not an easy balancing act, by any means, but Maxine is one of the best FLOs he's worked with. 'What do you make of the daughter?'

'Anna? Hard to read, sir. Pleasant enough, but it's like she's holding me at arm's length, you know?'

He does. 'Something to hide?'

'Maybe just her way of coping. She's certainly very protective of her parents. The father has a heart condition, and the mother—' she breaks off as a hammering at the front door announces Fergie's presence. 'Back in a minute.'

Mahler looks round at the living room. Pale walls, light oak furniture, a couple of muted prints of local settings . . . a room meant to be admired, this, not a room to relax in. The cream sofas are in pristine condition, the rigidly upright cushions positioned to repel all boarders. And everywhere he looks, there are images of Morven. Framed press cuttings, publicity shots, Morven at some sort of awards ceremony—

'Stunning, aren't they? The one in the middle is from *Fifteen Minutes*. It was her first big TV job, you know, straight out of university.'

He turns to see a small, sixty-something woman with Morven's

64

honey-coloured hair and her sister's wintry eyes, watching him from the doorway.

'You must be very proud of her.'

'My beautiful girl? Of course I am.' A momentary smile softening the lines of grief. 'I'm sorry. I should know your name, but—'

'This is Detective Inspector Mahler, Yvonne.' Maxine appears behind her, accompanied by an out-of-breath Fergie. 'He and DS Ferguson are here to talk to you—'

'Have you found him yet? The monster who did this to my Morven?'

'We're doing everything we can, I promise. Mrs Murray, we need to talk to you and your husband about Morven. Is he around?'

She gives a vague wave in the direction of the garden. 'Greenhouse or garage, one or the other.'

'And your daughter?' A look of incomprehension on her face. He tries again. 'Where's Anna, Mrs Murray?'

'With him, probably.'

A nod from Maxine. He leaves Fergie to talk to Yvonne Murray and sets off down the garden.

The garage is obviously unoccupied, but Anna is standing in the greenhouse doorway, talking to a tall, elderly man in an old-fashioned boiler suit. When she catches sight of Mahler her jawline tenses, giving him a glimpse of the woman he'd seen on the plane.

'Inspector.' She puts down the tray of plants she's holding and wipes her hands on her jeans. 'Dad, this is the policeman I told you about.'

'Is that right.' Robert Murray looks him up and down. A powerfully built man in his late sixties, Murray's face is gaunt with the marks of long-term illness, but his hands are clenched into capable-looking fists. And the look on his face tells Mahler exactly what he'd like to do with them.

The older man takes a step towards him, but Anna gives her father a reassuring smile. 'It's fine, Dad. You go in to Mam, and I'll be along in a minute. Go on, now.'

After a moment, Murray nods. 'Aye, well. A minute, then.' He gives Mahler a last suspicious glance and sets off down the path.

'Thank you for that.'

Anna shakes her head. 'That wasn't for your benefit. My father's not well and I don't want him upset.'

'Not my intention, I assure you.' He glances down at the tray of plants. Their sweet pungent smell sparks a near-forgotten memory from his childhood. 'Tomatoes? My grandfather grew them in bags, I think.'

'Ten out of ten, Inspector. But these are too small for that right now.' She taps out one of the fledgling plants and lays it on the bench, ready to be repotted. 'And I seriously doubt you're here to talk about gardening. So, what are we doing today – good cop, bad cop? Bad cop, psycho cop?'

'I'd assumed we'd be working together to find your sister's killer.' She starts to say something, but he holds up his hand. 'Look, the other day . . . it wasn't my intention to cause offence.'

Cool grey eyes flick over him. 'Was that supposed to be an apology?'

'Actually, yes.'

'Uh-huh.' California's rise and fall tones are colouring her voice, but the *aye, right* look she gives him is one hundred per cent Highland. 'You might want to work on your delivery there. Just saying.'

'I'll bear it in mind.' Though he suspects any apology he'd made would have got the same reaction. If Anna Murray's consumed with grief over her sister, she's doing a first-rate job of concealing it. 'The afternoon of Morven's murder, you said you'd argued over the wedding arrangements?'

She nods. 'I told her I'd come for a family wedding, not a media circus. When I got to Heathrow, she texted to tell me things had changed. A lot.'

'Oh?'

'It was a set-up. All of it. A quick makeover for the ugly duckling sister, then a touching reunion for the cameras. She'd already sold it to a tacky lifestyle mag, of course – to help finance the wedding, apparently. I told her I wasn't prepared to play ball, and things . . . escalated.'

'You couldn't come to some sort of compromise?'

'Morven didn't do compromise. Her negotiating technique was a little basic.'

'Sounds like you didn't get on with your sister.'

'No, Inspector, we didn't get on.' She picks up a seedling and puts it into a pot. 'It's not actually obligatory, you know. And we . . . we were very different people.'

'In what way?' Something in her voice there, the faintest lessening of control, as though he's touched a nerve. 'Tell me about her. The real Morven, not the made-for-TV version.'

'To her fans, that *was* the real Morven.'

'Not to you, though.'

A shake of her head. 'Morven . . . Morven could make you believe you were her best friend. And as long as you played by her rules, things would pretty much be fine. But if you stepped out of line . . .' Her mouth twists in a bitter smile. 'If you went against her, she'd run you down. No ifs, no buts, no second chances – my way or the highway, that was Morven. And yes, I know how that sounds. I just can't see how turning her into some kind of saint now she's dead is helping anyone.'

'I appreciate your honesty.' Though Mahler suspects Yvonne Murray had slapped a halo on her elder daughter some time ago. 'Still, this must be very hard for you. Watching your parents suffer, dealing with your own grief—'

'Of course it's hard!' Her hand knocks over the bag of compost, half-burying the potted seedling as she turns to glare at him. 'My mother's falling to pieces and my father's out here, fussing with his bloody tomato plants and trying to shut out the world. But I can't . . . I need to be here for them right now. Holding it together, any way I can. So frankly, you don't get . . .' her voice changes, her eyes widening as she stares at him. 'God, I was right. It *was* you on the

London flight, wasn't it? The angry man reading Dante and glaring at me across the aisle. I thought I recognised you at Bunchrew, but . . . what the hell gives you the right to look at me like that?'

An old, half-buried shame, rising to confront him. An angry man. After all this time spent remaking himself, is that still the face he shows the world?

He shakes his head. 'That wasn't—'

Her mobile buzzes into life on the bench. Mahler glimpses a 'stars and stripes' logo filling the screen before she frowns and hits 'decline'.

'I hope that wasn't important?'

'Yeah, me too.' She scrubs her hand across her eyes, sighs. 'Look, what is it you need from me, Inspector? I've told you everything I can remember. Every bloody thing. Don't you think if there was anything else, anything at all, I'd have been hammering on your door at Burnett Road by now?'

Irritation, turning to anger, mingling with near-exhaustion and what sounds like genuine puzzlement in her voice. At Bunchrew, until the very end, she'd seemed controlled. Detached, even – had that simply been a mask, a coping strategy? Or is the mask the one he's seeing now?

'Unfortunately, we've run into a slight problem with your statement,' Mahler tells her. 'Would it surprise you to learn that we haven't managed to corroborate your version of events?'

'What do you mean, "my version"? Surely Jamie—'

'Mr Gordon isn't returning his agent's calls, Ms Murray. And he certainly isn't talking to us. Can you give me any explanation for that, if what you've told me is true?'

'I . . . no.'

'No. So I'm going to ask you again, how—'

'Oh, thank Christ.' Her eyes flick to something behind him and her shoulders slump with relief. 'Thank Christ.'

Mahler turns to see a tall, dark-haired man in chinos and a denim shirt coming down the path. His jacket is slung over one shoulder, as though he's out for a stroll in the park, but his expression is anything but casual.

'Anna, I'm so sorry – I came as soon as I could. And you must be the policeman who's been leaving messages for me everywhere. Sergeant Ferguson, isn't it?' He turns to Mahler and holds out his hand. 'I'm Jamie Gordon.'

13

Seven-thirty a.m. briefing. The room air thick with the smell of bacon rolls and coffee, cut with the occasional waft of eau de last night's pub.

Mahler looks round at the faces, seeing the weariness setting in, replacing the adrenaline of the last few days. This is where it starts to become real for them, he knows, with the magic thirty-six-hour window come and gone without an arrest and progress beginning to slow. With optimism fading, and pressure building everywhere they turn to keep going, to put in just that bit extra – his job, now, to keep them focused. To keep them positive . . . and what he's got to tell them isn't going to make that any easier.

'Preliminary forensics on Morven Murray.' He nods to Fergie to close the door and gives them an overview of the latest lab results. It doesn't take him long.

'Not the most detailed findings I've ever seen,' Mahler finishes. 'What we have here is a list of "not founds" – no fibres, no DNA, no trace evidence of any kind. Witness statements are still being collated, and of course we'll talk to the owner of "Mitchell's Motorcycles" on the corner, but the location of Bunchrew House obviously means we can forget about any sort of door-to-door enquiries. On the other hand, we have now recovered her mobile, so let's hope there's something useful in her call logs. Otherwise, we're effectively working blind.'

A collective groan. And a voice from the back of the room – Pete, who's managed to sneak in on the stroke of half-past, avoiding the bollocking Mahler fully intended to deliver after the briefing. 'What about the champagne glasses? And the empty purse?'

Mahler shakes his head. 'No marks on the purse, and only one glass was used, by the victim herself. Dr McVinish's guess – and it's one I'm inclined to agree with – is that the killer was wearing protective clothing. Which presents us with a certain . . . challenge.' A pause while they digest that. 'But it also tells us this was no random act of violence. He knew exactly where to find the victim, and when she'd be alone. Make no mistake, this murder was planned down to the smallest detail. And that degree of planning is going to help us work our way back to him.'

'Ross Campbell, boss.' A gangly CID constable sticks up an eager hand. 'Champagne and two glasses – well, she wouldn't have been meeting anyone else at that time of night, would she? And he found the body.'

Fergie shakes his head. 'Not looking likely, son. Campbell was seen in the bar by half a dozen witnesses, sinking Laphroaig like there was no tomorrow. Helped upstairs to bed by the best man around eleven, blootered as hell and belting out "Flower of Scotland" to anyone who'd listen. I'm not saying it's enough to rule him out completely – but as alibis go, it's a bloody good one.'

'A "Yes" voter, then? At least his heart's in the right place.' Gary Matheson. Roughly six foot three of genial Aberdonian muscle, crossing his arms and sitting back as though he's waiting for the applause to start. Mahler looks round the room in case anyone seems remotely tempted. Four more months, he thinks. Four more bloody months of this.

'That wasn't a political comment, by any chance, Gary?' he asks. 'Because I seem to remember DCI Wallace specifically veto-ing anything—'

The door swings open. Karen's there waving a file in the air, trying to catch his eye. He tells Fergie to carry on and nods at her to follow him into his office.

'The hit-and-run on Kevin Ramsay.' She's out of breath, but there's no mistaking the excitement in her voice. 'Lukas, I think we've found the car.'

Finally. With no response to the public appeals and minimal evidence from the scene of Kevin Ramsay's murder, they've been scrabbling in the dark for too long and coming up with nothing. If this turns out to be a decent lead at last . . .

'Where?'

She opens the file, jabs a finger at the first page. 'There, in a field near Tornagrain. A late shift crew got a report of a burnt-out vehicle last night. Been there a few days, so the timing works, and it's a dark-coloured 4×4, which ties with what we know about the vehicle that hit Kevin. It fits, Lukas. It all fits.'

'Certainly looks promising.' Half a dozen miles out of Inverness, on the road to Elgin and Aberdeen. It's a busy stretch of road during the day, but if the car was torched at night . . . 'It's been cordoned off?'

'With a uniform standing guard until the forensic boys get there.'

'Good work.' Mahler leafs through the report. 'Keep on top of it, yes? We'll need to push hard on this one. What about the girl-friend, any progress there?'

Karen shakes her head. 'Gemma's still insisting Kevin was Mr Squeaky Clean. According to her, he'd turned his life around since they'd got together and dumped his old pals, all the usual shite.'

'You'd think she'd be a little more co-operative then, wouldn't you? What about the house-to-house, anything come from the follow-ups there?'

'Ach, you know what it's like down that end of Hilton when the cops show up. We're never going to be the good guys, are we? But I've put out some feelers, and guess whose name's come up a couple of times? Cazza bloody MacKay, that's who. Interesting, huh?'

'Very.'

Carl MacKay, aka Big Cazza, had started out as a small-time junkie and car thief who'd somehow managed to get off the gear after a spell in Porterfield prison. On his release, he'd worked his way up to become one of the names in Inverness's rogues' gallery, with fingers in so many pies he'd attained a kind of mythic status in what passed for the town's underworld. But these days, Cazza operates on the fringes of respectability, at least on the surface.

Mahler can see him sending a couple of heavies to rearrange Kevin Ramsay's face, if Kevin had blundered into something he shouldn't have. But murder? 'Do we have anything definite yet? Anything we can hang an interview on?'

'Just whispers at the moment, but I'll keep chasing.'

'Good. As soon as you get something solid, we'll have a chat with Mr MacKay – Gemma too, once the lab results are back. If we've something concrete to give her, it might convince her to play ball.'

Karen nods. 'Makes sense. And I could lead on this one for a bit, if you like – Andy lets me take on half his stuff anyway, and you're going to be tied up with our dead celeb for a while, aren't you?'

'Not exclusively. And Kevin Ramsay is just as important—'

'I need this chance, Lukas. Come on, just let me show you what I can do.'

A look of expectation in her eyes. A look of entitlement, at odds with her words, and Warren Jackson's fate lying between them like an open sore. Whatever she wants him to believe, Mahler knows it isn't him she's trying to impress.

He hands her back the file and stands up. 'She deserves to meet the officer in charge, Karen. After that, we'll take it—'

'Fine. I'll wait for you to give the word, then, shall I? Sir.'

Fergie, freezing in mid-sentence as Karen wrenches open the office door. Fifteen pairs of eyes watching her leave and swivelling back to him. A low buzz of chatter chipping at the silence. Mahler holds up his hand before it goes any further.

'Before the allocations, a couple of things to bear in mind. Firstly, I've referred to our murderer throughout as "he", but no assumptions are to be drawn from that regarding the perpetrator's gender. Is that clear?'

Some raised eyebrows at that, before a lone voice speaks up. 'You don't seriously think a woman—'

'I don't think anything yet, Pete. That's why we're going to look at every aspect of Morven Murray's life – relationships, career, finances, the lot. I want a full picture of everything that was going on, warts and all. But until it starts to come together, we work with what we've got. And that means these three.'

Mahler points to the names behind him on the whiteboard. 'Ross Campbell, the fiancé. Anna Murray, the sister. They were first on the scene, and they both admit arguing with Morven on the day of the murder. Let's check them out and either get them eliminated . . . or not. And Donnie Stewart, the kitchen porter who disappeared that evening and hasn't been seen since. Where has he gone? More importantly, why? Talk to his co-workers, his neighbours, anyone who might have seen him. And get him found.

'One more thing to be aware of. Dr McVinish raised the possibility of two assailants – for now, that suggestion stays within the confines of this room. Understood? If it pops up in print or online anywhere, I will find out. And I assure you, a visitation from Professional Standards will follow like the wrath of Almighty God.'

A collective intake of breath. *Good.* Leaks are going to happen, he knows that. But even after Warren Jackson's disgrace, spelling out the consequences never hurts.

'Look, I don't need to tell you the press are all over this. And the family . . .' He shakes his head. 'You can imagine the kind of attention they're dealing with right now. We can't change that, but we can use the publicity this case is attracting. People want to help us catch Morven Murray's killer, so let's use that. Talk to them – on the streets, on the phone lines – in the middle of bloody Tesco, if you have to. And anything that sounds remotely useful, I want to hear about it. Particularly if it's from someone with a personal connection to our victim.'

Groans from the back of the room.

'Morven grew up here, boss,' Pete points out. 'She went to Millburn, did that stage school thing . . . there's got to be hundreds of folk in the town like that. Just saying.'

'Then we'd better get onto it, hadn't we?'

Mahler ends the briefing and watches the team file out – some to cross-check information and chase up responses from other agencies, others to get out into the dreich, damp streets and annoy the good citizens of Merkinch until they find someone who recalls seeing Donald Stewart, the missing kitchen porter.

It's hard to see what connection he could have with Morven Murray, but the man's involved, Mahler's sure of it. Unlikely coincidences do occur in policing, but he refuses to believe Stewart's vanishing act is one of them.

On the face of it, Donnie Stewart's looking good as a person of interest. He'd have had the means, the opportunity . . . but the motive? What possible motive could the man have had to do something like this? If looking for a motive in the context of this case even makes sense. Oh, he's seen worse during his time in the Met, but not much. And not often, thank God. But the team . . . he'd watched them leave, seen the shock on their faces as they struggled to understand that this had happened here, in their home town.

Inverness might not be the sleepy Highland backwater they'd grown up in, but it's still the kind of place where people turn to see what's happening when they hear the sound of sirens. Where the

75

weekly paper runs a naming and shaming feature on local neds' appearances in the courts. Where crime happens, by and large, to someone else. Some*where* else.

And now? Suddenly, their Inverness is another kind of place. A place where two violent killings can happen within days of each other. The murder of Kevin Ramsay had been shocking enough, but Kevin had lived on the fringes of a darker world and his death had been more distantly shocking, like the report of yet another gun crime victim in the States. But Morven's murder . . . they're struggling to understand that their home town can also be a killing place for someone like Morven Murray. That hate can lie in wait for her, hiding in the shadows to deliver brutal, bloody death.

He opens Marco's report on Morven Murray, starts working his way through line by line. He's only a couple of pages in when Fergie appears in the doorway, a buff folder in hand. 'Got the background you wanted on Anna Murray – *Doctor* Anna Murray, as it happens.'

Mahler takes the file, scans the contents. Anna Murray turns out to be an associate professor of history, teaching at the University of California, San Diego. She'd moved over to the States within months of graduating from Glasgow University, done her Masters degree and worked her way through the academic ranks over the past fifteen years – an impressive career, and an explanation for her hybrid accent, Mahler concedes. If not an excuse. 'Nothing of interest to us, I take it?'

'Clean as a whistle, boss. Lives on her own since splitting with a partner last year – he's some hot-shot lawyer, apparently, with his eye on a political career.' Fergie shakes his head. 'Thought she'd have better taste myself, but I suppose it takes all sorts.'

'Allegedly so. Well, when Jamie Gordon comes in to make his statement we should be able to get a better handle on her movements on the night of the murder. What about Ross Campbell, anything emerging there?'

Fergie looks smug. 'Up until ten minutes ago, I'd have said not.

Nothing linking him to Anna Murray before the murder, alibi's rock-solid, no red flags or anything like that.'

'But?'

'I phoned to check a couple of things in his statement. No answer from his mobile, but he'd been in such a state at Bunchrew I thought maybe he'd gone off somewhere to get his head together. Gave his brother a ring to see what was up . . . and turns out he's been back at work since yesterday.'

'A couple of days after the death of his fiancée?' And it had been Ewan Campbell, Ross's best man and business partner, who'd supplied his alibi for the evening of Morven's murder.

Fergie nods. 'There's more. That info we were waiting for from Morven's solicitor in London? Here you go.'

Mahler reads through the letter Fergie passes him. And reads it again, just to make sure he hasn't misread the contents.

'Changes things a wee bit, eh boss?'

'Certainly does.' Mahler closes the file, stands up. 'I think it's time we had a more in-depth talk with Ross and Ewan Campbell, don't you?'

14

At first glance, the village of Struy seems an unlikely setting for a gin distillery, even one as small as the Campbell brothers' venture. It's only twenty miles from Inverness, but they're long Highland miles, hugging birch and fir-dense hillsides along the River Beauly – the vision of the Highlands most summer visitors are looking for, Mahler concedes, complete with lichen-covered drystone walls and fluffy, air-brushed sheep. Perfect during the long, never full-dark days of a Highland summer, when even the rain has a freshness to it. Not quite so perfect in the depths of winter with miles of black-iced roads to the nearest shop or doctors' surgery.

The distillery lies just outside the village, up a twisting minor road to what looks like a former school, or possibly a church. Just behind it, half-hidden by a cluster of trees, Mahler can just make out a large, hangar-like building in industrial green, which he assumes is where the distilling process takes place. But the former school itself has been transformed, with a smart glass-fronted entrance leading to the reception area and beyond it, a café-gift shop.

'Nice place, eh?' Fergie coaxes the Audi to a halt outside the entrance. 'They run tasting weekends sometimes, but they cost a bloody fortune, and – oho, looks like we've got a welcoming committee.'

'So I see.'

As Mahler gets out, the men in the doorway come towards him. Ewan Campbell is a slighter, more compact version of his brother, with sharper features and none of his high colouring. Maybe a couple of years older, Mahler reckons, and used to being in charge from the way he takes the lead, though that might simply be an attempt to deflect attention from his younger brother. Ross Campbell looks as though he's slept in his expensive suit, and his cheeks are alcohol-flushed, unshaven.

But it's the look on both their faces that catches Mahler's attention. There's a wariness, a tension that doesn't belong there, not for what he's been careful to pitch as a routine follow-up to their initial statements.

Ewan Campbell glances at their warrant cards, nods, and ushers Mahler and Fergie through reception to a bright, high-ceilinged office.

Tall, old-fashioned sash windows run the length of one wall, with a wood-burning stove at the far end. On the wall behind the polished mahogany desk, rows of framed certificates rub shoulders with photographs of major and minor celebrities posing glass in hand with one or both of the brothers. 'Eilean Dubh Brothers' may be a small undertaking, but it's clearly aiming high.

'Our hall of fame, Inspector.' Ewan Campbell follows the direction of Mahler's gaze. 'We're quite a young business, but we like to think we're going places. Don't we, Ross?'

'Got big plans, aye. Needs us both here, keeping an eye on things though.' Ross Campbell glances at his brother before turning to Mahler. 'And it takes my mind off . . . off what happened.'

'I'm sorry. We'll be as brief as possible, but we do need some more information from you about the day of Morven's murder. You'd been arguing, you said, and—'

'I never said that! We were talking about the wedding, and Morven got a bit het-up, that's all.'

'What about?'

A shrug. 'God knows. Something about the bloody flowers, I think. She liked things to go right, you know? The way she wanted them. But I . . . I'd had enough of wedding talk, and I sort of tuned her out after a while.'

Fergie sucks air through his teeth. 'Didn't go down well, eh? Got you. What happened then?'

'Morven said she had to meet her sister – some surprise she'd got planned – and I came here to find Ewan.'

'You came straight here?'

'No, I . . .' his eyes flick towards his brother. 'I drove around a bit, got my head straight first.'

Mahler glances at Fergie. It had been a little more than a minor disagreement, then. 'And you got here at what sort of time, would you say?'

'Early evening.' Mahler had directed the question at Ross, but it's Ewan Campbell who answers. 'I was just finishing up, so we went up to my flat and had something to eat. Then I took Ross back to Bunchrew – got there around eight, or thereabouts – and we went down to the bar to catch up with a couple of friends.'

Mahler nods. The timing tallies with what the bar staff had reported. 'But you didn't go round to Morven's suite? Or try to call her?'

Ross Campbell shakes his head. 'We were going to have breakfast together anyway, so I thought I'd keep my head down until then. But when she didn't answer my texts the next morning, I . . . I got worried. Found her sister and we went round to Morven's suite. And . . . and there she was.' His head droops forward, and Ewan Campbell puts a consoling hand on his brother's shoulder. He gives Mahler an irritated look.

'What's the point of going over all this again? My brother's

80

grieving, in case you'd forgotten, and he's on medication. Is hassling him really the best use of your time?'

Mahler glances at Fergie, who produces a sympathetic, sorry-to-mention-it look. And closes in on Ross Campbell.

'Not what we're here for, sir. We're sorry for your loss, and we'll not keep you longer than we need to. But we've spoken to Morven's solicitors, and it seems that she'd made you the major beneficiary in her will a couple of months ago. Did you know about that?'

'Of course he bloody knew.' Ewan Campbell glares at Mahler. 'They were engaged to be married, weren't they? And—'

Mahler holds up his hand. 'If you could let your brother answer for himself, please.' He turns to Ross Campbell. 'Sir?'

'Ewan's right. We both did it, in case . . .' Ross Campbell swallows, looks away. 'In case one of us fell under a bus, we said.' He scrubs at his eyes. 'Check with my bloody solicitor if you don't believe me.'

'I see.' Mahler glances at Fergie. 'Thank you for clearing that up. I'm sorry if it seemed intrusive, but—'

'What, you're just doing your job?' Contempt stamped across Ewan Campbell's face. 'Harassing a man who's just lost his fiancée?'

'I'm sorry. But he may also have been the last person to see or speak to Morven, and he's admitted to arguing—'

'It wasn't a fucking argument!' Ross Campbell shrugs off his brother's hand. His face is blotched pink and burgundy, sweat mingling with tears on his flushed cheeks as he jabs his finger at Mahler. 'You hear me, it wasn't—' he breaks off, shakes his head. 'Can't do this, Ewan. Can't—' He shoulders his way past Fergie and out of the room.

'Ross, wait!' Ewan Campbell shoots Mahler a vicious look and hurries after his brother. Fergie's heading to the door to follow when there's the sound of raised voices, then a car driving off. Moments later, Ewan Campbell returns alone.

'Is your brother all right?'

81

Campbell glares at Fergie. 'No, he bloody isn't! You practically accused him of having something to do with Morven's death. Do you seriously think Ross is some kind of psycho killer who'd murder his fiancée two days before his wedding? Jesus Christ.'

Mahler shakes his head. 'I don't think anything yet. We're just trying to piece together what happened – and they did argue, didn't they? Enough for your brother to drown his sorrows the night she died.'

For the first time, Campbell looks uncertain. 'He . . . he was upset, yes. But he couldn't have killed anyone. I got him upstairs and poured him into bed, remember? Anyway, Ross is the last person who'd have wanted Morven dead – personally and professionally speaking. Without Morven, "Eilean Dubh Brothers" might not even be here today.'

'What do you mean?'

'I mean . . .' Campbell shrugs. 'What the hell, the last tour should have just finished. Follow me and I'll show you.'

Campbell leads them out through reception towards the hangar-like building Mahler had noticed earlier. The car park, which had been half-full when they'd arrived, is empty apart from a sleek Mercedes people-carrier with the company's stylised thistle and berry logo on the side.

'We keep our tours quite exclusive,' Campbell tells them as they walk past. 'We've expanded a lot since our first distilling four years ago, but it's important to retain the artisanal feel of what we do. It's what attracted me to the industry, and of course it's what people expect from us after the TV series.' He raises an eyebrow at Mahler's blank look. 'The one called *Scots Wha Hae . . . Vision*, on STV?'

'I'm not sure—'

'God, yes!' Fergie nods. 'I remember now. They went round all these new wee businesses, trying to see who'd make it and who'd bomb. Morven was the presenter for your half-hour, wasn't she?'

82

'She was, yes. Things had been lurching along for eighteen months, I'd sunk all my savings into this place for bugger all returns, and I was starting to think I'd made the biggest mistake of my life. Then Morven made that half-hour programme – just thirty minutes' worth of exposure, sandwiched between two episodes of *Coronation Street* – and everything changed. Everything.'

They've reached the entrance to the building. Campbell opens the door and pushes it wide. 'This is where we are now. Bit of a turnaround, wouldn't you say?'

Mahler looks round at the building's interior. The walls are brilliant white, the lighting illuminating the trio of burnished copper stills to their left. Further down is an enclosed area of shelving, filled with rows of fat glass vats. The last third of the space could be the lounge of an upmarket boutique hotel, with smart contemporary seating arranged round a low oak table.

Fergie wanders over to inspect the selection. He picks up a boxed set of three miniatures, glances at the price tag. And puts it down again.

'We're concentrating on high-end marketing,' Campbell tells them. 'Artisanal Highland gin, flavoured with a range of native-grown botanicals. We're not cheap, but we're bloody good. And from next year, we'll be supplying a couple of very up-market London retailers. Not bad, considering I started up with a second-hand still, a couple of "how-to" books, and a glorified garden shed.'

'Impressive,' Mahler concedes. 'And you think Morven's TV programme made all this possible?'

Campbell shrugs. 'I'm not saying I wouldn't have got there, in time, but it certainly got the business noticed by the right people.'

'So you started up on your own? I assumed from the name—'

'Ross came on board officially last year.'

Something in Campbell's voice, there. Faint, ungraspable. But there. Mahler glances at Fergie, nods. 'I see. But you look after the day-to-day running of the business, while your brother . . . I'm sorry, what does he do, exactly?'

'Ross leads on PR initiatives. And he does an excellent job.'

'Must be a bit of a change for him, though,' Fergie puts in. 'After the football career, I mean. And he's still got his car showroom, hasn't he? Must take up a fair bit of his time, that.'

'That's up for sale. Look, Ross's injury hit him hard, and he . . . made a couple of false starts. But that's all behind him now, and we're concentrating on putting our energies into this place.'

Mahler nods. 'I understand. Though of course you'll be shouldering most of the load yourself while he comes to terms with Morven's death.'

'You think I don't know that? Ross is . . .' Ewan Campbell shakes his head. 'Ross is my little brother, Inspector, and I'll always look out for him. Now, if there's nothing else, I have a conference call I need to sign in to.'

Campbell leaves them at the car park and walks back towards reception. Fergie points the remote at the Audi, more in hope than expectation. When nothing happens, he resorts to his keys and yanks the passenger door open for Mahler.

'Watch that wee wet patch there, boss – I think my can of juice must have fallen over. So what do you make of him?'

Mahler gets in. Carefully. 'He didn't like being questioned about Ross's role in the business, did he? And he may be grateful to Morven, but I don't remember him expressing any sorrow over her death. There's something there, Fergie. And that will she made gives his brother one hell of a motive.'

'No argument there. But Ross Campbell was hammered on the night of the murder, boss. Half the hotel staff saw him staggering up the stairs on his brother's arm, tripping over his own feet. And either he's the best actor I've ever seen, or he's genuinely in bits.'

'I know.' And the bar bills bear witness to the amount of whisky the Campbell brothers had consumed between them. Or had ordered, at least. What if neither brother had been as drunk as they'd appeared? And Marco McVinish had mentioned the possibility of a second assailant. What if there had been two murderers after all?

Mahler turns to Fergie. 'For what it's worth, I agree with you. But that will . . . I think we'll take a closer look at Ross Campbell and his finances, including these false starts of his. Ewan too – let's turn over a few stones, Fergie. And see what crawls out.'

Fascinating how much consternation the taking of this one life has generated. Not a special life – not an illustrious, well-lived life, in spite of the hysterical breast-beating currently on offer throughout the press and social media. There are tribute Facebook pages and Twitter trends, and a stream of grieving halfwits intent on burying the hotel entrance under a slag heap of floral tributes and stuffed animals. All this to sanctify the overblown bottle-blonde bitch, turning her into a tabloid saint or a fearless campaigner for the global disenfranchised, depending on your particular taste. It's almost amusing. Almost.

Still, some of the coverage is interesting. According to the latest speculation, the violence is the mark of a psychopath. Some dangerous loner with a celebrity fixation, so the opinion pieces run . . . a predator, a half-beast in human form who's been stalking her for months. And while some of that is true, at least in part, how sad, how empty would a life need to be if stalking Morven Murray was sufficient to give it purpose?

And now? A life has been taken. An ending made, for now. But not without stumbling – not without the need to adapt, to improvise a plan that should have been fool-proof. And through it all, the calm-destroying, fury-inducing thought that refuses to be silenced.

Will it be enough?

15

Burnett Road Police Station

The interview room has had an upgrade since Mahler last used it. Mint-coloured walls have replaced institutional beige, and the seating no longer feels guaranteed to produce paralysis of the buttocks after twenty minutes. The smell, though . . . the smell is the same as it's ever been, sweat and old nicotine lingering like exorcism-resistant ghosts.

Not that it seems to bother James 'Jamie' Gordon. He'd given them a short statement at the Murrays' house, but assured them it would be no trouble at all to rearrange his diary and come in to the station for a voluntary interview.

When Mahler and Fergie enter the room, Jamie's sitting back in his chair, surveying his surroundings with a look of mildly detached interest, as though he's taking mental note. The faulty radiator in the corner is still blasting out heat, but Gordon looks cool and perfectly at ease in jeans and a linen shirt. Designer casual, Mahler decides, glancing at the neatly folded jacket by the writer's

87

side. Apparently writing mass-market drivel about hairy-thighed Highland chieftains pays considerably more than he'd thought.

'Sergeant Ferguson. And Detective Inspector . . . Mahler, isn't it?' The writer gets to his feet and holds out his hand. 'No relation to the composer, I assume?' He catches sight of Mahler's face, and shakes his head. 'Sorry, I can't imagine how many times you've heard that one.'

'Fewer than you might think in the course of my work.' Mahler starts to run through the usual preamble for anyone attending an interview voluntarily, but Gordon cuts him short.

'It's no problem, seriously. Least I can do . . . God, poor Morven. And poor Anna – she found her, right? I can't imagine what that must have been like.'

'Indeed. Have you known Anna Murray for long, Mr Gordon?'

'A while, yes. Morven and I were in a few of the same classes at uni, and Anna started first year as we were in our final year, so I got to know her then. Anna was the quiet one – scarily bright, though – and Morven . . . well, she was just Morven. Even then, you could see she was destined for—'

'Higher things?'

Gordon shrugs. 'Fame and fortune, I was going to say. She definitely had a plan.'

'Sounds like you didn't like her very much.'

'Everyone liked Morven. Though she could be a bit . . . full-on, sometimes. But I admired her guts, her determination to succeed.'

'And her sister?' Fergie puts in. 'Were they close, would you say?'

'Close?' Gordon sits back in his chair, considering. 'No, I wouldn't. I don't think they got on well at all, to be honest. Anna didn't attend Morven's graduation, I know that much – some sort of falling-out, I think.'

'Do you know why?'

'You'd have to ask Anna. But I suppose it must have been hard for her – she always seemed a little in Morven's shadow.'

'She came back for her sister's wedding, though.'

'She did, yes . . . surprised me a bit, actually. But maybe she decided it was time to kiss and make up.'

'And you didn't keep in touch with either of them?' Fergie asks him. 'Why do you think Morven invited you to the wedding?'

Gordon gives an apologetic shrug. 'Well, I'm not unknown, I suppose. And Morven was always very proactive where her career was concerned.'

'Meaning?'

'Meaning she'd have wanted a decent sprinkling of people in the public eye amongst her guest list. And I'm doing some research up here anyway, so it was really no big deal. Anyway, it's quite fun to catch up with old friends occasionally, see what they're up to . . . don't you think, Inspector?'

Mahler, who considers it as far from the definition of fun as it's possible to get, shakes his head. 'We're having a little difficulty putting together a timeline for the evening in question. Perhaps you could take me through it?'

He sits back and listens to the writer paint a picture of a few quiet drinks and a pleasant meal with an old friend – Anna Murray's version, almost to the letter. 'We got back to Bunchrew around ten, I think, and—'

'You're sure about that?'

'Pretty sure, yes. I wanted to drop Anna off and get back to my hotel at a decent time, because I was planning to drive up to Helmsdale early the next day – I've kept on my parents' old house and I use it as my base when I'm up here. I suppose I could check with reception, ask what time I picked up my key, if that would help?'

Mahler glances at Fergie. 'That won't be necessary, thank you. So you dropped Miss Murray at the entrance—'

'Well, no. Anna was feeling a bit woozy on the way back – jet lag, probably, starting to catch up with her. So I parked at the top of the drive and we walked down together for a bit of fresh air.'

89

'I see. So you would have noticed someone hanging around, someone who didn't seem to belong there?'

'We definitely didn't see anyone like that. No one around at all, actually – it was like the *Marie Celeste*. We were just talking about it when . . . oh, Christ.'

'What?'

'We heard . . .' Gordon's face has lost most of his colour and his voice is strained, as though he's fighting to get the words out. 'I've just remembered. Halfway down, we heard something moving over by the trees. I . . . I thought maybe a deer or a large dog. But it could have been him, couldn't it? It could have been Morven's killer.'

'This was where exactly, the trees in front of the hotel?'

'No, the other side. We stopped for a moment in case it was a deer and we spooked it, but it moved away towards the water. Maybe if I'd gone to investigate—'

'Probably not a good idea.' Fergie passes the writer a glass of water. 'You can't be a wee bit more specific about the time?'

'No, I'm sorry. But like I said, it couldn't have been much later than ten. Neither of us wanted to be out too late, and Anna had definitely had enough by then. She was still spitting feathers at the way Morven had set her up at the airport.'

Fergie leans forward. 'She was mad at Morven?'

'Absolutely raging! She . . .' Gordon's face changes as he realises what he's said. 'Now hold on! I mean, she was angry, but not . . . not like *that*, for God's sake.'

Mahler smiles his understanding. 'And when you heard about Morven, you didn't get in touch with Anna?'

Gordon shakes his head. 'I wanted to and then I realised I didn't have her phone number. I tried the hotel, of course, but the switchboard was going crazy. And doing anything more would have felt . . . well, pretty intrusive, really. But I did send flowers to the house.'

'Very thoughtful. And it didn't occur to you to come and talk to us?'

'About the noise we heard? It just went out of my head – I told you, we thought it was a deer. And it's not as though . . .' a look of shock crosses his face. 'My God, you are. You're checking alibis, aren't you? You surely don't think Anna – look, I said I wasn't sure about the time. Maybe it was a bit later? I don't—'

'We're just information-gathering at the moment, Mr Gordon. But we do appreciate you taking the time to talk to us.' Mahler closes the folder he's been studying and stands up. 'Obviously should we need to contact you again—'

'Yes, of course, just ring me.' Gordon scrubs his hand across his forehead. 'God, this is awful. You read about things like this in the papers, but when it's someone you know . . .'

'I understand.'

Mahler and Fergie accompany Gordon downstairs. They're almost at the front desk when chaos erupts behind them. A filthy, bare-chested figure in harlequin trousers is being escorted to the desk by two disgusted-looking PCs. His curtain of straggly, greying hair has fallen forward, obscuring his face, he's mumbling to himself, and there's something about the way his chest is heaving . . .

'Watch out!'

Mahler shoves Fergie to one side and puts out a hand to grab the writer, but it's too late. The mumbling man lurches forward, his mouth open like a dark unsavoury chasm, and projectile-vomits over the floor, the foot of the desk . . . and most of James Gordon.

'Ah, Jeez.' The custody sergeant rolls his eyes as the man slumps to his knees, his head lolling from side to side. 'My clean floor, man!'

The older of the two PCs gets a hand under the man's arm and hauls him to his feet. 'Think that's bad? You should see the bloody van. Come on, son, get a grip, eh?'

'We'll leave you to it, sergeant. Mr Gordon, this way.' Mahler steps over the spreading pool of vomit and guides the shuddering writer to the exit. 'No lasting damage, I hope?'

91

Gordon looks down at his ruined clothing and musters a grey-faced smile. 'Nothing the dry-cleaners can't cope with, I'm sure.'

At the door, he turns back to Mahler. 'About Anna . . . look, I know what I said, but she's not a murderer, Inspector. I'll stake my life on it.'

'Bit over the top, boss,' Fergie remarks as they watch Gordon cross the car park. 'That "stake my life" bit, I mean.'

'He's a writer, they tend to the dramatic. What do you make of him?'

'Thought he was going to throw up when he realised it probably wasn't a deer he heard. But we've been through those woods and along the shore – if the killer did go that way, he made damn sure not to leave any forensics behind. No trace of the weapon, either.'

'Which ties in with his MO.' And Mahler's betting he'd used his proximity to the water to get rid of any remaining evidence. 'But argues against Ross Campbell being involved, at least directly. Though I'd be happier if we could tie these timings down.'

Fergie nods. 'Gordon seemed awful keen to fit in with whatever Anna Murray told us, didn't he? Mind you, she wasn't sure about what time they got back.'

'She didn't seem very sure about a lot of things. I'll buy jet lag for some of it, but—'

A clanking sound announces the arrival of 'the cleaning crew' – a very young PC with a mop and bucket and an air of resignation. He surveys the scene, shaking his head as though in disbelief at the amount of bodily fluid one skinny, semi-naked drunk can expel, and gets to work.

'Boss.' Fergie leaps backwards, away from the swishing mop. 'You want me to talk to Anna Murray again?'

'Not at this stage. But check with the reception staff at both hotels and the bar staff at Bunchrew, see if we can get these timings cleared up. And then—' the swishing sounds have stopped. Mahler glances at the young PC and shakes his head. 'Time to reconvene upstairs. I'm out in half an hour, so I need you to sort out the actions from this. And see where we are with tracking down this missing kitchen porter, yes?'

'No problem. And if Braveheart comes looking for those end of quarter figures—'

'I'm supporting a junior colleague in a potentially challenging situation with the partner of a recent victim of crime.'

'You mean you're off out with Karen to get Kevin Ramsay's girlfriend back on side?'

'Wasn't that what I just said?'

'Aye well, good luck with that. So, Flash Gordon there . . . shame about his fancy jacket, eh?'

'I'm sure he knows a good dry cleaner.' The writer's car, a silver 4×4, is parked close to the barrier. Mahler watches Gordon rummage in the boot, his jacket held out in front of him as though it might burst into flames at any moment. An interesting morning, he reflects. Productive, even.

'Maybe.' There's a distinct smirk on Fergie's face. 'Never going to get the stink out though, is he? Not properly.'

'Not in a million years.'

16

2.15 P.M.

Kevin Ramsay's girlfriend lives in what Mahler's mother still calls 'New Hilton', a social housing development to the south-east of the town. Built largely in the 1970s, when Inverness was starting to expand in earnest, the area is starting to show its age. The harling on the older buildings has a grey, discoloured look, and there are tell-tale signs of neglect here and there . . . still, there are worse places to live, Mahler thinks. A lot worse. Though the look on Karen's face as they pull up outside Gemma Fraser's block of flats makes it clear she can't imagine many.

'Ned City, here we go again.' Karen gets out of the car and looks round. Her leather jacket is zipped to the neck, her burgundy hair gelled into don't-mess-with-me spikes. 'Oh, the joys. You sure you want to do this today?'

'You have a better day in mind?'

She shrugs. 'Just seems a bit knee-jerk after her rant to the *Highland News* last week. If it looks like we're harassing her—'

'We are not harassing her.' Mahler glances up at the third-floor window. No-one there now, but the blind is moving slightly, as though someone's just stepped out of sight. 'I'm introducing myself as senior investigating officer, and we're bringing her up to date with developments.'

'And sounding her out about Cazza MacKay.'

'That too. But softly-softly at this stage, please. I don't want her spooked.'

Though if Karen's CHIS is right and Cazza MacKay's been paying regular visits to Gemma since Kevin's death, she's probably spooked enough already, Mahler reflects. Even in his new, semi-respectable businessman guise, Cazza MacKay isn't the kind of man you'd want to get a social call from.

The communal entrance to the flats has been wedged open, so they make their way upstairs. There's no answer to Mahler's first three rings. But on his final try, as Karen's fishing for a card to shove through the letter box, the door to the flat eases open and Gemma peers out. She's a small, scrubbed-clean blonde with wary eyes and what looks like a new plaster cast on her right arm.

'I'm on my way out.'

Mahler holds out his warrant card. 'This won't take long, I promise.'

After a moment, she shrugs. 'Please yourselves. But watch my clean floor, I've just hoovered.'

She leads the way into a tiny, immaculate living room. The walls are decorated in shades of cream and aqua, and there are delicate glass ornaments on every gleaming surface. Mahler tries and fails to imagine Kevin Ramsay ever feeling at home here.

'Great picture.' Karen goes over to look at the studio portrait of two young children that's occupying pride of place above the fire surround. The boy has a crew cut and Kevin's pinched, old-young features. The girl, a couple of years younger, is posing, chin on hands, in a princess outfit and bright pink trainers. 'That place in the Market, was it?'

Gemma nods. 'Kevin bought her the fancy dress,' she tells them. 'The trainers too. Leanne pestered me for ages, but I said she had to wait for her birthday. Kevin wasn't having it, though – just went out and got them for her.'

'That was good of him . . . oh, let me.' Mahler bends to help her move the pile of paperwork she's struggling to fit into a folder. 'Awkward, isn't it, when it's the right arm.'

'My own fault.' She lowers herself into an armchair, grimacing as her plaster cast hits the edge of the coffee table. 'Tripped over Kyle's dumper truck . . . ach, just leave that lot, I'll sort them later.'

Mahler glances at the brochure on the top of the pile. 'You're going to college?'

'Health & Social Care, starting in September. At least, I was . . . Kevin was going to help me with the kids and I have a wee job, so we'd just about have managed.' Gemma gives him a bleak look. 'That's the end of that, isn't it?'

Mahler winces at the thought of Kevin Ramsay being in charge of a hamster, let alone two under-fives. But who's to say he wasn't a domestic goddess on the quiet? 'I'm sorry. But you should talk to the college. They might be able to sort something out.'

'Maybe.' She gestures at the couch. 'Go on then, you may as well sit. So how come I get a detective inspector this time? Because I spoke to the papers?'

'That isn't why we're here.' Mahler introduces himself as the officer in charge and explains about the burnt-out van. 'Believe me, I understand how frustrating it must be for you. We're doing our best to find whoever's responsible for Kevin's death, and we're making progress, but I do need you to work with us on this.' He takes out his card and puts it on the coffee table. 'If there's anything you think of after we've gone, anything that might help, please get in touch . . . and I promise to keep you informed of what's going on. Deal?'

Gemma looks at Karen, and back at Mahler. 'Aye, fair enough. But there's nothing else I can tell you. Kevin . . .' She shakes her head, blinking away tears. 'God knows, he wasn't perfect. But he was trying to sort himself out. Trying really hard.'

96

'Must have been rough on you, though.' Karen leans forward, a sympathetic smile on her face. 'Two young kids, and Kevin . . . half the folks he hung out with, I wouldn't have wanted anywhere near a wee palace like this. Didn't it bug you at all? Or did you just get used to it?'

'What's that supposed to mean?'

No. Mahler shakes his head at Karen. *Leave it.*

'Cazza MacKay.' Karen sits back, folds her arms. 'A friend of yours, is he? Because he's been seen leaving your place, Gemma. More than once.'

Silence. The shutters coming down on Gemma's face, ridding it of any kind of expression. Apart from one.

'You've been fucking spying on me?' She jumps up, knocking the pile of papers to the floor. 'You fucking bunch of . . . Cazza's one of the good guys, right? He came to see if we needed anything. What's wrong with that?'

'I'm sorry.' Mahler glances at Karen. 'We were concerned, that's all. Look, we'll let you get on . . . and I promise you, we're not going to give up on finding Kevin's killer, Gemma. We—'

'Aye, right. Well, I'll not hold my breath on that one, eh? Now bugger off. Go on, get out of my bloody house!'

The sound of the door slamming follows them down the stairwell and out into the street.

'Lukas, that wasn't—'

Mahler holds up his hand. 'Let's hold the post-mortem over coffee, shall we? I know just the place.'

Inverness's newest supermarket, perched above the Slackbuie roundabout, has what's probably the highest café in the town . . . and on a wet, miserable Friday afternoon, probably the least well-patronised. Mahler collects two mugs of hot brown liquid and brings them over to one of the window tables.

Karen stares at what he's just put down in front of her. 'That's a latte?'

97

'Think of it as a penance.' He glances at his mug. In need of caffeine, he'd bought it on the assumption it couldn't be as bad as it looked. He takes another look, revises his opinion and pushes it aside. 'Want to tell me what happened back there?'

She shakes her head. 'Don't lay this one on me, Lukas. I told you Gemma wouldn't give you anything.'

'She did give us something. She confirmed Cazza's been to see her . . . she might even have told us why, if you'd stuck to the script. What the hell did you think you were doing?'

'My bloody job. Cutting through the crap and getting to the truth.' She raises the mug towards him, parodying a toast. 'Cheers. So is that my bollocking over with for now? Great view here, by the way. Rolling hills to your left and bloody Jakeyville to the right.'

'It really gets to you, doesn't it? Why do you hate it so much?'

A hiss of exasperation. 'I don't hate it, Lukas – Christ, I was born there! I hate what guys like Cazza MacKay are turning it into.'

'Then it's a pity you spooked Gemma before we found out how she really broke her arm.'

'What are you talking about?'

'Don't tell me you bought that "tripped over a toy" nonsense? The place is like a bloody show home!' He shakes his head. 'Cazza came visiting, all right . . . to shut her up about something. And to make sure she got the message, the bastard left his calling card.'

'And you thought you'd . . . what, charm it out of her? For God's sake, Lukas – she might not like me, but at least she knows I'm real.'

'Meaning?'

'Meaning she knows you don't actually give a fuck about her sad wee life. As soon as Andy's back, you'll be off this case faster than shit off a shovel . . . and we'll be the ones left clearing up.'

So that's where this is going. Mahler sits back, crosses his arms. 'And you're willing to take up the slack, is that it? As acting SIO, no doubt. Karen, you know I can't—'

'June can. And you're her blue-eyed boy, aren't you? Look, it'll help both of us, for fuck's sake – you get to concentrate on your big, high-profile case, and I get a result here.' A flash of her old smile as she touches his arm. 'You know I can do this, Lukas. And I bloody deserve it.'

She pushes her latte aside and folds her arms, her posture mirroring his. She's a rising star, he's known that for some time – bright, tenacious, ultra-committed, Karen's got what it takes to climb the ladder at Police Scotland. Chief Superintendent? ACC, maybe, or even higher. Kevin Ramsay's case could be a stepping stone for her, and with Andy Black still on sick leave, Karen's hungry for the chance to show what she can do.

Mahler doesn't blame her – when he was starting out, he might have done the same. And June Wallace, under pressure from the higher-ups, has been pretty clear about which case should take priority. If he chose to pull back from the Kevin Ramsay investigation, let Karen take on more responsibility until Andy Black's return, June wouldn't question his decision, he knows that. But his conscience would.

Because death is the ultimate leveller. It doesn't discriminate by wealth or social standing or any other man-made marker – it equalises. He owes Kevin Ramsay the same commitment, the same attention, as Morven Murray, and that's what he's going to deliver. And if Karen can't see that, she isn't ready to take this on, not yet.

'Morven Murray's high-profile, yes,' Mahler tells her. 'But she's not more important, not in my book. The woman we just left has lost her partner. She's entitled to just as much effort from me as Morven's family is.'

'And what about Warren's family? Do you ever think about what they deserved? Because I'm damn sure it wasn't what happened.'

Warren Jackson again. Popular, salt-of-the-earth Jackson, the proverbial 'bad apple' Mahler had brought down with Karen's help. A year further on, is she still holding that against him?

'This isn't about Jackson. It's about a man who was run over and left dying in the street like a piece of bloody rubbish.'

She gives him a disgusted look. 'Christ, Lukas, get real, will you? You don't care about wee Kevin or his girlfriend – you don't even care about Morven Murray. This is about you keeping your career ticking over until your mother finally—'

Pushing back his chair, hearing it scrape along the floor as he stands. Looking down at her, a dark pulse stirring in the shadow-places of his mind. Wanting her to go on. Wanting her to push a little more, until the anger he's barely holding back finds the form, the voice it's reaching for . . .

'Don't,' Mahler advises. 'Don't follow that thought any further, Karen. For both our sakes.' He drops the car keys onto the table in front of her. 'When you're done here, go and find out what Gemma told A&E about her arm. Then make a start on matching those missing 4×4s. I don't expect you back at the shop for some time – in fact, I don't expect our paths to cross at all for the remainder of this shift. Is that clear?'

She gives him a bright, malicious smile. 'Pretty boy in a sharp suit . . . you think you're untouchable, don't you? Think you can come in and lord it over folk who've been here for years, grafting away and getting bugger all thanks for it. You need to stop kidding yourself, Lukas – you can stay here till they put you out to grass, but you'll never fit in. And it's fucking cold out there on your own.'

17

10.15 P.M.

When Fergie gets home, Zofia is in the living room, deep in conversation with Tomasz, her sister Gabriela's eldest. Fergie stifles a sigh. He's got nothing against Tomasz, but today has been a grade one on the bastard scale. The boss came back from visiting Gemma Fraser with a face like a thunderstorm looking for somewhere to happen, and Karen Gilchrist had stamped in an hour later, looking like fifty shades of pissed off. At which point Fergie had grabbed a spare DC and spent half the afternoon trying to track down Donnie Stewart, the missing kitchen porter.

They'd tried his flat to start with, on the off-chance Stewart would have been daft enough to go back there, but with no luck. After that, they'd spent a frustrating couple of hours flashing a decade-old mugshot of the man round his known drinking haunts, with bugger all success.

There had been a glimmer of hope when one old boy said he'd seen Stewart with Mina Williamson a couple of times. But when they'd tracked Mina down, she'd looked at them like they were idiots and told them she'd got better taste than that wino, thank you very much. Now if Fergie or his cute wee pal fancied buying her a drink . . . They'd exited the pub at a speed Usain Bolt would have been proud of, with Mina's cackling laughter ringing in their ears.

Now all Fergie wants to do is slump in front of the telly and watch something mindless, with a can in his hand and Zofia cuddled up next to him. Only Zofia has what looks like a maths textbook in front of her, open at a page of xs and ys, which means she's in the middle of a tutorial with Gaby's least academic offspring.

Zofia was working in Bar One when Fergie met her – an ice-blonde, tall and capable, with a no-nonsense manner about her. The best-looking woman he'd ever seen, Fergie had thought then, and no one was more surprised than he was when she agreed to go out with him. And when he'd learned she'd been a teacher at home in Poland . . . man, the whole station had been placing bets on how long it would last.

Apart from the boss, that is. The boss had taken him aside and told him to be bloody grateful she'd given him a chance. And to get a team of cleaners in if he ever wanted her to set foot in his flat. Or the Audi. Fergie had taken the advice about the flat, if not the Audi. And nearly a year later, much to his amazement, it still seems to be working.

'Ten minutes only, and then we finish,' Zofia assures him. 'Tomasz has worked hard today.'

'That's great. But let the lad have a wee bit of fun too, eh? He can't always be studying.'

Zofia frowns at him over her glasses. 'Why not? Tomasz knows this is important. To work hard and do well – see, he will be commis chef now for one week, for trial. And if he is good worker, then who knows? Maybe he can go to college and study to be chef.' She gives him a gently reproachful smile. 'You could do more too, I think, if you wanted.'

No, Fergie thinks, he's pretty sure he couldn't. Being Mahler's DS takes up all the time and energy he's willing to give . . . fuck's

102

sake, what about all this bloody work-life balance stuff everyone's supposed to be into these days? The boss hasn't got the memo, and he's pretty sure Zofia hasn't either. But he's learned to recognise when she's gearing up to give him a pep talk, so he opens his beer and puts on his listening face.

'I have to go now.' Tomasz gives him a grin that's doing its best to be sympathetic, and pushes back his chair. He must have come straight here after college, because he's still wearing his cheffing gear – a white, double-breasted jacket and a pair of garish, multi-coloured trousers. 'I am sorry for being so late here, but . . .' his grin fades to a look of confusion. 'My trousers have something wrong?'

Fergie stares at the trousers. Sees them superimposed on a skinny, vomiting drunk. Adds a ten-year-old police mugshot to the mix, one he's spent the afternoon flashing round all the pubs in Inverness. And dredges up a smile from somewhere while his stomach does a slo-mo forward roll.

'No,' he tells Tomasz, 'there's nothing wrong.' And if that isn't the biggest lie he's ever told, Fergie thinks, it's still too bloody close for comfort.

He goes out into the garden and hits a number on his mobile. It's late, but he knows Mahler will want to hear this. Even if it's going to bugger up the rest of the weekend for them both.

'Boss? It's about Donald Stewart.'

18

MONDAY, 9 JUNE, 9.30 A.M.

'Let me get this straight, Lukas.' June Wallace tosses Mahler's report onto the stack on her desk and sits back in her chair. 'You're telling me we had this kitchen porter banged up downstairs – safe and sound within our own bloody four walls – and we let him go.'

'Ma'am.'

'Uh-huh. And no bugger has seen hide nor hair of him since. That right?'

'Yes, ma'am.' Not the most eloquent response, Mahler concedes, but from the look on June's face it's probably the wisest.

As with all disasters there had been a window of about an hour where, if the gods of policing had been with him, he might have been able to retrieve things. As soon as he'd got Fergie's message, he'd rung the custody suite and told them to hold onto Stewart . . . and if it had been a weekday, Mahler reflects, he might just have been in time. But it was Friday night, and a wedding reception at one of the town's less upmarket venues had ended in a near-riot when the groom had been caught in one of the cloakrooms with the chief bridesmaid.

The bride, her father and three muscle-bound, shinty-playing cousins had objected. Strongly. Mass arrests had followed, and every cell at Burnett Road had been put into service. Forty minutes before Mahler's call, Stewart was hauled before the custody sergeant and was offered a night in the cells and court in the morning, or a fixed penalty notice with twenty-eight days to pay.

'And he took the ticket, right?' June glances at Mahler, sighs. 'Aye, of course he bloody did. No joy with family and friends, I take it?'

'Not as yet.' Mahler updates her on Fergie's encounter with Mina Williamson. 'Doesn't look like he has anyone close, ma'am. He kept a very low profile at work, by all accounts, and he hasn't been near his flat for over a week. We will find him, but with no idea where to look, it's going to take time.'

'The one thing we haven't got. Do your best, Lukas, we need to flush this guy out.' June gives him a hopeful look. 'He's not some sort of psycho fan, I suppose? Flat papered with press cuttings, victim's face tattooed on his arse, stuff like that?'

If only, Mahler thinks. At least a crazed celeb-worshipper would provide some sort of rationale for Morven Murray's murder. 'No links to the victim that we've found . . . which doesn't rule him out, of course.'

'But?'

'But everything points to a highly organised killer, and Stewart's a shambling, alcoholic mess.' Mahler shakes his head. 'He doesn't fit, ma'am.'

'He's a better fit than any other bugger right now. Means and opportunity, Lukas.'

'But as we've said before, no motive. And what about the champagne? Morven was expecting a visitor, one she thought worth splashing out on a bottle of vintage Moët for. And Ross Campbell's confirmed he had no plans to meet Morven that evening.'

'Another man, you think?' June nods. 'Fine, I'll buy that. So what's your team doing about it? Apart from playing bloody

Candy Crush when you're not looking, I mean! I gave you extra manpower to throw at this—'

'You gave me Pete. I'm still overseeing half of Andy Black's cases, and we've finally lifted Liam Gerrity for the Black Isle stabbing. We're pretty sure Gerrity's been doing business with Cazza MacKay's boys, and—'

June holds up her hand. 'Aye, aye, I get it. You're stretched. Welcome to my world.' She crosses to the window and waves him over. 'Notice anything different?'

Mahler glances out at the traffic rumbling past towards the Longman roundabout. And spots a late arrival in the car park. 'If it's about the Audi, I've told Fergie a dozen times—'

June gives him a look that would blister paint. 'Very funny. There are no TV vans cluttering up the place today, and that's just the way I like it. They'll be back, though, depend on it . . . and the Chief Super will be yelling for something to feed them. What about the fiancé – this thing with the wills has to make him a front runner, right?'

'On the face of it, yes. And I've got Pete and Donna looking into him as we speak – background, finances, the lot. But it looks like Ross Campbell spent the evening of the murder getting plastered. He was put to bed by his brother, who swears Ross couldn't undo his own shoelaces by eleven, so the chances of him committing such a forensically clean murder are minute.'

'But? Come on, Lukas, I know that look.'

Mahler shrugs. 'It doesn't rule out some sort of conspiracy. Campbell could have been tucked up in bed while someone else carried out the murder. But who? Without any sort of forensics to point us in the right direction, we're working blind.'

'Anything else?'

'We're taking a look at Morven's recent career too – there seems to have been a bit of bad blood between her and a couple of other presenters. Again, it's hardly a motive for murder on the face of it, though we'll keep digging. And there's a possibility of a recent fall-out with her agent, just to add to the fun. But finding Donnie Stewart has to be our main priority.'

'Aye, well.' June heaves a sigh. 'Never thought it was going to be simple, did we? But the clock's ticking on this one, son – the Chief Super's got the world on his back about Morven Murray, and he needs a bone to chuck at them. Quickly. Are we clear?'

'Ma'am.' Another press conference, Mahler thinks, that's what Chae Hunt will be yelling for. The family's grief laid out raw and bloody for a ninety-second soundbite on the evening news, sandwiched between the latest Referendum polls and Andy Murray's Wimbledon progress. 'If that's everything—'

He turns to go, but she shakes her head. 'Hold on a minute. I wanted to ask . . . your mother's been out of hospital for a while now, right? How's she doing?'

'Good days and bad days, ma'am.' His stock answer. But what is he supposed to say? Mina has gone. Moved on to easier pickings, he suspects, and he has no regrets about that, none at all. But his mother has refused to answer his calls, and her support worker says she's missed a couple of appointments. Right now, the bad days seem to be gaining the upper hand.

'Aye. Not easy on you, though, eh?' June sighs. 'Man, the way things turn out. She went out with my big brother for a while, did you know that? Mad keen, he was, not that it was ever going to last. Grace had twice the brains of our Iain, and with her looks . . .' she shakes her head. 'Don't suppose you remember what she was like before . . . well, you know.'

He doesn't. There are fragments, sometimes – an outing to the park, eating ice creams in the sun – but even there, Jochen Mahler's shadow hangs over them, bleeding the laughter from her eyes. *Tristi fummo nell'aer dolce.* Sad we were, in the pleasant air.

But June's waiting for an answer, and it seems simpler to give her the one she wants to hear. 'A little.'

'Uh-huh.' She darts a half-embarrassed glance at him. 'Only she's been making a few calls, Lukas. Like last time.'

'I'm sorry.'

'Ach, it's nothing we can't handle. But maybe you should drop in on her on your way home tonight, see how she's doing. And tell her June from school was asking for her. She'll know who you mean.'

Unlikely, Mahler thinks. So unlikely as to be off the scale, in fact. But he assures June he'll pass the message on and heads back to his office . . . where, for once, Fergie's waiting for him with some positive news.

The final lab reports are in, and fibres recovered from near Morven Murray's body look as though they may have come from the protective clothing worn by her murderer. 'Just a bog-standard polypropylene number from somewhere like B&Q,' Fergie tells him. 'But he must have caught it on something and not noticed. Not much chance of tracing it at the moment, but if we identify a suspect . . .'

Mahler nods. The chances of the coverall itself being recovered are minuscule – the killer will have disposed of it as soon as possible after leaving Bunchrew – but there's every possibility of finding further fibres on his clothing, or in his vehicle. 'What about the mobile, Pete? Anything of interest there?'

'I wish.' Pete takes off his glasses and rubs the bridge of his nose. 'I've been cross-checking the numbers, and it's all yawn-a-minute stuff. You'd think Morven Murray would have a few decent contacts, wouldn't you? A couple of footballers, one of those X Factor lassies maybe? But they're all to do with her work. Her agent, a solicitor, a firm of accountants. Bo-ring.'

'All of them?'

'Every single one. It's like she doesn't have a life outside work.'

'Or she had a second phone for personal use. But of course, we've already checked for that. Haven't we?'

Pete turns an unlovely shade of beige. 'Shit.'

A groan from Fergie, one Mahler's tempted to echo. A second phone means asking June to make a data access request to the service provider and rushing it through Fraser 'Lightning' Bolt, the force's Single Point of Contact Officer. Whose nickname, Mahler has learned to his cost, only applies when a visit to Wetherspoon's or the Heathmount's bar is on the cards.

'Agreed.' He picks up Pete's in-tray and glances through it. 'Bit to catch up on here, isn't there?'

'Ach, there's nothing urgent. And I've been concentrating on this stuff.'

'Then I suggest you concentrate harder in future. Because when you put your mind to it, you're actually an asset to this team, Pete.' Mahler pulls an overdue report from the bottom of the tray and hands it to him. 'But while you're working for me, turning up with your brain in neutral is not an option. Ever. Understood?'

'Sir.'

'Good. And just to be clear – if I ever have to stand in front of the DCI again and hear about you skiving off, you'll be pulling weekend shifts for as long as I can swing it.'

The door opens and the duty custody sergeant looks in.

'Any chance youse could sort out what you're doing with that Gerrity guy you parked downstairs? He's doing my flaming head in.'

'On my way.' Mahler puts the paperwork on the desk, and glances at Pete's screen. 'That local call on the seventh, what was that?'

'That place in the Eastgate that does all the Apple stuff. The boy said she was having problems with her iPad so he gave her a bit of advice over the phone.'

Mahler frowns. 'There were no iPads found at the crime scene. So now we're missing an iPad and her personal mobile.'

'Nicked by the killer, surely?' Fergie points out. 'Along with her other phone, probably, and the cash in her purse. Easy pickings, boss.'

'But he left her Rolex lying on the table? No way. The killer took them, but he wasn't looking for a quick windfall. There's something on her phone or on that iPad that links him to the murder and he couldn't risk us finding it.'

Pete frowns. 'Like a text, you mean? He must know we'll trace those.'

'Something else, then. Something we haven't thought of.' Mahler turns to his DS. 'Glyn Hadley said Morven had been discussing ideas for a new series – and one of them involved looking at cold cases and unexplained disappearances. What if there's some sort of connection?'

'With a TV programme? And Hadley said she'd gone off the idea.'

Mahler shakes his head. 'Hadley said *he* wasn't keen. But I can't see Morven giving up quite so easily, can you? Fergie, I need you to pay him a visit. Find out exactly what she was planning, whether they'd discussed any details. Talk to her colleagues too, see if you can find out what was really going on with her career.'

'To London? Ach, boss.' Fergie makes a face like a toddler confronting its first Brussels sprout. 'Do you not fancy it yourself? You could catch up with your old pals, have a nose round your old stamping ground.'

For a moment, Mahler's actually tempted. He could call in at Charing Cross nick, see who's moved where, whose career has taken off . . . and catch the pitying glances from his old squad. A transfer to Inverness? He might as well have gone to the dark side of the moon, as far as they're concerned.

Mahler shakes his head. 'Andy Black's off sick for another couple of weeks, so I'm still SIO on the Kevin Ramsay case, I need to review where we are with that. And Hadley's a pompous little show-off – he's more likely to open up to someone he thinks he can impress, someone who's a little out of their element.'

'Aye, well, that would be me all right.' Fergie looks resigned, then brightens up. 'Looks like I'll have to miss that gym induction day Zofia had booked for me, though. Can't be helped, eh?'

'Hadley's out of the country until the eighteenth, so I'm sure you can rebook.' Mahler turns to go, looks back at Pete. 'You said there were recent calls to her accountants? Get Donna to have a word with them, see what she can find out there. And that second mobile? I don't care what you have to do to Lightning to get things moving, but I want those call logs found.'

19

THURSDAY, 12 JUNE

The silence is the first thing Anna notices when she opens the door to the postman. The absence of clicks and whirrs from hidden lenses, the missing rise-and-fall hum of bored, journalistic voices . . . the press and TV vans have gone, slipped away under cover of darkness like a retreating army, leaving nothing but a few discarded sandwich wrappers and the odd drinks can behind.

'Tommy Sheridan,' Jamie tells her when he calls in. 'He's at the Spectrum Centre tonight, doing a referendum talk.'

'Really?' She realises she can't quite face talking to Jamie in the living room's chill formality, and takes him through to the kitchen instead. 'Which side is he on?'

'Oh, he's pro. In fact—'

'All this referendum hoo-ha.' Anna's mother looks up from the pile of newspapers she's poring over as they enter. 'Hot air and nonsense, that's all it is! Alex Salmond's face all over the papers, and not a word about Morven for days. Don't people care about her any more?'

'Of course they do,' Jamie assures her. 'But the papers will have to cover other things, Mrs Murray. They'll be watching for the next development, that's all.'

'And how long's that going to take? The police are doing nothing! And we're just supposed to . . . to sit here and *wait*, while everyone forgets about her.'

'That's not going to happen, Mam.' Anna takes hold of her mother's hand, squeezes the unresponsive fingers. 'I promise you. But we have to try to carry on—'

'Why? So you can get on with your precious work as though nothing's happened?' Her mother pulls her hand away. 'Good to know you've got your priorities straight, Anna – good to know you won't let a wee thing like your sister's murder get in the way!'

She stands up, scattering the heap of papers, and runs out of the room. The articles she'd been cutting out flutter to the floor like tired monochrome butterflies.

Anna turns to follow, but Jamie puts his hand on her arm. 'Maybe give her a minute? She . . .' he shakes his head, lets his hand fall to his side. 'God, listen to me, trying to tell you what to do. It's just . . . that thing your mam was doing with the papers—'

'I know.' Anna retrieves the cuttings and puts them on the dresser. 'Morven's agent suggested it. He said Mam might feel more in touch with her that way.'

'That Hadley guy who was on *Reporting Scotland* the other week? Jesus.'

She shrugs. Hadley's overblown, posh-boy persona sets her teeth on edge, but talking to him seems to help her mother. 'I don't think she knows what else to do . . . and she's right, I was trying to get on with some work today. I . . . I need to do something, Jamie. I need to think about something that isn't about . . .' she waves her hand at the pile of cuttings, 'about this. Does that make me heartless?'

'You're not heartless. But you do look knackered – why don't we go and grab a coffee somewhere? You look like you could do with getting out for a while.'

For a moment, she's tempted. How long has it been since she's ventured further than the local shop? Even their supermarket shopping gets delivered these days. And time has started running into itself, aimless, walking-on-eggshells days blurring into too-long, sleep-free nights. But her father's gone out to a 'Yes' supporters meeting and she can't leave her mother alone, not in her current state.

Anna shakes her head. 'Mam needs someone with her right now. But we can go down to the summerhouse for a bit of fresh air.'

She gets the Chablis from the fridge and a couple of glasses and leads the way past the clematis and the raspberry canes. Her favourite bit of the garden since she was a little girl, this part . . . the scruffy, untamed part hidden beyond the lawn and flower beds with their perfect, manicured edges.

She pulls out a couple of garden chairs for them to sit on. When she looks up from pouring the wine, Jamie's watching her. 'What?'

He shakes his head. 'You can't carry on like this, Anna. Supporting your parents is fine, but . . . what about the memorial service, who's organising that? Not Hadley the heavy-breather again?'

'Preparing "a few ideas for us to think about" as we speak.' Anna picks up her glass, half drains it and pours herself a generous top-up. 'Good old Glyn. What would we do without him?'

'Can't imagine. What about Ross? He doing any better?'

She shakes her head. Ross Campbell has turned up at her parents' house a couple of times since Morven's murder, barely coherent and reeking of alcohol. Both times, he'd looked like a man planning to climb inside a whisky bottle and stay there. How he's going to cope with the memorial service is anyone's guess.

'Not so you'd notice, no. But he and Mam get on really well, so I guess they're helping each other through this.'

'Yeah, looks like that's working.' Jamie glances at her. 'Look, I've got a completely selfish suggestion to put to you. It's more work, but I think the distraction might be good for you.'

He's in the early stages of negotiations with BBC Scotland, he tells her, for a historical documentary on the Highlands. 'Not the

114

Bonnie Prince and that tired old Jacobite guff, though. I want to concentrate on the Clearances and their aftermath, and I could do with some help putting it all together. How do you feel about it?'

She needs a moment to work out what he's asking her. 'You want me to get involved? Jamie, I can't. I need to be here for Mam and Dad right now.'

'You need a bit of breathing space as well. You can't carry on like this, Anna. Look, it wouldn't take long, I promise – and it would give you something else to focus on, wouldn't it?'

He has a point, she supposes. 'But the nineteenth century isn't exactly my period, Jamie. I'm not sure how much use I'd be.'

'Are you kidding? You've got the serious academic skills, you've got the background – and to be honest, I'm a wee bit up against it, time-wise.'

'What's a wee bit, exactly?'

'Enough to tell me I need to get a move on. Anyway, with you on board there's less chance of me getting completely up myself – hard to believe, I know, but it happens sometimes.' He shakes his head. 'Though compared to the giant ego I spoke to at the cop shop . . . God, what was his name? Sneery git in a suit three levels above his pay grade, looked like he'd a stick rammed up his—'

'Mahler talked to you? What did he want?'

'Well, that's the thing. He was asking about the night Morven was killed, and I . . . I may have dropped you in it a bit.'

'What do you mean?' Ice in the pit of her stomach. 'What did you tell him, Jamie?'

'Just that you were annoyed with her for setting you up for that stupid photoshoot. Well, you were, weren't you? And he gave me a funny look when I said I dropped you at the hotel by ten.'

'No, it must have been later than that, surely? I heard the clock in the hall—'

'Look, don't worry about it – you were probably still in shock when the guy spoke to you, and when he pushed me, I said I might have got it wrong. It's not like you lied to him, is it?' He glances at

115

his watch, frowns. 'I better go. Listen, let me know if this memorial service thing is going ahead, and I'll do my best to be there. And have a think about the Clearances project, will you? It'll take a day or two at most, and I'd really appreciate it.'

'I will. And . . . thanks, Jamie. Thanks for everything.'

He shakes his head. 'No thanks needed. What's happened . . . you don't deserve any of this stuff, Anna. None of you do.'

She watches him set off down the path, knowing she doesn't need to think about it. She's going to work with him, of course she is. Not because of what he'd said, but what he hadn't. Since the news of Morven's murder broke, Jamie's phoned or called round nearly every day . . . not intrusively, not pushing in, just doing what he could to show he was on their side. And neglecting his new project as a result, she suspects. The least she can do is help him out for a day or two.

Her mobile buzzes in her pocket. Nothing urgent, just a discreet enquiry from faculty admin about what's happening – not pushing her for a return date, which she's grateful for, though she's going to have to think about it at some point. She's already missed her final teaching week, and there's no way she'll be back in time for the round of meetings scheduled for July. Or the leaving bash for Chrissy, the departmental secretary, or Hannah's baby shower, come to that.

The thought is suddenly, stupidly, upsetting. Anna closes her eyes, and for a moment the smells and sounds of downtown San Diego are so intense it's as though she's back there, strolling through Balboa Park in the sunshine or taking in an exhibition at the Museum of Art. Driving up to La Jolla at weekends for brunch with friends, maybe, or walking along the beach. Enjoying the life she's made there, living it to the full . . . homesick, she thinks. She's come home to be homesick. In which alternative universe does that make any kind of sense? And what good is she doing here, anyway?

Supporting her parents, allegedly. Being there for them . . . only Dad's out of the house and into the garden as soon as he's up and dressed, incinerating weeds or pushing the lawnmower over the grass with a sleepwalker's unblinking gaze. And Mam is breaking apart, piece by brittle piece, and there's nothing she can do to stop it. Great job you're doing of supporting them, Anna. Really well done . . . and that's not even the worst of it, is it?

It's not like you lied to him. She pours herself the last of the wine and angles her chair round so she's facing away from the house. And wonders what Jamie would think of her if he knew the truth.

He's only been absent for a few days, but the house feels cold, uninhabited again, as though his presence is an anomaly, a temporary irritation it's trying to shrug off. He resets the thermostat and sorts through the mail – junk, most of it, but it never hurts to be thorough – and Morven's face appears, grinning up at him from the local free paper.

His stomach revolts, filling his mouth with bile. Another touching tribute to the sad media tart, no doubt. Christ, is she going to plague him for the rest of his life? Why can't the stupid bitch stay dead? Unless . . .

He speed-reads the article, feels his face relax into a disbelieving smile. The memorial service for poor murdered Morven is to be held at Bunchrew House. Unbelievable. Out of all the possible venues in the city, they've chosen the actual crime scene for their maudlin grief-fest. How twisted would you have to be to dream that one up?

He crosses to the dresser, takes out the ten-year-old Tomatin and pours himself a finger, irritated to see the faint but noticeable tremor in his hand. He can't afford to lose control, not now that things are finally going so well.

He turns on the TV, scrolls through the news channels. Alex Salmond and Alistair Darling are snarling at each other on a current affairs programme, two surly, long-toothed pit-bulls, desperate to bring each other down as the Referendum campaign heats up. A gift to him, this graceless cycle of never-ending posturing. Another week of Yes/No tedium, eating up the column inches, filling the TV soundbites. Another week that carries Morven's story further and further out of the headlines – almost a month, now, since that night at Bunchrew. A month of virtual silence from the police, which means they're floundering. As usual.

Oh, he's not out of the woods yet, he knows that. There are loose ends still to be dealt with – the kitchen porter, for one. If there had been a moment when all his plans could have fallen apart, that was it. The fool had come from nowhere, looming out of the half-dark at him, shocked mouth opening and closing like a gaffed salmon. If it hadn't been for the skull mask . . .

The mask had been a last-minute addition, a macabre fancy he'd indulged in against his better judgement, or so he'd thought. But he'd been wrong. The mask had calmed him, kept him resolute. Kept him focused. And shown him the kitchen porter for what he was – a skinny, trembling runt with red-rimmed drinker's eyes, the kind of man you'd walk past a hundred times and never see. A nothing man, easy to threaten. Easy to buy. Easy, as it turns out, to make use of.

For now.

20

MONDAY, 16 JUNE

After a week of grey, unsettled skies, the sun decides to make an appearance on the morning of the memorial service. It's still only June, and not even the ever-optimistic Fergie would suggest that summer has finally arrived. But as Mahler pulls up at Bunchrew House the clouds are starting to clear and the firth is a still, dark blue.

'Jesus, Lukas, you're cutting it fine!' June Wallace is standing in the doorway, mobile clamped under her jaw while she fiddles with an e-cigarette. 'The Chief's hopping about like a hen on a hot girdle and the hotel manager's getting twitchy about a bunch of journos cluttering up his nice clean hotel.'

'Out in force, I take it?'

'Them and half the bloody town, thanks to that open invitation in the *Courier*.' June gestures towards the roped-off area serving as a temporary car park. It's already half-full, and Mahler can see a steady stream of vehicles making their way down the drive. 'Going to be a nightmare, son, you wait and see. Ach, sod it!' She gives up on the e-cigarette and stuffs it in her pocket. 'Come on, family's in here.'

Mahler follows her to the oak-panelled room that serves as a bar and informal lounge for hotel guests. Chief Superintendent Chae Hunt, immaculate in full dress uniform, is at the far end of the room, issuing instructions to an aide. He looks up as they enter and beckons them over.

'Found our lost sheep I see, June.' He nods a dismissal at the aide and turns to Mahler. 'Detective Inspector, good of you to join us.' A pause. A glance at his watch. And in case Mahler's somehow missed the point, the flash of a razor-wire smile. 'Eventually.'

'Sir, I was delayed—'

'You're here now. Let's move on, shall we?' The smile reappears for the space of a millisecond. 'The family's trusting us to get results, Inspector, and we're going to deliver for them. Aren't we?'

Mahler contemplates a response involving rabbits and hats. And possibly a magic wand. 'Sir.'

He scans the room. A young, dog-collared man with a hipster beard and a nervous expression is making last-minute amendments to a page of handwritten notes. Robert and Yvonne Murray are seated by the fire, deep in conversation with Maxine. Robert Murray has lost weight and there's a disturbing greyness to his features, but his wife looks infinitely worse. So why is there no sign of the one person he'd expected to be there, offering them support?

He looks round again, sees the French windows standing open and, beyond them, two figures by the drystone wall. 'Sir, ma'am, if you'll excuse me? Someone I need to see.'

Anna Murray, pale skin and graphite dress light-and-shade sombre, is talking to the half-slumped man beside her on the wall. He's shaking his head and grunting annoyance, but not making any kind of intelligible reply. As Mahler comes closer, he realises why.

Ross Campbell's dark suit, too heavy for the warmth of the day, is a crumpled mess and his shirt has come untucked, pink hairy belly exposed between gaping buttons. His eyes, half-closed in his sweat-sheened face, are rimmed with red, and the smell of alcohol on his breath is overwhelming.

'Is he okay?'

Whirling round to face him, anger flushing her cheeks. 'Of course he's not okay! I've been trying to get some water into him, but—'

'How much has he had to drink?'

'Enough.' She shakes her head. 'Look at him! There's no way he can do this.'

Mahler has to agree. How could Maxine have allowed Campbell to get into this state? 'Help me get him inside and we'll find someone to look after him'

Mahler bends to take Campbell's arm, but the man's eyes snap open and he pulls away.

'Get off me.' He struggles to his feet, glaring at them. 'I've a right to be here, haven't I? And your boss man says it's important, so I . . . I'm staying.'

He finger-combs his hair, gives them a last defiant look and lurches towards the French windows.

'Mr Campbell, wait. Where's—'

June Wallace appears at the French windows. She ushers Campbell inside, looks back at Mahler and holds up her wrist, pointing at her watch. At his nod, Anna gives him an incredulous look.

'You're not letting him go through with it? Ross isn't fit—'

'His choice.' Harsher than he'd intended, because she's right. If Campbell gets through the morning without throwing up over his shoes, it'll be a miracle. 'Look, if things become difficult, I promise I'll intervene. But we do need to go in now.'

'It's already difficult, Inspector.' She straightens her shoulders, her jawline rigid with tension. 'But thank you for that. Right, I'm ready.'

She isn't ready, of course, he knows that. None of them are. Maxine's done her best, but how could she have prepared anyone for this? Even Chae Hunt looks taken aback at the size of the crowd shoehorned into the makeshift enclosure by the side of the firth. In front of it, a horseshoe of chairs sits facing the lectern for the main part of the service, and the tributes which will follow.

Mahler catches June's grim expression as they walk across the lawns. She's scared up extra uniforms from somewhere to provide a decent level of presence throughout the grounds but she's clearly not happy, and he doesn't blame her.

Faces turning towards them as they take their seats. The buzz of chatter from the waiting journos cutting off, and cameras bursting into clicking, flashing life. Mahler hopes the minister isn't as nervous as his deer-in-headlights look suggests.

He steers Campbell to a chair next to Anna and positions himself on his other side. Campbell's face is shiny with sweat and he probably shouldn't stand too close to a naked flame, but the sight of all those pointing cameras seems to have sobered him up temporarily.

At least the Chief doesn't seem fazed by the numbers. He looks round the enclosure, nods at a few favoured faces, and starts his intro speech. Chae Hunt's camera-savvy style isn't universally popular at Burnett Road – rumour has it his youthful looks aren't solely down to good genes and clean living – but there's no denying he knows how to work a crowd.

By the time Robert Murray starts his tribute to his murdered daughter, everyone is hushed, receptive. But Ross Campbell's contribution is what really gets them straining on the edge of their seats – tearful, shambolic, his drink-trembling fingers clutching what Mahler hopes is a glass of water, Campbell is car-crash TV made flesh. Mahler's leaning forward, ready to make good his promise to intervene, when the man erupts in a coughing fit. Red-faced and sweating, he's un-telegenic enough for the cameras to lose interest and move on to Anna Murray's pale, exhausted features. Mahler passes her a glass of water, leaning past Campbell to obscure the cameras' view, and is rewarded with a nod of thanks.

As the minister delivers his homily, Mahler scans the crowd. So many people, the hotel's had to set up an additional parking area to the rear of the hotel to accommodate everyone. Had Morven really been that popular? Or have most of them just come for a good gawk and the chance to get their faces on the telly?

He follows the cameras' progress. A couple of passes over the mass of heads and back to home in on the family, lingering over Yvonne Murray's tear-stained face before they cut to the Chief for his closing remarks.

'None of us here today feels untouched by the loss of Morven Murray. It has devastated her family and, indeed, our entire community.' A pause and sideways glare at a still-spluttering Ross Campbell. 'I would like to offer my sincere sympathies to Mr and Mrs Murray . . .'

Movement by Mahler's side. He turns to see Anna fumbling with a strip of pills – she's trying to be inconspicuous, but it's making her clumsy and the strip flutters to the ground. As the minister begins a closing prayer, Mahler bends to retrieve it for her. Painkillers? A US brand, maybe. He files the name away to look up later. And finds himself returning her smile of thanks.

It catches him, somehow, that smile. Catches and holds him unexpectedly, showing him a time-stopped fragment of something new, something unquantifiable . . . and then everything falls apart.

Campbell cries out, a quick sharp sound of mingled shock and pain. He gets to his feet and takes a couple of steps, but his face is contorted and he's hunching over, clutching his left arm. Before Mahler can reach him Campbell crumples to the ground.

Silence, complete, appalled, for a couple of microseconds. Then chaos. Yvonne Murray screaming, an eerie, klaxon wail as June shouts into her mobile. Mahler makes for the unconscious man, but Anna's there already.

'Is he breathing?'

Shaking her head, not looking up. 'Can you keep everyone back, please?' Quick, efficient hands locating the end of Campbell's sternum and moving into the CPR position – she obviously knows what she's doing, and Mahler leaves her to get on with it. He works with June to hustle the media and civilians away from the scene, makes sure Maxine's looking after the Murrays and doubles back to Anna.

'Ambulance is on its way.'

A gathering panic in her eyes when she looks up. 'How long?'

Thirty minutes, according to Ambulance Control. Twenty if they're really lucky. But it's been nearly fifteen and Campbell's showing no sign of responding. And as far as Mahler's concerned, lucky is not exactly how the day has panned out so far.

'Let me.' She shakes her head, but he strips off his jacket and kneels down. 'You're tiring. Take a break.'

Readying his hands in position, showing her he knows what to do. Waiting until she nods and her fingers pull out from under his. Then pushing down, *one-two, one-two*, finding the rhythm and working to it as time falls away from him, back and shoulder muscles straining, *one-two, one-two*—

'Wait, I think he's breathing!'

She's right. Mahler lifts his hands, watches Campbell's chest rise and fall with a series of rasping breaths. He drapes his jacket over the man to conserve his body heat and slumps down beside Anna on the grass. And offers his thanks to the God he no longer believes in.

'Ambulance is here!'

June, running across the grass with a uniform in tow. Moments later, the ambulance pulls up and its doors are flung open. Mahler brings the paramedics up to speed and, within minutes, Campbell is hooked up to monitoring equipment and stretchered inside.

'Lucky man.' June watches the ambulance speed off down the drive, and turns to Mahler. 'If it hadn't been for you two . . . Lukas, I'll see you back at Burnett Road after you've taken Ms Murray home.' Anna starts to say something, but June holds up her hand. 'It's no trouble. Is it, Lukas?'

'Ma'am—'

'I'm free after two.' June spots the uniformed officer still stacking the chairs and waves him over. 'Come on, son, back to the ranch.' She sets off for the car park, the uniform trailing in her wake.

Mahler turns to Anna, but she shakes her head. 'Don't worry, I'm sure you've got better things to do. I'll call a cab, and – God, my parents! They'll be looking for me—'

'Maxine will have taken them home. And my boss is right, it is the least we can do. Campbell should be bloody thankful you were here today, Anna.'

A blink of surprise at his use of her name. 'Call it a team effort. But okay, I'm convinced.' She gets up awkwardly and looks round. 'There was a jug of water on the lectern, wasn't there? I was going to take some medication when everything kicked off.'

'Wait there, I'll find you some.' He spots one of the hotel staff heading back towards the entrance with the water, and sets off in pursuit.

When he gets back, she's sitting on the grass, her face tilted towards the sun.

'Not quite up to San Diego standards, I'm afraid, our Inverness weather.' He passes her the water. 'Do you miss it?'

'Only every day.' A barely there tremble in her fingers as she takes two pills from the blister pack. She looks up, sees him watching her. And sighs. 'They're just painkillers, Inspector. I had an . . . an injury . . . eighteen months ago. Sometimes I push myself too much, that's all.'

'An accident?'

'Something like that. I manage without them most days, but—'

'Not today?'

'They make me too fuzzy. And I knew this bloody memorial service would be hell for everyone.' A struggling bleakness in the look she gives him. 'Got that right, didn't I? Poor Ross. I was so focused on my parents, and all the time—'

'You're blaming yourself? Don't. You tried to stop him taking

126

part, that's where your responsibility ends. If not . . .' A memory-image, rising out of nowhere, of a slumped dark shape painted against the light. Mahler shakes his head. 'There has to be a limit, Anna.'

She stares at him. 'You're being kind. And that's twice you've called me by my name. It's a little . . . weird, you know?'

'I know, I surprised myself.'

A smile, and then she looks away. 'I thought . . . when Ross finished speaking, he seemed okay at first. But then he looked round, and I guess it must suddenly have hit him. He was just . . . staring at the crowd, looking like all his nightmares had come at once.'

'Today can't have been easy, I imagine. For anyone close to Morven.'

He hadn't meant the implication, not consciously. But there it is, hanging in the air, beyond recall. Beyond apology.

'Oh, I see.' Her mouth twists in a splintered-ice smile. 'So I've been judged and found wanting, is that it? Let me guess – if I could weep on cue, you'd find that more acceptable, right? Sorry to disappoint, Inspector, but I don't tear up to order. Not for the cameras, and not for you.' She gets to her feet, brushes down her dress. 'I'll call a cab from the hotel, thanks.'

Mahler watches her make her way across the grass. The woman from the plane is back – tense-jawed, wintry-eyed. Angry. Because he'd implied she wasn't grieving for her sister? On the face of it, not an unreasonable assumption. He's seen no tears, no visible emotion from her since the day of Morven's murder – which could mean nothing, of course. There's no template for grief, he understands that well enough. He suspects the cameras won't have liked it, though. Composure plays badly for the media, in his experience. And composure when dealing with the loss of a sibling . . .

Mahler starts back towards the car park. And stops short as he realises what had been bothering him ever since he'd seen Anna and Ross Campbell together. There's someone else who should have been there today, another absent sibling.

When he and Fergie had visited 'Eilean Dubh Brothers', Ewan Campbell had been fiercely protective of his younger brother. He'd told them he'd looked out for Ross ever since they were children.

So today, on what had to be the most traumatic, most gruelling of days for Ross Campbell since the discovery of Morven's body – why wasn't Ewan Campbell by his brother's side?

21

TUESDAY, 17 JUNE

Eilean Dubh Brothers, Struy

'Inspector.' Ewan Campbell walks across the rain-soaked car park to meet Mahler. His smile is the grimace of a man preparing to hustle an unwelcome but necessary visitor inside his premises as quickly as possible. 'You'll forgive me if I don't say it's good to see you again. I thought we'd gone over everything we needed to on your first visit?'

'Just a few additional queries, if you don't mind.' Mahler glances at the near-deserted café as they walk past. 'Quiet day today?'

'The first tour doesn't start until eleven. And weather like this doesn't do wonders for our casual footfall, of course.' He leads Mahler through to the office and closes the door. 'Anyway, I'm sure you didn't come for a rundown of how my business operates.' He sits at his desk, gestures to Mahler to take a seat. 'To be honest, I'm not sure why you've come at all – surely we could have done this over the phone?'

Mahler shrugs. 'Sometimes it's more helpful to talk face-to-face, don't you think? It makes it easier to avoid any crossed wires.'

'Not really, no. I'm pretty careful to say exactly what I mean, and I manage to make myself understood perfectly well most of the time.' A flicker of irritation crosses his face as Mahler doesn't reply. 'Fine, then. What do you need to know, Inspector? I'll do my best to make sure there are no crossed wires this time.'

'Just a couple of things,' Mahler assures him. 'I would have asked you at the memorial service for Morven the other day, but it didn't seem like quite the right occasion – though I don't actually recall seeing you there, now I come to think of it.'

'That would be because I didn't go.'

A reasonable comeback, Mahler supposes. If a little surprising. 'I see. It's just that your brother found it quite traumatic, and I'm sure he would have been glad of your support. Can I ask why you didn't you go with him?'

'If there was any way I could have been there, obviously I would have been. But this is a small company, and I had commitments I couldn't get out of.'

'Business meetings?'

'Exactly.' Campbell looks down at his desk diary, as though for confirmation. 'And no, I couldn't reschedule. Believe me, if I'd had any choice, I would have.'

Something in his voice there, something genuine enough that Mahler accepts he's telling the truth. About that, at least. 'I understand. How is your brother now?'

'Still in hospital, but they say it's just for observation. He needs to rest, but they think he just needs his medication reviewed.' A pointed look at Mahler. 'And not to be put under any further stress.'

Mahler nods. 'Of course. Does he have anyone who'll be able to oversee the running of his other business, while he's recuperating? It must be quite challenging, operating his car sale-room as well as fulfilling his PR role here.'

'Ross knows I'll take care of everything until he's on his feet again.' Campbell glances at Mahler. 'Is that it? Because I do have things to get on with—'

'Not quite. When we spoke last time, you said you were grateful to Morven for featuring your business on the, er . . .' Mahler consults his pocketbook, 'the *Scots Wha Hae . . . Vision* documentary. I was just wondering how that came about.'

'I'm not sure what you mean.' Campbell pours himself a glass of water from the tray on his desk, drops in a chunk of ice. 'I heard about it, saw it looked like a good opportunity to put us on the map, so I applied. And we were lucky enough to be chosen as one of the featured businesses.'

'Oh, I understand that. But didn't the rules specifically state . . . I don't know, the usual caveats about not having any connection with the organisers of the competition?'

'Probably, but I'm not sure—'

'Morven.' Mahler watches the colour leave Campbell's face, apart from two dull flushes of red. 'I'm not mistaken, am I? Before starting up the distillery, you'd worked with Morven on *Fifteen Minutes* for a couple of series?'

'Not exactly. Close but no cigar, as they say . . . whatever the hell that means.' Campbell reaches for his water glass, the barely there tremor in his hand the only hint that Mahler's rattled him.' Yes, I was in television for a while, but behind the scenes. I'd worked on the forerunner to *Fifteen Minutes* and when it bit the dust, I tried out as a presenter. But Morven came along, and . . .' he shrugs. 'She was just what they were looking for, and I wasn't.'

'That couldn't have been pleasant.'

'It was bloody awful at the time. But I picked myself up, took a couple of interesting courses, and sort of . . . fell into this business. And I've never looked back.' There's a glint of malice in the smile he gives Mahler. 'What, were you hoping I'd say I've hated her for years? Afraid you're out of luck, Inspector.'

'It might have made my job a little easier,' Mahler concedes.

'Unfortunately, things aren't usually that straightforward. You didn't like her though, did you?'

Campbell puts down his glass. 'Not much, no. I knew her vaguely through friends at Glasgow uni, and I didn't think much to her then. Frankly, she was a smug, self-satisfied bitch with a galaxy-sized ego. But my little brother was crazy about her, and that was good enough for me. So if you've come here looking to add either of us to your list of suspects, you're wasting your time.' He stands and crosses to the door, opens it wide. 'Unless there's anything else. . .?'

'I don't see the need to keep you back any longer,' Mahler tells him. 'At least, not at the moment. Thank you for your time, Mr Campbell.'

As Mahler's leaving, the sun comes out. He walks across the car park at a leisurely pace and turns to raise a hand at the figure watching him from the reception area.

Ewan Campbell had sensed he'd come on a fishing expedition, and he hadn't liked it. But most of the time, he'd been telling the truth. An easily angered man, Mahler thinks. The kind of man who bears grudges, maybe? It might have been worth pushing him a little harder, particularly about his brother's other business, up for sale for nearly a year with no takers and reported to be dying on its feet.

But Ewan Campbell had been honest enough about his dislike of Morven – and about his brother's apparently genuine love for her. Which might mean nothing, in the end. But right now, there's nowhere further Mahler can go with this, not until Ross Campbell's fit enough to talk to.

He pulls out of the car park and heads back to Burnett Road for an update on the search for the missing kitchen porter.

22

THURSDAY, 19 JUNE

Merkinch, Inverness

When Donnie opens his eyes, the rain is dripping down his neck. Soaking his skanky hoodie, making it smell worse than the bin store where he's just spent a stinking, miserable night. He gets to his feet and peers over the slatted wood door. No one around, not even the bouncer guy upstairs who says he's training for a marathon. Training for a heart attack, more like, the fucking poser. Even runs home from the club he works at, the new one down Academy Street . . . though with a boss like Cazza MacKay, maybe he needs to be fast on his feet.

He gives it a few more minutes then works his way over to the communal entrance, keeping the hoodie tight around his face. A glance left and right to check there's no one watching. Head down and through the door. Up the stairs at a run. Outside his flat, fumbling with the key. Then inside, lungs bursting, heart thumping like it's going to fly out of his chest. *Made it.*

Donnie eases the door shut and looks round. Surprise, surprise, he's had a visit from the polis. They've left a fucking mess, too – cupboards standing open, drawers pulled out and emptied, bin bags sitting on the kitchen floor and stinking the place out. Bastards. Why were they ripping his place apart, for fuck's sake? What did they think . . .? His heart starts tripping so fast he thinks he's going to fall down dead on the spot. *Oh, Jesus.*

He sinks to his knees, guts cramping, and last night's White Lightning spews out of him. The shadow in the skull mask. The knife, glinting in the half-dark. *They think it's him. Oh Christ, oh Jesus, they think the man in the shadows is him!*

Dry-heaving now, little bursts of light behind his eyes. Donnie sits back on his heels, scrubs his hand across his mouth. The man had known this would happen, he'd warned him to stay away – but what was he supposed to do, freeze his arse off in that manky shed forever? He'd been going off his head in there, and all the time, the cash the guy had given him was just lying around. No good to him there, was it? So he'd stashed an emergency tenner in his shoe and gone to get hammered on the rest. And man, it had been great. Really fucking great . . . until he'd lost the head at some wifie and got lifted by the cops. Christ, he'd thought he'd had it then. His guts give another heave at the thought of what they'd have done, if they'd worked out who they'd got in their stinking wee cell.

When they let him out, he couldn't believe it. He'd slunk back to the shed and hid there, jumping every fucking time a car went past. Waiting for the polis or the knife guy to come knocking, until he couldn't stand it any longer. He'd made his way back here – the long way round, he's not an eejit – and staked the place out. Spent the whole night in that minging bin store to make sure he hadn't been followed. Making sure he was safe.

Safe. Aye, right. Fucking joke that is. No job, no booze, no cash. No girlfriend either, not after he'd worn out his welcome at her place and stood her up at McCallum's. Nowhere he can run to. *Nowhere.* And there's a nutter in a skull mask coming for him, if the polis don't get to him first. All because he'd skived an extra fag break on that late shift – ten bloody minutes, and his life is down the pan. How is that fair? How is that fucking *right*?

Donnie shakes his head. It isn't right. But maybe there's something he can do to change that. He thinks about what he's got stashed in the shed, and what it might mean, and the cramping in his guts starts to calm. Maybe he can keep the knife guy happy and get himself a bit of insurance at the same time. Play it smart, for once in his life. But he'll need to clean himself up first.

He gets to his feet, starts stripping off the manky hoodie the cops had given him before they chucked him out, and heads for the bathroom. A wash, a shave, maybe, and back to the shed for the wee toy the guy in the shadows had left in his keeping. And then a trip down town to see who'd like to play with it.

It's still raining as he sets off – solid, slanting stuff, bouncing off the pavement like the middle of bloody winter – but it doesn't bother him, not today. More rain means fewer folk around to notice him when they should be minding their own business. And the cops are all hiding in their wee cop cars eating burgers and pretending they're on a stake-out somewhere sunny. Still, he keeps his head down as he passes McCallum's, just in case.

The jakey begging outside the shop sees him coming and starts mumbling something, his hand held out for change, but Donnie pushes past him and goes inside, unzipping his jacket. The guy in the shop is sitting by the till, a can of Red Bull resting on a stained copy of the *Highland News*. He takes the iPad from Donnie, taps the screen a couple of times. And names a figure that's about a quarter of what Donnie's expecting.

'You're joking, man! Latest model, this.'

A shrug. 'What I'm offering, pal. Take it or leave it. And I'll need to see your ID.'

'What for?'

The guy looks at him as though he's just crawled out of a bog. 'Records, pal. We all need records these days, don't we? Just a bill or something with your address on it will do. Or your driving licence?'

Driving licence. Aye, right. Donnie shakes his head. 'Not got anything with me. I'll come back later, aye?'

He makes a grab for the iPad – and knocks over the can of Red Bull. Sticky red liquid shoots out, covering the counter, and the guy goes mental. Wheechs the paper out of the way, calling him everything under the sun, and drapes it over the till while he mops up the mess with a couple of tissues.

'Fucking numpty!'

Donnie isn't listening, He's staring at the face looking out at him from the paper's front page. And the red-stained strapline underneath it. While the guy's searching for more tissues, Donnie grabs the paper. He stuffs the iPad down his hoodie and runs out of the shop, nearly tripping over the guy begging in the doorway. Running down the street, trying to ignore the cramping in his gut. Morven Murray's blood on the knife that night. *Morven* fucking *Murray* – and the guy's trying to buy him off with a handful of tenners?

People are looking at him. He makes himself slow to a walk, and ducks down Bank Street towards the river. He needs to think this through, needs to work out what happens next. But one thing's for sure, it won't go the way the knife guy's expecting. He'll think it all through, then he'll ring the knife guy, the man from the shadows. And the guy will listen to what he's got to say. Or else.

Donnie glances at the photo again and a slow smile spreads over his face.

Or fucking else.

23

HMP Inverness (Porterfield)

Built in 1902 to house 103 prisoners, Porterfield is the country's smallest prison – and, Mahler's convinced, its most discreet. Tucked away between the genteel streets of Crown and the Castle's selfie-friendly views, it's so easy to overlook that he's willing to bet a surprisingly high percentage of the city's inhabitants would struggle to pinpoint its location.

Out of sight, out of mind, apparently – which, apart from some residual paperwork, was how he'd regarded the Black Isle Slasher, as the local weekly paper insisted on calling Liam Gerrity, the man Mahler had recently lifted for attempted murder. Until Gerrity's lawyer had got in touch, that is. And told him Gerrity was in the mood for a chat.

'We're wasting our time, Lukas.' Karen presses the intercom and waits for them to be buzzed in. 'Gerrity doesn't know a bloody thing about Kevin Ramsay's murder. He's winding us up, that's all. And we've fallen for it.'

Mahler shrugs. She's probably right, and this is nothing more than an elaborate 'make the cops look stupid' wheeze cooked up by Gerrity. But five weeks after Kevin's murder, the only leads they have are minimal forensics from a burnt-out 4×4 and a few fuzzy CCTV images of a pub car-park. And Mahler's only too aware that he's had to concentrate more and more on the Morven Murray killing as the weeks have passed. If Gerrity has anything to tell them that might redress the balance, Mahler's more than willing to listen.

He passes through the metal detector in reception, waits for Karen to do the same, and follows the prison officer through to the Links Centre, a temporary-looking suite of offices housing support services from counselling to benefits advice. They're shown into the conference room, where Gerrity's waiting.

He's leaning back in his chair as they enter. His eyes are half-closed and there's a bored, hard man smirk on his face. But Gerrity's leg is twitching, beating an edgy tattoo against the table, and deprived of his usual sunbed tan, his complexion's nearly back to its natural, indeterminate porridge. Which, Mahler supposes, is pretty appropriate in the circumstances.

'Aye, aye.' Gerrity watches Karen sit down and treats her to what he probably imagines is an inviting grin. 'Thinks are looking up. You an upgrade from this guy, doll?'

Karen gives him her permafrost glare, and opens her pocket-book to make a note.

Mahler shakes his head.

'Not a good start, Liam. Let's try again, shall we? DS Gilchrist and I are running late and we're severely caffeine-deprived – trust me, this is not a good combination. So let's hear it. What do you know about the night Kevin Ramsay was killed?'

The hard man smirk makes a reappearance. Gerrity sits back, shrugs. 'Maybe something, maybe nothing. Depends on what you can do for me, know what I mean?'

'You're joking.' Karen glances at Mahler and puts down her pen. 'Been watching too much *CSI*, hasn't he, sir?'

Mahler nods. 'Certainly sounds like it. You're in no position to make demands, Liam, believe me. If you're hoping to have a year or two knocked off your sentence when it goes to court—'

'Fuck's sake, man, I'm not daft.' Gerrity scrubs the sleeve of his prison-issue sweatshirt across his shiny forehead. 'Not got a date yet though, have I? And in the meantime, I'm stuck up here in teuchter town.'

'You're on remand,' Karen reminds him. 'What's the problem?'

'Aye, in fucking community prison. Know what that means? It means folk know who you are. And if they know who you are . . .' he wipes his forehead again. 'I want a transfer. Perth, maybe, or Saughton. Somewhere big.'

Mahler stares at Gerrity. Porterfield is an overcrowded Edwardian fortress, entirely unsuited to a modern prison population. Its facilities are stretched almost to breaking point, but relations between staff and inmates are good and incidents of any kind are remarkably rare. What would make Gerrity so keen to get away?

'Finally run out of friends up here, Liam? Shame. But being banged up isn't like booking a holiday, I'm afraid – you don't get to choose from a list of preferred locations.'

Gerrity shrugs. 'Maybe I do. The hit-and-run on wee Kevin Ramsay? No names, mind, but maybe I can point you in the right direction. You know "Working Girls", don't you? That place down the Longman?'

Working Girls. Tacky as its name suggests, Cazza MacKay's most recent business venture is a bargain basement answer to a marginally more salubrious establishment at the other end of town. Mahler glances at Karen, nods. 'Go on.'

Gerrity tells them his ex had worked there until a couple of months ago. At first, she'd enjoyed it – decent money, punters mainly stag parties high on booze-fuelled bravado – but then things had gone downhill. The clientele had changed, and new staff had

139

appeared, mainly of the shaven-headed, slab-faced variety. One in particular had put the wind up Lisa sufficiently that she'd started looking for a new job.

'He was a big English guy – Manchester, Liverpool, somewhere like that. Said he was a barman, but Lisa never saw him pulling a pint. Saw him doing plenty of other stuff, though – good with his hands, know what I mean? Then the day after Kevin's murder, he was gone. Pal of his, too, just like that.' Gerrity leans back, grinning. 'Interesting, yeah? So, we talking transfer now or what?'

Interesting, yes. But not enough. Mahler leans forward. 'Need to do better than that, Liam. There's nothing there for us, not without names.'

'You're joking me.' Gerrity's smile disappears. 'I'm telling you, Kevin was a problem, and these guys sorted it out. Is that the kind of sorting out you want going on in your shitey wee teuchter town?'

'A problem to Cazza? Why?'

Gerrity shakes his head. 'Think I'm doing your fucking job for you? I told you what I want – that's all you're getting until you make it happen.' He nods at the prison officer stationed by the door. 'We're done here, pal. See the polis out, will you?'

Mahler and Karen are escorted back through the succession of doors and down to reception. As they walk over to the car, Karen looks back at the prison walls. 'Mad keen to get out of Sneckie, isn't he? What do you think?'

'I think you drag Pete away from his Candy Crush fixation and go and annoy the manager at "Working Girls". Feel free to be creative. And persistent.'

'Major annoyance or minor irritation?'

'Oh, the full works, I think – licence compliance, health and safety, employment status if you can get Immigration on board.'

'Happy to, if you think I can handle it. Sir.'

Ah, the return of the Attitude. How he'd missed it. 'Have I ever suggested you couldn't? You're a bloody good officer, Karen, and you'll make a bloody good DI some day.'

She shakes her head. 'Not if I don't have the chance to show what I can do. Donna and I could have handled today, Lukas – but every time someone mentions Cazza, you're there like Pavlov's sodding dog.' She looks him up and down, gives him an exasperated look. 'And you look bloody knackered, by the way. Would it kill you to delegate sometimes?'

A truce? Maybe the beginnings of one. And she's right, Mahler realises. He's been trying to run both cases at the same level of intensity, but there's only so far he can stretch the team's resources. Or his own, for that matter.

'I suspect the DCI might agree with you,' Mahler concedes. 'Okay, you're leading on "Working Girls". And talk to Gerrity's girlfriend while you're at it. Maybe she'll be a little more forthcoming now she's not connected with the place.'

'Fine by me.'

He glances at his watch. 'I've got a meeting in half an hour, but I'm clear at three to run over some actions. After that . . .' he tries to remember the last time he'd gone home, other than to check it was still standing. Or left the office, come to that. He makes a decision. 'After that, unless the sky falls in or a zombie plague breaks out, I'm going home.'

24

SATURDAY, 21 JUNE

Four fifteen a.m. His mobile lit up and buzzing, zig-zagging across the bedside table. Control room? June? Mahler reaches for the phone, his head already halfway into duty mode, when he reads the number on the display.

'I've seen him!' His mother's voice shrilling through the speaker, raw-edged with panic. 'I couldn't sleep so I got up to make some tea, and he was out there in the garden, just staring up at me! And you said not to call the police again, but I'm so scared, and—'

'I know.' Out of bed. Pulling on his clothes as he searches for his car keys. Rehearsing all the coping strategies they've practised with her care manager, though he can tell from her voice they're not going to work this time. 'But you're going to be fine, I promise. I'm on my way over, and—'

'What if he gets in? I'm calling the police—'

'No! Look, you don't need to do that. I'll be there—'

Silence. The kind that tells him he's talking to a dead line. He grabs his warrant card and drives at borderline bat-out-of-hell speed, up through Drummond and into Crown. As he'd expected, the genteel streets of Crown are deserted and he slows to something more sedate as he approaches the church. It's a fairly safe bet most of the local Neighbourhood Watch members are asleep, but he doesn't fancy dodging the business end of a shinty stick, wielded by one of the group's elderly insomniacs in full vigilante mode.

Mahler parks by the old academy and walks to the flat. No external signs of anything out of the ordinary, but the door is unlocked and the place is in total darkness, which isn't part of her usual pattern.

He hits the light switch and makes his way along the hall, opening doors and calling out as he goes. No answer. If something else had spooked her before he'd got here, spooked her badly enough to leave the flat . . . he's got his finger on the emergency number for the on-call CPN when the bathroom door opens a couple of inches and his mother's anxious blue eyes peer out at him.

'Lukas? Is that you?' A huge flashlight clutched in her hand, big and clunky enough to do some serious damage if she'd mistaken him for the putative prowler.

He slips the phone back into his pocket, nods. 'I'm going to take a look round. Do you want to stay here, or—'

She peers down the hall, shakes her head. 'I'm coming with you.'

'Okay. But I'll take the torch, shall I?' He waits until she's pulled on a dressing-gown, and leads the way. Always the same order, always checking behind the door first, the beam from the massive torch floodlighting each corner of the room. Kitchen next, then the utility room and out into the garden, all the way down the path. Opening the shed door, holding it wide so she can see.

'No one here. Not him, not anyone. See?'

'I . . . yes, I see.' Embarrassment pinking her cheeks, a small defeated smile. 'I'm sorry. I woke up, and . . .' she shakes her head. 'This isn't the life you should have, is it? Stuck in Inverness looking after me. Maybe if you'd stayed on at Cambridge, not joined the police . . . you'd have been happy there, wouldn't you?'

A life spent writing obscure papers on Dante and the Italian

143

renaissance. Would it have been a refuge, or a prison? His day job is only partly to blame for his storehouse of bad dreams, he knows that. And she would have been alone, defenceless. Broken.

He shakes his head. 'I made my choice. I'm good at what I do, Mum – and my life is fine, I promise. Are you feeling better?'

'A little. Would you like some tea?' An attempt at a smile. 'I'm going to have some.'

It's five a.m. Five a.m. on his first day off in nearly three weeks. Sleep is what he wants, unthinking, semi-comatose hours of it, unpopulated by Kevin Ramsay and Morven Murray's bloody, reproachful ghosts. But since that isn't going to happen . . . 'Tea would be great. Thanks.'

He watches her potter around the kitchen, rummaging for the lemon shortbread, hunting for the best mugs. Humming to herself. *Humming*, for Christ's sake. Is he here so rarely that his visiting in the middle of the night is enough to make her happy?

He glances at the dresser, frowns. Shouldn't the silver tea caddy be on that middle shelf? He'd thought the room looked neater, that she'd finally got round to tidying up. But a closer look reveals spaces on the shelves, things moved around. And on top of a pile of magazines, a cigarette lighter in neon green plastic.

'It belongs to Mina. She . . . she's been staying with me again.'

A slow, dark anger burning through the guilt. Mina, with her skinny avaricious fingers and her calculating eyes. He looks round, taking a mental inventory of the room's contents. Wishing he could whistle up a spare SOCO to do a bit of light dusting of his mother's cash tin.

'I'm not sure Mina's much of a friend, Mum. She . . .' *nicks anything that's not nailed down . . .* 'borrows things, and she doesn't always bring them back.'

She's still rooting in the cupboard for the bloody shortbread, her back towards him. He sees her shoulders tighten as she closes the cupboard door and turns round, her eyes wide, disbelieving.

'You . . . you mean she steals?'

144

'Look, I'm sorry. I—'

A snort of laughter from her stops him in the middle of the rambling apology he'd been cobbling together. She abandons the shortbread quest and sits beside him, shaking her head as though he's just told her the best joke she's heard in ages.

'Did you really think I didn't know? Lukas. I'm ill, not stupid. Yes, I keep some money in the tin. But not all of it – and if she needs an extra pound or two from what's there, so what? I've got everything I need. And she's going through a bad patch right now. She's drinking more, and I don't think she's very happy.'

'So it's fine for her to take your things?'

His mother sighs. 'Lukas, listen to me. Mina . . . she's not perfect, but she understands what it's like to . . . to never feel safe. Oh, I know he's not coming back. In the daytime, when the sun's out and the TV's on, of course I know that. But when everything goes quiet, I . . . I hear him, Lukas. I hear him *breathing*, close to me.' Her hands are kneading the tea towel, scrunching it between her fingers as though she's trying to squeeze it into nothingness. 'And that's when I'm glad Mina's here. That's when I *need* her here. If not—'

'It's okay. I understand.' He doesn't. There are very few people he would choose to share living space with, and he can't conceive of a universe in which Mina Williamson would be one of them. But he has no alternative to give his mother, no assurance of security to fight the fear that's stalked her for more than twenty years. Except for one.

He eases the towel out of her grasp and takes her hand. 'Listen to me. What happened . . . I don't know how to make it easier to live with. But I promise you this – I absolutely promise my father will never get close to you again. Never.'

Five-thirty. Not dark, not at this time of the year, but greyish, the pre-dawn light painting the city in shades of charcoal and graphite.

Mahler pulls into his parking space and kills the engine. He sits there watching the light change over the river, until he realises his forehead is threatening to hit the steering wheel as he loses the battle to keep his eyes open.

He makes himself get out of the car and walk towards the entrance to his block of flats. He's almost there when the prickling on the back of his neck makes him stop and start to turn. A huge dark shape appears from the side of the building, and something explodes out of the shape, something he barely has time to register as a fist the size of a small ham before it crashes onto his jaw.

When he opens his eyes, he's lying on a brown leather couch in a room he's never seen before. The sunlight is streaming in through a vast picture window and hitting the crystal pendants on an oversized table lamp directly in his eyeline. Wincing, Mahler reaches up to cover his eyes. And finds he's been swathed in what he suspects is a dog blanket, judging from the smell.

As he's trying to work out which particular level of hell he's been sentenced to, a round, solicitous-looking face bends over him, making sympathetic noises. 'Sugar in your tea, son? Looks like you could do with it.'

Mahler peels his face from the couch and discards the dog blanket. He sits up groggily. 'Assaulting a police officer – not your usual style, Carl. What's going on?'

Cazza shakes his head. 'Ach, it was just a wee tap. Wullie didn't mean anything by it. Did you, Wullie?'

The man-mountain on the beanbag in the corner gives Mahler a mock-penitent grin. 'Got a terrible twitch, me. Didn't even know I'd done it until I saw you hit the deck.' He glances at Cazza, gets to his feet. 'You need anything else, boss?'

'Just see we're not disturbed, son. Mr Mahler and I need to have a wee chat.'

The door closes behind Wullie, and Mahler lets himself relax a fraction. From the bruise rising on his jaw, he's guessing Wullie's contribution to any discussion would be strictly non-verbal, so it's safe to assume Cazza doesn't plan to damage him physically. For the moment.

He shakes his head to clear it. And decides not to try that again for a little while. 'So are you going to explain what I'm doing here? Before I add abduction to the assault charge, that is.'

Cazza spreads his hands. 'No need for that, surely? I just wanted a wee word, confidential, like.'

'My door at Burnett Road is always open. And I'd be very happy to see you there—'

'Aye, I'd get a warm welcome from all the cop-shop boys, all right. But seeing as I wasn't born yesterday, we'll do things my way. On neutral ground, so to speak.' Cazza puts a mug of tea on the table in front of him. 'Look, one visit from those two lassies – fair enough. Got to show your faces, haven't you? But since then, your big hairy polis have been making a right nuisance of themselves at my wee club. Turning up at all hours, harassing the girls and putting off the punters. The fuck do you think you're up to, son?'

'I'm running a murder enquiry into Kevin Ramsay's death. And I need to talk to one of your ex-members of staff about it. Perhaps you know the man I'm looking for? Manchester accent, not into small talk, but lets his fists do the talking. Ring any bells?'

Cazza shrugs. 'I've a manager there deals with staffing. I'll ask him the next time I'm down.'

'We've already spoken to him – but curiously your staff records seem to be incomplete. Which is why you'll continue to get little visits from HMRC and various related bodies. And if this missing Mancunian turns out to have been acting on your orders—'

'You want to be careful, son.' Ice displacing the veneer of affability in Cazza's voice. He leans forward in his chair, bringing his face level with Mahler's. 'You want to be really careful making accusations like that. Wee Kevin was a bit of an eejit, but there was no harm in him. And more than that, he was family.'

'He was what?'

'You didn't know? Gemma's my cousin Mandy's girl. I used to

147

give her a lift to school, sometimes, when Mandy wasn't up to it. I'd no' harm a hair on the girl's head, son . . . and that goes for her daft boyfriend too.'

Gemma Fraser's related to Cazza? It's just about possible, Mahler supposes. The MacKays' network of familial relationships is complex enough to make a genealogist break down and cry. And if he's telling the truth, it might put a different complexion on things. Though if family got in the way of business, Mahler's not sure how far Cazza's loyalties would stretch.

'And you've got no idea who might have done it? Doesn't sound like you, Carl, not knowing what's going on in your own backyard.'

Cazza's face darkens. 'Don't you worry, I'll get there. And when I do—'

'You'll pass the information on to me, of course.'

'Goes without saying.' Cazza gives him a look that tells him it does nothing of the sort. 'But seeing as we're getting things off our chests, I'll tell you this much. The wee jakey was mixed up in something – God knows how he managed it, but I think his big lugs were flapping when they shouldn't have been.'

'Like what?'

Cazza shakes his head. 'If I knew that, do you not think I'd have done something about it? But maybe you and me could . . . what would you call it in the job, now, pool our resources?'

It takes Mahler a minute to work out what Cazza's suggesting. 'You want us to work together?'

'Why not? You lot aren't going great guns on your own, are you? Listen, I'm taking a risk here – how do you think it would look if word got out I was helping the cops?'

'Not good, I imagine. So I'm supposed to believe you're doing it out of a sense of public duty, is that it?'

'Believe what you fucking like, son.' Cazza's smile turns feral, long enough for Mahler to glimpse the man behind some of the stories he's heard. 'My reasons are my own business. Now, are we going to find out what happened to wee Kevin, or what?'

Mahler lets himself imagine, just for a moment, the look on June's face if he introduced Cazza as a CHIS. 'You think he heard something he shouldn't have, you must know whose nose he put out of joint.'

'Guy further up the food chain, of course. He's the one you need to go after.'

'Who is he?'

Cazza shrugs. 'Goes by the name of Hollander, that's all I know. All anyone knows.'

'And he's into . . .?'

'You name it, he's got a finger in it. Drugs, mainly, though he has a nice line in people transport too.'

'How do I track him down?'

Cazza gives him a look. 'Man alive, son, what do I pay my taxes for? You're the fucking cop here! But you need to watch your back, because they're not all as squeaky clean as you are down at Burnett Road. And if this guy gets wind of what you're up to . . .' he shakes his head. 'You do not want to get on his radar, believe me. Not you, not your friends or your family.' Cazza puts down his mug, leans over and waves a pudgy hand in front of Mahler's face. 'How many fingers?'

'Three.'

'No concussion.' Cazza gives a satisfied nod. 'Fine, then. I'll get Wullie to drop you back at your place.'

Getting dropped off by Cazza's neanderthal henchman. He can just imagine how that would go down at Burnett Road if anyone got to hear about it. 'Thanks, but I'll walk.'

Cazza gives him a pitying look. 'Not with that lump on your napper, son. You'd keel over into the fucking river and you'd be useless to me then. Hold on there and I'll get you a taxi.'

25

MONDAY, 23 JUNE

London in late June had been everything Fergie expected – hot, smelly and full of too many people, packed into the tube's sweaty, airless hell. After he'd spoken to Morven's agent and a couple of her colleagues who had supposedly known her best, he'd headed back to Inverness on the first available flight, his shirt sticking to him and his sensible shoes all but melting to his feet. God, it had been good to be home. And even with the boss in his current mood, it still is. Sort of.

'Satnav thinks we're here now.' Fergie pulls over to the side of the road as a tractor rumbles down the single-track road towards them. 'Though I reckon it's just having us on. Who the hell would want to live up here? Arse end of bloody nowhere, if you ask me.'

Mahler looks up from his mobile, indicates the rutted side-track they've just passed. 'Owen Taylor, apparently. That looks like the turn-off on Google Earth, unless you were planning on finding another scenic route?'

'Sorry, boss.' Once the tractor's manoeuvred itself past them, Fergie gives the gear lever a thump and swings the car round.

They'd both managed to miss the first turning, but he isn't planning to point that out, not this morning. Mahler had come in half an hour later than normal in a filthy mood and sporting a lump on his jaw the size of a hen's egg. Fergie isn't planning to ask him about that either.

Mostly, Mahler's a decent guy to work for. Mostly. But since Fergie got back from London, Mahler's been haunting Burnett Road like a vampire in search of a blood bank, wanting everything done yesterday and looking like he hasn't slept in a week . . . Braveheart on his case, most likely. Two murders in the last month – in Inverness, for God's sake, how mad is that? – and sod all in the way of leads in either case. Christ, who'd be a DI?

'Owen Taylor's been living like a hermit for years, boss,' he points out as the Audi rattles down the track. 'We don't even know if he *is* the guy Hadley said they argued about, the one Morven was planning to talk to.'

Mahler gives him the sort of look Zofia uses when she's trying hard not to call him an idiot. And runs through all the reasons Owen Taylor had jumped straight to the top of their interview list when Fergie had got back from talking to Morven's agent.

Hadley had insisted Morven had abandoned her idea of a series looking into famous 'cold cases', but he admitted she'd mentioned a local unsolved disappearance she knew about, that of a missing teenage girl, to get him interested. According to Hadley, they'd had a 'robust' discussion about it, which Fergie's guessing is agent-speak for they ended up screaming at each other. But no, he was sure Morven hadn't pursued it any further. Why would she, when he'd talked it through with her and offered a couple of much more interesting alternatives to think about? Hadley had planned to email her about them, but hadn't got round to it. But by sheer dumb luck, he had remembered the name of the missing girl.

'Casey Taylor disappeared while on a family holiday up here,' Mahler finishes. 'Almost ten years ago this month. It broke her family apart, and her brother bought a house less than twenty miles from where she was last seen. If Morven was looking to move on to something harder-hitting than her usual brain-dead fluff, Casey's disappearance ticks all the right boxes.'

'Bit harsh, boss. She— man alive, what's *that*?'

The track comes to an abrupt end in front of a five-barred wooden gate. Fergie can just about make out the outline of a single-storey house, with a long gravel driveway guarded by what looks like a procession of garden gnomes in camouflage gear. But his view of both keeps disappearing as the gate shudders under the weight of the largest, least friendly-looking dog he's ever seen in his life. The beast is flinging itself against the posts in a frenzy of non-stop barking. As Fergie pulls up, the thing pauses to look their way, and he catches the gleam of amber-yellow eyes in a massive, furry head.

'I take it Hadley didn't mention the hellhound?' Mahler pushes his door open a cautious six inches and steps out.

Fergie's edging his way towards the gate when a huge man in a Black Watch body-warmer, his long, greying hair in a ponytail, comes out of the house. He walks down the drive towards them. And Fergie's stomach does a sudden backflip.

'Boss, he's got a—'

'I see it.' Mahler keeps his eyes on the man holding the shotgun. And takes out his warrant card. Slowly. 'Mr Taylor?' He holds it up and nudges Fergie to do the same. 'DI Mahler and DS Ferguson from Burnett Road. We're here to talk to you—'

'I know why you're here.' Taylor lowers the shotgun and puts a hand out to the snarling fur-mountain. 'Bella, down. You'd better come in.'

Inside, the house looks like a show home. According to the electoral roll, Taylor's been here for over a decade, but apart from the garden gnomes on guard duty up the drive, there's none of the normal clutter of day-to-day living to suggest the place is inhabited. And it's almost completely monochrome – ice-white walls, pale carpets, and sleek black couches arranged with mathematical precision on either side of a polished granite hearth.

No sign of a dog basket, so Fergie lets himself relax a fraction, hoping the beast's confined to the garden. And then he spots the only personal touch in the entire room. Dividing the room into two parts is a tall canvas and wood screen, over three metres wide, its entire surface covered with glossy black and white prints.

Mahler walks over to the screen, turns to Taylor. 'Yours?'

'Gets me out of the house. Why?'

'They're excellent. You should think about going professional.'

Taylor shrugs, mutters something about getting them coffee and disappears into the kitchen.

Fergie glances at the images, trying to see what's got the boss so fascinated he's snapping them with his smartphone. No colour anywhere, just endless shades of black and white – they might be arty, but they're the most depressing set of photos he's ever seen. And that includes the ones from his first wedding.

Stark, misshapen trees and derelict buildings glower under grim dark skies, with the occasional dead bird or burst bin-bag in the foreground to draw the eye. Clever, maybe, but he sees plenty nightmarish visions in the course of his work without having those things in his living room.

'You really rate them, boss?'

Mahler's mobile beeps before he can answer. He glances at the text and starts to say something, but Taylor reappears with coffee mugs on a tray. He passes them one each and puts a plate of short-bread in front of Fergie.

'Maybe you'll like these better, fatty. But don't drop crumbs on the floor, mate. I don't like mess.'

'Watching my figure, thanks.' Fergie glances at Mahler, gets the nod to go first. 'You said you knew we'd want to talk to you, Mr Taylor. Why was that?'

'You've got a high-profile murder on your patch, and you've got no bloody leads to speak of. So you're going through the dead bint's contacts, and guess who turns up? An ex-army weirdo, living on his own up a dirt track in the bleedin' Highlands.' Taylor gives him a grim smile. 'Be a funny sort of copper if you didn't want to talk to me, wouldn't you?'

Mahler leans forward. 'So Morven Murray was in contact with you. And as you say, this is a high-profile case – but you didn't think that might be useful information to share with the police?'

Taylor's smile dies. He puts down his mug, centring it carefully on his coaster. And a faint warning bell starts chiming, somewhere in the back of Fergie's head. *Careful, boss. Go easy here.*

'We appreciate you talking to us now,' Fergie assures him. 'So Morven did come to see you?'

'Twenty-fifth of May, yes – I don't exactly get many visitors, so I remember the date. Wouldn't get out of the car until I'd locked Bella in the shed, mind, and then she sat on the edge of her chair, like she thought she'd catch something. She liked my shortbread, though.'

Fergie nods. 'And you talked about your sister?'

Taylor looks down at his hands. 'After a bit. Still chokes me up, and . . . it's tough, mate. Brings it all back, you know? And that messes with me bloody head. She asked me some family stuff, asked to see a couple of pictures of Casey. Then she asked if I'd take part in this series she was planning.'

'How did you feel about that?'

Taylor shrugs. 'Said no at first. Had my fill of journalists the first time round, when Casey went missing, didn't I? But that Morven . . . she had a way with her. Bit of a smooth-talker, you know? Made you think you were something special.'

'Good-looking woman, wasn't she?'

Taylor grins at Fergie. 'Easy on the eye all right, mate. Wouldn't have chucked her out on a cold night, know what I mean? And in the end I thought, what harm can it do – our Ma's gone now, and nothing can hurt her any more. Might even turn up something, who knows? And if there was even that small chance, and I didn't

154

take it . . .' he shakes his head. 'Couldn't do it, could I? Couldn't close the door on the possibility, even after all these years, that someone might remember something about the night Casey went missing.'

Mahler leans forward. 'So you told Morven you'd do it?'

'Said I'd think about it. Wasn't going to say yes there and then, was I? Didn't go down well, either – counting on me being a push-over, I reckon.' He gives a grim smile. 'Wiped the smirk off her face and no mistake.'

'What happened then?'

Taylor shrugs. 'She had another go at getting me to sign up right away. But when I wouldn't play ball, she made a couple of notes on her iPad, finished her tea and left.'

'How was her mood? Would you say she seemed angry or upset?'

'More surprised, I'd say. Don't think she was used to people saying no to her, know what I mean? Left me her card and asked me to give her a ring if I changed my mind. Next thing I know, her face is all over the bleeding news. And there's no chance of getting her programme made now. Is there?'

Mahler shakes his head. 'So you argued about your decision? And this was the last time you saw or spoke to Morven Murray?'

'I never said we argued.'

'You didn't deny it either. And you haven't answered my question.'

The alarm goes off inside Fergie's head. Only now it's not a bell, it's a bloody great klaxon. He glances at Mahler. Christ, what's wrong with him today? Taylor had been co-operating, talking freely, and now it's as though a switch has been thrown, erasing the rational, matter-of-fact man they've just been speaking to.

Taylor stands up, knocking over the coffee table, and the mugs tip onto the vanilla carpet.

'Might have bloody guessed. Your investigation's going nowhere, so you're looking for someone to pin it on – and your local ex-army nutter with a missing sister is as good a bet as any, eh?'

'No, of course not!' Mahler eye-signals to Fergie. 'That wasn't—'

Taylor shakes his head. 'Go on, get out, the pair of you! You've got thirty seconds until I let Bella loose. You should be fine, she's not as young as she was.' He grins at Fergie. 'Not putting any money on you though, fatty. Plenty for old Bella to get a hold of on you, ain't there?'

'Mr Taylor, I'm sorry.' Mahler backs up, still talking, and eases the door open. 'You've been very helpful, and—'

'Twenty-nine, twenty-eight . . .'

Through the door and down the drive, the monster barking its head off as it takes off after them. Mahler's in the lead, but not by much, and Fergie's damn sure he's not getting left behind. Mahler reaches the gate, clears it and turns back to help, but Fergie's already airborne. As he sails over the gate, he feels the heat of the dog's breath on his rear as it makes a last-minute leap, but its jaws snap shut on empty air.

Before Taylor decides that opening the gate would be a fun way to end the proceedings, Mahler and Fergie sprint for the car. Mahler gets there first and throws himself inside, but Fergie's only seconds behind. He jams the key in the ignition and reverses down the track at a speed that would normally have Mahler threatening him with a stint on traffic duties. And he doesn't ease off until they're back on the main road and heading for the A9.

'That was . . . informative.' Mahler glances at Fergie. 'You okay?'

'Arse is still in my trousers, if that's what you mean. Jesus God, did you see the teeth on that thing?'

'Oddly enough, I didn't stop to examine it.'

'Fair enough. You want to call Taylor in once he's calmed down a wee bittie?'

Mahler shakes his head. 'He's told us what we needed to know. And he's suffering from severe, stress-induced anxiety.' An awkward silence. 'Which I knew, and I still misread him. My fault.'

'Ach, he was like a pressure cooker, man. No telling when he

156

was going to go off.' Except the signs had been there from the start, Fergie thinks. And you didn't just misread him, boss. You didn't read him at all. He glances at Mahler, clears his throat. And plunges in. 'You all right, boss? It's just, you know, if your Mam's not so good . . .' He lets the sentence hang. Too close to the line? Aye, probably. 'Look, I didn't mean—'

'There are . . . issues at the moment. A new support worker, and she doesn't cope well with change.'

'Shit.' That explains the stream of text messages. Christ, does he get any peace? 'I'm sorry, boss.'

Mahler shrugs. 'It's hardly an excuse. I lost focus, that's all – but we're still a lot further ahead than we were this morning.'

'We are?'

'Taylor said Morven was taken aback when he didn't agree, but no more than that.'

'Because she thought he'd change his mind.'

'Maybe. But Morven doesn't strike me as the kind to give up that easily – she'd want to keep her options open in case of any setbacks. So maybe she had a plan B lined up, someone else up here she was planning to talk to.'

'Could be, aye.' Fergie launches the Audi into the Inverness-bound traffic. 'And he said she had her iPad with her, didn't he?'

'Which wasn't recovered from her room. Exactly. So, the killer took it. The question is, what did he do with it?'

'Drive over it. Drop it in the firth,' Fergie suggests. 'What I'd do if I wanted to get rid. So where now, back to the shop?'

Mahler shakes his head. 'Not right away. I think we'll take a little trip over to the Black Isle first.'

'Boss?'

'You weren't impressed by Taylor's photographic talents, were you?'

'Not much, no.'

'Pity. You see, Taylor was obviously more taken with Morven Murray than he let on, because he made a trip to Bunchrew for her memorial service. And he took a couple of really interesting snaps there.'

Mahler takes out his smartphone, holds an image up in front of Fergie.

'Recognise those two? Cazza MacKay's heavies, both of them. And somehow I don't have them down as grieving fans. Anna Murray said Ross Campbell had been staring at the crowd before he collapsed – in a sort of daze, she assumed. But what if he was staring at something very specific? *Someone* very specific.'

'You think there's a connection?'

'I bloody know there is. And it might just explain—' Mahler's mobile buzzes. The boss listens for a moment, nods . . . and utters three words Fergie would have laid odds on never hearing him use in the same sentence.

'Good work, Pete. Yes, right away.' He ends the call and turns to Fergie. 'Morven's second mobile's been traced, and the call logs are in.'

26

TUESDAY, 24 JUNE

Seven-fifteen a.m. An early-morning chill, already burning off as Anna leaves the house. Back in San Diego, the city would already be alive – traffic humming on the 15 and the I-5, KPBS playing on the drive into work. But Inverness doesn't do rush hours, not at this time in the morning. A couple of cars pass her on Drummond Road and there's a dog barking somewhere in the distance, but her footsteps are the only ones she hears as she walks down to the school.

Jamie's silver 4×4 is waiting in the car park. The place is deserted, but she still glances over her shoulder as she gets in the car.

'Someone tailin' you, babe?' He glances at her face and drops the cop-show villain impression. 'You all right?'

'Fine.'

'That good, huh?' He turns onto the main road, heads towards Inshes. 'Look, if this is a bad time, we can always reschedule. The last thing I want to do is make your life any harder right now.'

'It's not that. It's just . . . we got a few crank calls yesterday evening.'

'Because of the *Crimewatch* thing? Yes, I can see that'd stir up the nutters. How are your folks bearing up?'

'How do you think?'

Lukas Mahler had called to warn her the day before the broadcast, an odd, stilted kindness in his voice. She'd worried about her mother's reaction when the programme aired, but in the end it was her father who'd got up and walked away, helpless to stop his imagination supplying the unvoiced horrors in Mahler's careful narrative.

'Sorry, stupid question. Listen, if you need to offload—'

'Thanks, but today's supposed to be about your project.' She finds a smile from somewhere. 'How about we focus on that right now?'

'Works for me.' As they cross the firth, Jamie outlines his plan to feature one family caught up in each of the most infamous Clearances and follow their stories in his documentary. 'I've roughed out a quick draft, if you want to take a look?' He indicates a folder lying in the footwell on her side.

She pulls out the folder and starts to read, mentally cross-referencing Jamie's draft with the notes she's made from the source material. But after a few pages, the words are jumping in front of her eyes. By the time they're coming up to the Cromarty Bridge, her head is nodding forward and the folder slides to the floor.

'Sorry.' She bends to retrieve it, but he shakes his head.

'Leave it. Look, we've got a tractor and two bloody caravans in front of us so we're going nowhere fast. Why don't you close your eyes for a bit? Don't worry, I won't dock your pay!'

'Very funny.' She starts to make a half-hearted protest, and gives up. Why? He's right, she's shattered. And a ten-minute catnap can't hurt . . .

When she opens her eyes, the 4×4 is slowing outside a small, white-washed church, enclosed by moss-covered drystone walls.

'We're here?'

'We are.' Jamie pulls over on a patch of rough ground opposite the entrance. 'Built by Thomas Telford, no less, in 1827. See, I've been doing my homework. Impressed?'

'Very.' Though as soon as she'd seen it, Anna had recognised one of Telford's 'parliamentary kirks', intended to provide rural highland communities with places of worship. But none of the others, she suspects, is as intimately connected with the story of the Clearances as the one she's looking at now. She gets out of the car and walks over to the gate.

'Built to serve a community of more than two hundred souls,' Jamie tells her. 'Hard to imagine now, isn't it?'

'Just a bit.' Anna looks down the long, empty valley. In March 1845 the people of Glencalvie had been served with writs of removal . . . and told it was their landlord's wish to see them gone, not just from the strath, but their homeland itself. By 24 May, having nowhere else to go, ninety newly homeless people had built a makeshift camp in Croick churchyard. And had left a lasting memorial to their plight.

'They're down here.' Jamie leads her past the weathered headstones to one of the side windows. 'The messages are pretty hard to read, but the transcriptions—'

'I know what they say.'

Anna walks round to the entrance and pushes open the door to reveal plain white walls, austere dark pews. And a century-old chill that all the central heating in the world isn't going to shift.

'They held out for three years, though,' she points out when Jamie reappears. 'And at least the reporter from the *Times* made sure their story got a hearing.'

He gives her a reproachful look. 'So that makes it all right? When those ninety people walked out of this strath, they were walking away from everything they'd ever known. Not for dreams of a better life, not chasing an easier option – these people were forced from the lands they'd held for generations.'

'I know. Jamie, I understand. I'm just . . . being a historian, I guess. Being balanced. It doesn't mean I don't care about what happened here.'

'But you can't—' He glances at her, sighs. 'I was preaching at you, wasn't I? Sorry. I just . . . it gets to me, that's all. I'll shut up now.'

'Nothing wrong with being committed to your subject. And preaching here would be kind of appropriate, wouldn't it?'

'I suppose. Look, I'm going to see if I can find the land agent's grave. Rain a couple of curses down on him or something.'

Anna watches Jamie make his way across the grass. Odd to see this seriousness, this driven quality in him when his jokes are what she remembers most from university. But perhaps he'd played up the mischievous side of his character because he'd known that's what she needed most? If so, she'll always be grateful to him for that.

She takes a couple of snapshots of the church interior, including the transcriptions from the window, and starts to head back to the car. After years in the Californian sunshine, she's forgotten how changeable the Highland weather can be. The sky, ice-blue when they'd arrived, is clouding over now as the warmth leaches from the day, but the light still lingers on the green and brown-gold hills. Hollywood's version of the Highlands, this view she's looking at. Stark and beautiful . . . and empty. And by the roadside opposite the church, with no irony at all, someone's placed a neat placard advertising holiday lets at Croick manse.

A burst of anger, sparking through her veins. Holiday lets, for God's sake.

'Nice touch, isn't it?' Jamie comes over to stand beside her. 'That's what happens when people disconnect from their past, Anna. They forget it's what made them. I know I got a bit carried away earlier, but—'

'It's okay. I get it.' She'd been on the point of telling him she couldn't continue working on his project. Her role has already grown beyond the few hours' research they'd originally talked about, and it would be so easy to get drawn in even further. Easy, and oh-so tempting. What she's seen and felt here . . . she could wrap the work around her, use it like a shield against the memories that won't leave her, of walking up to Morven's suite and opening the door to find—

Anna shakes her head, pushes the images away. She'd told herself spending time on Jamie's project would be wrong, that her parents need all her attention right now. But he's right, she's shattered. Keeping the household running, fielding calls from exclusive-hungry journos . . . if she could sleep nightmare-free for more than a few hours, she could just about manage. But she's getting close to running on empty, she knows that. If working with Jamie can give her something else to focus on, something to help blot out the images, even for a while . . .

'We'll make sure this isn't forgotten,' she tells him. 'Remind people what happened here.'

He gives her his old grin, the one she remembers from uni. 'For a moment I thought I'd frightened you off. How about I buy you brunch in Dornoch to celebrate?'

'Find me a decent cup of coffee and you've got a deal.'

The restaurant is on Dornoch's main street, not far from its tiny but picturesque cathedral. While Jamie orders, Anna reads through the rest of his draft proposal. And looks up to find him trying to gauge her reaction.

'I amended the Culloden references after we talked last week. You think we've got the right opener now?'

'It's your project. But yes, I do. What sort of timescale have the production company given you?'

He looks blankly at her. 'What do you mean?'

'I thought you said BBC Scotland—'

'They're looking at it, yes. I can't jump at the first offer I get, though, can I?'

'I suppose not.' Though she'd got the impression it was pretty much a done deal. She reaches for the folder to check something, and catches the gaze of a couple at a nearby table. Who immediately start studying their menus in sudden, unconvincing fascination, as though they hadn't been listening in to every word.

'Think you've got a couple of fans there,' Anna stage-whispers to Jamie. 'Over by the window, see? The ones carefully not looking at us.'

He glances casually over, shakes his head. 'No way. With my glasses on, I've a very forgettable face, and—'

'What?' She looks round as the woman says something to her companion. The man looks up, turns towards them. And stares straight at Anna, the local paper in his hand. She can't read all of the headline. But the first word . . . the first word is enough.

She pushes back her chair and runs for the entrance. In the shadow of the cathedral, she slumps down on the only tourist-free bench and shuts her eyes. Shuts out the world. Or tries to.

'Anna, I'm sorry.' Jamie standing in front of her, his shirt pulling out of his trousers, the way it used to when he was at uni. 'Bloody *Crimewatch*! I'd hoped you could put the whole Morven thing out of your head for a few hours.'

Yes, because it's that easy. 'It's always in my head, Jamie. What I saw won't just go away.'

'No, I . . . God, what a stupid thing to say.' He sighs, sits down on the wall beside her. 'Look, you've not said much about what happened. Do you think it would help? I'm told I'm a good listener.'

It won't. But she tells him anyway, the words a rough and bleeding rawness in her throat. Tells him about the figure sprawled on the rug, blonde hair painted with darkness. The rug stickily damp beneath her knees as she reached out . . . She looks up to see him watching her, his eyes stunned, unfocused. 'Who would do that to her, Jamie? To anyone?'

'God, I . . .' he makes a hopeless gesture with his hands. 'I don't know how to answer that. A crazed fan, a random psycho? Anna, there are nutters everywhere.'

She shakes her head. 'What if that's not how it was?'

'What do you mean?'

'I just think . . . you didn't see her. Whoever did it, it was like they were trying to destroy her. Like they hated her so much, they were trying to obliterate her.'

He shrugs. 'Maybe that's exactly what it was. Maybe it's like . . . I don't know, a serial killer's calling card or something.'

'In Inverness? And if it's a serial killer, why haven't there been more murders?'

'How do you know there won't be?' She starts to say something, but he holds up his hands. 'Sorry, that was a horrible thing to say. But I think I know where this is coming from.' He puts his hand on her shoulder, gives it an awkward squeeze. 'Look, don't hate me, okay? But you and Morven, you lived in different worlds – you were strangers, really, until this crazy wedding stuff came up. And maybe you hoped the wedding might be a chance to straighten things out, yes? But it's too late for that, so you're trying to deal with it any way you can.'

'That sounds like a plot from one of your novels.'

'I'm right though, aren't I?'

She swallows down the sudden rawness in her throat. 'Maybe.' But it's more than that. She needs to understand what happened. Needs it to make *sense*. 'Morven wasn't some random victim on a psychopath's hit list, Jamie. She was chosen.'

'Oh, for God's . . .' He gets to his feet, dusts a scatter of gravel from his chinos. 'OK, fine. She was chosen. By some unknown nutjob, for unknown nutjob reasons. Look, no offence, but can we drop it now? This wasn't exactly how I'd seen us spending today.'

His face is ashen, carved into shocked, rigid lines, and she feels a twinge of guilt. She hadn't wanted to talk about what happened, Jamie had encouraged her. But the little she'd told him was more than he wanted to hear, that much is obvious. 'Fine by me. So where next, Badbea or Helmsdale?'

His phone is buzzing on the wall next to her. He glances at it, hits a key and shoves it in his pocket. 'No, let's leave it for today. I don't think your head's in the right place for this right now, and I'm bloody sure mine isn't.'

Jamie walks back to the car, leaving her to follow. On the drive back to Inverness he's uncommunicative, resisting her attempts at conversation until she's had enough and asks him to drop her on the main road rather than at her parents'. As he drives off, Anna catches a look of relief on his face. And wonders if it mirrors her own.

She walks down to her parents' house. There's a sludge-coloured Audi parked outside with a 'Bairns Not Bombs' sticker on the rear window – one of her Dad's friends, she thinks at first, come to rope him into leafleting duty for the 'Yes' campaign. But when she gets inside, there are voices coming from the living room.

She pushes open the door. And Lukas Mahler turns towards her.

'Miss Murray. Might we have a word?'

'What is it?' Steadying herself against the doorjamb, a sudden sick foreboding curling round her insides. 'Have you found someone?'

Mahler and his sergeant exchange a look. But before they can say anything, her mother shakes her head.

'They want to talk to you.' Her voice is tight, accusing. 'About Morven.'

He opens his eyes to darkness; an unreal, all-encompassing absence of light that seems to have physical mass, weighing him down and robbing him of any possibility of movement. It's only when he grows accustomed to the gloom that he makes out the straps around his naked torso, pinning him to the cold metal gurney on which he's lying.

Fear, sharp and sudden, cramping his guts. Flooding his throat with bile as his vision adjusts to his surroundings. More straps round his wrists and ankles, the leather biting into his skin. A steel trolley over to his right, holding what looks like a collection of surgical instruments – not clean and pristine-shiny, but dull, bent-bladed, spotted with splashes of brown.

The fear has him now, a vicious, clawing thing tearing at his insides as he struggles to get free, his skin raw and bloody. He has to get away, has to try and save himself before . . . a door opens in the middle of a wall, flooding the room with light. Showing him what's waiting there for him.

Morven comes towards him – drags herself towards him, her hands cupping her abdomen and the things that ripple and move there. And her face is like the sum of every horror flick he's ever seen, grey-blue, bloated, the eyes sunk into their sockets but still alive. Still knowing.

One hand reaches out towards him, and something breaks inside him. He opens his mouth to yell—

He wakes with the scream still building in his throat, his hands clenching and unclenching around the sweat-soaked sheets. The dream so impossibly real that he scans the room, his heart jumping in his chest, until the contours of his world return to normal.

Christ. He gets to his feet, staggers to the bathroom. Turns the shower on full and douses himself in cold water until every inch of skin is stinging and he's certain he's awake.

Towelling himself down, he catches his reflection in the mirrors. Anger courses through him, stiffening his spine, pulling his shoulders back. Remaking him into the man he's become. The man in charge of his own fate. The man who acts.

He walks through to the living room in search of the Lagavulin he'd opened the night before and finds it next to the armchair, a third of the bottle gone. An inherited weakness, this craving that comes on him in times of stress. One he can't let himself indulge in, not now when things are finally starting to go his way. He opens the bottle, takes it through to the kitchen and lies it on the draining board. And watches the whisky empty with exquisite, teasing slowness down the sink.

The dream had been a warning, that's all, a sign not to let his guard down. Now more than ever, he needs to hold his nerve. It's taken a while, but the saccharine tide of grief over the bottle-blonde bitch's passing is finally starting to ebb. He's seen the coverage slowly wane as the weeks go by, and in a few months, Morven Murray will be just another dead has-been. Her choice, in the end, not his. She'd held his destruction in her hands and refused to let it go. What was he supposed to do, let her destroy everything he'd achieved?

There are still one or two loose ends he needs to deal with, though. He'd dismissed the police's efforts at first – that had been a mistake, and one he's not intending to repeat. Oh, the Crimewatch charade was a surprise, but it's hard to see what they'll gain from it. There is no new information to be uncovered, nothing that will lead them back to him . . . nothing, apart from those loose ends. But very soon they too will cease to be a problem.

This time, he's laid his plans even more carefully. And this time, there will be no witnesses.

Of any kind.

27

TUESDAY, 24 JUNE

Burnett Road Police Station

The interview room reminds Anna of her UCSD office, right down to the mint-green walls and utilitarian beige floor-covering. All she needs now is for Chrissy the departmental secretary to bounce through the door, and she'll know this is some sort of sick, unfunny wind-up.

She shifts in her seat, tries an experimental shuffle forward, but the chair doesn't move. Bolted down, she suspects. A metallic sourness fills her throat, the first stirring of fear she's let herself feel since she'd got home to find Mahler there. Waiting to have a chat, according to his sergeant – just to clear up a couple of details, that's all.

Anna looks up at the video camera mounted on the ceiling, and the sourness crawls a little higher. This doesn't feel like a room where people have any kind of chats. This is a room where people like Mahler ask questions. And don't stop asking until they get answers.

She reaches for the awful coffee someone's brought her, but her hand's shaking and the coffee slops onto the table as Mahler comes in. He's carrying a folder and there's a spiky-haired, impatient-looking woman with him who introduces herself as DS Gilchrist. She gives a brief, unconvincing smile and rattles through an explanation about the interview, but Anna isn't listening. She's staring at Mahler, the pulse jumping in her neck as he opens the folder and starts to read aloud.

She makes herself listen, makes herself not look away as he takes her through her initial statement – the argument at Mam and Dad's, meeting up with Jamie and going into town – and she still has no idea why he's brought her there. Not until he finishes reading and looks up.

'Did you know your sister used two mobiles, Miss Murray?'

She tells him no, she hadn't known that, and Mahler nods.

'One for work, one for family and friends. The messages from the second mobile have now been recovered – and I have to tell you, they make very interesting reading. Would you like me to explain why?'

Oh, Jesus. She licks her dry lips. 'Go on.'

'When I spoke to you with DS Ferguson at Bunchrew, I asked you if you'd had any contact with Morven after coming back to the hotel. Do you recall that?'

'Yes, of course. Look, I told you. I hadn't slept for nearly twenty-four hours, I had a couple of drinks with Jamie, and I guess it all just . . . caught up with me. When I got back to the hotel, I felt really woozy. The last thing I wanted was another fight with Morven.'

'But you did have contact with her. Didn't you?' He turns to another section of the file. 'You weren't too "woozy" to conduct an abusive conversation with her by text. You do recall that, I take it? If not, let me refresh your memory. There are five unanswered messages from Morven's phone, all saying "Where are U Midget". The last three are accompanied by triple exclamation marks and are in upper case. You remember receiving these, yes?'

A twist of nausea, rising from her stomach. 'Yes.'

'Thank you.' He turns over a page. 'The exchange continues:

'"Morven: Don't you dare bail on me, I'm warning you! I need you at my rehearsal tomorrow with your smiley face on. Got it?"

'"You: I'll be there. For Mam and Dad, not you."

'"Morven: Jesus Christ. Still sulking about the Con-man after all this time?? U need to get a life, Midget. He was out of your league anyway."

'"You: Fuck off, Morv. Just fuck off and die." Do you remember sending these texts?'

Mahler and the spiky-haired DS staring at her. The silence growing, finding a weight of its own. *It's not like you lied to him, is it?* 'I . . . yes.'

'Yes. But you didn't see fit to mention them to me or Sergeant Ferguson when I asked if you'd been in contact with your sister.'

'I said I hadn't spoken to her, and I hadn't. The texts . . .' God, why hadn't she told him about the bloody texts? It doesn't even make sense to her, looking back. 'I'm sorry. I should have told you about them, but I wasn't thinking straight – I don't make a habit of sending texts like that, and I suppose I was embarrassed. It was stupid of me.'

Mahler gives her a look she's pretty sure translates to *you think?* 'Moving on . . . in her last text Morven refers to a con man. Do you know who she's talking about?'

Colour, rising to burn her cheeks as the silence lengthens. DS Gilchrist's pen tapping an impatient tattoo. And still she can't find the words.

'Ms Murray, I asked who—'

'Connor Ryan. He was my tutor at uni, and we . . . we were involved. And yes, I know how it sounds. But Conn was just starting out on his academic career. Not that much older than his students, and getting a hard time in tutorials because of it, I think. And somehow we just . . . fitted.'

171

Gilchrist leans forward. 'What happened?'

A bitterness at the back of her throat. 'Morven happened. I've no idea how she found out, but she did. And she made it her business to put an end to things. She told him if he didn't finish with me, she'd make sure everyone in the department knew about us.'

'And he went along with it to save his career?'

Anna shakes her head. 'Conn was ... I'd never seen him so angry. He was ready to brazen it out, said it would all blow over if we stood up to her. But I knew Morven, knew how far she would go. So I finished with him.'

Mahler glances at the file. 'I see. And then?'

'Conn left the following term. Went back to Ireland for a time, I think, then to St Andrews. We kept in touch for a while, but then ... then we didn't.'

'And you haven't spoken to him since? Do you know where he is now?'

'No, I told you, we lost touch.' She watches Mahler and the woman exchange glances. What the hell ...? And then it hits her. 'Wait, you seriously think Conn – that's crazy! Conn couldn't kill anyone. And we broke up fifteen years ago, for God's sake!'

'Believe me, the ability to harbour grudges is not time-limited. Tell me, why did you wait nearly an hour to reply to Morven's texts?'

'I didn't. I answered them as soon as I got back to my room and switched my phone on.'

Mahler shakes his head. 'Your replies weren't sent until eleven-thirty and we've confirmed Mr Gordon was back at his hotel by ten-twenty. Could you have fallen asleep and not replied until later?'

'No, I ...' It couldn't have happened like that. She knows it didn't, because ... she tries to pin down the reason she's so sure, but it's hopeless. The little she remembers is faded, washed away by the memory of what followed. 'God, I don't know. Maybe.'

'I see.'

An odd dissatisfaction in his voice. Is Mahler actually trying to intimidate her? Anna stands up and the spiky-haired DS shoots her a look of surprise.

'Look, you said this was voluntary. I've answered all your queries, and now I'd like to leave. I have the right to do that, don't I?'

With the least convincing smile Anna's ever seen, Gilchrist tells her yes, she has that right, and Mahler terminates the interview. Another learned-by-rote speech from Gilchrist she doesn't listen to, a signature on a form, and she's being taken along the corridor back to the reception area.

'So that's it? What happens now?'

'Now?' Mahler takes out a card, hands it to her. 'I thank you for coming in and ask you to call me if you think of anything else – or if Mr Ryan gets in contact.' He glances at his watch, turns to Gilchrist. 'I'll see Ms Murray to the exit. Briefing upstairs in ten, yes?'

It sounds like a dismissal, and from the look on her face, that's exactly how Gilchrist takes it. She gives a curt nod and goes back through the last set of security doors.

'I'm fine from here, thanks.' Anna turns to go, but Mahler's there before her.

He holds the door open, waits for her to go through. 'I'll walk with you as far as the main road.'

'Is this where you tell me not to leave town?'

'No, this is where I tell you to drop the attitude and start co-operating with this investigation.' Outside, he looks less polished than usual, his features almost gaunt in the glare of the sun. 'For God's sake, Anna, I'm not your enemy – I'm the man who's trying to find your sister's killer. I'm trying bloody hard, as it happens, because I want him downstairs in one of my cells, waiting for his trip to the High Court. Isn't that what we both want?'

Frustration in his voice. And a ragged edge of weariness, surprising her into an unwilling compassion.

'Of course it is. It's just . . .' she shakes her head. How to make him understand? 'Morven's death . . . I know it's real, I *know* she isn't here any more, but I don't feel it, not really. It's like it happened to someone else. Does that make me sound as crazy as I think it does?'

Silence as he looks at her. Then a sigh. 'Actually, no. I had a friend who died, and that's exactly . . .' he shrugs, looks away. 'You should have told me about the texts.'

'I know. And I'm sorry – but you're wrong about Connor. The man I knew – there's no way he could do something like this.' She glances up at him. 'I suppose you hear that all the time, don't you?'

'Doesn't make it a lie. Anna, people are like Russian dolls – they have faces under faces, masks under masks. And the worst ones, the really monstrous ones keep them bloody well hidden. My job is to strip those masks away, if I can. And show their naked faces to the world.'

They've reached the exit to the main road. At the car-park barrier, he turns to look at her. 'You've said you weren't close, but you must have spoken sometimes. Did Morven ever mention any worrying incidents, any arguments she felt unsettled by?'

Anna tries to imagine Morven being unsettled by an argument. And shakes her head. 'I'm sorry, but we . . . look, we hardly ever talked, not really. I honestly know very little about her life. Why?'

Mahler's silent for a moment, as though he's deciding how much to tell her. 'We think it's unlikely Morven was killed by a total stranger, which means we're looking at someone she either knew personally or had dealings with in the course of her work. We're following various leads, but if there's anything you think of that might help, even if it doesn't seem important—'

'I'll get in touch. I promise.'

He gives her a weary nod. 'That's all I ask.'

She watches him walk back across the car park. An odd sort of policeman, with his just-so tailoring and his interesting take on people skills. Smug, Jamie had called him, but that's unfair. There's an awkward kindness in him, a compassion that must make his job a kind of purgatory at times. Under the Oxbridge polish, Mahler seems like a man constantly unsure of himself, a man who takes nothing for granted. A man with his own masks, perhaps. But what he'd said about the killer just confirms everything she'd been trying to tell Jamie. Of course Morven must have known him – how else could he have got close enough to do what he'd done?

She'd told Mahler she knew very little about Morven's life, and it had been the truth. But perhaps it's time that changed.

28

Ness Islands, Inverness

Donnie zips up his hoodie and pulls it round his face – there's no CCTV this far past the castle as far as he knows, but he's not taking any chances. He walks on, past Bellfield Park, past the posh flats before he turns down into the Islands. Fucking stupid place to meet, he thinks. A crazy place. It had been fine a couple of hours ago, when the sun was out and there were still folk around – kids mucking about, bairns playing in the park, tourists taking selfies on the bridge. But the kids and the tourists are gone now, and the Islands are dark and quiet, the only sounds the rushing water and the hitch of his own breathing, quick and nervy like a young lassie on her first date.

Standing out here on the bridge gives him an odd, exposed feeling. He looks round and finds a spot on the bank, near to the trees where he can watch for someone coming from both directions. He wipes his damp palms on his jeans, his eyes darting from side to side as the darkness takes hold and the shadows lengthen.

Fuck, what is he doing here? This whole thing had been a bad idea, right from the start. Oh, contacting the knife guy to tell him things had changed, that had felt good. He'd been calling the shots for once – him, wee Donnie Stewart, showing he couldn't be pushed around. And it had gone great, just the way he'd planned . . . only there's no sign of the guy, and the dark, the trees, the fucking *silence* is doing his head in. Making him see things, remember things—

The bushes beside him explode into life. He spins round, his hands bunching into fists . . . and a wee brown and white dog bursts onto the path, trailing a long, sparkly lead. It takes off for the bridge, little legs going like the clappers, and though its owner is only a couple of minutes behind, Donnie's betting the beastie will be halfway to Bught Park before she catches up with it.

No sign of the knife guy yet. Donnie pulls out his mobile to check the time, wishing he'd got a video of the wifie chasing her dog. Put that on YouTube and he wouldn't need the guy's money, he'd be fucking coining it. He glances at the display, and a finger of cold touches the back of his neck. Twenty-five past? Christ, the guy's nearly half an hour late.

Donnie thinks about calling him. Thinks about it for all of five seconds, as the cold feeling inches its way down his spine. Because this is starting to feel all wrong. *Bad* wrong, like that night at Bunchrew. What the fuck is he supposed to do if the guy doesn't turn up – he can hardly go to the bobbies, can he? He'd taken the guy's money, made himself a fucking accessory or something. And—

Footsteps coming up behind him. Fast, determined. Donnie's stomach gives a quick, acid lurch. Fuck, why hadn't he taken some insurance along with him? Because he's suddenly, sickly sure whatever the man's bringing him, it isn't wads of cash.

He hefts the phone in his hand and starts to turn, ready to slam it into the guy's face – and pain explodes at the back of his skull. His knees buckle and he pitches forward. He tries to get up, but

177

a foot comes down on his neck, mashing his face into the gravel. Fuck, he thinks, no fucking *way*, this isn't—

Punches to his kidneys, one after the other. Tears running from his eyes, the pain vast, unmanageable, like nothing he's ever known. Frantic, he reaches for his attacker's ankle, trying to pull him off balance, but something smashes down onto his hand and he hears the crack of bone as his fingers shatter in a white-hot flare of agony.

'You wanted to talk to me?' The man bends down, the hiss of his voice so close Donnie can feel the man's breath hot against his ear. 'Here I am.'

29

FRIDAY, 27 JUNE

Morven's flat is in Glasgow's West End. Not quite Kelvinside, Anna realises, in spite of her mother's insistence, but definitely within spitting distance. Not that you'd want to do something quite as uncouth in the upmarket air of Cleveden Street, of course.

She walks up the drive, Morven's keys in her hand, two letters stuffed in her pocket. The one from Morven's solicitor, telling her the flat was hers – if it hadn't been followed by a long telephone call, assuring her that it was genuine and offering her any assistance she might need should she decide to put it on the market, she'd have been convinced she was the victim of a particularly sick practical joke. But the other letter he'd sent on to her . . . Three days later, she's still trying to make sense of it. She'd told her mother she'd look in on Morven's flat, make sure the police hadn't left it in too much of a mess after they'd finished there. If it's not a total lie, it's not the whole truth either. But it's as much of the truth as she suspects her mother can bear at the moment.

And even now, she's not sure what she's hoping to find here, in this pale Victorian sandstone with its perfectly tended grounds.

Morven had lived her life in London, in the chic Clerkenwell town-house she adored. She'd only stayed in her Glasgow flat a couple of times a year, on her brief trips back to Scotland. How can there be anything of her life to discover in this place she'd so clearly outgrown?

Anna goes up the steps to the main door. And walks into a wood-panelled entrance hall that looks to be approximately the size of her entire North Park condo. Her footsteps echoing across the tiles, she crosses to Morven's ground-floor flat, turns the key. And stares.

The flat is stunning, its high-ceilinged, corniced elegance so completely unlike what she'd been expecting that Anna double-checks the keys again to make sure she's in the right flat. She wanders through the rooms, looking for something – anything – to connect it with Morven, but there's nothing. The flat feels eerily empty . . . of Morven, of anyone. Like a disused film set, or an abandoned television studio. Had Morven simply not cared enough about the place to make it feel like home? Or had she been unable to stop playing a part, even here? Anna shakes her head, an odd, unwilling twist of pity taking her by surprise.

She tries a couple of doors, peers into what are obviously guest rooms. And then, at the end of the hall, she finds what can only be Morven's bedroom, a huge black and gold boudoir of a place with vast floor-to-ceiling wardrobes along one wall. And photographs.

There are photographs of Morven everywhere, glossy, air-brushed images on every available surface, with a few smaller ones of Ross looking uncomfortable at various black-tie events. The only family photos are clustered on one of the bedside tables, next to a vase of skeletal roses, the petals long since shed. And in the far corner of the room, a tall bookcase with a selection of tasteful *objets* in her favourite blacks and golds, interspersed with pastel-covered lifestyle guides and celeb biographies.

Anna looks round at the room. Tries to rid herself of the feeling that this, too, is posed, that there's an odd desperation to the gallery of photographs on show. Did Morven need them to show herself, as much as anyone, how far she'd come?

She pulls out the other letter, the one the solicitor had included with his couple of dry, legalese-filled pages. The one dated eighteen months ago, written in Morven's trademark violet ink.

Hiya Midget,

Surprise! Okay, that's pretty tasteless, considering there's only one reason you're reading this. But I'll be an optimist and assume I went out with a bang around fifty, the way I always said I would – old enough to have done everything I wanted, young enough not to look like a total hag. So what do you think of your present? Not quite what you were expecting, I'll bet.

Look, I know what you think of me, and I sort of don't blame you. I was always going to get somewhere, Anna, and you – you weren't. Just how it was, right? Doesn't mean I didn't have to work for it, though. You think it just happened? No way. And don't think my life is a bed of roses, either. 'On' all the time, smiling though you feel like shit, dragging yourself out of bed at stupid o'clock to interview some spotty moron who got lucky on a talent show and think they're God's gift – could you do it, Midget? Doubt it.

Look, I'm not big on saying sorry. Feels like apologising for being me, and you know I don't do that, not ever. But maybe I don't want you to go through your whole life thinking I'm a total bitch, either. And what you did for that poor cow in the Women's Refuge in San Diego – Jesus, Midget, that took more guts than I have. Did they ever get the bastard who shoved you down those stairs? Bloody hope so.

Anyway, I'm giving you my Glasgow flat. I don't need it – don't even know why I bought it, to be honest. Seriously, does it look like the sort of place I'd want to live in? I bet you will, though. I bet you'll love it when you see it. So take it. And enjoy.

Morv

Anna swallows down the obstruction growing in her throat. Eighteen months ago, she'd been in hospital in San Diego, recovering from surgery that had saved her life but left her lower leg a scarred, misshapen version of itself. And Morven . . . Morven had chosen to do this for her.

The room is closing in on her. She needs to go, get out of here . . .

Anna turns to leave, and the book on the bedside table catches her eye. Not quite believing what she's seeing, she picks up a copy of *Monstrous Regiment: Sixteenth Century Women of Power.* Compiled a couple of years ago, it was the only publication she'd ever contributed to that had made it out of academia into 'real' publishing – and, she suspects, helped her hold on to her position at UCSD when so many of her colleagues had been dropped.

The book looks like it's never been opened, which doesn't surprise her in the least. But it's there. It's right *there*, by Morven's bloody bed. And she can't talk to Morven about it, can't ask her any of the things she needs to know. Not now, not ever again. Because it's too late now, isn't it? Too late for either of them. *Too bloody late.*

'Stupid cow.' The grief she'd pushed away for so long is creeping up on her, wrapping its ghost-grey hands around her throat. Bringing the tears at last, raw, acid trails of them, falling faster than she can scrub away as her knees buckle and she sinks onto the bed. 'Morven, you stupid bloody cow!'

30

MONDAY, 30 JUNE

Fergie's Audi groans its way over the Kessock Bridge, sounding like a pre-war plumbing system in its final death throes. Mahler opens the window to clear some of the permanent fug that clings to the car's interior, and re-reads the email Donna had sent last night. She's done an excellent job in piecing together the various strands of information about the Campbell brothers' finances – and with Ross Campbell finally fit to talk to them, it's time he gave them a few answers.

Campbell lives on the doubly misnamed Black Isle, Cromarty's fertile green peninsula across the Beauly firth. Before the 1980s, travelling to and from the Black Isle would have meant a ferry ride or a longish drive along the coast. Back then, few Invernessians would have chosen to move across the firth and face that sort of commute on a daily basis. But with the coming of the Kessock Bridge, everything had changed. The Black Isle's pretty little villages had become increasingly attractive to affluent Invernessians looking for a picturesque faux-rural lifestyle, and the villages have been expanding ever since, clusters of shiny executive villas climbing the hillsides.

Campbell, of course, has a cathedral-windowed mini-mansion in the primest of prime locations, overlooking the firth. Not a gated community, not quite, but the lawns look like dense green velvet and the vehicles on the driveways are a mix of top-of-the range 4×4s and sporty little Beamers. There are a couple of smaller cars dotted here and there, some of them almost as old as Fergie's, but Mahler's guessing they belong to the garden and cleaning staff the homeowners undoubtedly rely on to maintain their pristine environment.

'How the other half lives, eh?' Fergie points to the L-shaped house at the end of the road. It's slightly set back from the others, with a pair of wrought-iron gates that wouldn't look out of place on a stately home, complete with lions rampant on the posts. 'You sure his posh car sales place is really going down the pan?'

Mahler nods. 'In turbocharged fashion, according to Donna.' Which is the only reason he can think of which might explain how he'd got entangled with someone like Cazza MacKay. 'Let's see if Mr Campbell feels like talking to us today, shall we?'

They trek up the drive and ring the bell. The door is opened by Campbell's sister, a thirty-something woman with his broad shoulders and ruddy colouring. She gives their warrant cards a suspicious glance, and when Mahler asks to talk to Campbell her face manages to look both unimpressed and wary.

'You know my brother's not long out of hospital, right? Can't it wait?'

'I'm afraid this is rather urgent, Ms—'

'*Mrs* Jamieson. And it had better be.'

She takes them through to a large conservatory, housing an indoor swimming pool and a small sitting area next to a poolside bar. Campbell's in the water, ploughing up and down in a graceless mechanical crawl. As he comes in to turn, Mahler walks to the edge of the pool.

'Mr Campbell? Sorry to interrupt your exercise session.'

Campbell's head jerks up. He's wearing mirrored goggles, so

184

Mahler can't see his full expression, but the jut of his chin suggests it isn't one of unalloyed delight.

'What do you want? I'm meant to be convalescing.' His sister starts to explain, but he cuts her off. 'Never mind, Lynne, they're here now. Get me that robe, will you?'

She stalks past Mahler, picks it up. 'They shouldn't be bothering you at home, Ross. I'll stay with you, make sure —'

'No need.' Campbell heaves himself out of the pool, the displaced water lapping at their shoes, and takes the robe. He wraps it round himself and pushes past Fergie to the bar. 'Probably just an update for me, right?' He shakes his head. 'Could have saved yourselves the bother – unless you've come to tell me you know who killed Morven, you've got nothing I want to hear.'

A challenge in his voice. Itching to take them on, Mahler thinks, now he's on his own turf. Show them who's boss. But there's a tension in his body language, an unease at their presence that tells a different story.

'Just a couple of things to clear up, sir. Good to see you're feeling better, by the way.'

'I told you, I'm recuperating.' Campbell watches his sister leave. He opens a bottle of Corona and takes a long swig. 'The doc gave me some pills, told me to watch my stress levels and look after myself.'

'Aye, very wise.' Fergie glances at the bottle of beer. 'No need to go overboard though, eh?'

'You trying to be funny? Look, if you want me to do an appeal or something—'

'We're concentrating on Morven's memorial service at the moment, Mr Campbell – specifically, the people who were in attendance.' A flash of uncertainty in his eyes, enough for Mahler to know they're on the right track.

'I don't remember much about it. I was ill, remember?'

Mahler nods. 'Of course. The stress of the day, no doubt – only it was a little more than that, wasn't it? Anna Murray remembers you staring at something, just before you collapsed. Something over by the trees.'

'That's rubbish!' Campbell scrubs his hand over his mouth. 'I told you, I was ill – you'd no business letting me go out there in that state!'

'I seem to remember you were quite insistent. But yes, that's what I thought . . . until I had one of the still shots from the service blown up.' Mahler takes out the image and holds it up. 'You were staring at these two men, Mr Campbell – staring straight at them. Friends of yours, are they?'

'Never seen them before in my life.'

'They work for a man called Carl MacKay. A businessman, of sorts.'

'The club guy?' Campbell's shrug looks almost convincing. Until he scrubs the sleeve of his robe across his sweating forehead. 'Don't know him either.'

'No? He's got several strings to his bows, our Mr MacKay. Extortion, money-lending, protection rackets – any of that sound familiar to you, Mr Campbell?'

'I told you, I don't know him!' Campbell's voice has a strained, unhappy edge to it. 'Why would I know someone like that? I've never—'

'I think you have.' Mahler steers Campbell to a seat. 'I say that, because you've got a habit, Mr Campbell – you're a gambler, aren't you? Oh, you're a drinker too, but it's the gambling that's got you by the throat, and you don't know how to get clear of it. Which is why you've bled your own business into the ground, and got into debt with a thug like Cazza MacKay.'

'No!' Campbell's legs are jittering like a junkie twitching for their next fix. He pulls the robe over his knees and stares down at them as though he's trying to work out why they're shaking so much. 'It's a lie! You don't know—'

'I know you need to start talking to us. Or we'll start wondering whether Morven signed her own death warrant when she made a will in your favour. Is that what you want us to start wondering, Mr Campbell? Because—'

'What's going on in here? I heard shouting.' Campbell's sister appears in the doorway, mobile in hand, and glares at Mahler. 'I told you, my brother's not long out of hospital, and you're harassing him! If you're not out of this house in two minutes—'

'We wouldn't dream of taking up more of your time. Mr Campbell, you've been very helpful.'

'I haven't told you anything—'

'Believe me, you have.' Mahler nods at Fergie, who's already heading for the exit. 'And we're very grateful for your assistance. Mrs Jamieson, we'll see ourselves out—'

'You bloody won't!'

The door slams closed behind them with enough force to topple one of the artificial bay trees in the porch. Fergie rights it quickly and picks up his pace, glancing right and left as they walk down the drive. 'Don't think they have a dog, do you?'

'I suspect we'd have found out by now.'

'Aye, probably. You don't think – I know it looks bad, boss, but I can't believe he killed her.'

'It looks bloody awful. Cazza's heavies were there to put the frighteners on him, which suggests he's in pretty deep. And he seemed pretty desperate to—'

Mahler's mobile buzzes. *Hell.* June Wallace's number, flashing up at him – wanting to know why he's been running around the Black Isle harassing local worthies, he assumes, instead of sitting at his desk staring at a spreadsheet of staffing forecasts.

'Ma'am? Yes, just outside. But even in the Audi, we should still make it in about twenty minutes.'

He ends the call, and turns to Fergie. 'We need to get back to town asap. A body's been found in the Ness Islands – and it looks like it's our missing kitchen porter.'

31

Ness Islands, Inverness

To most true Invernessians – and in spite of everything, Mahler's beginning to think of himself in those terms – they're just 'the Islands'. Set in the middle of the river and linked to each other by elegant Victorian footbridges, the Ness Islands are less than twenty minutes' walk from the centre. Less, perhaps, if you cut down from the castle and walk along Ness Bank.

Green, thick with birch and fir, the Islands are where the respectable folk of Inverness come to walk their dogs, or turn their shrieking offspring loose to play amongst the undergrowth while they enjoy a temporary respite. And where the less respectable ones find suitably shaded hideaways to get intimate with their recreational drug of choice.

The crime scene tent is just visible from the footbridge, a flash of white amongst the green. Mahler ducks past the hopeful-looking reporter from Moray Firth Radio and picks his way along the approach path towards the blue and white tape, wondering what it is about the Islands that always sets the hair prickling on the back of his neck.

It's the way the light changes, he tells himself, the switch from sunlight to gloom as the paths lead deeper into the trees, but he knows it's more than that. In the centre of town, the river is sun-painted, silver-bright, a backdrop to a thousand tourist selfies. But at the Ness Islands, it's faster, darker. More treacherous—

'Careful, sir, it's slippery as hell just there!' Cath Fraser holds up a warning hand as Mahler climbs down the bank. 'We've already had to fish a wee SOCO out of the burn.'

'No wonder.' Fergie, following on Mahler's heels, swears as he trips over a fallen branch. 'All that rain last night, eh? Going to bugger up the forensics, that.'

Cath runs through her report as Mahler looks round at the scene. A jogger out for a run had seen it and called it in. 'Thought someone had been fly-tipping and dumped a bag of old clothing at first. That, or a wino sleeping off a skinful of White Lightning. Then he took a closer look, and . . .' she pulls a face. 'Got a hell of a shock, poor guy.'

'Hardly surprising.' A white-clad figure backs out of the tent and turns to face them. 'Your man here is definitely not looking his best.' Marco McVinish pushes back his hood and wipes his sweat-damp forehead. 'Fiscal's been and gone, by the way – and giving lunch a miss today, I suspect. Lukas, Fergie, you ready? I warn you, it isn't pretty.'

'Is it ever?'

Mahler pushes back the tent flap and looks in. A bundle of old clothing, or a semi-comatose drunk sleeping off his hangover? Yes, he can see why the runner might have thought that, at least at first glance. Half-hidden by the brambles and dock leaves, Donnie Stewart's body would have been a slumped, amorphous heap. Until the lumpy, bloated things like deformed starfish resolved themselves into fingers on bruised and bloodied hands. Until he'd seen the dark, misshapen football with its ooze of grey matter and the empty eye-socket staring skywards . . .

'Poor bugger died hard, I'm afraid.' Marco holds back the tent flap to let them out. 'Seems to have pissed someone off very badly indeed. A seriously unpleasant someone.'

'Remind you of anything?'

'Come on, Lukas, you know better than that. Yes, the level of violence used is on a par with Morven Murray, but that's about all.' He glances at Mahler, sighs. 'Fine. I can't rule out the same person being involved in both murders. That do you?'

'For the moment. Any sign of defensive wounds?' From the position of the body, it looks as though Stewart had been attacked from behind. But if he'd managed to fight back, even a little, there's a chance some forensic evidence will have survived the previous night's rain.

'Hands are such a mess, it's impossible to say at this stage. But I'm hoping he landed a punch or two on the bastard, aren't you?'

'Crazy place for the killer to pick, though,' Fergie points out. 'If he wanted to top Stewart, why do it somewhere so public? There's always folk down here, the place is hoaching with dog walkers.'

Mahler shrugs. 'Stewart and the killer decide to meet for some reason. But they don't trust each other enough to choose somewhere too obviously deserted. Why not pick here?'

And though people walk through the Islands at all hours, they tend to stick to the main walkways. After the first bend, this path gets steeper, the trees and bushes encroaching more and more. If the runner hadn't taken that second look . . . *Mi ritrovai per una selva oscura,* Mahler thinks. I found myself in a dark wood. And for Donnie Stewart, this had been the darkest wood of all.

Fergie nods. 'Aye, maybe. And it would fit with the Doc's theory about two people being involved in Morven's murder.'

'It would.' And yet, something's not quite right. The shape of it's too unformed, too plastic . . . too many unknowns, Mahler thinks. Had Stewart been a willing accomplice? Or even the instigator – but no, that doesn't fit either. There had been nothing at Stewart's flat to show he'd had the slightest interest in Morven. The man had been a loner, a drunk fighting the battle for sobriety and losing it little by little every day. But he'd been a peaceful drunk, mostly. And crucially, one with no history of violence against women.

The scene team is still working around them, tagging, photographing. Mahler turns to ask McVinish a question, and a glint of white by one of the bushes catches his eye. He waves over one of the SOCOs. 'Something?'

The white-suited figure inches its way down the slope. 'Could be, aye.' A purple nitrile glove brushes a residue of mud from the object, and holds up a fragment of white plastic. 'Looks like the casing from a smartphone or a mobile. Well spotted.'

'Just the casing?'

More brushing and peering. The man marks the spot and straightens up. 'So far, yes. But we're still working our way down the bank, so we'll see what we get.'

Mahler nods. An intact phone would have been too much to hope for, he supposes. But if the SIM card or any of the memory chips can be recovered . . .

'Mightn't be our boy's, of course,' Fergie observes. 'You'd think the killer would have made off with it, wouldn't you?'

Mahler glances at the tent, and back up at the path. 'If he'd seen it, yes. But in the heat of the struggle, he might have missed it – or simply not had time to search for it.' And given all the hours invested in this case with so little to show for it, surely they're overdue a run of better luck? He turns to Marco McVinish, who's stripping off his nitrile gloves.

'As much as you can give us, Marco, as soon as you can, yes?'

The pathologist gives him a weary look. 'Naturally, Sherlock, naturally. Let's hope this marks the end of our rather bloodthirsty summer, shall we? It's not what Inverness is used to – in fact, by my reckoning, we've just used up our unexplained deaths quota for the next five years.'

At Burnett Road, Mahler leaves Fergie assembling the team for a briefing while he reports to June.

191

'In the Ness bloody Islands?' She shakes her head. 'Unbelievable. But at least we can tie him into the Morven Murray case now. How are the forensics looking?'

Distinctly damp, due to the recent rain. And the man who'd discovered the body had promptly gone into meltdown, tripping over his own feet and generally stamping all over the immediate locus as he scrambled to get away from the corpse. Neither of which, Mahler decides, is going to brighten June's day.

'The scene was . . . as you'd expect,' he tells her. 'Confused. But the search for the rest of the mobile is ongoing. If anything's found, it could be the breakthrough we need.'

'Good. What else?'

'The PM's this afternoon. I'll be attending as soon as I've briefed the team, and—'

June shakes her head. 'Fergie can do that. You need to be here, doing your job – which is overseeing your team, by the way, not harassing bereaved relatives.' She opens a file, slides a sheet of paper towards him. 'Ross Campbell. I've had my ear bent by his sister about you haranguing a sick man in his own home.'

'She's made a complaint?'

'No, thank Christ, but it was bloody close. What the hell did you think you were doing?'

'Campbell's in major financial trouble. And I think Cazza MacKay's got him over a barrel.' Mahler tells her what Anna Murray had observed at the memorial service and how Campbell had reacted when challenged. 'Cazza MacKay's boys don't strike me as grieving fans, ma'am. They were there to intimidate Ross Campbell, and they scared him half to death.'

'Is that what he said?'

'He denied it. But he was clearly agitated, and—'

'And you carried on questioning him. A man only recently out of hospital with a heart condition.' June shakes her head. 'Christ, Lukas, what were you thinking?'

'I was thinking we were this close to getting something concrete to pin on Cazza MacKay, ma'am.' And Mahler's betting once they'd got that, a proper, drains-up investigation of the bargain-basement *mafioso* would turn up skeletons by the closetful. Including any dealings with the man called Hollander. If he actually exists, that is. As far as Mahler's concerned, the jury's still very much out on that one.

June nods. 'I get that. I do – and if we'd the slightest chance of Campbell standing up and telling us that's how it was, I'd let you off the smacked wrist. This time. But how do think what you did would stand up against an actual harassment charge, if Campbell decides to take it further?'

June opens the bottom drawer of her desk, glares at the empty space formerly occupied by her stash of fags, and shuts it again. 'Look, I'm not saying you're wrong. God knows, there's a nice wee cell in Porterfield I'd love to introduce Cazza to. But Cazza MacKay doing a bit of dodgy business with Ross Campbell is not our priority right now.'

'Surely being hassled by Cazza's heavies for money strengthens Campbell's motive for killing Morven? Her will makes him the main beneficiary.'

'True. But you can't tie him into Stewart's murder, can you?'

Mahler shakes his head. Since leaving hospital, Campbell's barely set foot outside his house. And according to his neighbours, his 4×4 hasn't moved from his drive in days. 'Not at the moment. Not physically.'

'No. And without that link, you're nowhere. So either find something that'll stick, or get off the man's back. What about this Ryan guy Anna Murray told you about, the one you're meant to be prioritising?'

'At St Salvator's College, St Andrews, until three months ago, then the trail goes cold – but he's an Irish national, so he may have returned there. We're checking call logs, trying to tie down his last known movements and liaising with the Gardai as a matter of urgency.'

June nods. 'Urgent. Fine. That's what I'll be passing on to the Chief when he gets back from his strategy meeting at Tulliallan – and these two murders are what you'll be focusing on. Which means directing the enquiries, not dotting about all over the place, playing cops and robbers with Cazza MacKay. That clear?'

Has she forgotten about Kevin Ramsay? 'Three murders, surely, ma'am?'

June shakes her head. 'Morven Murray and Donnie Stewart – there's a clear link there, so you carry on leading them. But I've just got word that Andy Black's finally got the all-clear from the Doc. He's back on Monday, so he'll be taking over Kevin Ramsay. You and Karen can bring him up to speed first thing.'

32

TUESDAY, 1 JULY

Her parents' house is silent when Anna lets herself in. Not unusual these days, but the quality of the silence feels subtly different. She drops her bags in the hall and stands still for a moment, listening. There's no answer when she calls out, no sound of movement in response. When she still can't hear anyone she checks the kitchen and the living room, but there's no sign of her mother. And the back door is locked, so her father can't be working in the garden.

Anna touches the side of the kettle. Completely cold, which is even more unusual. Her mother's usually never without a cup in her hand – she runs on tea, according to her father. So why—

Movement in the garden. Swift, fleeting, just on the edges of her vision. A figure? She unlocks the door and runs down the path, but there's no one there. She turns to go back indoors. And a hand touches her arm.

'What are you doing out here?' Her mother, headphones round her neck. An iPad raised aloft as though she'd been planning to bring it down on the back of Anna's head. 'I thought you were a burglar!'

'Christ, Mam, you gave me the shock of my life! Didn't you hear me calling you?'

'Do you have to use that kind of language?' Her mother lowers the iPad. 'If you must know, I was listening to that Radio Scotland interview with Morven, the one they did when she got the *Elevenses* job – they're repeating it, seeing it's a month since . . .' she takes a ragged breath, looks away. 'If you were looking for your dad, you'll not find him here. He's out defacing lamp posts with his "Yes Inverness" pals. Not that the other lot are any better, mind.'

'I thought . . . it doesn't matter.' She was sure she'd seen something. Some*one*. But it had been the merest glimpse, more a suggestion of movement than anything concrete – it might have been one of the neighbours' cats, for God's sake. Is she really going to say anything to unsettle her mother, when she's looking a little more together for the first time in weeks?

'Do you fancy a cup of tea?' Anna puts her arm round her mother's shoulders and steers her back inside. 'I've brought back some things from Morven's flat I thought you might like to see.'

'Was everything okay? I always thought it was such a shame she didn't use it more often. That lovely flat, lying empty half the year.'

'Fine.' Anna puts the kettle on to boil, gets two mugs from the dishwasher. 'I checked the locks, turned the heating down, that sort of thing. And I found a few bits and pieces I hadn't been expecting.'

And this is the moment she's been putting off, the moment when she tells her mother about Morven's letter giving her the flat. It shouldn't be so difficult, she knows that. Why can't she find the words? For a moment, as the kettle boils, they hang there on her tongue. And slide away, unspoken, as she watches her mother rummaging through the holdalls full of Morven's things she'd brought back from Morven's flat.

'You know, I haven't seen half of these.' Her mother looks up and gives her the closest thing to a smile Anna's seen since Morven's death. 'And where did you get these albums? They're beautiful!'

'I thought you'd like them.' Before catching her train at Queen Street, Anna had gone into Paperchase and bought half a dozen scrapbooking albums. 'I know you handed over all your clippings to the police, but I found these at the flat, stuffed in the back of a cupboard. They're not in any sort of order, but I thought we could work on them together. Build a collection, if you like, to remember her by.'

Her mother looks up, the glint of tears in her eyes. 'That's such a nice thought. I know you didn't always get on, but she was your sister, Anna. And she was really proud of you. I still have some of the older cuttings, though. Let me go and see what I have left.' She dabs at her eyes and stands up. 'I always meant to get everything organised, but . . . you always think there'll be another day, don't you? You always think there'll be plenty of time.'

Anna watches her mother go. She's looking better – sounding better, too, now she's got something concrete to do. She'd refused any sort of counselling when it had been offered, but maybe putting together this collection could prove to be a kind of therapy for her. If it does, it'll help Anna assuage some of the guilt she's feeling right now. Because when she'd loaded up the bags, she hadn't been thinking of her mother. She'd been thinking *research*.

Morven wasn't big on IT, but she'd been big on her own publicity. The flat had been stuffed with it – photos, press clippings, even old publicity shots, all jumbled together. And now it's here, the record of Morven's entire existence contained in these two holdalls. Waiting for Anna to give it form again. To give it *life*, if she can.

Morven had known her killer, Mahler said, known and trusted him enough to let him into her suite late at night. Not room service, because she'd ordered the champagne earlier in the evening – so she was expecting someone to call. Someone important. Someone she'd thought it worth making a fuss of, at any rate. Or someone she needed to placate.

Connor. The name flashes into Anna's mind before she can stop it. That and Mahler's comment about masks. But it isn't him. It can't be. Conn didn't do masks – whatever he felt, whatever he thought, it was written on his face. And he was crap at keeping secrets. *Except you*, her mind whispers. *He was pretty good at keeping you a secret, wasn't he? Until Morven found out . . .*

No. She can't – *won't* – believe Conn capable of something so brutal. And if she's right, she's looking at the means to prove it. What she's brought home in these bags is Morven's entire life from university onwards. More than the collection her mother had given the police, much more. What she's looking at is an *archive*.

And somewhere in that archive is the clue to Morven's killer.

33

WEDNESDAY, 2 JULY

Burnett Road Police Station

Another 7 a.m. briefing. Another victim's bloodied remains, disassembled in brutal monochrome and pinned across the whiteboard. Mahler listens to Fergie's summary of the post-mortem on Donnie Stewart. Fergie's doing his best to keep his voice matter-of-fact as he recites the list of injuries the man had suffered, but Mahler can feel the atmosphere in the room changing as the team take in just how badly Stewart had been beaten.

'And a ruptured spleen,' Fergie concludes. 'Report's on its way to you, boss, but basically the guy was beaten to death. And if I don't have to see what that looks like ever again, I'll be a happy man, believe me.'

'Okay.' Mahler looks round the room. They're struggling with what they've just heard. Feeling angry, feeling frustrated. Feeling sickened. But not helpless – he can't afford to let them feel that, even for a moment. He points at the whiteboard. 'Donnie Stewart and Morven Murray. Two brutal murders and a killer running around free – not in Glasgow, not in Edinburgh, not in London. Here. Not how things are supposed to be, is it? Not in Inverness. But this is what we've got. And it's up to us to deal with it – not the big boys from down south. Us.'

A quick look round the room while that sinks in. 'I know there's a lot of stuff in the media right now about what a sterling job we're doing. Or not, right? Well, forget that. Put it right out of your minds. Because I know the effort we're all putting into this, and I know it's going to pay off.'

A voice from the back of the room. 'We're assuming it's the same guy, right?'

'Treating them as separate but linked, yes. So what we need to look at is—'

Heads turning as the door opens. A bulky presence fills the doorway, dark, grey-flecked hair cut to accentuate an imagined resemblance to George Clooney – just about possible, Mahler concedes, if Clooney lived on a diet of Big Macs and pints of heavy – and sporting purple-yellow bruises round each eye, like a particularly ill-advised pair of shades. Andy 'Marmite' Black, Burnett Road's finest. At least, according to Andy Black.

'Feeling better, Andy?' Mahler makes his mouth approximate a smile. 'We'll be done in ten minutes.'

Black takes a long, leisurely look around the room until he catches sight of Karen. 'No worries. I'll catch up with DS Gilchrist in the meantime—'

'As I said, we'll be free in ten minutes. There's an office booked upstairs, if you check with Admin.'

Silence. Black's jaw working what's either a wad of chewing gum or the inside of his cheek as Mahler waits. Then a grudging nod. 'Fine. See you in ten.'

As the door closes behind Black, Mahler hands over to Fergie for the duty allocations. Digging deeper into Donnie Stewart's life falls to Gary, backed up by a couple of uniforms, and Donna's tasked with tracking down Connor Ryan while Pete starts piecing together everything they have. House-to-house enquiries haven't yielded much so far, but Mahler's not ruling them out yet. The properties near the Ness Islands are a mix of care homes, flats and B&Bs with a sprinkling of larger houses, many still in single ownership. And the greater the mix of properties, the greater the potential pool of witnesses.

'Talk to everyone,' Mahler finishes up. 'Nursing staff on late shifts, delivery drivers, insomniacs – anyone who might have been around on the night of the murder. Anything they mention that might be relevant, let's get it noted. Remember, we had Stewart downstairs in the custody suite not that long ago, sleeping off a drinking bout. I'll leave you to imagine the headlines once the press get wind of that one. So we go back to the beginning with this, right back – where was Stewart hiding out? What was he living on since Morven's murder? He must have had funds from somewhere.'

'Could have been living rough,' Gary offers.

'So ask around again – usual places, usual faces. And take a look at any break-ins to unoccupied buildings recently – garages, sheds, anywhere he could have holed up. He was a functioning alcoholic, so flash his mugshot in the pubs, the supermarkets, anywhere he might have got booze from. Look, this is Inverness, not London – people interact. Someone will know where Stewart's been living, what he's been doing. We just have to find them.'

'Do you think there's a connection, boss?' Fergie asks when the team's left. 'Between Stewart and Connor Ryan, I mean?'

Mahler shrugs. There has to be a connection between Stewart and Morven's killer, and Ryan might have had – *might have* – had a motive after Anna had broken up with him. But fifteen years later? He looks across at the whiteboard image of Connor Ryan, culled from a now defunct Facebook page.

Taken on a skiing holiday with a group of colleagues, it shows Ryan giving the obligatory thumbs up for the camera. Suntanned, athletic, sporting the kind of wide, half-vacuous grin the unimaginative like to call 'infectious', Ryan looks like no one's vision of a multiple murderer. But then, Mahler reflects, neither had Ted Bundy.

'It'd be nice and tidy, wouldn't it? And God knows, we could use some of that right now. But take a look at this.' He holds up a battered red-top decorated with the ghosts of abandoned coffee cups, and flips it open. 'From our showbiz correspondent: "The truth behind the smiles – Morven Murray's colleagues speak out." If one-eighth of these comments are actual quotes, Morven was about as well-loved by her co-workers as the Grim Reaper.'

Fergie peers over his shoulder. 'Nice. "Selfish control freak Morven made my life a misery" – Christ, that's from one of her co-presenters! Didn't take them long to get the knives out, did it?'

Not the best choice of words, Mahler reflects. But the article provides more confirmation that Morven hadn't been as universally adored as her mother had chosen to believe. People who'd cosied up to her on TV were coming forward to air ancient grievances, certain of their audience now Morven could no longer face them down.

'These people are the harmless ones, though,' he points out. 'They're just venting. We're looking for someone with enough of a grievance to kill for – and it looks as though our pool of potentials just keeps getting bigger.'

'So where do we go next?'

The call logs. Most of the numbers have been accounted for, but there are a couple of numbers on the list that Pete hasn't managed to trace. Mahler tells Fergie to get him to take another look at them. 'And talk to Glyn Hadley again. Don't stand for any waffle about client confidentiality – he was Morven's agent for years, he knows who she had major fall-outs with.'

Mahler glances at his mobile. A message from Karen, with a scowling badger emoji, indicating Black's about to enter carpet-chewing mode. 'Right, I'm needed upstairs. If anything comes in about Connor Ryan or Donnie Stewart, I want to know right away.'

*

Forty-five minutes later, Mahler's back at his desk. The handover briefing with Andy Black and Karen had been scheduled to run for a full hour, but he'd already ensured Black had been emailed all the relevant updates beforehand. True, the rest of the time could have been used for an informal discussion about the way forward, but Black had made it clear he'd be looking at the suggestion that Gemma, Kevin's girlfriend, had been having an affair with Eddie Scrimgeour, a gaunt and vicious house-breaker with a string of violent offences to his name.

According to Black's 'source', Scrimgeour had taken it badly when she'd ended the affair and vowed revenge. But as there's no evidence that Gemma even knew Scrimgeour and the source happens to be Kevin's embittered alcoholic ex, Mahler had resisted the urge to suggest Black stops mixing his painkillers with strong drink. He'd invented an urgent phone call and made his escape. Karen had given him a reproachful look, but it was either that or introduce Black's face to the surface of the desk. Repeatedly.

He opens his emails and watches the screen populate with a forest of red flags. Crime statistics response to be actioned. The latest overtime totals versus projected figures, with a comment from June that looks to be ninety per cent exclamation marks and scowling emoticons. And two requests for annual leave or a duty swap next month, one from Pete and one from Gary, both pleading special circumstances. Both just happening to coincide with the Tartan Heart music festival at Belladrum. As Fergie would say, *aye, right*. He sends them a one-line reply and opens the crime statistics report.

'Boss—'

He doesn't bother looking up. 'No chance, Pete. Not even if your long-lost brother is headlining at Bella with—'

'They've got the rest of the mobile.'

While he'd been briefing June, word had come in that the crime scene search had been completed. Stewart had been standing near the footbridge when he was attacked and the initial struggle had taken place there, not far from where Mahler had seen the shards of plastic. But his assailant had dragged him further down the bank towards the burn, presumably to minimise the chance of being seen, and continued the attack there.

'It's in a hell of a state,' Pete warns him. 'Smashed to bits. But the motherboard and chips are in reasonable nick, so there's a chance the tech guys at Gartcosh will recover some data from it. Good one, eh?' Pete's grin wavers as he looks down at the Post-it stuck to his hand. 'Oh, aye, and we've got some more info on Connor Ryan.'

The look on Pete's face tells him he's not going to like this one. 'He's inside? Or joined a religious order? Left the country?'

'I wish. If he was banged up, at least we'd be able to find him. But since he left his job, he hasn't gone anywhere or done anything – it's like he's dropped off the edge of the world.'

'He can't be living on fresh air. Cash point records? Supermarket shops? Online purchases? The man can't have just vanished!'

Pete shakes his head. 'Sorry, boss. But it looks like he'd been planning to do just that. The week before he disappeared, he told his bank he needed readies for a building project he was planning. He closed two ISAs and withdrew the money over three days – not transferred, just withdrew it. As far as we can see, he's gone to ground with over fifteen grand of ready cash.'

He's driving in the early morning, through the grey half-light that's as close as the Highlands get to darkness in these long summer months. Driving through the mountains, over the pass at Drumochter and the Slochd Summit, the only car for miles like the last survivor of some global catastrophe.

No boats, no bridges left for him to burn, not now – for better or worse, all his choices have been made. But he imagines the road boiling behind him as he drives, fiery rivers of lava-flowing molten in his wake. Time, his ally for so long, has turned against him. And everything he thought he could rely on has begun to fall apart.

He glances at the road sign as he passes. Another eighty miles before he's reached his destination. Another eighty miles before he can let himself relax. A surge of anger grips him, tensing his shoulders, making him hunch over the wheel.

He'd made his plans so carefully, worked out every step. And nothing had fazed him, not even when he'd had to improvise. Stewart, though – letting Stewart live had been a mistake, he sees that now. But what should he have done, killed the man for an accident of timing? He's not a monster, whatever the world might think.

And at first, Stewart had seemed like a gift from the gods. A weak man, a frightened man, too stupid to raise the alarm and save himself. A man to be made use of, or so he'd thought. Only he'd got that badly wrong. Dangerously wrong. And everything may hinge on how well he's managed to put that right.

Coming up to the turn-off in the early morning mist. Leaving the main road behind him, slipping through the silent villages like a ghost, his anger slowly ebbing as he drives. He needs to think things through, to make sure he's left nothing to chance this time. But his memory . . . he suspects his memory is lying to him, showing him things that didn't happen. Hiding things that did. How is he supposed to know what to do if nothing it shows him is real?

Walking down to the Ness Islands to meet Stewart, he remembers that. Waiting for the light to fail, his mind clear, his breathing calm, unhurried. Knowing what had to be done. Thinking it would be easier, this time. Then when the kitchen porter appeared, when everything seemed so perfect . . . his body had failed him. He'd stood frozen, arms clamped to his sides as the seconds passed and Stewart grew increasingly nervous, muttering to himself and stamping his feet in the evening chill. Another minute and the man would have turned and run, he's sure of it—

Then the runaway dog had burst through the bushes. It bounded across the footbridge, its owner hurtling past a few seconds later. And he'd known then why he'd been made to wait. This wasn't meant to be easy – this was to test his strength, his determination. To show how far he'd come. And what he was willing to do.

Is it any wonder he can't remember it all? Oh, there are moments when the images are there in front of him, sharp and bright and terrible. But they are moments only, disconnected things that have no power over him, and he pushes them away without hesitation. What he's done hasn't been through choice and it doesn't make him a monster. Maybe there are no monsters, he thinks, only people like him, people who'd been forced to act to save their own lives.

In the end, he can't regret Stewart too much. Stewart had tried to trick him, and he'd paid the price. But what he's contemplating now . . .

Another loose end to be dealt with. The most dangerous act of all, this one, because if he makes a single mistake there's no way back, not this time. And even if he's successful, he can't be completely sure he's safe. But doing nothing isn't an option either

– and he's never shied away from hard choices, has he? The choice, if you can call it that, was made a long time ago. Fifteen years ago.

34

If he's got nothing to hide, Ryan's done a suspiciously good job of disappearing, Mahler concludes. Not only has he withdrawn enough cash to see him through several months of modest living – and a couple of really immodest ones, if such is his plan – but he's been bright enough to stop making any calls on his mobile or carrying out any sort of activity online.

'Sold his car around the same time.' Fergie adds another note to Ryan's section of the whiteboard. 'For cash, of course. And the rent's paid up on his flat for six months in advance. He really doesn't want to be found, does he?'

'Apparently not.' Mahler stares at the lecturer's smiling mug-shot. 'What about friends, colleagues?'

'Bit of a rolling stone, by all accounts – loads of friends, but no really close ones. And I drew a blank with the colleagues too.' The departmental secretary at Ryan's college described him as a lovely man. But yes, he did have a bit of a temper. And he'd seemed a little moodier, a bit preoccupied before he left. But all the staff got a bit grumpy around finals time, and she'd assumed he was just stressed. 'He sent in a letter of resignation dated the day he disappeared, all i's dotted and t's crossed, and just buggered off.'

'And hasn't been seen since.' There's a gathering pain at the base of Mahler's skull. He reaches in his drawer for a pill, dry-swallows it.

'You all right, boss?'

'Fine. So Ryan was last seen on' – he checks his notes – 'the fifteenth of April. He's got no car. None of his colleagues gave him a lift anywhere, which leaves—'

'Taxis? Buses? Trains?' Pete offers.

Mahler nods. 'All of the above. So start with the local taxi firms and see if anyone remembers picking him up – I know, it's a long shot. But right now, that's all we've got.' And most people, Mahler reflects, are creatures of habit. In a small university town like St Andrews, there will be two or three firms the staff and students use most regularly – and if they're lucky, Ryan will have done the same. 'If you've no joy there, he must have gone by bus. See if the bus station has CCTV, and work from there.'

Pete gives him a dubious look. 'They won't have kept the images, not after all this time.'

'So let's hope he took a taxi to wherever he was going, yes? And keep hassling his phone provider about his mobile – if he so much as orders a pizza on it, we'll have him.'

He leaves Pete grumbling over his keyboard and asks Fergie to chase up the CCTV images from the nearest locations to the Ness Islands for the night of Donnie Stewart's murder. The chances of finding anything useful on them are close to zero, but it's just possible Stewart's killer might have been caught on camera as he made his way to his meeting with the kitchen porter. Assuming he came on foot, of course. Assuming he didn't arrive from the Drummond direction and walk down Merlewood Brae. Assuming a whole raft of scenarios which, Mahler concedes, basically boil down to a bloody house of cards.

The pain in his skull is building, a slow relentless pressure heading for his temples. He goes downstairs and out through the custody suite for what passes for fresh air this close to the station, and finds Karen sitting on the courtyard wall, attempting a post-mortem on the remains of a sausage roll. From the look on her face, the filling appears to have died of extreme old age.

'You could take it back and get a refund. If it's that bad.'

She shrugs. 'I've had worse. Just needed to get out for a minute, you know? Clear my head.' She shrouds the sausage roll with a paper napkin and gives it a decent burial by lobbing it into the bin. 'Don't tell me you're actually planning to walk over to the garage and buy something to eat like us common folk?'

'You were eating that? I thought it was some sort of experiment.'

'Funny guy. I've got a bag of brownie bites we can go halfers on if you want.'

'I'll pass, thanks.' He has, after all, his reputation to consider. Most of his junior colleagues assume he gets his nourishment by rising from his tomb to feast on the blood of the living, and he sees no reason to disabuse them of the notion. 'Everything okay? Apart from your impending death by junk food, I mean.'

'Kevin's girlfriend, Gemma Fraser. She's done a bunk. Went round to see her with the FLO and her place is all locked up. I checked with the nursery and the bairns haven't been for a week.'

'You talk to her neighbours?'

Karen nods. 'Told them she was going on holiday. Two weeks in Mallorca with the bairns – a big surprise for them, apparently, so she asked her pals to keep it hush-hush.'

'It's possible, I suppose.' Possible, but barring a lottery win or the intervention of a fairy godmother, not exactly likely. 'You didn't buy it?'

'Would you? Christ, Lukas, the lassie's not got two pennies to rub together. How could she afford a bloody holiday? Andy said give it a few days and do a follow-up on Monday, but . . .' she shakes her head.

'You happy with that?'

The look on her face is answer enough. Andy Black's officially in charge on the Kevin Ramsay case, of course, and all the lines of enquiry should originate from him. Mahler's job is to concentrate on Morven Murray's case, June's made that perfectly clear. Abundantly clear, in every briefing Mahler's had with her since Black's brow-ridged features had returned to grace Burnett Road's MIT again. But she hasn't said anything about taking a short, therapeutic stroll to ward off an impending migraine. About twenty minutes ought to do it, Mahler reckons. Twenty minutes to see off several birds with one projectile. Because he's got a pretty good idea what might be behind Gemma's sudden disappearance. And it certainly isn't a fairy godmother.

He comes to a decision. 'You know, I think a certain local businessman is overdue a visit to discuss the rise in complaints about some of the patrons of "Working Girls". Anti-social behaviour, petty vandalism, that sort of thing. What do you think?'

'Has there been a rise?'

'Almost certainly. Fancy a walk?'

Built on the site of a 1930s civilian airfield, over the years, the Longman industrial estate has gradually split into two distinct sections. From the level crossing at Millburn to the Harbour Road roundabout, sleek, glass-fronted car showrooms alternate with the premises of small local traders. Over on the west side, as the road curves round towards the harbour, the site takes on a more run-down appearance, the units becoming scruffier and more utilitarian.

A bizarre choice of location, Mahler always thinks, for a so-called gentlemen's club. No doubt Cazza had snapped up the former builder's yard at a knockdown price, but getting the change of use permissions through the council's planning department must have been almost impossible. And yet there, on the scruffiest corner of the scruffiest side road, lies the latest jewel in Cazza's crown . . . covered in scaffolding and surrounded by half a dozen white vans.

'Hoi!' Karen leaps to one side as a vanload of greenery reverses towards them. 'Watch where you're going, you effing lunatic!' The van comes to a juddering halt and the doors swing open, depositing a pair of canvas-wrapped bay trees at their feet.

The driver, purple-faced and sweating in a hi-vis jacket three sizes too small for him, gets out. He starts walking round to the back of the van, catches sight of Karen . . . and turns tail, heading for the rear of the building with, Mahler concedes, an impressive turn of speed for someone of his proportions.

'I know that guy.'

Karen starts towards him, but Mahler shakes his head. 'Organ-grinder first, monkeys later. Come on.'

They pick their way round pallets of gravel and bark chippings towards the entrance, a massive, double-doored creation Mahler suspects is strong enough to withstand assault by a small tank. As he reaches for the bell, the door opens inwards, and one of Cazza's minions holds up a hand to bar their way.

'We're closed until Saturday night. Renovations.'

Karen gives him her unimpressed look. 'God's sake, do we look like bloody punters? We're here to see Cazza.'

'Mr MacKay's busy right now. If youse would like to make an appointment—'

'Consider it made.' Mahler flashes his warrant card. 'Now move. Or DS Gilchrist here will make a call to our friends in the HSE about being nearly mown down just now by half a ton of foliage. And don't even think about texting Cazza a warning, because that would annoy DS Gilchrist – and believe me, you don't want to do that. Got it?'

Mahler leaves the man processing that and nods at Karen to follow him. The reception area of 'Working Girls' seems to have had a makeover too. With its sleek leather seating and muted silver and grey décor, it could almost be mistaken for the foyer of a smart boutique hotel. Though he suspects the black and white prints adorning the walls might be a little too X-rated for the standard clientele of most hotels.

Cazza's office is on the first floor, up a flight of blonde-wood stairs. When Mahler pushes the door open, the first surprise awaiting him is the sight of Cazza in successful businessman mode – sharp suit, a whiff of Tom Ford cologne and a pair of designer frames. The second surprise is the man sitting across the desk from him.

'DI Mahler.' Cazza offers him a flint-edged smile. 'And DS . . . Gilchrist, isn't it? Well, well. If I'd known I was having visitors, I'd have got some cakes in. Wouldn't I, Ewan?'

Ewan Campbell's face looks like a paint selector card for fifty shades of porridge. He starts to get up, but Cazza's hand shoots out to grip his arm, and he subsides. 'Hold your horses, man. Not in a rush, are you? Ewan here just dropped in for a wee chat, Inspector.'

'I didn't realise you were such good friends.'

Cazza shrugs. 'We know each other through Ross. Don't we, Ewan? Ross and me played together in Clach's youth team for a while – before your time, that. Then Ross went on to bigger things—'

'And you began your criminal career? I see.' Mahler glances at Campbell. There's a padded envelope by his elbow with a bundle of cash poking out of it, and Mahler's willing to bet it's connected to the man's obvious discomfort. 'Are you all right, Mr Campbell? You look a little pale.'

'He's fine,' Cazza snaps. 'What's this about, son? You're on a meter here, in case you didn't realise.'

'Gemma Fraser. Since we last spoke, she seems to have disappeared. I don't suppose you'd know anything about that?'

'Of course I do – she's having a wee break at my place in Marbella. Thought she could do with it after what she's been through.'

'Just out of the goodness of your heart, eh? Funny she never mentioned it to anyone.' Karen makes a show of consulting her pocketbook. 'Not her FLO, not her neighbours. No one. Why do you think she'd do that?'

Cazza shrugs. 'Haven't a scooby. Look, the lassie's fine

213

– roasting herself by the pool and having a great time, last I heard. If you don't believe me, give her a ring. I've got her number here somewhere—'

'Don't worry, I will.' Karen gives him her permafrost smile. 'Back at the station, where Gemma and me can have a good long chat in private. Boss, we done here? There's a lad downstairs I need a word with, and—'

Karen's mobile bursts into life. She glances at the display and looks at Mahler. 'Sir, I need to take this—'

He nods towards the hallway. 'I'll catch you up outside.'

As the door closes behind Karen, Campbell reaches for the envelope, but Mahler's there before him. He picks up the envelope and empties it onto the desk. Half a dozen bundles of neatly wrapped banknotes spill out, and Campbell's face loses its last tinge of colour.

'Well, well. Either the membership fees here are getting ridiculous, or I've interrupted a spot of cash-in-hand trading.' Mahler glances at Cazza. 'A little clichéd even for you, surely, the used notes in a brown envelope routine?'

'Ross and I had a wee wager, that's all. Gentleman's agreement, just between the two of us. But he's not feeling too well right now, so Ewan here came to drop off my winnings.'

'Is that correct, Mr Campbell?'

'Perfectly.'

'There you go – all cleared up.' Cazza gives Campbell his version of a cheery grin. 'I'll not keep you, Ewan. Things to see, people to do, eh?' When Campbell doesn't move, the smile grows a layer of ice. 'Go on, fuck off. Tell Ross I was asking for him, aye?'

Campbell makes a faint, disgusted noise and gets up to leave. Mahler holds up a hand. 'So you were just doing a favour for your brother, Mr Campbell. Have I got that right?'

Campbell's expression holds layers of weariness. And a bitter, unwilling acceptance. 'It's not the first time, Inspector, and it won't be the last. I told you, I'll always look out for Ross.'

214

And clear up his messes, Mahler realises. No matter how degrading it gets, no matter how expensive, Ewan Campbell will be there to watch his brother's back. 'In that case, I won't keep you. Goodbye, Mr Campbell.'

Once Campbell's gone, Cazza opens his desk drawer and takes out a bottle of Laphroaig. He waves it at Mahler, who shakes his head.

Cazza sighs. 'No drinking on duty, eh? Ach well, down to business then. What can I do for you today, DI Mahler? Now we've cleared up those two wee misunderstandings.'

'Until Gemma contacts us herself to let me know she's safe and well, I'll keep an open mind on that, thanks.'

'See, that's interesting.' Cazza pours himself a finger of the Laphroaig, raises the glass at Mahler. 'Slàinte. First of all, no one's reported her missing, have they? So you're basically chancing your arm, son. And wee Kevin's not even your case any more – Andy Black's back, so I heard.' He shakes his head in mock-dismay. 'Cops telling me porkies, who'd have thought it. Can't believe anyone these day, eh?'

'But I'm supposed to believe your heavies turned up at Morven Murray's memorial service about a gentleman's agreement? Come off it, Carl.'

'Believe what you like. I thought you were chasing murderers, not wasting your time with eejits like Ross Campbell.' He glances at Mahler, sighs. 'Fine, the man owes me money. A fair bit of it, as it happens. But if you're trying to fit him up for Morven Murray, forget it – he's falling to pieces over the death of that lassie, and his so-called business is going down the tubes. You think I'm the only one he's been borrowing off? Trust me, a wee talking-to from Billy and Jez is the least of his problems.'

From what Donna's managed to uncover about Campbell's finances, that part's probably true, Mahler concedes. 'And you're telling me all this just to be helpful, right?'

'No, I'm doing it to get you lot off my fucking back. You're bad for business, and you're doing fuck all to catch the real bad guys here.'

'Guys working for Hollander, is that what you're saying?'

Cazza shrugs. 'I'm saying I gave you a lead, son, and frankly I'm a bit disappointed in you. Why are you boys not on his case?'

'I talked to people, Carl. No one's heard of him. No one – but I'm guessing it would suit you just fine if we wasted our time chasing someone that doesn't exist.'

'Maybe you've not been talking to the right people, then.'

So he's supposed to believe this Hollander is someone neither Police Scotland's glory boys at Gartcosh or his Met contacts have heard of? Mahler shakes his head. 'I've passed on everything relevant to DI Black. But a vague hint about some mystery man who might not even exist? We'll need more than that to take it seriously.'

'Want it spoon-fed, don't you? OK then, try this. Kevin had some new pals. A couple of ex-army boys from down south.'

'Glasgow?'

Cazza shakes his head. 'English. They were bringing in supplies for the party girls and boys. That good enough for you?'

'Not without names, Carl.'

MacKay sighs. And gives him a couple of nicknames that sound just stupid enough to be worth passing on. 'Talk to your pals at SOCA, son – they're supposed to be keeping an eye on the buggers, but I reckon they're just pissing in the wind. And that wee eejit Kevin got mixed up in it somehow. Heard something he shouldn't have, and thought he could play with the big boys.'

'Should have stuck to the straight and narrow like you, you mean?'

'If he'd stuck with me, he'd still be alive.' Cazza takes another sip of the Laphroaig, leans back in his chair. 'Now you trot back to Burnett Road with your wee pal and see if you can't get Andy Black to get his finger out.'

As he goes down the stairs, Cazza calls after him. 'And Hollander? He's as real as you or I am, son. Don't you ever doubt it.'

216

35

When he gets outside, there's no sign of Karen or the Health and Safety-flouting van driver. Mahler's about to ring her when she texts to say she's gone to see the van driver's ex-partner, who works nearby – after enduring a lengthy period of abuse, the woman had taken out an interdict on him. He shouldn't have been anywhere near her place of work, and she needs to be warned in case he's planning any mischief.

Mahler heads back to Burnett Road, where for once Pete and Fergie have some good news for him.

'I found Connor Ryan! At least, I found the taxi driver who picked him up when he left St Andrews,' Pete tells him. 'You were right, he did use the same firm all the time.'

'So what have we got?'

Pete checks his notes. 'A decent break – well, sort of. On Sunday, 4 May, Ryan calls a taxi just after 12.15 p.m. Even better news, he's going to the railway station in Leuchars. The bad news is, it's well past the thirty-day period they retain images for, so there's no chance of picking him up on CCTV.'

Mahler nods. It's still potentially the best lead they've had so far. 'Looks like we're going to do it the hard way, then. St Andrews to

Leuchars is only about fifteen minutes' drive, so assume he could be getting any train from 12.45 onwards to, say, 13.30.'

'Why no later?'

'Makes no sense to hang around a tiny station like Leuchars longer than you have to – I'm guessing he got a train no later than 13.30, which should help us a little.'

Pete stares at him. 'How? He could have got a train to bloody anywhere!'

'At least it was a Sunday,' Mahler points out. 'We've probably got a fairly small number of trains to look at. And don't forget, if Ryan was involved in Morven Murray's murder, he'll have had to have been within easy travelling distance of Inverness.'

'Unless he hired a car. Or bought one.'

Mahler shakes his head. 'Hiring would leave an audit trail. And why sell your car to buy another one? He'd still need insurance, which needs paperwork – and I'm pretty sure that's what he's trying to avoid. So let's look at the possibilities, and draw up a list of places he could have left the train at. After that . . . well, we'll take stock once we have the list.'

'Going to be a bloody long list, boss.'

'Then you'd better get started, hadn't you?'

Fergie goes after him. 'You're not serious? Pete's right, the man could have gone anywhere – and how do we know he didn't get another train from wherever he did get off? Or a bus?'

'You have a better idea?' And Mahler's noticed Pete has an odd sort of talent for making connections and seeing patterns in apparently random pieces of information. If anyone can track Connor Ryan down, he has a feeling it might be Pete.

'Look, we have a man with good reason to dislike Morven Murray who clears his bank account and walks out of his job two weeks before her murder. A man who hasn't been seen since – so if there's the slightest chance of tracking him down, we need to try.'

36

WEDNESDAY, 9 JULY

'Anna, how lovely to hear from you!' Glyn Hadley's posh-boy voice, purring fruitily down the phone at her. Pretending this isn't the fifth time she's called his office since she got back from Glasgow, and the only reason he's talking to her today is because the tabloids, bored with taking pot-shots at Alex Salmond, are running with an interview with one of Morven's exes, Gavin Hunter.

They'd broken up over four years ago and Hunter, a failed entrepreneur and committed substance-abuser, has been in and out of rehab three times since then – hardly a reliable source, Anna would have thought, even for the red-tops. But there are enough insinuations scattered throughout the article to make Morven newsworthy again. And for Glyn Hadley to finally deign to take Anna's call.

'Deeply distressing, all this muckraking.' Hadley's voice slides effortlessly into sympathetic mode. 'Only thing you can do is keep a low profile until it dies down – and not add fuel to the fire, obviously. From what I understand, you didn't always . . . well, you weren't exactly close, were you?'

'We hadn't been, no. But she was so excited about the wedding, I'm sure we would have reconnected over that. And she had such an amazing career, didn't she? Morven always kept me up to date with what she was up to when we spoke.'

'I hadn't realised.'

'Oh, yes.' She injects as much enthusiasm into her voice as she can manage. 'You know, the fascinating people she met, the ups, the downs . . . all of it, really.'

'She talked to you about these plans of hers?'

'Well, not in detail. I mean, she was still thinking things through, you know, and . . .' She can hear herself floundering, playing for time. *What* bloody plans? 'How did you feel about it?'

As soon as the words are out, she knows she's made a mistake. She can feel the drop in temperature on the other end of the phone. When Hadley speaks again, the faux-chumminess is encased in layers of ice.

'Morven hadn't spoken to you about it at all, had she? If she had, you wouldn't have needed to ask.'

'I'm sorry. I was only trying—'

'Don't bother trying to wriggle out of it. You rang me up on a fishing expedition, and you are, as they say, busted. So what exactly are you planning, Anna? Something bigger than Gavin Hunter's interview, obviously. Let's see, a quick hatchet job masquerading as a biography, is that it? I hope you're not angling for representation from this agency, because that isn't going to happen – not now, not ever.'

Before she can explain, he hangs up. She doesn't blame him – he'd thought he was defending Morven's memory, and she finds herself liking the man a little more for it. But she's just blown any chances she had of finding out if Morven had had any serious fallings-out with anyone connected to her career.

Mahler had said they were looking at both Morven's personal and professional life, hadn't he? Though if he starts investigating every bust-up Morven's had in the course of her career, Anna's guessing it'll take him a hell of a long time. But if it's nothing to do with her job . . .

Anna looks at the pile of documents she's spread across the dining-room table, still waiting to be sorted. There's probably enough material left for one more scrapbook to add to her mother's collection, focusing on Morven's career highlights. At least Morven had been disciplined enough to date everything, so sorting them into chronological order had been relatively easy.

But the earlier records, the ones Anna's most interested in, are something else entirely. Dating from Morven's first forays into student broadcasting, they're little more than a few scribbled notes, a couple of bad editorials from long-gone student magazines, and a tatty A4 envelope stuffed with photographs.

Anna empties them out and sifts through the pile. Some snaps of family holidays – days out on the beach at Nairn, two windswept little girls grinning for the camera – and then a whole stack of later ones documenting Morven's time at university.

She turns them over, one by one. There's something oddly comforting about the feel of them in her hands, like a memory she can touch. A disappearing feeling, she realises, because who bothers to print actual photographs these days?

Memories, maybe. But as she goes through the pile, it becomes clear she's wasting her time looking for answers there. What had she been hoping to find, a Jack the Ripper clone caught snarling at the camera? There's no one in these later images but Morven. Morven posing model-style, head tilted, hand on hip, smoky-eyed and pouting. Morven in a club, drink in hand. Morven putting on her make-up, getting ready to go out . . . Morven, the original party girl. Yet somehow, she'd still managed to scrape through her finals. Anna gathers the photos together, ready to stuff them back into the envelope. And one of them catches her eye.

At first, she has no idea why. At first, it's just like all the others – look, there's Morven at another party, mugging for the camera with a Corona in her hand. Surprise, bloody surprise. Only there's another girl in this one, an unknown, dark-haired girl with her arm round Morven's shoulders. The photo's a little faded and out of focus, but there's something about her, some sort of memory that's hovering just out of reach . . .

Anna picks up the photograph and stares at the dark-haired girl, willing her name to come to mind. Because she does know her, she's sure of it, and . . . oh, Christ, it's Janis. *Janis Miller.*

Fifteen years ago at the end of a damp, unsunny June, the whole country had known her name. Janis Miller, one of Morven's band of sleek-haired, caramel-tanned BFFs. Janis Miller, who'd astonished everyone by taking her election to the Student Representative Council seriously and had put in the hours to make it a success. Janis Miller, who'd fallen to her death from a top-floor balcony during her flatmate's graduation party. Anna hadn't known her personally – she'd been in Morven's year, not Anna's – but the accident had sent tidal waves of shock throughout the entire university.

No date on the back of this one. Which, Anna finds, she's suddenly grateful for. She starts to turn it over again, but changes her mind. Too much death, she thinks. Too much death not to look at their faces and see it written there, like history-book images of doomed young men smiling in the Flanders trenches. Better to remember them like this—

'When were you going to tell us, Anna?'

Her mother, standing in the doorway, a bulky padded envelope in her hand. Looking at her as though she was five years old again and had been caught crayoning on the living-room wallpaper.

'Jamie Gordon came round while you were down town – on his way to Helmsdale, he said, so he couldn't stay. He took a cup of tea, though. And we had a nice wee chat about this TV programme you two are making.'

'Mam, it's Jamie's programme! I'm helping him with a bit of research, that's all.'

'That's why he left this for you, is it?' Her mother drops the package onto the table, sending Anna's pile of photographs flying.

'Only a rough draft, he said, but he wants to know what you think of it. Of your *script*.' The look on her face is a mix of anger and contempt. 'Do you really think I don't know what you're up to?'

And here it is. The fight they've been dancing around for days. For weeks, if she's honest. Anna sits back, folds her arms. 'Sorry, you've lost me. What is it you think I'm up to, Mam?'

'You were always jealous of her. Always. Do you think I didn't see the way you looked at Morven? Like you wanted everything she had – and now you've finally got your chance. Jamie Gordon was her friend, not yours! But here you are, pushing for a part in his bloody TV programme. Trying to grab your fifteen minutes' worth, now Morven's not here to get in your way.'

Jesus Christ, what has Jamie been telling her? 'I told you, this is Jamie's script – I'm helping him pull it together, that's all. Tidying up any inaccuracies, that sort of thing.'

'That's not the way it sounded to me. It sounded as though he'd got great plans for the two of you to work together.'

Straw, camel, back. It's a fight that's been coming for weeks now, ever since she started working with Jamie, but the surge of anger Anna feels still takes her by surprise. 'Okay, that's it.' She starts gathering her papers together. 'I'm not doing this, Mam, not now. I know you're hurting, but—'

'He asked her first.'

'To help with the documentary? I don't believe you.'

A joyless smile etches her mother's mouth. 'You don't seriously think you were his first choice, do you? For something like this? Oh, I know I can't stop you. But don't think I'm going to make it easy for you to . . . to steal everything she had.' She holds out her hand. 'I want her keys back. The keys to Morven's flat, Anna – give them to me!'

And she almost does. Because even now, with her mother's face a rigid mask of fury inches from her own, the instinct to give way, to play the quiet, unassuming daughter is still there. And because this small victory might calm her mother, draw her back from the precipice of rage and grief and bitterness she's been living on since Morven's death. Until the next time. But what will save her then?

Anna shakes her head. 'I can't do that. Sorry.'

She takes out the solicitor's letter, hands it to her mother with the one from Morven. And watches her face come undone, slack with incomprehension. With betrayal.

'You said you were just going down to check on it. And when you brought back all this stuff – I thought you were trying to help me remember.' The glint of tears, misery warring with disbelieving anger. 'You were just clearing it out, weren't you? I wondered why you were down there the whole weekend – but it all makes sense now. You were throwing away your sister's life before you moved in and took it over.'

'What's all the shouting for?' Her father, standing in the door-way. How long had he been there, listening? 'Yvonne, I could hear you halfway down the path!'

'Back from your flaming meeting, are you?' Her mother spins round, thrusts the letter at his chest. 'I suppose you knew all about this!'

Silence while he reads the letter. When he's finished, he hands them back to Anna. 'Sounds like Morven was trying to make things right between the two of them – and don't tell me there was nothing to fix, Yvonne. We both know what she could be like.'

Her mother gasps. 'Don't you dare say that – don't you dare! Our daughter's dead, Rob!'

'Anna's our bloody daughter too!'

Silence. Only for an instant, but long enough for Anna to see the look on her mother's face before it rearranges. A look of sadness, yes. But also of regret . . . and with it, a relationship breaking. Shattering into smaller and smaller pieces.

'I know that.' Her mother's hand reaching out, her mouth trying to form a smile. 'Anna, you know I didn't mean—'

'Didn't you?' She pulls her hand back and turns away. Gathers up everything on the table and sweeps it into her holdall. Not saying anything else, because really, what is there left to say? She goes up to her room and gets her suitcase out of the wardrobe.

'Anna, don't be daft.' Her father's following her, trying to catch his breath after taking the stairs too fast. 'Look, your mam's just upset. Seeing you getting close to Jamie, hearing about the flat – it's all too much for her. Can't you understand that?'

Does he really think that's all this is about? 'I'm trying to. Believe me.' She looks round for the holdall, slides her laptop inside. 'I think we need a bit of space right now, that's all.' She zips up the case, pulls on her jacket. And attempts a reassuring smile. 'I'm not going far, don't worry – I'll find a B&B in town. You've got my mobile if . . . if anything happens.'

Down the stairs and out the front door. Her mother calls after her, but Anna shakes her head. Not now. Not until there's a chance they can stop doing this to each other.

She slings the holdall over her shoulder and walks up to Culduthel Road, past the elegant pastel boutique hotel on one side and the more traditional lines of the Beaufort to her right.

The sun is starting to break through the watery clouds, and the summer visitors are out in force, disgorged from the giant tour buses parked by the river. The B&Bs are doing good business, too. She walks past half a dozen 'No Vacancies' signs on Ardconnel Street before finding somewhere she can stay for more than a couple of days.

'Town's packed for some reason,' the owner tells her as she hands over her credit card. He's a big, round-faced man with mad professor hair and the remnants of a Caithness accent. 'Have you been down the High Street today? Can't move for the tourists. And there's that *Question Time* thing tomorrow night, of course.'

'In Inverness?'

'At Eden Court, aye. Wee Eck Salmond's not on it though, just some singer guy and a journalist wifie. Shows the polls must be getting tighter, eh, for the BBC to bother trailing up here? I'm going along myself, just for the craic. Here, I'll take your case for you.'

225

He shows her to a small room on the first floor. It would probably give most of her Californian friends claustrophobia, but there's a dressing table she can use as a desk, and if she stands on tiptoe at the window she can just about see the river.

'No en suite, I'm afraid, but the bathroom's just across the landing. So, you just back for a visit, then? Bet you're seeing a few changes in the town, eh?'

Her Bank of America credit card. Of course. She tells him she teaches history in San Diego and he looks impressed. 'Good for you. Better weather, eh? Went out to Oz a few years ago myself, but . . . ach, the folks were back here and getting older, so you know . . .' he shrugs. 'You picked an interesting time to come home, with the Referendum in full swing.'

'How do you think it's going to go? The vote, I mean.'

'No idea. I know how I'd like it to go, but . . .' he shakes his head. 'Ach, I think maybe we've missed our chance. Too long being told we're not big enough, not good enough, all that stuff. But I'll tell you one thing – if it's a "No" on the eighteenth, see on the nineteenth? We're going back in our box for the rest of the decade, Westminster will make bloody sure of that.'

When he's gone, Anna lets herself lose the cheerful smile. She unzips the holdall and takes out the padded envelope Jamie had left for her. It's not his fault her mother had heard the word 'script' and jumped to conclusions, but why the hell would Jamie have said he'd spoken to Morven first? Assuming he *had* actually said that, of course. It wouldn't be the first time her mother had rearranged facts to suit her own narrative – and that narrative would always see Morven as the natural first choice for something like this.

Anna stuffs the script back into the envelope and tosses it onto the floor. She needs to talk to Jamie, but she needs to get her head together first. In the days after Morven's murder, she'd felt weirdly disconnected – the police interviews, the photographers camped outside her parents' house – everything felt as though it was taking place behind a barrier. And she'd welcomed the feeling, used it to keep functioning for her parents' sake. To be *useful*.

But now the barrier is crumbling and everything she does feels like whistling in the wind. As the weeks pass, the effects of Morven's murder are growing, not dissipating, like the aftermath of some massive explosion. Her parents are ground zero, and everyone else is collateral damage – even Mahler, who every time she sees him looks more and more like a man fighting a battle on half a dozen fronts at once.

And after today, it would be so easy to walk away. She has a life waiting for her in San Diego – a good life, with a job she loves and friends she misses. But she'd walked away once before, hadn't she? Let the rift with Morven deepen as the years passed and their lives grew further apart. If they hadn't argued on the day of Morven's murder, if she hadn't gone into town with Jamie instead of trying to sort things out with her sister, would Morven still have died?

She'll never know for sure. But leaving now, without doing everything she can to find out who killed Morven, would feel like giving up on her all over again. And there's no way she can do that.

37

FRIDAY, 11 JULY

High summer, or what passes for it in Inverness. The rains at the beginning of the month have dispersed, giving way to long, crystal-bright days when the river moves like liquid silver.

In the centre of town, the city is setting out its stall for the summer visitors. The floral display beneath the castle is being coaxed into weed-free civic neatness, and hanging baskets are sprouting everywhere. Busking pipers are duelling across the High Street, facing in opposite directions like kilted bookends while shortbread-tin muzak blares from the gift shops. And posses of uniformed officers are out on charm patrol, moving on the winos from their debating benches outside McDonald's and chasing the Poundland shoplifters down Bridge Street.

In the mid-morning sun Mahler is dressed for the gym, running along the river on a rare few hours off. Over the footbridge at the Islands, down past the former Royal Northern Infirmary, its out-dated Victorian grandeur now home to the admin centre for the University of the Highlands and Islands. Then further down Ness Walk – stopping before he reaches the sign for the new Archive

Centre, because he's winded, no point denying it, the worst shape he's been in since last summer.

Not exercising, not eating properly – all he needs, he suspects, is Fergie's alcohol intake and June's nicotine addition to turn him into everyman's identikit Scots DI. Though right now, he'd happily trade a little clean living for the clear-up rate of any fictional detective. Or failing that, a decent night's sleep, undisturbed by Kevin's and Morven's bloodied, reproachful ghosts. Donnie Stewart hasn't appeared yet, but Mahler knows it's only a matter of time.

His calf muscles are starting to protest. He does a couple of stretches and turns back towards town, heading for the Infirmary Bridge. Wondering how the hell Stewart had stayed beneath their radar for so long. If they'd moved faster, put in more resources . . . but Stewart hadn't just been hiding from the police. Morven Murray's killer had been hunting him too, Mahler's sure of it – so had Stewart been an accomplice who couldn't be trusted, or a witness who'd seen too much? Either way, the killer had to have contacted him to set up the meeting. And if enough information can be extracted from the call log for Stewart's phone . . .

His own mobile buzzes against his arm, flashing up Anna Murray's number.

'Inspector?' Her voice is hesitant, tinged with an odd embarrassment. 'I'm sorry, but I'm with a . . . a distressed lady here who gave me your number to ring. She says you're her son.'

And in the background, the sound of weeping. Quiet, desperate. Familiar. His gut tightens.

'Where are you?'

'At your mother's flat. I . . . I think you should come over.'

He's home in under ten minutes, showered, changed and on his way five minutes after that. Anna Murray must have been watching for his arrival. Before he's halfway up the path, she's standing in the doorway, waiting.

'Inspector.' She steps aside to let him through. 'I was just passing, and . . . well, you'd better come in.'

It's going to be bad, he knows that as soon as he gets inside. Every available surface is littered with books and overflowing carrier bags and all the cupboards are standing open, as though a poltergeist had rampaged through the entire flat. Christ, how can it have got so bad, so quickly? But he knows the answer to that, of course he does. If his mother stopped her meds, it wouldn't have taken her long to go downhill.

He goes into the living room, but at first he can't see his mother. He's turning to ask Anna where she is when he spots her, crouched between the dresser and the wall. Her hair is matted and her knees drawn up to her chest, as though she's trying to make herself as small as possible.

'Mum?' He goes over to her, but she cowers away. 'Mum, what is it? What's wrong?'

'I saw him. He was there, Lukas! Waiting in the garden. Waiting for me to . . . to . . .'

Her voice falters, breaks into splintered, rasping sobs. Anna kneels down beside her and touches her arm.

'I was thinking I'd make a cup of tea for us. We were standing outside for quite a while, and it got cold once the rain started, didn't it, er . . .' She looks at him and mouths a question.

'Grace,' he says. 'My mother's name is Grace. Mum, if I make the tea, would you like Anna to get your dressing gown?'

A slight movement of her head, something that might be a nod. He shows Anna to his mother's room, waits until she's collected the dressing gown and his mother is wrapped inside it and seated on her favourite chair before motioning to Anna to follow him to the kitchen.

'You said you were passing?'

'I'm staying at a B&B round the corner.' Anna pulls the door closed. 'I . . . I needed a bit of space for a few days.'

'I see.' Why hadn't Maxine told him? He makes a mental note to speak to her later. 'Was my mother . . . did she call out to you?'

Anna shakes her head. 'Grace was just standing on the doorstep, in a short-sleeved top and no shoes. At first I thought she'd just locked herself out, but then . . . well, I realised it was a little more than that.'

'My mother's unwell.' Which clearly isn't much of a revelation. But understanding – or worse, sympathy, from Anna Murray isn't something he's comfortable with. 'She was . . . attacked some years ago, and very badly beaten. It's left her with some mental health issues.'

'I thought maybe something like that . . .' A quick, embarrassed glance at him. 'I used to volunteer at a women's shelter in San Diego, you see. Some of the stories I was told . . . no one could have survived what they'd gone through and not been changed by it, Inspector. No one. Does your mother live alone?'

He nods. 'She has spells – quite long ones, sometimes – when she copes well. But if something triggers a relapse . . .' he shrugs. 'I transferred from the Met last year to be on hand if things deteriorated again, but—'

'You don't think you're helping that much. But if you leave, the guilt's going to eat you alive.' She gives him a weary half-smile. 'Welcome to my world. But you shouldn't feel guilty – your being here *is* helping her, I'm sure.' She glances at him, sighs. 'Not my business, right? I'll shut up now.'

'I suspect guilt is one of those emotions that feeds on itself. But thank you.' He puts the kettle on, looks round for the mugs his mother keeps for visitors. 'Is that the reason you moved out?'

'One of the reasons.' She tells him about the letter from Morven's solicitor and everything that it had set in motion 'And before you ask, yes, I'll take the letters in to show you. I'd have done it right away, only I assumed they'd have been in touch. And my head was all over the place, to be honest.'

'Understandable.' And it had obviously been dealt with separately to Morven's will, presumably through a Scottish solicitor, which is why the settlement hadn't shown up in their enquiries. 'Will you keep the flat?'

'I wasn't going to, not at first. But now I think Morven wanted to put things right between us, and this was her way of doing it. So, yes, I think I'll keep it – and maybe I'll find a way to . . . I don't know, reconnect with her through it.' She pulls a face. 'That sounded horribly Californian, didn't it? Sorry.'

'Appallingly so. But the apology gets you a free pass. This time.'

He finds himself smiling. Finds the smile returned. What is it about Anna Murray that draws his smiles in spite of himself? Whatever it is, she shouldn't be here, comforting his mother. Drawing his smiles. She's a witness in a murder investigation. A *current* investigation, for God's sake.

The kettle's boiled. He throws a couple of teabags into the pot, adds the water. Puts two mugs on a tray before he turns to her. 'I'll need to take a look at everything you found at the flat, see if there's anything we've missed. Can you call in to Burnett Road tomorrow?'

'I assume that's not really a request. Don't worry, I'll be there – no need to send a car this time.' She picks up her bag, offers him a chilly smile. 'I think I should be going now, don't you? Tell Grace I said goodbye.'

'Anna—'

The sound of a car pulling up outside drowns out whatever he'd been going to say. He takes the tea through to his mother – who's still sitting in her chair, thank God, wrapped in her dressing gown – and tells her Anna had to leave.

'That's a shame. She had kind eyes. Is she a friend of yours?'

'I met her through work.'

'Kind eyes, and a pretty smile. Don't you think?'

'Mum—'

Her hand finds his, holds it. 'Lukas, you mustn't . . . you're not like him. You know that, don't you?'

Movement outside, saving him from answering. The slam of a car door and footsteps coming up the path. 'I think that's Ruth.

You remember Ruth, don't you? She's taken over from Siobhan. She's here to talk to you about what we do next, and—'

'She wants me to go in for respite. That's why she's here, isn't it?'

'It's your choice, you know that.' But he has no idea what they're going to do if she refuses. She needs care, and she needs to feel safe. And he can't offer her either of these things. 'It might help, though. What do you think?'

'Maybe. I don't want to stay here, not by myself.'

'You won't have to,' he assures her. 'But I wish you hadn't stopped taking your meds, Mum. Why did you do that?'

A look of confusion on her face. 'I . . . I didn't mean to. But when I went to the packet, it was empty, and I couldn't find any others. I must have run out, mustn't I?' When he doesn't answer, she gives him a worried look. 'Lukas? That's what happened, isn't it?'

'Yes.' Except that she'd had a couple of months' supply left the last time he'd visited. He'd checked it, the way he always does. How could all those meds have simply disappeared? Only one way, that's how. 'Has Mina been staying with you again?'

A hesitant nod. 'Last week, I think. Or maybe it was it before that, I . . . I can't remember.' Her mouth trembles. 'I think . . . sometimes I wonder if I'm going mad, Lukas. I forget the stupidest things, and—'

'You're not going mad. You need a break, that's all – listen, that's Ruth knocking.'

He gets up to go and let her in, but his mother grabs his hand again. 'Last week – yes, that was it! Mina was staying with me last week. She's just lost her boyfriend, and she was really upset about it. Do you think you could find her for me? I . . . I'm a bit worried about her.'

Mina Williamson. Opportunistic, light-fingered *Mina*. And the meds had been sitting in a plastic tub in the kitchen, for God's sake. Nice and convenient for his mother. Jesus Christ.

'Lukas, what's wrong?'

233

His mother's hands are starting to shake again. He rescues the mug of tea and puts it on a side table. 'Nothing. Don't worry, Mum. I'll find her.'

By some miracle, Ruth has managed to arrange a couple of weeks' respite at a local recovery unit, where his mother knows and trusts the staff. Mahler walks her to Ruth's car and watches them drive off – Ruth trying to make conversation, his mother hunched in her seat as though she's trying to make herself as small as possible – and he feels the anger pulse through him.

Anna Murray had tried to tell him he shouldn't feel guilty. But she doesn't know what he did, all those years ago. What he *didn't* do. And how his mother had paid for it. There are things he can never change now, things that have broken and can never be repaired. But there are still some things he can do to make his mother's life a little better. Things to keep her safe from lying, thieving little 'friends' like Mina Williamson.

Find Mina. That's one promise he fully intends to keep . . . before the day is out, with a little luck.

'Mina's not been seen at her flat since yesterday,' Fergie tells him when he calls. 'Heading down Castle Street now and there's no sign of her on the corner. She's barred from McCallum's, so—'

'I know, she'll be at worship. Fine, I'll see you there.'

Mahler leaves the car where it is and runs down the Market Brae steps. Mina's a creature of habit, and unless it's raining hard enough to keep most people indoors, she can usually be found contributing to the alternative street theatre on offer between Poundland and McDonald's, where the council have thoughtfully provided benches for the boozed-up performers' comfort. But Mina is a sun-worshipper, and in weather like this, if she's not at her flat or lurking outside McDonald's with her drinking pals, Mahler knows there's only one other place she's likely to be.

At the far end of Church Street, the Old High is the oldest

religious site in Inverness. Saint Columba preached here, or so the story goes, finally converting Brude, the Pictish king, to Christianity by ordering the Loch Ness Monster to stop snacking on his subjects.

A place of execution, too, Mahler recalls, despite its sanctity. In the months after the Battle of Culloden, Jacobite prisoners were dragged into the churchyard and shot, earning the site a lasting reputation for paranormal happenings. And on a warm summer afternoon like this, he's pretty sure the spirits will be out in force again . . . only they'll come via bottles of Buckie or six-packs of value cider, as the members of Inverness's alternative café society stretch out between the graves with their firewater of choice.

By the west door, a huddle of tourists are peering at the headstones as a tartan-draped tour guide gives them a history-lite version of Culloden and its bloody aftermath. Mahler stations himself by the Robertson mausoleum to wait. When Fergie arrives, the tour guide is in full dramatic flow, only slightly hampered by bursts of heckling from further down the graveyard.

'Any sign?'

Mahler points to a row of headstones by the far wall. 'Spotted a couple of our regulars over there. And—'

A sound of breaking glass. A yell like a banshee on helium, followed by a ragged cheer. And the unmistakeable sound of two people doing their best to knock seven bells out of each other.

Mahler races across the grass with Fergie on his heels. Halfway down the path, being egged on by half a dozen onlookers, Mina's wrestling with 'Midden', a grizzled veteran of Burnett Road's temporary accommodation, over what looks like a battered Union Jack backpack.

As Mahler reaches the first set of headstones, the onlookers scatter, shambling off between the graves to a chorus of shrieks from the tour group. At the commotion, Mina's head jerks up. She bares her teeth at him, shoves her sparring partner aside and hurtles down the grassy slope towards Bank Street. If she makes it to the bottom in one piece, Mahler knows she'll head for Johnny Foxes, the pub on the corner, and he'll lose her.

'Stop! Mina, I'm warning you—'

She sticks two fingers in the air, risks a look round to see where he is, and loses her footing. Mahler reaches for her arm—

'Hey you, let go of her!'

A yell from one of the tourists. Mahler only hesitates for a split second, but Mina makes the most of it. She sinks her teeth into his hand and bolts for the street, but Mahler lunges after her and gets her on the ground.

'Don't move,' he warns her. 'Not a bloody muscle, Mina.'

'You're breaking my fucking arm, ya bastard! And you're not fucking lifting me, no way – I've not fucking done anything!'

She's writhing as though he's pulled a taser on her. And as Fergie puffs over, Mahler spots the tour group snapping away on their smartphones. 'Oh, for Christ's sake. How about assaulting a constable in the execution of his duty?'

'Boss—' Fergie, sounding uneasy. Mahler shakes his head, tightens his grip on Mina's arm.

'Or how about stealing prescription drugs with intent to supply?'

'I didn't—'

'What did you think would happen to my mother when you stole those pills, Mina? Did you think she'd just carry on, somehow? Did you?'

'Boss!'

Enough of a warning in Fergie's voice to make him move away from her. But not too far. 'Newsflash, Mina. She didn't just carry on. She couldn't – you left her without any medication, and thanks to you, she's back in bloody respite. So I'm warning you, don't push me.'

'I needed them more than she did! My man—' her voice cracks and she rubs a grimy hand across her nose. 'My man's gone, and instead of doing your job, you lot are fannying about harassing me and my pals! Why don't you fuck off and—'

236

'Right, that's it. On your feet.' Fergie hauls her up, adjusts his grip on her wrist and reaches for his cuffs. 'Mina Williamson, I'm detaining you for—'

'Wait.' Mahler holds his hand up. 'My mother said you'd lost your boyfriend.' Shapes coming together inside his head. Patterns forming. Was this the unknowable thing, the thing he'd missed? 'Who is he, Mina? What's your boyfriend's name?'

Mina starts shaking. Her whole body is shivering so violently that she looks as though she's having some sort of seizure. Mahler's turning to Fergie, ready to have him call an ambulance, when Mina grabs his wrist.

'Donnie.' She licks her lips, her eyes darting from side to side. 'Some bastard killed my Donnie. And he said he's going to get me too!'

38

'She swore blind she wasn't involved with Donnie Stewart when we were trying to track him down,' Fergie tells Mahler as they wait for the duty GP to finish examining Mina. 'Made us look like total numpties, and I bloody fell for it. Sorry, boss.'

'At least we know now why no one had seen him around.' On the way back to Burnett Road, Mina had admitted hiding Stewart in her flat for a couple of nights. After that, according to Mina, he'd slept rough. 'Though I suspect there's more to it than that. He—'

The door to the doctor's room opens and Mina emerges, still clutching the backpack. To her obvious disgust, the duty GP confirms she's fit for interview. The doctor shakes her head at the sight of Mahler's bruised hand, but lets him off with a reminder about his tetanus booster after he promises to come back to let her look at it later.

'You've to be nice to me.' Mina gives him a baleful look over her mug of tea as he catches up with Fergie and Mina in the interview room. 'The doctor said so. She said—'

Mahler holds up his hand. 'Not in the mood, Mina. Seriously not in the mood. Let's just get on with it, shall we? Why was Donnie hiding from us – was he involved in Morven Murray's death?'

'He wasn't hiding from you! And Donnie wouldn't kill anyone. He . . .' she puts her tea down, wipes her mouth. 'He was scared. Dead scared. And . . . and so was I.'

It hadn't been Donnie's fault, she tells them. He'd seen a guy at Bunchrew on the night of the murder, and the guy had seen him too. Donnie wouldn't tell her what the guy had threatened to do to him if he told anyone, but it hadn't been hard to guess.

'You could have come to us. And if Donnie had told us about this man—'

'Youse lot would have listened to him, would you? Aye right.' Mina glares at him. 'You'd have wheeched him down into a cell and, there you go – one sad alky bastard banged up for it and that's that. All done and dusted, and a nice wee box ticked off your list. Anyway, Donnie never saw his face. The guy had a mask on – all bones, like a skeleton head.'

'A skull?'

Mina nods. 'Donnie was shit-scared. Told me he had to do what the guy said, or the guy would sort him out. And then he . . . he'd come for me.'

Plausible enough, Mahler supposes. But how had the man kept Stewart onside for so long? Mina swears she doesn't know, but Mahler suspects hard cash, either on the night or promised at some future date. Backed up with threats if Donnie had started getting difficult. 'What about his voice? Was he local?'

Mina shakes her head. 'Donnie said he talked like a fucking headmaster, all big words and sneering at him like he was rubbish.' Mina's lip curls over one yellow incisor. 'You know, like you do.'

Fergie shakes his head. 'Not good enough, Mina. No way. You'll have to give us more than that, unless you fancy a spell down-stairs for a couple of nights. You gave my boss here a hell of a nip, and he's not exactly the forgiving type. So I'll ask you again – did Donnie say or do anything else that could help us?'

And there it is. So fast, Mahler almost misses it . . . her eyes flicker to the battered Union Jack holdall balanced on her lap.

A glance at Fergie – yes, he's seen it too. Mahler leans forward. And lets the anger come through this time. 'I'm afraid there's something you're missing, Mina. Something you haven't quite grasped yet, so let me spell it out for you. If you'd told us this – any of this – earlier, there's a good chance your boyfriend might be alive today. Banged up, maybe, but alive. So how does that feel, Mina? Tell me, how does that bloody feel?'

'Bastard!' Mina leaps to her feet, pulling her fist back to get an optimum angle to aim at his jaw . . . and crumples suddenly, slumping back into her chair and wailing like an injured animal. Fergie goes towards her, but Mahler shakes his head. He passes her the tissues and waits until her shuddering dies down.

'Look, you're grieving, and you're scared,' he tells her. 'I understand that, Mina, I really do. It's too late to help Donnie now, but you can still help us find his killer. Fergie will get you a cup of tea—'

'Two sugars. And a KitKat.'

'And a KitKat. Absolutely. And you're going to sit there and tell me every bloody thing you can think of. Starting with whatever's in that bag.'

'There's nothing—'

'Open. The bloody. Bag.'

Mina bares her teeth at him. And opens up the backpack. 'Here. It's not working anyway. Doesn't even switch on.'

Mahler looks at what she's just placed on the table. And nods at Fergie. 'You think you could find another couple of KitKats from somewhere?'

Despite inhaling Donna's entire stash of chocolate-covered biscuits, Mina doesn't have that much more to tell them in the end. She knows Stewart went back to his flat a couple of times but he never told her where he hid out between visits. He'd been given money by the man in the skull mask – it hadn't lasted long, but

240

then Stewart had come up with a plan to extort more from him. A plan involving the iPad he'd given Mina to keep safe for him.

'He said it was insurance, so the guy couldn't double-cross him. Said if his plan worked, he'd be fucking rolling in it.' Her mouth twists in a bitter half-smile. 'Aye, right. Folk like us, our big ideas always turn to shite, don't they?'

'I'm sorry,' Mahler tells her as he walks her back to reception. 'But there's every chance the information you've given will help us catch his killer.'

Mina squints up at him. 'If you get the guy, what happens then? A big court case? My face in all the papers, maybe?'

'Very likely, yes.'

'And he'll get banged up forever, right?' She drops the backpack into the litter bin by the entrance. And gives Mahler a look of pure contempt. 'Aye, right. And even if he is, big fucking deal. My man'll still be dead, won't he?'

Eight-thirty that evening. Mahler's MIT room deserted, silent, dark, apart from the ghost-glow from his laptop. The pain at the base of his skull is inching its way upwards. Gathering its strength for an all-out assault soon, he suspects. But there is medication in his desk, if necessary. And caffeine should hold it back a little longer—

'Not going home?' Karen stops in his office doorway. 'Watch out, the Chief'll find a way of charging you for out-of-hours electricity.'

'In a while.' Mahler closes the file he's been working on. 'Putting in a few extra hours yourself, aren't you? Any developments on Kevin Ramsay?'

'Just following up a few things while there's peace and quiet.' She comes in, perches on one of the desks. 'You know how mad it gets here sometimes.'

He does. But he suspects that's not the only reason. 'How's Andy – still the same devastating combination of charm, intellect and industry?'

241

'Ach, Andy's OK, you just need to know how to handle him.' A pause. 'Anyway, I've seen a couple of jobs I'm thinking of applying for.'

'Out of area?'

'Not going to get much further here, am I? Look, I'm not blaming you. It's just . . . I don't know, maybe it's time to move on.' She darts a glance at him. 'What about you – don't you miss the buzz of the Met? Always being at the sharp end, never knowing what you'll be dealing with?'

A chair kicked over. A slumped dark shape, painted against the light. Sirens wailing and a rising scream behind him . . .

'Trust me, the sharp end is overrated. And my mother's had a setback.' He tells her about Mina. And watches an awkward sympathy flit across her face.

'Christ, that's rough. I . . . I'm sorry. But this sort of thing . . . she's always going to be vulnerable, isn't she? Maybe if she was living somewhere more, well, residential—'

'Somewhere with visiting hours, you mean. Maybe a communal lounge and a nice sing-song every Thursday?' Anger, rising to fill the back of his throat. Hot, acidic. Burning. 'How long do you think my mother would last in a place like that?'

'I didn't mean . . . ach, forget it. Time I was off, anyway.' At the door, she looks back at him. 'Your mam's not going to get any better, Lukas. You know that, don't you? You can't save her, and you can't put your bloody life on hold for her. And . . .' she glances at him, sighs. 'Never mind. Don't stay too late, eh?'

The sound of the door closing. Her footsteps moving off, heading for the stairs. Mahler opens the desk drawer, takes out a blister pack of tablets and dry-swallows two. They feel rough in his throat, their taste dark and bitter as failure. No, he can't save anyone – not his mother, not Raj. Not then, not now. *Tant'è amara che poco è più morte*. Only Dante had got it wrong, Mahler thinks. It's not death that takes the harshest toll. It's living. His mother understands that, and so, he suspects, does Anna Murray.

He stares down at the file images of the iPad Mina had – eventually – handed over to them. According to Pete it's been wiped, whether by accident or design, restoring it to its factory settings, so the iPad itself won't give them anything. But the fact it had been in Stewart's possession is fascinating enough. If it's Morven's iPad – and that at least shouldn't be too hard to check – how had Stewart ended up with it?

There has to have been something on it, something the killer wanted to keep the police from finding out. But why not get rid of it himself? Why take the risk of involving Stewart? Unless it hadn't seemed like a risk, of course. Unless it had seemed like the perfect way of incriminating Stewart and keeping him in line. There's no chance of getting any useable prints or DNA from it, but Mahler's betting Stewart wouldn't have known that.

So what does that mean for Marco's theory that there had been two killers? The use of two weapons, the differing methods of attack – the precision of the fatal throat wound, contrasted with the other frenzied slashes – on the face of it, they're strong supporting evidence for Marco's hypothesis. But the shape of it . . . feels wrong. In spite of the evidence, Mahler's becoming more and more convinced they're dealing with just one man – a clever, ruthless man, who'd planned his murder of Morven Murray with infinite precision.

The killer had tried to buy off Stewart, used him to cover his tracks. And when Stewart had proved a threat, he'd lured the man to a miserable, lonely death. Resourceful, adaptable, cold-blooded – despite Anna Murray's protests, Connor Ryan is starting to look like someone they need to find. Fast.

The pills are starting to take effect. Mahler can feel his concentration start to waver, the screen shimmering in front of his eyes. Luckily, he knows a quick fix for that too. He opens his desk drawer and takes out his stash of decent coffee. While the kettle's boiling he rings the recovery centre. His mother's asleep, but the team leader on duty promises to tell her he's rung.

243

When he gets back to his desk, there's a new email in his inbox. It's from Pete's infinitely more industrious counterpart at Gartcosh's digital forensics lab, who's been working on the shattered mobile found near Stewart's body:

> Hi Lukas
> Not a lot of info on this one, I'm afraid. As you'll see, this phone was activated on 21 May and was last in use on 26 June. Only four outgoing calls were made (details in attachment) and two incoming received (ditto). Bad news is, it's not on contract, so almost certainly a burner. Sorry!

Burn phones. Cheap, untraceable mobiles, bought and discarded as soon as they'd served their purpose. Makes sense, Mahler concedes. The phone found near Stewart doesn't match the one they have on record for him, so either the killer had carelessly lost the burner he'd been using or it's one he'd given Stewart so they could keep in contact. And nothing the killer's done so far has been remotely careless.

Mahler drinks his coffee and reads through the attachment. One incoming call to the burner phone on the day of Stewart's murder – was that to arrange a meeting? Mahler makes a note to check with the lab at Gartcosh tomorrow to see if there's any way to narrow down the triangulation data they've got. Pete and Donna are wading through the lists of possible short-term lets Ryan might have found, concentrating on rural areas within reasonable travelling distance of Inverness, but it's thankless, needle-in-the-haystack work. Christ, why can't they find any trace of the bloody man?

He thinks of Connor Ryan, holed up somewhere out of their reach, with enough cash to see him through pretty much anything. Ryan had wanted to disappear, and he'd planned it with infinite care. The kind of care the murderer had shown when covering his tracks. Circumstantially, everything's starting to come together around Ryan. Everything except the timing.

Mahler takes a mouthful of now-cold coffee and stares at the screen. No time limit on revenge, he'd told Anna Murray, and broadly speaking, it's true. But most people who dream of taking revenge do exactly that, in his experience. They fantasise about it, imagine how good it would feel . . . and that's where it stays. As a fantasy. So what had changed? Why, fifteen years after his affair with Anna had ended would Ryan suddenly have turned to murder?

He takes out a notepad and begins to rough out another timeline, this one taking the first call as its starting point. And realises he's missed something – something that's been staring him in the face since he'd opened the email. All the outgoing calls had been made to the same number. And he's seen that number before.

He starts working through all the call logs on file. The mobile he's looking for ends in 360, and it's somewhere in the file, he *knows* he's seen it somewhere . . .

Speed-reading now, page after page, the print blurring in front of his eyes as the headache starts to creep back past the pills . . . and there it is, on the very last page.

At 11.55 p.m. on 27 May, the day of Morven's murder, the mobile found near Stewart's body had been called by an untraced number, ending in 360. A number that also appears in Morven's call logs.

39

MONDAY, 14 JULY

'You remembered one number out of those pages and pages of calls?' Pete, who's back at work looking remarkably healthy after a sudden bout of food poisoning, stares at Mahler. 'Respect, boss. Ever fancy doing my job?'

'I think we'll let the current arrangement stand. For the moment.' Three days off work, coinciding with a well-known music festival in the Perthshire countryside. Not for the first time, Mahler wonders if it's possible to swap Pete with something more useful. Like an espresso machine. 'Fully recovered now, I take it? Good. Because there's something I need you to check out.'

He pulls up the file listing outgoing calls made from the mobile number he'd found in Morven's call logs. 'Let's call this phone 1, okay? This mobile is activated on 27 May. It calls Morven Murray's personal phone once and only – on that same day, the day she was killed. The next day, 28 May, phone 2 is activated. It makes two calls to phone 1, one on 28 May and the other on 24 June, which just happens to be the day Stewart died. Now take a good look at the mobile numbers. Notice anything?'

'The one Stewart had ends in 366, the other one 360. So?' The colour drains from Pete's face as he stares at Mahler. 'Oh, wait a minute. You're not seriously thinking we can trace them?'

'I just want to know if it's possible they could have come from the same shipment. Look, two mobile phones, only a few digits apart, activated on two consecutive days – talk it through with your friend at Gartcosh, see what she suggests. And report back to me by two this afternoon, yes?'

'Boss, I'm not sure—'

Tapping on the glass of the partition wall. Mahler looks up to see Karen with a coffee in each hand, nodding at the back stairs leading to what passes for a courtyard. He nods an acknowledgement and turns to go. 'Oh, and Pete . . . I suggest you make sure you're in perfect health for the Belladrum weekend. Understood?'

Pete starts to say something, and decides against it. Wisely, Mahler feels.

He leaves Pete staring at his computer screen and goes downstairs to meet Karen. She's slumped against the wall, looking as though she's had an even later night than he has, without the satisfaction of having anything to show for it.

'You know he was at Balado, don't you?' Karen gestures up at the incident room window where Mahler suspects Pete is making whimpering noises down the phone. 'Wee chancer.'

'Pete the mad festival-goer? I don't know that for sure, no. But I do know if he tries it for Belladrum, I will personally go down there, extract his arse and drag it into June's office for whatever level of kicking she feels appropriate.' Mahler tries the coffee – not as good as his, but it isn't terrible either. 'Is that what you wanted to talk to me about?'

She shakes her head. 'You know that guff Cazza tried to feed us about him treating Kevin Ramsay's girlfriend to a holiday? Well, I finally caught up with Gemma this morning.'

'And?'

247

'She confirms every bloody thing he told us.'

'No suggestion that one of his heavies had her in a headlock at the time, I take it?'

'Sounded like she was having the time of her life. I could hear the bairns splashing in a swimming pool all the time we were talking, laughing their heads off.' She sighs. 'Hate to say it, but I think Cazza's on the level with this one.'

Unwillingly, Mahler nods. He supposes it's possible Cazza could be indulging Gemma as a cover for his involvement with Kevin's murder, but it suggests a level of subtlety not usually associated with Cazza MacKay. So does that mean his story about a man called Hollander might be worth a second look?

He thanks Karen for keeping him informed, something he suspects Andy Black would not be impressed by. 'So what now? Is Andy still looking at Eddie Scrimgeour for Kevin's murder?'

Karen shrugs. 'Scrimgeour's been acting the big man in front of his pals for weeks now, and there's something going on, that's for sure. Nothing we can take to the PF yet, but Andy's like a dog with a bone when he gets going – the man never gives up, I'll say that for him. He's got me looking at that gang of shoplifters that did all the supermarkets in May, for God's sake – if I look at any more bloody CCTV I swear I'll go mental.' She stares at him, her face flushing. 'Christ, Lukas, I didn't mean—'

'I know. It's fine.' He drains his coffee, and finds a smile from somewhere. 'Thanks, Karen. Good luck with the shoplifters.'

He heads back upstairs to see if Fergie's finished the follow-up interviews he'd been doing in connection with Stewart's murder. And meets Donna on the landing, looking as though she's won the lottery.

'Boss, it's Ryan. I think we've got him!'

Connor Ryan had been impressively successful in staying offline since leaving St Andrews. He'd not used any social media and he'd conducted all his financial transactions in cash. All except one.

Two days ago, after almost three months of leaving no digital footprints whatsoever, he'd ordered a delivery of flowers online for his sister's birthday. 'And rang her landline from his mobile last night,' Donna tells Mahler. 'To check the flowers had arrived, probably. We'll have to wait for triangulation to get a better idea of his likely whereabouts, but—'

'Chase it. Have we spoken to the sister again?' She'd originally claimed she and Ryan weren't particularly close, but birthday flowers followed by a phone call suggest otherwise.

'Left a message, but she's not answering her phone. I'll keep trying.'

Mahler nods. 'And let me know as soon as the triangulation data's in.'

It won't allow them to pinpoint Ryan's location – in an area as geographically wide and as poorly served by phone masts as the Highlands, that kind of accuracy simply isn't possible – but it will help them concentrate their efforts within a more manageable radius. It's tangible progress, at last. And when Fergie returns, there's even better news.

One of the last follow-ups he'd done was to a woman who'd spotted an unfamiliar vehicle parked by a neighbour's house around 11.30 p.m. on the night of Stewart's murder. The car was empty, but she was certain she'd seen someone walking quickly away towards the Islands.

'Noticed it right away, apparently,' Fergie tells him. 'She knew the neighbours were away and couldn't think of anyone else who would have a legitimate reason to be parking there at that time of night. She wondered if they might be – her words – "casing the joint", and thought about ringing us. But when she looked again, about half an hour later, the car had gone.'

Half an hour. And a dog walker had come forward to say she remembers seeing Stewart around eleven-thirty. The dog had made a dash for freedom so she'd only seen him for a moment or two, but he'd been alone, she was sure of that. And by the time she'd retrieved the mutt and retraced her steps, around half an hour later, there was no sign of him.

Mahler feels a twist of adrenaline jolt along his spine. He looks round the room, sees the same spark take hold in all their faces. The first actual sighting of the murderer. Giving him form, Mahler realises. Making him, finally, a knowable thing. A discoverable thing.

'Right, folks.' Crucial, now, to keep them focused. He looks round at them again, allows himself a smile. 'We've now got an approximate time of death and unconfirmed but promising sightings of the murderer and his vehicle. We could wish for a better description of the car than "big and light-coloured", perhaps, but we'll work with what we have.'

And given when the murder took place, he reflects, big and light-coloured might just be enough to help them pick up the vehicle on CCTV. Even in the summer, by eleven-thirty at night the traffic in the centre of Inverness varies from sparse to practically non-existent. He tasks Donna with getting hold of the footage they need and gets Gary to agree a viewing roster with her.

On his way back to his office, Fergie updates him on the latest findings from the post-mortem. According to Marco McVinish, the murder weapon had been something like a metal bar, possibly a wheel wrench. A blunt instrument, in other words. Which, Mahler points out, isn't exactly a revelation. 'And unless we recover it with both sets of DNA all over it, I'm not sure how much further that gets us.'

'Aye, right enough, it's a bit of a long shot. But we will get him, boss, if that's what's bothering you.' A pause. And a sideways glance. 'You wondering about the car?'

'Partly.' There are ways and means of acquiring a reasonable set of wheels for hard cash, no questions asked. He could probably do it himself, if he had to. But an academic like Ryan? 'The phone call, though . . . the phone call doesn't fit, Fergie. After going to all that trouble to disappear, after not using his phone for months, why risk it all to wish someone happy birthday?'

Fergie shrugs. 'Not saying it makes sense. But where would we be without criminals doing something daft, eh? Half the time, that's the way we bloody catch them.'

'True.' But Mahler has a sense of the pieces not quite fitting, all the same. If Ryan *is* the killer, why the sudden carelessness? Morven's murder had been meticulously planned and carried out, Stewart's hugely risky by comparison. Is that because killing Stewart had been a complication he hadn't counted on?

'Stewart was a loose end,' Mahler tells Fergie. 'Killing him wasn't part of the original plan. And I think Mina can thank her lucky stars the killer didn't know she had that iPad. Have we definitely identified it as belonging to Morven yet?'

Fergie shakes his head. 'Maxine was going to ask the parents—'

'Leave it for the moment. There's someone I want to talk to first.'

40

Evicted from its home on Castle Wynd in the 1980s, Inverness Public Library sits on the edge of town, sandwiched between Farraline Park bus station and the Rose Street multi-storey. The former courthouse building has a gaunt, institutional feel, at least from the outside. But the interior is bright and welcoming enough to attract a number of people through its doors, even on a bright July morning with a promise of real heat by lunchtime.

If she doesn't look at the messages filling up her inbox, Anna can just about make herself believe she's back in the reading room at Glasgow University, revising for her finals. Just about. Until a text from Jamie flashes up with yet another amendment to the draft script she's working through.

She scans the message, allows herself an internal eye-roll and switches the phone to airplane mode. The script's gone through so many changes she's starting to regret ever getting involved with it. Her mother's convinced she's planning a showbiz career as a direct insult to Morven's memory, and Jamie . . . Jamie is concentrating so hard on fine-tuning his script that she's starting to wonder if the production companies he's been talking to are a little less enthused by his project than he's led her to believe.

Time to walk away? God knows, she can think of several pretty good reasons to do just that. But when Anna looks down at the notes she's made, she knows it's not an option.

She'd been researching Patrick Sellar, one of the most infamous figures in the history of the Highland Clearances. Acting as the Duke of Sutherland's agent, Sellar had evicted his lordship's tenants with sufficient brutality, even by nineteenth-century standards, to be brought to trial in Inverness. Unsurprisingly, the jury of local landowners and merchants who depended on them for patronage had acquitted him – in about fifteen minutes, according to the court records.

History had judged Sellar and his kind more severely, and Anna's not about to argue with that. But Jamie's script reduces a complex situation to a morality tale for five-year-olds, painting an idyllic, soft-focus version of Highland life pre-Clearances, ripped apart by an evil cabal of absentee landlords. It's a lazy, simplistic treatment – how the hell did he hook multiple TV companies on the strength of what she's seen? But reading through the latest research, another story's starting to emerge.

A story of resistance, this one – futile, in the end, like all last stands of a dying culture, but none the less inspiring for that. A story of women fighting the evictions, shoulder to shoulder, in defence of the only life they'd known. Women beaten unconscious, jailed, abused – dying, sometimes, of their treatment. Jamie had wanted something fresh, hadn't he? Something to bring his project alive. Well, she's just found it for him.

Anna notes down a couple more additions to her reading list, reaches for her laptop . . . and sees Lukas Mahler making his way across the room towards her. He looks shattered, his expression so sombre that a chill runs through her.

'What is it?' She starts to gather up her things. 'Has something happened to my father?'

'Nothing like that. I'm sorry, I did try to ring, but . . .' he indicates the other tables, where the discreet tapping of laptop keyboards has fallen strangely silent since he walked in. 'Is there somewhere we can talk?'

There isn't. But she's been working all morning and a caffeine-deprivation headache is hovering somewhere above her right eye. 'I could do with a coffee break, actually. I sometimes go across the road, or there's Caffè Nero—'

'I was thinking of somewhere less crowded. And a little more appropriate, if you don't mind a short walk?'

Appropriate. She takes a gamble that he doesn't mean Burnett Road police station this time. And musters a smile. 'If you can guarantee good coffee, I'm in.'

The walk, down Queensgate and along Church Street to Leakey's bookshop, turns out to take all of five minutes.

'Café's rumoured to be closing down soon, I'm afraid,' Mahler tells her. 'But it's usually quiet around this time, and . . .' He glances at her. 'Oh, I see. You were expecting somewhere more inquisitorial? I'm afraid we're hosing down the cells at Burnett Road at the moment. Flat white or espresso?'

An attempt at humour. As though having coffee with Mahler isn't disturbing enough. She asks for a double espresso and makes her way to a table looking down on the huge wood-burning stove and row upon row of bookshelves. Located in the former Gaelic church next to the Old High, Leakey's is one of her favourite places in the town – a home from home, more or less, when she was growing up.

She watches Mahler carry their coffees over. And a thought strikes her.

'How did you know where to find me? I didn't tell . . .' At the look on his face, she shakes her head. 'The B&B guy, right? He saw me heading out with my laptop.' She hadn't said she was going to the library, but he'd known she was a historian working on the Clearances. 'That's Inverness for you, Inspector. We make it our business to know what everyone's up to.'

He shrugs. 'Less true than it used to be in our parents' day, perhaps. But Mr Cummins definitely enjoyed telling me how he worked out where you'd gone.'

'I thought . . . I mean, your mother's obviously local, but your accent—'

'I was sent to school in England when I was seven. My accent was the first casualty of that.'

Seven? Christ. 'That must have been hard.'

'There were reasons.' He tips a pack of sugar into his espresso, knocks half of it back. 'I didn't thank you properly, did I? For helping my mother the other day.'

'I didn't do that much, not really. How is she now?'

'A little better. But if you hadn't been there . . . you said you stopped volunteering at the women's shelter in San Diego? That seems a pity, seeing how she responded to you.'

A burn of heat rising in her cheeks. 'I hadn't intended to. But one day, there was an . . . an incident, and I was injured. I tried to go back once I'd recovered, but I . . . I couldn't go through the door.' She clamps her hands round her empty cup to stop them shaking. 'Just couldn't do it. So when I saw Grace, I . . . I understood a little of what she was going through, that's all.'

'Anna, I . . .' he glances at her cup, rattling on its saucer. And places his fingers on top to silence it. 'I'm sorry. Truly. And I'm sorry to have to do this to you now, but I need to ask you something.'

He takes out his smartphone, touches an image to enlarge it and holds it out to her. 'We're hoping you might be able to identify this iPad. Have you ever seen it before?'

She leans forward and studies the image. The iPad has a distinctive monogrammed cover that she recognises as a famous designer brand, but other than that . . . she shakes her head.

'I'm sorry, no. Morven would love it, though, she's a real labels girl, and—' the look on his face stops her in her tracks. 'You think it was hers, don't you? Where did you find it?'

'It was in the possession of a man called Donnie Stewart.

He worked as a kitchen porter at Bunchrew House, and—'

'The man who was found murdered in the Ness Islands? How did he get Morven's . . . oh, Christ.' A sudden bitterness painting the back of her throat. 'You think he killed her.'

Mahler looks as though he's trying to pick his words carefully. 'We think it's probable Stewart was involved, yes. But it's unlikely he was working alone. Is there anything else you remember about that evening, anything at all that could help us?'

Does he really think she hasn't asked herself that? 'I've gone over it in my head so many times, but it's all . . . jumbled, like bits and pieces of a dream. Sometimes I wonder . . .'

'What?'

She shrugs. 'It seems like the harder I try to remember, the more confused it gets.'

'Then don't. Stop trying for the whole picture, and look for just one element – a sight, a sound, maybe – that you can focus on. If you can find that, we'll work from there. Make sense?'

'It does, actually. Thank you.'

'Good.' He glances at his watch. 'Are you going back to the library after this?

'Too much going on in my head right now, I think. Why?'

'The B&B, then.' He drains his coffee, stands up. And produces what could almost pass for a smile. 'Shall we? I think better when I'm on the move. And you can tell me about your research as we walk.'

A police escort back to the B&B? So much for keeping a low profile while she gets her head straight. But Mahler's already heading for the stairs – and maybe he's right, she concedes. Maybe she'll never make sense of that night if she keeps trying to force things. And the memory he's just made her live through again is plenty to cope with for one day.

They walk up Queensgate and through the Victorian market with its mix of quirky shops and inevitable tourist traps. It's the first time Anna's spent much time in the city centre, and although she can see some of the positive effects of the council's much-vaunted regeneration plans, there have been casualties too. Some of the old established businesses have disappeared, the premises either left empty or occupied by charity or pop-up shops. Inverness has always been a fairly prosperous town, but even here, the lingering after-effects of the recession are obvious.

At the foot of the Market Brae Steps, there's a 'Yes Inverness' stall, decked out in blue and white saltires, its supporters studiously ignoring the group of 'Better Together' workers waving Union Jacks outside McDonald's. Mahler dodges a couple of attempts to present him with a balloon from both camps, and waves Anna on towards Stephen's Brae, the hill leading up to Crown.

'Should be a little less fervent this way, thankfully. Unless you're keen to be harangued relentlessly by born-again activists of either stripe?'

'I didn't notice any haranguing.' As far as she could tell, both sides had been well-behaved, taking any heckling in good part. 'And this is a massive thing we're living through. You can't just pretend it isn't happening.'

'And yet here I am, doing exactly that. On the nineteenth of September, half the country— Anna, what is it? What's wrong?'

'Nothing. I just . . .' A memory, rising up to take her by surprise. 'Morven would have loved all this, you know. She wasn't political, but she'd have made sure she was in the spotlight somehow – when one of her friends ran for the student council at uni, Morven was in there with her, getting her face all over the campaign. Which reminds me, I wanted to ask when I can have those papers back – the ones I brought back from Glasgow? I need to do a bit more work on them.'

'I thought you'd finished the scrapbooks for your mother?'

'I have. But you said Morven must have known her killer – and you're right, she'd never have let someone she didn't know and trust into her suite. So I thought if I went through her papers and put a proper archive together, I could—'

'I don't believe I'm hearing this.' They're walking past the abandoned shell of the old Inverness Academy, boarded up and dilapidated behind its rusting fence when Mahler turns to stare at her. 'Please tell me I've got this wrong. Please tell me you haven't been running round the town playing Miss bloody Marple with a double bloody murderer on the loose!'

'Do you want to shout a little louder? I'm not sure they got all of that.' Anna nods at the group of Japanese tourists gathered by the church. Mahler barks an explosive curse and produces a terrifying smile as the group files past. As soon as they've gone, he turns to glare at her.

'Let me try to explain. My team and I, we're the police. We're the ones you call to investigate a crime, because we're the trained professionals, the ones who're out there day after day, chasing your sister's killer—'

'And getting nowhere!'

Silence. Layers of weariness in his face before he nods, looks away. 'Sometimes it feels like that, yes. But we do it anyway. Because it's our job to be at the sharp end, not yours. Look, Donnie Stewart is dead – lured to an isolated spot and killed in a spectacularly brutal fashion. What does that suggest to you?'

Put like that, the answer's obvious. 'It was him. The other person involved in Morven's murder.'

Mahler nods. 'Stewart represented a threat to the killer, and it got him killed. You're raking through Morven's past, turning over every rock you can find and hoping something crawls out. Do I have to spell it out?'

Does he really think she hasn't thought of that? 'Now you're trying to scare me. But I'm not a threat to him – and I'm not an idiot, Inspector. If I did turn up anything, I'd tell you right away. I just . . . I need to do this.'

'For Morven? Or for yourself?'

'Does it matter?'

'If you put yourself in harm's way, yes. Very much. I understand the need for action, believe me, but I can't sanction this.'

'I'm pretty sure I didn't ask you to.' She tries another tack. 'Look, you think it might be someone from her time at uni, don't you? That's why you asked about Conn.'

'It's something we're looking at. We're also looking at her social media interactions, her professional contacts, her future plans, so— What is it? What's wrong?'

'Her plans.' She swallows the raw sourness in her throat. 'When I spoke to Glyn Hadley, he told me she was making plans for . . . something to do with her work, that's all he'd tell me. But that's not . . . why would you be interested in that?'

Silence. Mahler staring at her as though he's making up his mind about something. Finally, he nods. 'Okay. To convince you finally to walk away from this . . . Morven was researching a new series. She wanted to investigate cold cases – unsolved murders, unexplained disappearances, that sort of thing. We know she'd already talked to one family, and we're pretty sure she had another couple lined up.'

'You think that's why—'

'I don't know!' They've reached the entrance to the B&B. Mahler scrubs his hand across his forehead. 'Sorry. I don't know for sure, of course. But if she'd uncovered something about an unsolved murder, the killer would need to prevent it getting out. Having thought he'd got away with it—'

'I see.' Trying to keep her voice steady as what he's telling her sinks in. 'And if he thought I was following in her footsteps, he might not be too keen on that, right?'

'Anna, I don't want to alarm you. But I'm asking you not to continue your research – and I think it would be a good idea if you went back to your parents' house.' She starts to say something, but Mahler holds up his hand. 'That one's not negotiable. Maxine's your family liaison officer, I need you to stay in contact with her – and if you're planning any more day trips, I'm asking you to let me know.'

Day trips? She shakes her head. 'The furthest I'll be going from now on is Helmsdale – Badbea, maybe, if Jamie wants to work on his final scenes. And I'll tell Maxine—'

'Not Maxine. Me.' The faintest lightening of his expression as he looks at her, something that in anyone but Mahler she might have called a smile. 'One of my tutors used to say historians were the guardians of our past and protectors of our future. I feel losing one unnecessarily would be very careless of me.' He looks at his watch again. 'Please, think about what I've said. And if you re-member anything else—'

'I'll get in touch.'

She watches Mahler walk back towards the Market Brae steps. And waits until he's out of sight before she slumps down on the wooden bench by the B&B's entrance. Unsolved murders. Cold cases. Christ, what had Morven been thinking of?

Anna looks down at her hands, waits for them to stop shaking. Mahler's right, she needs to go back to her parents' house. If she's going to continue her research, it has to be somewhere she feels safe. Safe*r*, at least, after what he's told her. Somewhere to get her head together, maybe. Because in spite of her fighting talk to Mahler, inside she's quivering with fear.

She's never been a risk-taker, never been the idiot victim in the slasher movies, skipping down the cellar steps to face the monster in the shadows. And after that day at the women's shelter, her store of bravery is all but gone, used up in those long, terrifying moments before help had arrived. But this . . . she can't walk away from this now, however much she wants to.

Mahler's talking about cold cases, but he's still investigating Conn. It's a legitimate line of enquiry, even she can see that. But he's wasting time – Conn didn't kill Morven, one of her cold cases did. And there's only one person left who knows how to find which one. One person who knows how Morven's mind worked, how she'd have chosen which case to follow, which to let go.

Her sister.

41

When Anna calls at her parents' house, they're in the garage. Her father's kneeling on the garage floor and wrestling with a new pressure washer while her mother's squinting at the instruction leaflet, trying to read the tiny print without her glasses. It's so absurdly normal, this vision of the life they used to have, that it makes her feel like an intruder.

She turns to walk away, but she steps on a piece of packaging and the cardboard crunches underfoot. Her mother spins round, her face tightening into wary lines.

'Sorry. I should have rung—'

'Don't be daft.' Her father abandons the pressure washer and gets to his feet. 'Good to have you home, lass. Isn't it, Yvonne?'

'Of course it is. Oh, for heaven's sake, Rob, there's water everywhere! Anna, we'll go and get the kettle on while your father tidies up his mess.'

Inside, Anna looks round. She's only been away a few days and nothing's changed that she can see, but the house feels subtly different. And there are scents in the air, warm ghosts of ginger and cinnamon she remembers from years ago. 'You've been baking?'

'A wee bit of gingerbread, that's all.' Her mother switches on the kettle and passes her the biscuit tin. 'See if there's anything left in there. Is tea all right for you?' She opens the cupboard with the 'for best' mugs and takes out three. 'I was going to make a pot, but—'

'Tea's great. And our normal mugs are fine, too. I'm not a guest, Mam.'

'You're staying, then?' One of her mother's no-smile smiles as she lines up the mugs on the worktop. 'Only I can't see your bags anywhere. And he's missed you.' A pause. 'We both have.'

'I'm sorry. Has Maxine been round recently? I know you get on well with her.'

A shrug. 'She has to get on with victims' families, doesn't she? It's her job. And that's all we are to her, just a job. That detective inspector too.'

'Mahler's been here?'

'Said he'd just come to see how we were doing.' Her mother's mouth draws into a tight line. 'I told him we'd be a lot better if he did his job properly and caught the man that killed Morven. Then he asked about you.'

'Me?'

'Wanted to know if you'd said anything about coming back. I told him no, but we were quite used to you going off and doing your own thing.'

And there's a scab just waiting to be picked. 'Mam, I . . .' she shakes her head. This isn't what she's come for. 'Look, I want to help. If there's anything I can do—'

'Think I've got it sussed now.' Her father, standing in the utility room doorway, brandishing the instruction leaflet. 'Is the tea poured yet? If not, I'll maybe just try this—'

'I'll take it out to you.' Her mother hits the kettle switch again, throws a couple of teabags in the pot. And gives him her leave-my-kitchen-now look. 'Off you go, you're dripping on the floor.'

Anna watches her father retreat down the path. He's walking more slowly, and his leg is dragging slightly. 'He's not doing too much, is he?'

'He says keeping active helps him. And he's sleeping better – we both are. Other than that . . .' her mother shrugs. 'Like your Inspector Mahler said, it's not like a dose of flu, is it? Not something you get over.' She pours the tea, hands Anna a mug. 'Here, take this out to him. I'll need to get your bed made up.'

'I'll do it. Duvet covers in the airing cupboard, right?' At the door, she turns back. 'Look, about the flat . . . it was as much a surprise to me as it was to you.'

Her mother starts to say something but Anna shakes her head. 'It's fine, I know you don't believe me, but it happens to be true. Morven wanted me to have her flat. Yes, I'm having trouble processing it too, but that's what she said. But I don't want us to fall out again, Mam. Not over this. So I was thinking, if I made the flat over to you and Dad—'

'No! I just . . .' grief flooding her mother's face, overwriting the lines of anger. 'I want it to still be hers. I want her to be there, that's all – and that's just stupid, isn't it? Because the truth is, she never even liked the bloody flat that much.' She gives Anna a defeated look. 'Do what you want with the place – what does it matter now? Sell it, rent it out, whatever. Just don't use it as a rock to tie yourself here.'

'What do you mean?'

Her mother sighs. 'I mean, we don't need a babysitter, Anna. You've been here since Morven died, and . . . and we appreciate it. We do. I know I'm not . . . not the easiest person to get on with sometimes. But you've got your own life waiting for you, and we all need to start putting ourselves back together. Don't we?'

'I guess so.' Her mother looks thinner, and Anna's not sure how much better she's been sleeping, in spite of what she'd said. But there's something different about her today, something more focused, as though she's learning to reconnect with a world that doesn't have Morven in it. Maybe they all are. And maybe Anna's part in that is done.

Oh, being back in Scotland had started to work its spell on her, of course it had. Being back in Glasgow, even briefly, had felt invigorating. And the old guilt about being so far away had gnawed at her again, tormenting her with *what ifs*, so much so that she'd thought about talking to her old friends at the university, maybe putting out a few feelers. But her mother's right, her life is in San Diego, not here. And maybe it's time she started focusing on that.

'I want to finish work on Jamie's documentary first,' she tells her mother. 'I know you don't like him, but I promised—'

'I never said I didn't like him. It's just . . . he was so keen on Morven, I always think of him as her friend.' She sighs. 'I'll need a bit of time to start seeing him as yours.'

'Jamie was keen on Morven?' She tries to think back to her first year at uni. Jamie had been part of Morven's entourage then, true. But a jokey, irreverent one, as far as she remembers.

Her mother is smiling, a faraway look on her face. 'Oh yes, he absolutely worshipped her – you just had to look at him to see that. In fact, I often wondered if that's why he stopped coming round after a while. Didn't you know?'

'Oh, God.' Jamie's voice on the phone manages to pack more embarrassment into two short syllables than she's ever heard. 'Your mother's got a memory like a bloody elephant! Yes, I did the whole secret crush thing when we were in first year – had it bad for a couple of terms. Obviously wasn't that much of a secret, was it?'

'I'm sorry. I honestly had no idea.' Which is not that surprising, when she stops to think about it. Morven was three years older, in her final year when Anna had just started her first, and apart from Jamie, their circles of friends hadn't exactly coincided. And then there had been Connor Ryan. Once she'd started seeing Conn, everyone else had pretty much faded into the background. 'How long did you two . . . I mean, Morven never said—'

'What?' A shout of laughter at the other end of the phone. 'Get real, Anna. Morven wouldn't have looked twice at me, and you know it. Anyway, she wasn't—'

'What?'

A sigh. 'Nothing. Look, we were just friends – well, sort of. You and I were always a bit too uncool for the in-crowd, weren't we?'

'Maybe we were just ahead of our time.' She tells him about the rest of the conversation with her mother. 'We're still tiptoeing around each other a bit, but we're getting there. Even about Morven's flat.'

'I told you she'd come round. Did she like those albums you made for her?'

'Loved them. It was harder than I'd expected, looking through all Morven's stuff. But I'm glad I did it – now more than ever.' She tells him about the archive, and Mahler's reaction when she'd told him about it. And listens to the growing silence on the other end of the line. 'I needed to do something, Jamie. If there was anything the police might have missed . . . you'd do the same, you know you would.'

'Would I? Anna, I don't know – Mahler's a smug little prick, but he's a cop, after all. Maybe he knows what he's talking about this time. Please tell me you've done what he said and stopped poking around? This psycho guy's still out there, for God's sake.'

'Of course I have. I'm not an idiot.' The lie slides out, smooth and quick and seamless, before she can recall it. But he sounds genuinely worried for her and she's got an even trickier subject to broach next. 'Listen, I've been thinking. We'll be nearly done with your draft treatment in a couple of weeks, so it's probably time—'

'That's what I wanted to talk to you about, actually.' Excitement colouring his voice, turning him into the cheerful, larger-than-life character she remembers from uni. 'Remember I told you about Blue and White, the production company from Glasgow? They're not huge, but they've done some good docu-dramas recently. And they're making very encouraging noises about our project.' A pause. 'Thing is, they're interested in two presenters, not one . . . and I sort of suggested you might be interested in doing a couple of on-camera pieces.'

'You did *what*?'

'Anna, just hear me out. Please? You know your stuff and you've got a great way of condensing it into bite-sized chunks. And we've worked together really well. I think we'd make a great team. Don't you?'

Christ, she should have seen this coming. He'd been tinkering with the script recently, dividing it into segments which, she realises now, could work for either one or two presenters. If he'd so much as mentioned that possibility when he'd spoken to her mother, no wonder she'd gone into meltdown.

'Jamie, I'm flattered, honestly. But I don't—'

'No need to make a decision now. Look, why don't you come up to mine on Friday? We can have a read through and talk it over - I'll even do lunch up at the house for us. And if it's your folks you're worried about . . . maybe it's too soon for them, that's all. Why don't we keep everything under wraps from now on? Until things have settled down a bit and you feel the timing's right.'

To do what, step into Morven's shoes? There's no way she'd contemplate that, even if she hadn't been planning to leave in a few weeks' time. But doesn't Jamie deserve to hear it from her face-to-face, not over the phone?

'Lunch sounds great. But if you're hoping to talk me round—'

'What do you think?' She can hear the smile in his voice when he answers. 'See you Friday, Anna.'

Friday. She hangs up, looks down at the notebook she's been using since her conversation with Mahler at the B&B.

She'd started with a list of a dozen possible cold cases, and now she's down to just three. The end of the road now, or close to it. She picks up her pen, circles the middle name . . . and stares at the photograph pinned inside the notebook.

Janis Miller. Not a cold case, not a disappearance. Just a tragic accident, according to the findings at the time. No logical reason for Janis Miller's name to be on her list, but it's there all the same. Because of the dreams. Because of the whispers, late at night, when she can't sleep. Pushing at her, crowding her like pale, insistent ghosts . . .

Anna draws a line under the final name and closes her notebook. She'll finish her research, and when she's certain she's got it right she'll send it on to Mahler. Give him and Morven what they've both been looking for – the truth for one of them, release for the other.

And then she'll finally be able to go home. Wherever the hell home turns out to be.

42

WEDNESDAY, 16 JULY

Six a.m. The sky ice-blue, a faint promise of sun through the early-morning haze. Mahler's running again, following the river along Ness Bank this time as far as the Three Graces. Possibly the most dour-faced rendering of Faith, Hope and Charity he's ever seen, the three statues peer grumpily across to the Episcopalian cathedral, looking as though they'd prefer to be almost anywhere else. With only four hours' sleep under his belt and a progress report due for June later that morning, Mahler knows exactly how they feel.

Even out of shape, he usually enjoys the illusion of freedom his runs bring. They're a time to contemplate, to let his mind run on unfamiliar tracks about the cases he's working on. But lately the exercise endorphins are refusing to kick in and every run he does feels like a penance.

He's pushing the team hard – too hard, sometimes – and the only reason June hasn't hauled him in for a discussion of the overtime budget is that he's shouldering as much of the load as possible himself. And for the moment, Morven's murder is high-profile enough for Chae Hunt to cut them a little bit of slack . . . at least, until the next gathering of senior management at Gartcosh.

After that? Another team brought in, he's guessing, to 'lend assistance' to what they'll call his floundering enquiry. To pick over what's been done, to scrutinise, to re-examine. To judge. Before he lets that happen, he'll take a sleeping bag into his office and spend every waking hour he has going over the case files. And re-interview everyone personally if he has to.

Back at the flat, he showers, changes and heads for Burnett Road. And gets his first surprise of the day – either Pete has managed to turn himself into a hologram or he's already at his desk, apparently hard at work. If it wasn't for the trail of biscuit crumbs down his front, Mahler would be betting on the hologram.

'Got something for you, boss.' Pete pulls up a PDF file and angles the monitor towards Mahler. 'Normally, we'd have no chance of tracing burners – it'd be real needle-in-a-haystack stuff. But my pal at Gartcosh is a bit of a phone nerd, and she found this.'

'Which is?'

'Probably the most misguided attempt at phone styling ever to hit the market.' As Fergie arrives, Pete launches into a long explanation of why the phone detailed on the PDF was a crime against technology, but Mahler holds up his hand.

'Fine, we're convinced. But this helps us how, exactly?'

Pete grins. 'This is why.' He scrolls to the next page of the document. 'It was launched last year, but it was such a clunker, sales practically fell off a cliff. Most places either didn't stock it at all or only stocked it in fairly small quantities. Assuming the killer didn't have a cache of them stockpiled somewhere and he didn't buy them too long before the murder – well, it's still going to be a big job to try and trace where he got them from. But I don't think it's going to be impossible.'

Mahler nods. 'If he bought them in this area, he'd avoid the smaller stores, surely? More chance of an unusual purchase sticking in an assistant's mind.'

'And if it's Ryan, he'll have bought them for cash.' Fergie shrugs. 'Hell of a lot of assumptions there though, boss.'

'Perhaps.' And perhaps it's a house of cards they're building, not an evidence chain. He doesn't do hunches, doesn't trust the 'copper's gut' adrenaline twist he's feeling right now. But something has changed in the room, an intangible something that brings Donna over to peer at the screen with them.

'It won't take long to get a list together, if we're concentrating on this area. And then we can—'

'Busy little bees in here today, eh? It's usually so quiet I have to check I'm on the right floor . . . apart from the sound of Pete playing Candy Crush, of course.'

Mahler looks up to see a leather-jacketed Andy Black lurking in the doorway, like a cross between a nightclub bouncer and a badly upholstered sofa. Karen's with him, the look on her face suggesting she'd prefer to be somewhere else. Almost anywhere else.

The words *what fresh* and *hell* flit briefly across Mahler's mind. 'Something I can help you with, Andy?'

'There is, aye.' Black walks over to the whiteboards, looks them up and down as though he's conducting an inspection, and stops in front of Cazza MacKay's mugshot. 'Something we need to get straightened out, you and me.' He jerks his head in the direction of Mahler's office. 'It won't take long.'

Mahler shakes his head. Something's rattled Black's cage and he's come looking for a fight, but Mahler's not inclined to give it to him. He's got a briefing with June in twenty minutes and some real progress to report this time. 'We're in the middle of something right now. Can it wait until we're—'

'Cazza MacKay.' Black jabs a stumpy forefinger at the mugshot. 'What did you think you were playing at, dragging my DS down to that bloody club of his on a wild goose chase? Last time I looked, you'd plenty to be going on with yourself without sticking your nose into my investigation.'

'As I'm sure Karen's explained, Carl MacKay forms part of my investigation too, which is why we went to talk to him.' A nod from Karen. 'We asked questions and we got answers – no wild geese involved, just solid police work. What part of that do you have a problem with?'

Black glowers at him. 'Don't get it, do you? I'm back. That means I run my cases my way – I say where we go, who we talk to. And when we fucking do it. You clear on that?'

'Perfectly.' Fergie shoots a glance at him, but Mahler shakes his head. Black's trying to mark his territory, that's all. He hadn't managed it last year, and this time isn't going to be any different. 'Happy to let you have your cases back, believe me . . . minus the half dozen or so we've cleared up for you while you weren't here, of course.' As Black starts to say something, Mahler holds up his hand. 'No need to thank us, Andy. Just doing our job.'

'I was on bloody sick leave!'

'I know. Maybe remember to duck, next time? Blows to the head can be tricky things, I've heard.'

'That your excuse, is it? I hear your mam's back in hospital again.'

A phone ringing, somewhere to his left. As he stands up, Mahler sees Donna make a grab for it. She listens, turns to look at him, but he shakes his head. Not now. Whoever it is, not now.

He closes the file he'd been working on, hands it to Fergie. And walks over to the desk beside the whiteboard. 'Short-term respite. And that's your business how, exactly?'

Black shrugs. Smiles. 'Just saying. Runs in families, doesn't it? Going mental.'

An intake of breath, somewhere behind Mahler. The anger rising to the surface, quick and bright and joyous. Karen shaking her head at him. Too late, far too late.

Mahler's shoving the desk aside and moving towards Black. Pulling back his fist, seeing it streak out and catch Black under the chin to lift him off his feet. Waiting for the sound, the meaty, satisfying smack as it connects with Black's jaw.

Only it isn't happening. Fergie and Karen are there, one on either side of him, gripping his wrists like manacles as the door opens and June walks in.

'Morning all.' She looks round the room, frowns. 'Grand day for it, eh?'

A quick glance at Fergie and Karen. And a longer look at him.

'Lukas, Andy.' June gestures towards the stairs. 'My office for a wee chat. Fergie, go and see if there's any French Fancies left at the Nessie garage. Karen, I'm sure you've got stuff to catch up on, haven't you?'

June takes the stairs two at a time. By the time they reach her office, Andy Black is wheezing, his sweating face a colour chart of glistening pinks and purples.

June sighs and waves him to a chair. 'Gave up the gym membership then, Andy? Aye, I thought so.' She looks them up and down, and gives them her Hannibal Lecter smile. 'Right, then. I don't know what I walked in on down there, but I'm damn sure I won't be doing it again. Professional? No. Getting the job done? No. Thinking about the victims or their families? Of course you bloody weren't! So knock it on the head, both of you.'

There and then, Mahler abandons any thought of mounting a defence. In the first place, he doesn't actually have one. Secondly, when June flashes that particular smile, trying to flannel her is the worst of all possible tactics. Black tries it anyway.

'Ma'am, we were just discussing—'

'Ach, for pity's sake, Andy.' June treats him to a chillier version of the smile – Hannibal Lecter crossed with Chae Hunt, Mahler decides. 'Save the fairy stories for the bairns, eh? I've bloody heard them all. And I'm still waiting for your update on Kevin Ramsay – how about you and Karen get your heads together and bring me something that won't make me look a complete numpty in front of the Chief? Unless you need another wee minute to talk things over with your pal here, of course.'

'Ma'am—'

'Now, Andy.'

Black leaves in a cloud of wounded dignity. June watches him go and turns to Mahler.

'Just a wee discussion, eh?'

'It may have got a little heated.'

'Uh-huh. Were you actually going to thump him, Lukas? If Fergie and Karen hadn't been there?'

'Of course not, ma'am.'

'Aye.' She looks at his face, sighs. 'Aye, that's the right answer. Trouble is, I don't believe you.' She hits her keyboard and a spreadsheet appears. 'So, you had a couple of days' annual leave for your pal's funeral, but nothing else this year. And you've still got a carry-forward balance of . . .' she raises an eyebrow. 'Bloody hell, son, how did you get that past me? Right, unless a spaceship full of little green men lands on Castle Street and tries to abduct Nessie, you're on your holidays until next Monday.'

'Ma'am, I can't—'

'You bloody can! And if you don't want me having an official word with welfare about your current situation, you will. Go and spend some time with Grace. Binge-watch that Scandi-crime thing, the one with that sour-faced wifie in the big jumpers that Fergie's always on about. But if I see your face back here before Monday, you're in trouble.' She waves a hand at him. 'Go on, get out – and tell Fergie to get his arse up here with my bloody cakes.'

'Ma'am—'

'Go. Now.'

He goes. Because the look on June's face is telling him he's a sentence or two away from a reprimand, and he doesn't blame her – a few days' gardening leave is more lenient than he deserves. He'd let Black get to him, let the anger burn through his control. Let it *rule* him. If June hadn't appeared . . . His father's rage, beaten into him year after year. Hardwired into his genes. Dark. Corrosive. *Tainted.*

273

When he gets downstairs, the Incident Room is near-deserted. There's an illegible Post-it on Pete's computer and no sign of Andy Black – roaming the corridors looking for a couple of innocent uniforms to harass, Mahler assumes. Fergie and Karen are sitting in his office, a selection of cakes spread out on the desk in front of them. With, he can't help but notice, one significant omission.

'Boss.' Fergie looks up as he enters. 'Everything okay?'

'Everything's fine.' Mahler walks over and picks a box. 'Lemon slices. No French Fancies?'

'Garage was out of them. Do you think she'll mind?'

Mahler looks at their hopeful faces and risks his second lie of the day. 'I'm sure she won't. I'd wait a bit before taking them upstairs, though.' A pause. 'Half an hour ought to do it. Oh, and I'll be taking a few days off. Back on Monday, but I'll be keeping in touch in the meantime. Fergie, get Pete to ping me over that list of holiday cottages and short-term lets he's been putting together – I want to see if there's any way of speeding up the search for Ryan. And keep on his back about the triangulation data.'

'Boss. Just a few days' leave, is it?'

'Exactly.' He picks up his phone and iPad, turns to go. 'Right, then. Try not to commit major mayhem while I'm away. And by the way, what you two did back there—'

'We were saving your stuck-up, grumpy-faced arse. Sir.'

'I worked that out, Karen. Thanks.'

He turns down Fergie's offer of a lift and sets off walking. He needs to walk, needs to do something physical to lose the after-traces of his anger, burning in his bloodstream like spoiled and bitter wine. He'll walk, and later he'll run, until his head is clear and the vision of his fist connecting with Andy Black's face begins to leave him.

And then he'll get to work. June's banned him from Burnett Road until next Monday, but the updates from Fergie will keep him up to speed with progress. With Donna and a couple of uniforms working through the mobile phone outlets, they're closing in on Connor Ryan, he can feel it. But not fast enough. Not nearly fast enough.

Donnie Stewart had died because he'd got in the killer's way. An accomplice in the beginning, he'd turned into a threat . . . a threat that had ended up a bloody, battered corpse in the Ness Islands.

But Stewart's murder hadn't gone the way the killer planned. It had been messy, unscripted. Careless. And right now that carelessness is haunting him. It's knocked his confidence, made him second-guess himself. Made him wonder if he's made other mistakes, left other loose ends he needs to tidy up.

Other threats he needs to deal with.

43

Connor Ryan's sister lives in Kinsale, the small Irish town they'd grown up in. 'Did my nursing training in Dublin, spent a few years working in the UAE,' she tells Mahler when he rings. 'But the parents were getting older, you know, so . . . that's how it goes, isn't it? One day your life is your own, the next . . .' Her sigh is audible over the phone. 'Look, I've already spoken to one of your detectives, Inspector. I'm not sure what else you think I can tell you. Conn and I, we've never been that close.'

'He sent you flowers for your birthday, though.'

'He did, yes. The first time in years he's even remembered it – and no, I've no idea why.' A muted, off-mike sound like a child's complaining cry. She sighs again. 'Was there anything else now? If not, I'll need to go.'

Mahler quizzes her about Ryan's sudden departure from his job. She admits to being surprised, but not concerned. Connor had always done his own thing, ever since they were teenagers. And apart from a quick phone call at Christmas and the odd card, he'd never been one for keeping the family updated with his comings and goings.

'After a while, we got used to it,' she finishes. 'Conn's the original rolling stone, and—' A rising wail in the background. 'Hold on a minute, Mam. Inspector, if that's all—?'

There seems little point in pressing her any further. Mahler thanks her and ends the call.

'You think she was lying?' Fergie asks, when he rings with the first of his updates.

'She was uptight about something. Talk to the college departmental secretary again, see if she wants to add anything to her statement now she's had time to think things over.'

'Will do. Or I could take a trip across to Ireland, if you think—'

'And leave Pete thinking he's in charge of two murder enquiries?' Not to mention blowing a hole in the travel budget. 'No, concentrate on the college angle for now. What's happening with the triangulation data?'

'Pete's chasing it up, we should get something today.' A pause, the kind Mahler would call embarrassed in anyone but Fergie. 'Look, boss, there's something you need to know. Karen said she'd ring later, but I thought I'd give you the heads-up myself first. Just in case she forgets. Or something.'

As though the day could go any further downhill. 'Whatever it is, let's have it. Just spit it out—'

'Kevin Ramsay. Andy Black's brought Eddie Scrimgeour in for it half an hour ago.'

Six-thirty in the evening. Emails sent, phone calls made. Actions signed off for Pete and Donna and follow-ups sent to Fergie. No call from Karen, but Fergie's probably spoken to her by now. And what could she have said, anyway? Scrimgeour's a vicious little ferret of a man, but he's not a killer. And Karen's too good a cop not to know that. So what the hell has Andy Black got on him?

He gets up from his laptop, rolls his shoulders to ease the spreading tightness in his neck. Not his case, not any more. But Black's got it wrong. And while he's playing Supercop at Burnett Road, the real killer's out there. Laughing.

Mahler walks over to the balcony and opens the sliding door. The chimes of an ice-cream van at Bellfield Park drift in on Inverness's version of a summer breeze, fresh with a hint of bracing. No pipers today though, thank God. Like traffic noise and police sirens in London, the wail of bagpipes during Inverness's tourist season is everywhere, an ear-bleed-inducing white noise he's still not able to filter out.

Still, there are compensations. The city's clean, cool air is one of them, and this flat is another. Even with the antique wooden monstrosity that's currently lurking in his eyeline.

When he'd decided to return to Inverness last year, he'd known that London property prices were ridiculous. He just hadn't realised how ridiculous until his flat had sold for enough to fund two properties in Inverness, his own and his mother's. With the exception of his books and his music system, his London flat had contained nothing worth transporting five hundred miles. A bed had been acquired, a table and armchair had followed, and that had been that. Or so he'd thought.

Until he'd taken his mother on one of the few outings she could bear to leave her flat for – a trip to an antiques centre in a former manse near Auldearn. Half an hour later, he'd been several hundred pounds poorer and the unwilling custodian of an art deco drinks cabinet she'd fallen in love with but had no room for in her own place.

'But you should take it, Lukas,' she'd insisted. 'For when you have your friends round, you know. When you're more settled.'

So many things wrong with that statement. He'd opened his mouth to argue – and watched the shadow of apprehension creep across her face, her body language start to alter. Looking up at him, but seeing . . . someone else.

Two days later, the cabinet had been delivered. And there it squats, underneath the window in his living room, a hulking round-faced presence in burr walnut and glass. With his one and only concession to his heritage, a bottle of twelve-year-old Lagavulin, on the otherwise empty shelves.

Not much of a drinker at the best of times, Mahler had bought a bottle of his grandfather's favourite whisky a couple of years ago and put it in the cabinet on an 'emergencies only' basis. He picks up the bottle, holds it to the light. And decides Fergie's news pretty much qualifies.

He pours a finger of the Lagavulin and takes the bottle over to the table with him. Breathes whisky fumes over the printouts he's been working through all afternoon. And weighs the probability of another brain-crushing headache against the not-unpleasant prospect of getting completely off his face for once—

Knocking at the door of his flat. Loud. Persistent. Irritating.

Mahler puts the glass down. He picks up the dog-walking woman's statement again, and tries to ignore the knocking . . . until it becomes clear the knocker has no intention of giving up until he answers, or the residents of the entire building come over to complain. Either way, he's obviously not going to get any peace until he deals with whoever's there.

He puts down the statement, hibernates his laptop and goes to the door.

'Finally.' Marco McVinish looks up from his smartphone. 'Another minute, and – oh, hold on, I think I've got it. Aha!' He taps the screen a couple of times and a GIF of exploding fireworks fizzles briefly across its surface. 'Been puzzling over that one for days. Right, where were we?'

'You were battering down my door, and I was about to call the police. Since when do you play video games?'

'It keeps the brain cells active. And it's surprisingly relaxing – you should try it sometime.' Marco raises an eyebrow at the glass he's holding. 'Hitting the hard stuff, eh? Looks like I'm just in time.' He produces a bottle of red wine from inside his jacket and gives Mahler an expectant look. 'Aren't you going to invite me in?'

'I'm working.'

'No, you're not. You're lurking in here, feeling sorry for yourself.'

'You spoke to Fergie.'

'We compared notes. Oh, don't worry, he was very discreet. For Fergie. Can I come in now?'

'I'm not . . . oh, fine.' What was he going to do, drink himself into oblivion with a hundred and twenty pound bottle of whisky? He can hear his maternal ancestors spinning in their graves from here. 'You know the way.'

'Good decision.' Marco hands over the wine. 'Give it a few minutes to breathe, I would.' He strolls into the living room, flops onto the sofa and looks round. 'Decorating's going well, I see. You do know there are alternatives to builders' magnolia, right?'

'It suits me. Come on, Marco, what are you doing here?'

'Call me an angel of mercy.' He glances at the pile of paperwork on the table and shakes his head. 'Look, Duncan's off to another bloody "InverYes" meeting, so I'm free to provide a friendly ear and a decent Malbec. Tell me, did you really threaten to cut Andy Black's nuts off? Not that he doesn't deserve it, mind. The guy's an arse, Lukas.'

'An arse who gets results.' Mahler stares at the suddenly empty glass in his hand. And decides perhaps another twenty quids' worth wouldn't hurt. 'Seeing you're here . . . you said the level of violence used on Donnie Stewart was comparable to that inflicted on Morven Murray. But Morven suffered two distinct types of injuries, and it looks like Donnie was killed by someone acting alone. Could Morven's two sets of injuries have been caused by a single attacker?'

Marco frowns. 'I came to take you out of yourself, Sherlock, not to talk shop. But yes, of course it's possible – almost anything is, given enough determination. And the seeming frenzy of the post-mortem injuries always seemed a little like . . . well, overkill, if you'll forgive the expression. But if it's the work of one person

280

. . .' he looks at the empty glass in Mahler's hand. 'I think maybe we could both use a drink.'

By the time Marco leaves, the light is beginning to fade. Mahler stares at the half-empty Lagavulin. An expensive habit, if he ever acquired a real taste for it. But the effects of alcohol have never really appealed to him, the inevitable lessening of control least of all – some of the worst cases of assault he's seen have been fuelled by alcohol or drugs, often both. Though his father couldn't claim even that in mitigation for what he'd done.

He crosses to the window, looks out towards the river. A short walk, just ten minutes or so, would take him to the place where Donnie Stewart died. If Connor Ryan's the man they're looking for, he might have walked past Mahler's flat – if not on the day of the murder, then earlier, when he'd laid his plans.

If. Even now, with the weight of circumstantial evidence piling up against him, Mahler's struggling to see an obscure academic suddenly turn brutal killer, not once but twice. And yet . . . and yet, Ryan's in hiding. A couple of weeks before Morven's murder, he'd walked out of his job, walked out of his life. If he's got nothing to hide, why would he do that?

Unless something had changed. Something that meant carrying on with his normal life was no longer an option. Something about Morven? Something she'd done, or—

An answer. A new shape, this one fully formed, joins the pattern Mahler's building inside his head. *Something she'd been going to do.* Something like the 'new direction' TV series she'd been researching. The one about missing persons and cold cases.

The visit to Owen Taylor to talk about his missing sister hadn't gone the way Morven planned, but it hadn't bothered her because she'd got someone else to talk to – her plan B, all lined up and ready to go.

What if that person had been Connor Ryan? What if Ryan had

281

a deeper motive than a broken love affair for silencing Morven? Something darker.

Something deadlier.

FRIDAY, 18 JULY, 8.00 A.M.

A chill grey morning when he wakes. The house is fusty, clammy-damp, the Rayburn dead or dying, resisting all his efforts to heat the place. After an hour he gives up, makes an indifferent breakfast and eats it on the front step.

Tired, he thinks. The house is tired of him, tired of his presence and what it brings. Sometimes he swears it seeps into his dreams, this stink of disapproval. Can a house hate? If so, this one wants him gone, he's got no illusions about that. Well, it can rest easy – however today pans out, he knows it's time to move on.

But still, he thinks, today will be a good day.

The phone call doesn't matter, he can see that now. Sure, it was a blow at the time – caught him off guard, wrong-footed him. But it's a temporary setback, no more than that.

He still knows people, doesn't he? Still has friends. Still has contacts. And in this business, contacts are what count.

He gets to his feet, tips out the rest of his coffee over the yellowing corpse of some pot-bound plant, and looks down at the still-sleeping village. From up here, the houses look like hobbit-holes, squat and dull and charmless. Weird, though he'd loved the whole Lord of the Rings *thing when he was young, he'd never reckoned much to hobbits. Hairy-footed, greedy little peasants, happy to live their dismal little lives while others dared the darkness for them. No, he's never been a fan of hobbits.*

Aragorn, though, or Legolas ... typical nerdy misfit in his teens, he'd bought into the heroic adventurer fantasy big-time. Even played an online version of the game, for a few months. But after a while, acting in someone else's story had bored him. And heroes, he'd come to realise, might start off golden. But the shine wears off everyone in the end.

Still, today is going to test him. Today is the day he'd hoped would never come, the day when everything hangs in the balance. Success or failure. Security or flight – whichever it is, he'll win through in the end, the way he always does.

And then, in spite of everything, today will be a good day.

44

9.30 A.M.

Tomintoul. *Tomintoul*, for fuck's sake. Fergie coaxes the Audi round another uphill bend on the never-ending A939 and wishes to Christ Connor Ryan had found somewhere more accessible to hole up in than the highest village in the whole of the bloody Highlands.

When Donna had finally tracked the slippery little bugger to a cottage outside the village, the whole team had cheered. Actually cheered – after all the weeks of frustration, all the time they'd spent chasing their tails on leads that went nowhere, they were closing in on their first strong suspect at last. And God, it had felt good.

Even the boss had perked up when Fergie had rung to update him – wanting to jump into a car there and then, from the sound of his voice, and hare off to Tomintoul himself.

'Push Ryan as hard as you can,' Mahler had told him. 'Set off early enough to catch him off balance and keep him there. See how he reacts when you mention Morven Murray, and play on how badly it's affected Anna. Then just follow where it leads you. And if you get the slightest whiff of non-cooperation—'

'I go with my gut?'

285

'Don't detain unless you have to – I don't want the clock to start ticking until we've got something solid to hit him with, and if we end up charging him it's got to be rock-solid. But if you pick up anything that gives you pause, anything at all, you get him in. If Ryan's our man, he's already a double murderer. He's not getting the chance to make it three times lucky.'

Fergie glances at the satnav. Another eight miles. Eight miles climbing up through the Cairngorms on what's quickly heading for most hellish road status on his personal list of hellish bloody roads. And it doesn't matter. Forget all the techno stuff Pete's into, forget all the guff about triangulation data and digital footprints – this is real policing, the kind that grabs you in the guts and doesn't let you go, the kind it all comes down to in the end. The kind that tracks down bad bastards like Connor Ryan and brings them in to answer for what they've done.

Six miles. Four. Then two. Finally, the satnav wifie tells him he's reached his destination. As Fergie's pulling up outside the police station, a big, cheerful-looking PC comes out to meet him.

'DS Ferguson? You made it in good time, didn't you? Roads must have been quiet.'

'Oh, aye.' Of course they were quiet. Who'd trek all the way up here if they didn't have to? Which is just why Ryan had gone to ground here, of course. 'We ready to go?'

Andrews points to a police Land Rover parked across the road. 'Place you're looking for is a wee bit out in the sticks, so we'd best be on our way. If there's anything you need me to do, you can fill me in as we go.'

A wee bit turns out to be five miles out of the village, up an even smaller, even twistier single track road through miles of scrub and heather moor. By the time the single-storey cottage appears round a bend in the road, Fergie's mouth feels desert-dry and his heart is thumping in his chest. There's a battered-looking Fiat parked outside, and a thin plume of smoke rising from the chimney.

Fergie glances at Andrews. 'Looks like he's got a nice fire on for us, eh? Very hospitable of him.'

As they pull in, another car is just driving off. Andrews raises a hand in greeting to the driver as she goes past.

'You know her?'

Andrew nods, frowning. 'One of the district nurses. Looks like your guy's a bit under the weather, eh? Hope you've not had a wasted journey.'

'As long as he's got a pulse, it'll not be wasted. Come on, let's make a wee house-call.'

There's no answer to Fergie's first couple of knocks, but Andrews points out a movement behind one of the curtains. As Fergie's about to knock again, there's a shuffling sound from behind the door. The handle turns jerkily, as though someone's fumbling with it. And the door swings slowly open to reveal a gaunt-faced man in pyjama bottoms and a T-shirt. He's thin, near-emaciated, with a stubble of hair and purple shadows under his eyes. Apart from the eyes, there's no resemblance at all to the man Fergie's come to see.

'Connor Ryan?'

The man glances at the warrant card Fergie holds up, nods. 'You'd better come in.'

He leads the way into a small, sparse-looking living room. There's a wall-to-ceiling bookcase at the far end, and a tripod walker by the sofa. Ryan waves Fergie and Andrews over to the sofa and lowers himself carefully into a high-backed armchair.

Christ. Fergie exchanges glances with Andrews. What the hell have they walked into? He starts to explain why he's there, gets as far as mentioning Morven Murray and breaks off halfway through as Ryan starts to cough. 'Mr Ryan, are you all right? Is there any-thing I can get you?'

More coughing. Ryan sits back, breathing hard, and shrugs. 'A merciful death, perhaps? Sorry, that was blunt of me. But I don't really have time for anything else, you see. I've got what's almost certainly terminal pancreatic cancer.'

Jesus. Fergie shakes his head. And wishes himself anywhere but here. 'Look, I'm sorry . . . but shouldn't you be in hospital?'

'Until I discharged myself a couple of months ago, I was.'

'Why the f— why did you do that? Sir.' Fergie's never seen anyone look more like he needs to be in a hospital bed, preferably hooked up to a dozen bleeping machines. With wall-to-wall nurses, just in case.

Ryan sighs. 'How would you like to go, Sergeant? In hospital, surrounded by harassed NHS staff? Or in your own home, where your indignities belong to you and no one else?'

'What about your family? I don't understand why you'd cut yourself off from them. Surely they'd want—'

'To look after me? Yes, they probably would. Why the hell do you think I didn't tell them?'

Fergie stares at him. 'They don't know? Didn't they worry when they couldn't contact you by phone?'

Ryan shakes his head. 'We're not particularly close, and they're used to me dropping off the radar for months at a time if I'm finishing off an academic paper. Now, you said you wanted to talk to me about Morven Murray – well, ask away. My diary's a little full, but I can just about spare you half an hour.'

Jesus Christ. Fergie glances at Andrews, sees the same hot, embarrassed pity on his face Fergie knows is stamped on his. This is pointless. Worse than pointless, but he rattles through his questions anyway. When was the last time Ryan had seen Morven, what had she said to him when she confronted him about his relationship with Anna? And when he'd learned of Morven's murder, how had that made him feel?

Ryan makes an odd, rasping sound and bends over, clutching his middle. It takes Fergie a moment to work out the man's laughing.

'Unbelievable. You're seriously looking at me as a potential suspect? Let me lay this out for you, Sergeant. I am dying, slowly and bloody painfully.'

'I'm sorry, I—'

Ryan holds up his hand. 'Pancreatic cancer has a lousy survival rate, even if it's caught early – and it's hardly ever caught early. Even with the most optimistic of forecasts, I've probably got less than a year to live. Do you honestly think when my oncologist sat me down and took me through all this, my first thought was to do away with Morven Murray?'

'She wrecked your relationship with Anna. You must have hated her for that.'

Ryan leans forward. 'Anna chose to end things, Sergeant. Not me. And you know what? She was right. Oh, I made a lot of noise about standing up to Morven, but the reality was that mud sticks. The rumours would have followed us around, stalling our careers, and we would have ended up hating each other for it. Anna was ambitious and so was I, and we both had too much to lose to let her bitch sister screw it up. So in a way, Morven did us a favour. Anna most of all.'

'And you never tried to get back in touch with Anna?'

Ryan scrubs at his forehead. 'It was fifteen years ago. Sometimes you have to decide to let things go – and Anna's done well, hasn't she? Done really well.'

The man looks shattered, and he's given Fergie more than enough of his time. Fergie thanks him, and gets up to leave. At the door, he turns back. And asks Ryan one last question.

'Anna Murray. Is there anything you want to say to her?'

'Give her my—' Ryan stops, shakes his head. 'Actually, no. Don't tell her anything. She has a . . . a certain way she remembers me. Let's keep it like that.'

Fergie nods. And takes a long, shuddering breath once he's closed the door behind him.

Andrews gives him a sombre look. 'Poor guy, eh? I'm guessing you'll not be needing to talk to him again.'

'Christ, no. So what happens when . . . I mean, he doesn't want to go to hospital, does he? And living up here—'

'There's an ambulance practically on his doorstep,' Andrews

289

points out. 'And we can get a chopper in from Aberdeen in an emergency. Whether we'll get the chance . . .' he shakes his head. 'The man seems determined to do things his way. And who's to say he doesn't have the right?'

Back at the police station, Fergie starts to thank him for his help, but Andrews cuts him short. 'What, for hassling a guy with terminal cancer? Forget it – no offence, but that's the kind of co-operation with you boys up in North Div I can really do without. Safe drive back to Sneckie.'

Once Andrews has driven off, Fergie heaves at the Audi's door until it finally decides to play nice and let him back in. He's got no mobile signal and the boss doesn't have a radio while he's on leave, so he can't update him right away – Christ, he should have asked Andrews to get a message through, shouldn't he? But there's nothing he's learned here that needs to be acted on, nothing that takes the enquiry any further forward. All he's done is find another bloody dead end.

He winces at the unintentional pun. And decides this is one update that will keep until he's back in Inverness.

45

Morven Murray. Donnie Stewart. Connor Ryan.

Mahler's running again, taking his usual route through the Islands and back over the Infirmary bridge in the chill half-light. No music pounding in his ears today, the headphones silent as he waits for Fergie's call. And tries to argue away the doubts that had jolted him to early morning wakefulness.

Tightness inching up his neck. He stops and rolls his shoulders, trying to ease the pressure. Connor Ryan is the best lead they have – the *only* lead they have, for God's sake! – and when Fergie had phoned to say they'd found him, Mahler knew something had changed. He'd *known* it. And he'd waited for the pieces to come together, to show him the shape of the case he'd begun to build. Only it hasn't happened. Nothing's come together, nothing has formed. Which means there are other pieces out there. Other shapes he needs to find.

Back at his flat, showered and caffeine-energised, Mahler stares at the makeshift incident room he's constructed around the drinks cabinet from hell. Three names on the sheet of A3 blu-tacked to its door – two sisters and a lover. Another three, a subset of the first. And beyond that, nothing to link them, apart from their time at university. Nothing . . .

And there it is at last, the whisper of a grace note. Not one that makes any sense, not one that's even possible. The surge of adrenaline he's feeling has nothing to substantiate it, nothing that isn't made of supposition and hunches. And he doesn't do hunches.

And yet . . . Raj's voice in his head. Telling him to listen for the grace notes. Telling him to look in the one place he's ruled out. Until now. *Copper's gut. What's your gut telling you, Lukas?*

Mahler stares at the board. Adds another name, draws a connecting line. And wonders if he's finally found the mask that he's been looking for.

Inverness, 10.15 A.M.

Jamie had wanted to come and pick her up from her parents', but Anna had insisted on driving herself. She's re-forging her relationship with her mother, link by fragile link . . . and however much her mother insists she's fine about Anna working with Jamie, it's not something Anna's planning to put to the test.

Having Jamie pick her up would feel a little too much like rubbing her mother's nose in it, as far as Anna's concerned. And once she's broken the news that she's decided to go back to San Diego, Jamie's going to be hurt and more than a little disappointed. The last thing either of them will want at that point is to suffer a seventy-mile drive back to Inverness in each other's company.

Anyway, she's looking forward to doing the drive herself – taking it at her own pace, enjoying the feeling of having no one to worry about but herself. And maybe once she's back in SD, it might be time for her to move on professionally. She loves the city, but career-wise she's starting to realise she's been treading water for a while. And since she'd broken off her engagement, she's got no personal ties to hold her back if she does decide to move on.

She tries to call Lukas Mahler, to let him know she'll probably be out of mobile range for most of the day, but it goes straight to voicemail. She starts to call Burnett Road, but hangs up before the call connects – it's not like she's going far, for heaven's sake, and he knows she's planning to take a trip to Helmsdale so she and Jamie can finish up their research at the Timespan visitor centre. She tells herself she'll catch up with him once he's had time to read the email she sent him in the early hours, and takes the dual carriageway over the Kessock Bridge onto the Black Isle.

'You do know I have other work to get on with, right? Sir.'

Karen's voice holds all the warmth of a walk-in freezer when Mahler explains what he needs her to do. Hardly surprising, he supposes, given she's been tasked with putting together an evidence file that will stop June bawling out Andy Black when he asks to charge Eddie Scrimgeour. Andy Black should be doing most of it himself, of course, but if there's one skill Black's an unsurpassed master of, it's delegation.

And given that there isn't actually any evidence to place Scrimgeour anywhere near the locus, Mahler wouldn't put it past Black to be setting Karen up as a potential scapegoat when things fall apart.

'I know But I wouldn't ask if it wasn't urgent, Karen.'

A sigh. And the rustle of what sounds like a caramel wafer being unwrapped. 'Go on, then. What exactly do you want me to look up?'

'Suspicious or unexplained deaths between the dates I've given you.'

'In Glasgow? Have you any idea how long that's going to—'

'Not the whole of Glasgow. I'm only interested if there's a link with the university, and only in that four-year period.'

Another sigh. 'Fine, I'll see what I can do. Anything else?'

'Those names I gave you? If either of them come up in connection with anything you find, I need you to call me.'

'How much of a connection?'

'A mention is all I need.' He hears the tap-tap of her keyboard

293

as she starts inputting the parameters he's given her. 'So how are things?'

'How do you bloody—' a rumble of voices in the background. The tapping stops abruptly. 'Fuck. Look, I have to go. I'll get back to you as soon as I can.'

Before he can thank her, Karen hangs up.

Mahler looks at the board again. The last name he's added makes no sense – the man has an unshakeable alibi, the strongest of anyone connected to the case. For him to be Morven's killer, he'd have to have been in two places at once. And even then . . . Mahler shakes his head. There's no way this could be the connection he's been looking for. No way. Except. Except . . .

Copper's gut, Lukas. Copper's gut.

46

11.10 A.M.

Anna listens to the end of the news on Moray Firth, and turns off the radio. She'd told Jamie she'd be with him around midday, and so far she's been making good time – she's loved driving ever since she passed her test, loved it for the sense of freedom it gives her.

The weather is starting to turn, though. When she'd set out, the sky had been cloudless, iced turquoise blurring into the bright blue sweep of water as she'd crossed the Moray firth. But by the time she'd reached Tore, the colour had started to leach from the day in typical Highland fashion.

Now, as she crosses into Sutherland, the Dornoch firth is leaden, gunmetal sea meeting graphite sky, the Meikle Ferry bridge a thin charcoal strip of land between the two. Summer rain, summer chills – two of the things she won't miss when she's back in California. Wimp. *Wuss.* She shivers for another couple of miles before she gives up and turns on the heater.

The A9 is taking her steadily northwards, up the rocky coastline into the heart of Sutherland. Embo. Golspie. Brora. The blink-and-you'll-miss-it cluster of houses at Portgower. And finally, Helmsdale . . . where the rain that's been threatening since Ding-wall finally breaks. Sullen clouds opening, hiding the sea behind a curtain of grey as she passes the emigrants' statue at the entrance to the village.

Anna eases the Volvo over the bridge, doing her best to follow Jamie's directions since the route the satnav wants her to take doesn't make any sense. Surely he hadn't meant her to come this far out of the village?

She turns round and heads back towards the A9 to see if she can work out where she's gone wrong, but the satnav's insist-ing she'd been right the first time. Cursing, she swings the car round and heads back in the direction she'd come from. After ten minutes' driving, the B-road becomes a single track, winding higher and higher up the hill. Anna pushes on, the car bump-ing over cattle grids and potholes, until she spots a building up ahead.

She pulls up by the gate, frowning. This can't be right – Jamie had said he'd bought his parents' old house a couple of years ago and was slowly renovating it, but this place looks as though no one's lived here for years.

She's turning round again, heading back to Helmsdale to ask directions, when Jamie appears from around the side of the house. He's smiling, but there are lines of strain around his eyes, as though he's been working too hard.

'I was starting to think I'd have to send out a search party! My directions weren't that bad, were they?'

'Think I took the scenic route – I'm just a tourist here these days, remember.'

'You're getting used to being home again, that's all. Come on, I'll show you round – watch your step though, it's still a bit of a building site in places.'

Inside, it's obvious what he means. The house *is* being reno-vated, but the work is oddly haphazard. The ancient wiring hasn't been replaced and the tiled floor in the hall is cracked, uneven, but the living room looks like something from an interior decorator's portfolio, all edgy statement wallpaper and designer sofas. Most of the far wall is taken up with a huge picture window.

'My bolthole,' Jamie tells her. 'Internet's crap and the only place to get decent phone reception is in the bathroom, but I come here to work, not mess around on Twitter, so that's fine by me. What do you think?'

'It's a great location.'

'Isn't it? Views right over the water, when it isn't chucking it down.' Jamie lifts a pile of papers off one side of the couch, waves at her to sit down. 'I hope it doesn't get any worse, or we'll hardly be able to see anything at Badbea. You don't mind if we take a trip out there after lunch, do you? It's such an atmospheric place, I really want you to experience it for yourself.'

The Clearance village? She hadn't realised he wanted to go today. Still, it's only a few miles further on up the A9, and she'd planned to visit it herself anyway. 'If the weather holds, why not?'

'Great. So, how do you feel about the script now – happy with the changes I've made?'

'I think it works well, I really do. But—'

'That's all I wanted to hear. This documentary is a real op-portunity, Anna – for both of us.' He sighs. 'Look, I need to tell you something. It's sort of embarrassing, but what the hell. We're friends, right?'

'Of course.'

He attempts a smile. 'Right, here goes. I wasn't going to say anything, but my last couple of books didn't do that well.' His face darkens. 'Then some other opportunities I'd got lined up all fell through. Never rains but it pours, huh? Anyway, things were look-ing . . . well, not so good. And then I ran into you at Bunchrew, and it just seemed like fate. Don't you think?'

Oh, Christ. Guilt rising up, threatening to make her chicken out

297

of what she's come to tell him. But she can't let this go on. She has to come clean about the decision she's made before this gets out of hand. *More* out of hand. 'Jamie, listen – I've enjoyed helping with your research, I really have. But as for doing anything in front of the cameras,' she shakes her head. 'I'm sorry, but I can't. I won't be here.'

'I don't understand.'

She tells him about the conversation she'd had with her mother. 'I've stayed until now because they needed me. But they need their own space to grieve, too . . . and so do I, I think.'

'You're not serious. Anna, this is your project too – you've worked so hard on it, and now you're just turning your back on it? Look, if you're worried how people will react, don't be. If anything, they'll be even more interested now—'

'Now I'm the sister of a dead celebrity?'

'That wasn't what I meant.'

It was, though. She can see it in his face. And that's not the only thing wrong with what he'd said. 'My mother seemed to think you'd talked to Morven about it.'

Colour flushing his cheeks. 'Oh, for God's— look, Morven was a "name" – something to hook the suits with at the production companies. But you . . . I knew we'd work brilliantly together, you and I. But I know how she made you feel, Anna. Like you were always second best, right? I didn't want you to feel like that again.'

'I'm a big girl now, Jamie. I'd have handled it. So you asked Morven to take part before I'd even got here?'

'The day before, yes. I'd called round to see her and we spoke about it. What's wrong?'

'Nothing.' But there *is* something. The room feels suddenly stuffy, as though it's been left unaired for too long. 'I . . . I wish you'd told me, that's all.'

'I get that.' He spreads his hands, produces a conciliatory smile. 'You're right, that was . . . Look, Anna, I really want you with me on this. You can hold off going back to the States for a while, can't you? It would mean a lot to me.'

'Maybe. I suppose I haven't actually booked anything yet.' Matching his smile, his tone of voice as the stale air catches in her throat. 'Have they given you any sort of timetable yet?'

Letting his voice wash over her as he talks about setting up meetings with the latest production company he's been talking to. Not that they're tied to that one company, of course. If what they're offering doesn't come up to scratch, there are plenty— He breaks off mid-sentence to turn and look at her.

'Okay, what have I said now? Come on, Anna, you may as well tell me—'

She looks down at her hands. Exaggerates the unevenness in her voice, the tremble of her fingers. And hopes the craziness she's contemplating is just that. This is Jamie, for God's sake. *Jamie.*

'You remember that research I started doing, to see what I could find out about Morven's plans for her new series?'

He stares at her. 'You said you'd given up. That cop at Burnett Road—'

She shakes her head. 'I didn't. Couldn't. And what I found out . . . Jamie, I need to tell you something. Something that happened a long time ago.'

The hotel Mahler's standing outside is a building with an impressive history – according to the receptionist it dates back to the late eighteenth century. The CCTV system by the entrance isn't exactly discreet, but it looks over ten years old and Mahler reckons it's got at least two blind spots. Which answers one of the queries he's been wrestling with right away.

When he explains what he wants to do, the receptionist shakes his head. 'Sorry, no can do. We've got guests in that room today.'

Mahler glances through the door to the dining room. 'Where are they now?'

'Brunch. But—'

'No buts. Give them a Buck's Fizz each, and tell them it's on the house.' He extracts a suitable denomination note from his wallet and puts it on the desk. 'And have one yourself.'

'I can't just . . .' the man looks down at the second note Mahler's placed on top of it, and sighs. 'Fine. But I'll need to come with you.' He calls something to a colleague in the back office, and grabs a set of keys.

Upstairs, the building retains a lot of its original layout, the corridors high-ceilinged and corniced. The room Mahler's shown into has a state-of-the-art bathroom, but the windows overlooking the golf course are sash and cord. Original, not modern lookalikes, which means there's nothing to restrict their opening. And that, he realises, answers query number two.

'This is definitely the room he stayed in? You're sure?'

'Of course.' A hint of wounded pride in the man's voice at the implication that he might have made a mistake. 'We keep very careful records, especially of our returning customers. We like to give them little thank you cards when they come back, make them feel valued. It's all part of the service, isn't it?'

Mahler opens the window and looks out. Not a great view on this side of the hotel, just a small paved courtyard and a couple of trees next to a flat-roofed storage area of some sort. No parking for staff or visitors. And crucially, no CCTV.

His mobile pings an email alert. Karen? He glances at the preview. It isn't her. But another grace note whispers in the air.

'Will you be much longer?' The receptionist is casting nervous glances at the door. 'It's just I should be getting back—'

'Thank you, I've got everything I need.'

Mahler thinks about going in to Burnett Road and talking to June. Making a case with what he's worked out, getting her onside . . . thinks about it for the space of half a dozen heartbeats, and then dismisses it.

He doesn't have a case, not yet – even with what he's seen here, all he's got is a theory without any evidence to back it up. And a crawl of unease between his shoulder blades, telling him to find some. Fast.

47

12.30 P.M.

She's standing in the tiny, Rayburn-warmed kitchen with Jamie, looking out at the green and gold patchwork of the Helmsdale hills. Anna watches him put together a salad, slices a lemon for him to go with the sea trout. And wonders if she's losing her mind.

She tells him about Connor – all of it, starting with her affair at university and Morven's part in its ending, to Mahler's questions when she'd gone to Burnett Road. When she's finished, she looks up to find him staring at her. 'I know. Sounds crazy, doesn't it? I couldn't believe it at first.'

'But now you do?'

She lets her shoulders slump. 'You remember I said Morven was looking into cold cases? There was a photo of Janis Miller amongst Morven's things.'

'Who?'

'Janis Miller. She fell from a balcony during a student party in Anniesland.' Keeping her voice level as she glances up. 'Don't you remember? It was all over the papers.'

He looks blank for a moment, then nods. 'One of Morven's

302

friends, wasn't she? Name rings a vague bell. That wasn't a cold case, though – I had glandular fever at the time, so I don't know much about what happened, but she was a party girl, right? Probably preloaded before she even got there. Carried on drinking, maybe had a smoke or two, and fell. What?'

She moistens her dry lips. 'Maybe Morven found something that proved it wasn't an accident. There has to be a reason the police were asking me about Connor. And I know he lived near there.'

'Bloody hell.' Jamie stares at her. 'You really think . . . bloody hell, Anna.' He gets the fish from the fridge, lays it on the chopping board. 'I said you should let the police do their job, didn't I? No wonder you're spooked.'

She nods. 'I can't stop thinking about it. If he killed Janis, he must have killed Morven too, once she started getting too close.'

'Wow.' Jamie shakes his head. 'Well, it all fits, I suppose. Except you don't really believe it – do you, Anna?'

A dark, metallic sourness at the back of her throat. 'I don't want to, of course. But—'

'But it's better than thinking the real killer's still out there. And he's about a hundred times smarter than Inverness's idiot cops. Yes, I get that.' He takes a knife from the rack and glances at her. 'You might want to look away while I do this. I'd have cleaned it already, but—'

'I'm fine.' Making herself stand there and not flinch as the knife slides along the bone. A quick, expert flick and the innards spill out. Pink, glistening. Slippery.

'Told you to look away.' He disposes of the fish guts, rinses his hands. 'Just the filleting now, and we're done.'

'You're very good at it.'

He shrugs. 'After uni, I learned to look after myself. Eat well, exercise, all the things I didn't do back then – remade myself, I suppose. God knows, I needed to.' The knife moving faster to reveal the fish's pink flesh. Its rhythm harsher. Angrier. 'I'd had enough of being the jolly fat guy by then, you see. Being the butt of everyone's jokes.'

'Jamie, no one thought like that—'

'Of course they did.' The knife pauses mid-stroke. 'You don't have to lie to me, Anna – a rubbish English teacher in some rubbish school, that's all they thought I'd amount to. But I kept writing, kept going until the rejections stopped being rejections and the books took off – then surprise, surprise, suddenly I had friends.'

'You always had those.'

'Like Morven?' His voice changes. Roughens. 'That's crap and you know it. All those pretty little bitches wouldn't have given me a second look back then – but get myself some decent clothes and a flash car, and suddenly they all wanted to know me. But I wasn't going to let them fool me. Not again.'

Ice shivering down her spine. The sound of her own heartbeat deafening in the sudden silence as she looks at him and he looks back. *Idiots. Bitches. Smarter.* And everything she's been trying to deny, everything she's been trying not to see since the night of Morven's murder slams into her, driving the air from her lungs when she tries to breathe. Sealing the words inside her throat when she tries to speak.

She runs instead. Not for the outside – he's stronger and faster, and that's what he'll expect her to do. She races for the bathroom, slamming the door shut and ramming the bolt home. It won't hold for long, but maybe she doesn't need long. Anna pulls out her phone, tries it all round the room until 'no service' disappears and two small signal bars pop up.

'Anna? Anna!'

Thudding against the door, making it shake in its frame. Christ, he's hitting it with something big and solid, like a makeshift battering ram. He'll be through it in no time.

Heart hammering in her chest, she selects Mahler's name, types a two-word text with shaking fingers. Hits send. And waits.

More thudding. Crazy to let herself be trapped in here, but what else can she do? The window's too high and too small, and getting a message out to Mahler is her only hope.

As the door bursts inwards, the message finally disappears. She hits 'delete' and presses herself back against the wall.

Jamie holds out his hand for the phone and glances down at the display. 'Told you the reception's crap. Let's go back through, shall we? Time we had a little chat.'

As soon as Mahler pulls up outside the Murrays', he knows he's too late. Their Clio's gone from the drive and the space where Maxine usually parks is empty. When there's no response to his ring, he checks the back garden and the garage. Both secure, no sign of anything amiss, but the twitch between his shoulders refuses to go away.

He calls Maxine's mobile, then Anna's – voicemail, both of them. What the hell is Maxine doing, not answering her phone? Unless . . . last week Yvonne Murray had talked about another visit to Bunchrew. If Anna had gone with her parents, Maxine would have accompanied them. *If.* But why hadn't Anna mentioned it in her email? He scans it again. And realises there's one other place she might have gone. One other person she'd talked about going to see.

Mahler leaves messages for them both and one for Fergie, asking him to double-check as soon as he gets back from Tomintoul. He hasn't heard from Karen yet, but if he's right he can't afford to wait.

Back at the car, a quick check of his kit. No Airwave – he'd had to hand in his radio before going on leave, which means relying on his mobile for contact with anyone at Burnett Road – but at the moment, what he's planning isn't exactly by the book. As soon as he has something concrete to give June, he'll do it. But right now all he has is a prickling between his shoulder blades. And an urgent need to take a fishing trip.

To Helmsdale.

Mahler's driving up the A9, heading north under rapidly darkening skies as the Highland weather closes in around him. Flying over the rain-dulled Cromarty firth, thanking God for the light traffic as the slow creep of unease between his shoulders starts to grow. Too many loose ends from the beginning, this investigation, too many leads that took him nowhere—

Outside Tain, heading for the Dornoch firth bridge, his mobile finds a signal. Mahler pulls into a side road, hits 'accept' as Karen's number flashes up at him.

'Lukas?' Her voice is oddly tinny, as though she's talking inside a metal box. 'Listen, I've only got a minute, but I've found what you were after. In 1994, a girl called Janis Miller died at a student party at Glasgow uni.'

'How?'

'Took a header off a balcony. It wasn't treated as suspicious – everyone was hammered, and there was nothing to suggest it wasn't an accident. But Janis was in Morven Murray's year – quite good pals with her for a while, hung out together, stuff like that. And so was Jamie Gordon.'

'They were friends?'

'No connection that I can see. But you said a mention was enough.'

More than enough. Shapes, forming and reforming. Coming together in his mind. 'Did Gordon make a statement? Why didn't it come up when we looked into him earlier?'

'Because he wasn't at the party – ill, or something. Almost everyone else in her year was there, that's why his name stood out. And it was treated as an accident, remember?' A pause. 'This is important, right? Even though he wasn't there?'

'It's important. Very.' Another shape, moving to join the others. Mahler looks at the satnav and does a rapid calculation. 'Karen, this is what I need you to do.'

1.40 P.M.

Anna's walking back to the living room with Jamie's hand clamped on her arm, her legs shaking so badly she can hardly make them move. Still telling herself none of this is real, none of this is truly happening . . .

'Sit.' Jamie lets go of her arm, shoves her towards the couch. 'May as well be comfortable while I work out where we go from here.'

She looks round the room. The door to the hall is open, but Jamie's got the knife and he's standing between her and the only exit. And she's got no doubts about what he'll do if she tries to get away. None at all.

She risks a slight move sideways, a little closer to the armchair, to increase the distance between them. 'I'll stand, thanks.'

'Suit yourself. Christ, Anna what did you think feeding me all that guff about Connor bloody Ryan was going to do? Did you think I'd suddenly bare my soul to you or something?'

'It wasn't guff. The police really are looking for Conn.'

'For killing Morven? Bloody hell. You didn't believe it, though. That was just to try and trap me.'

She wills herself not to stare at the knife. He's relaxed his hold on it, but not by much. Not enough. 'I wasn't . . . I came here to let you down gently about your documentary, Jamie. That's all I was going to do.'

'So what changed?'

'You lied to me. You told me you'd asked Morven first, and that had to be a lie – if you'd asked her, she'd have been bending my ear about it before I even boarded the bloody plane. She wouldn't have been able to stop herself.'

'That doesn't prove anything.'

'It proves you lied to me. And you lied about knowing Janis – you had classes with her, for God's sake! Everyone at the uni knew

307

her name that summer. Everyone. The only reason you'd try to deny knowing her is if you . . .' Her voice shaking again, in spite of herself. 'If you killed her. And you killed Morven, too. Jamie, I don't. . . how could you do that? Why?'

'Because I'd no bloody choice!' The knife as punctuation, slicing through the air, making her shrink back. 'Morven was droning on about her stupid fucking wedding, and out of the blue she started talking about this great new series she'd got planned.'

'So that's how you knew about it.' Anna takes another half-step sideways. And prays he hasn't noticed.

'She'd been looking into some teenager who disappeared, but the family weren't co-operating so she'd had to rethink. And she'd come up with Janis bloody Miller.' He shakes his head. 'One of her own BFFs from uni, a nice, easy story to research – Morven always was a lazy cow, wasn't she? It was treated as an accident at the time, of course, but I couldn't risk her digging it all up again.' A shrug. 'If you'll pardon the expression.'

Staring at him as the ground shifts under her feet again. This man she'd thought she'd known. A man she'd thought of as a friend, turning violent death into a one-liner. Smirking at his own wit, as he threatens her with a knife.

'The police must have questioned you.'

Jamie shakes his head. 'I was tucked up in bed with glandular fever, remember? Even had the doctor's note to prove it, had anyone asked. Which they didn't, by the way. Because fat, scruffy Jamie might have been good for a laugh, might have been good for borrowing lecture notes and helping out with coursework, but he wasn't the kind of guy cool girls like Morven and Janis invited to parties, was he? Not the sort of guy they wanted to date.'

'You said it was just a crush . . .' she looks at him, and the last piece falls into place. 'It wasn't Morven, was it? It was Janis who wasn't interested.'

'You seriously think I tried? Even then, I wasn't that bloody stupid. But everything comes with a pay-off, Anna – and that night at the party was Janis's time to pay her dues.'

She tries to think back, tries to find the seed of what he's become in the memories she has of him. But she was in her first year, her head buried in her books as her exams loomed. The whole university had been in shock over Janis's death, but Anna hadn't known her personally, and Jamie had been the same as always. How could there have been so much darkness in him, so perfectly hidden?

'Someone must have seen you. Didn't they?'

'At a student party in full swing, with everyone half-cut and the lights on low? No one saw me. And if they had, you know what? Their eyes would just have glided over me. Because I was invisible to them, Anna.' His eyes distant, lost in an old bitterness. 'To the whole fucking lot of them.'

He's still holding the knife, but loosely, as though he's forgotten about it. She risks a glance at the open door. If she can keep him talking . . . 'Is that why you killed Janis?' Forcing the shudder from her voice. 'Because she didn't notice you?'

For the first time, he looks uncertain. 'I only meant to talk to her, at first. She'd got a job as an intern, working for some fashion house in bloody Florence – beat off loads of competition, played a blinder.' His face darkens. 'A complete success. You know why? She'd come to me on the quiet, begged me to write a crib sheet for her interview – and it worked. One of the best they'd ever done, apparently. Only I didn't even rate a bloody thank you. Tried to talk to her about it a couple of times, and she laughed in my face, told me to fuck off.'

Anna stares at him. That's what Janis Miller had died for? Two minutes of thoughtlessness? Maybe something about that night had always nagged at Morven, some unvoiced, barely-there unease. Until she'd started digging, almost twenty years later. And died for what her searching had uncovered. A swell of anger, cutting through her fear. No, not died – she'd been killed. Call it like it is, Anna. Call *him* what he is.

'You murdered my sister. Butchered her, as though she was a piece of meat. And you used me to give yourself an alibi.'

'I did what I had to. It needed to look like some sort of psycho killer's work, so I . . . made sure that's what the cops saw. And don't give me any phoney grief about your darling sister – you couldn't stand the bitch either. Christ, Anna, why couldn't you have just let it go?' He grabs the copy of the script, waves it at her. 'You see this? This would have bloody made us, you stupid—'

Anna tips the chair over, shoving it towards him as hard as she can. Taking him by surprise and running past him, out into the hall, making for the front door—

Her fingers are reaching for the handle when she feels him start to drag her back. She struggles, trying to pull free, but the uneven tiles are slippery where the rain has seeped under the door, and she stumbles backwards, hitting her head on the wall as she goes down.

Fuzzy. Staring up at a cobweb trailing from the faded lampshade. Greyness filling the world. And Jamie, grunting in satisfaction, as he bends towards her.

Jamie Gordon's House

2.20 P.M.

The 4×4 Anna had hired is parked by the gate. Mahler grabs a pair of nitrile gloves from his kit and approaches. No one inside, a light jacket folded on the passenger seat and no sign of a struggle in or around the car, but the pull between his shoulders is tightening with every passing second.

Mahler checks his mobile – still no reception. If back-up's on the way, he's got no way of knowing. And no time to wait and see. He grabs two rapid shots of the car with his phone, interior and exterior, before the rain washes away the tracks. Then he's walking up the path, calling out as he goes. His training kicking in, holding back the adrenaline need to run. To find her.

The door is open. Wide open. And just above the skirting in the tiny hallway, the wall is smeared with blood.

Mahler exhales. Focuses. And bends to examine the mark. Bright, still red, so recent. A couple of splashes on the tiles. A fall? Only a small amount of blood, thank God. Did Gordon overpower her here?

A glance at the living room shows him the overturned chair, the coffee table lying on its side. A struggle, then. But no blood, no signs of violence. No knives. Which means wherever he's taken her, there's still a chance.

He walks down the L-shaped hall, checking the rooms in turn. Two small, old-fashioned bedrooms, one on either side. A larger one that could be Gordon's. And the bathroom.

Bile rising in his gut as he takes in the burst lock, the cheap door hanging by one hinge. He steps over the plywood debris. And his phone bursts into crackling, distorted life.

'—Chief's doing his nut! What's going on, for God's sake? What are you doing in Helmsdale?'

June. Mahler fills her in on what he's found. And what he hasn't. 'Gordon's got her. And his car is missing, so—'

The beep of an incoming message. Anna Murray. He taps the screen to bring it up as June's voice fades in and out.

'—Christ's sake, Lukas! Where's Gordon taken her? I can get a chopper, if you've an idea where to—'

Mahler stares down at the text. Time-stamped forty minutes ago. Just two words, all she'd had time to write.

Jamie help

Forty minutes ago. Forty minutes for Gordon to have overpowered Anna, to have taken her – where? Somewhere isolated, but reachable by road. Somewhere random? No, it has to be somewhere he'll feel safe. Somewhere he knows well. Somewhere the setting will feed into whatever craziness Gordon's planning as his final act. And where had Anna said the documentary was going to end?

'I know.' The thing between Mahler's shoulder blades has a voice now. Harsh. Accented. Familiar. He tunes it out, forces it into silence. 'I know exactly where he's taken her.'

48

2.00 P.M.

Badbea Clearance Village

Anna opens her eyes to darkness. Lying on a floor, she thinks, except the floor is moving, the jolting motion sending flashes of pain along her shoulder blades. She tries to raise a hand to her face, but both her hands are tied behind her, and there's something covering her mouth. Panicked, she tries to sit up, but she's jerked sideways and her forehead slams into something hard and sharp before she's thrown back down again.

Roughness under her cheek, and the stink of petrol, making her stomach roil with every breath. She's in a car? The boot, she thinks. The boot of Jamie's car. The memory of what had happened rears up, filling her throat with vomit, making her retch, making her— No. *No!* She can't throw up. *Can't.* If she does, she'll suffocate.

Forcing the sickness down. Forcing herself to stop shaking. Breathe. *Breathe!* And think. At least she's still alive, for now. But how long has she been out? They could be bloody anywhere

313

by now. Going anywhere. And if she's wrong, if her message to Mahler hasn't got through—

Copper and salt in her mouth from where he'd hit her, mingling with the taste of her fear, making her retch again. The jolting suddenly intensifies, but the car's moving more slowly now, as though they're travelling over rougher ground. Where, though? *Where?*

Slowing down. Stopping. The slam of a car door and footsteps coming closer. Coming towards her. And she's praying, *don't let him, please don't let him—*

The boot lid is thrown open, the grey light blinding after the darkness. And Jamie's peering down at her. Looking the same as he always does. Looking like her friend. How can he still look like Jamie, after everything he's done?

'We're here. Do I have to carry you, or will you walk? Be easier on both of us if you do.'

Walk. Yes, she'll walk. She nods frantically, and he hauls her out of the boot, cursing as the leg pocket of the cargo trousers she's wearing snags on the catch. He dumps her on the ground – gravel, she thinks, it's gravel, they're in a car park somewhere – and reaches in to the boot. He stuffs something inside his jacket, and turns back to her. And when she sees what he's holding, her breath freezes in her throat.

She scrabbles backwards, her top rucked up behind her, her world shrunk suddenly to the scrape of the wet gravel on her skin. And the dull glint of the knife in his hands.

'Stop it, Anna.'

Jamie, walking towards her. Not fast, not hurrying, because there's no need, is there? The car park's deserted, and he's got all the time in the world.

Half a dozen paces and he's caught up with her. He grabs her shoulders, forces her to lean forward. Something cold and hard whispers against her wrist, and then her arms are free. The pain in her shoulders eases, but her arms are on fire now, pins and needles rushing in to torment her as she tries to make her fingers work again.

He slices through the rest of the tape and rips off the strip covering her mouth. 'There. Better? Right, up you come.' He watches her struggle to stand for a moment, then puts a hand under her arm and hauls her to her feet. 'Steady, now! Don't want you taking a tumble, not here.'

She stares up at him. Still trying to find a way for this not to be real, not the rain plastering her hair against her skin, not the terrified shivering she can't make herself stop . . . until the look in his eyes punches through her shock, her disbelief. The calm, unhurried, *purposeful* look. And the last hope she had of this being some mad hallucination leaves her.

'Jamie . . .' Her voice husky, pitted with fear. She licks her dry lips, tries again. 'You don't have to do this. You can drive away, just leave me here—'

'Oh, for God's sake – you're not stupid, so don't act it. You think I wanted this? I'm not a monster, Anna. I gave you every chance to walk away, but you just kept pushing – this is down to you, not me.' A dark amusement in the look he gives her. 'What, no playing for time, no sudden bid for freedom? Very sensible. Though there's nowhere to run if you did, of course.' His grip tightens on her arm. 'Come on then, let's walk.'

Understanding flowing through her, then. Ice in her veins, sharp and quick and painful. But with it, a kind of freedom. Anna takes a shuddering breath, lets her shoulders slump in defeat. 'Here?'

Jamie shrugs. 'It's what we planned, isn't it? The closing scenes here at Badbea, where the Sutherlands and the Grants and the Gunns scratched their living on the edge of nowhere while their landlords filled the straths with sheep.' He puts his hand under her elbow, guiding her along the path. 'Come on, the monument's this way. Badbea should be seen on a day like today, don't you think? With a chill in the air and a good haar coming in off the sea. How else can we show what it was like for them?'

315

Fear creeping up her spine, making her throat close up. She shakes the hair back from her face. *Keep talking.* She's got to keep him talking. Keep his mind off the knife, and what he's planning to do with it. 'You're right. But you don't—'

'Over there, can you see it?' He jerks her to a halt, waves the knife at what looks like a tumbled drystone wall to the left of the path. 'The first of the abandoned houses – Sutherlands, I think, or Gunns, I forget which. And right down there, the final shot we'd planned, down by the cairn. That's what we were doing, you see, when you missed your footing and slipped. I tried to grab you, but . . .' he shrugs. 'Obviously, I'll be devastated.'

No. Not this. Not here. She shakes her head. 'You . . . you're not thinking straight. No one's going to believe we'd have come out here on a day like this, are they? The police aren't stupid, Jamie! They'll work it out—'

'No, they won't. Mahler and his dopey sidekick might wonder, but they won't be able to prove anything – and I'm a bloody good actor, when I need to be. I fooled you, didn't I?'

'Because I trusted you. Because I thought you were my friend, for God's sake!'

Letting the fear colour her voice. Letting herself tremble, her leg drag slightly as he urges her further along the path. 'Look, Jamie, I understand! You think I don't know what Morven was like? She just pushed you too hard, and—'

'Shut up!' The knife, slashing through the air. Freezing the words in her throat. 'You made your choice. Now move.'

'I'm trying!' Stumbling now, as the path gets steeper. Rockier. This is where he's going to do it, here as they approach the cairn, rising out of the sea mist beside the ruined dwellings. In a few seconds, this barren strip of coastline will be the last sight she sees.

Anna takes a last look round. And pitches forward with a cry of pain. 'My leg! Jamie, please . . .'

Shielding her hand with her body as he hauls her upright. And then moving, slamming the rock she's grabbed into the side of his face, as hard as she can. Feeling it connect, feeling the sudden hot spurt of blood, hearing the crack of bone and his howl of pain and shock.

Releasing her, he drops the knife and staggers backwards, hands clutching at his face. And she's rooted there, watching, as though she's turned to stone. Until the screaming voice in her head tells her to run, to move. *Now!*

She runs. Stumbling, tripping in the rutted ground with its gnarled heather and bog-myrtle tufts. Feet slipping, sliding in the muddy channels, heart hammering. Running against the rain, against the wind, praying she's picked the right direction, praying—

A noise behind her. Footsteps? Yes, footsteps – slow, half-muffled by the rain and wind, but definitely footsteps. Getting nearer? Don't look back. *Don't.* She forces herself on, dodging between the rocks and drystone ruins, thanking God she's wearing dark, hard-to-spot clothing.

'Anna!'

Before she can stop herself, she half-turns. And without warning, her ankle fails her.

She pitches forward and rolls into a waterlogged gully. An instinct she didn't know she had makes her pull into a ball, arms raised to protect her head, but the ground is littered with stones and she feels herself being battered as she falls.

Scant inches away from the ruins of an abandoned dwelling, she manages to grab the stump of a broken-off fence post. She clings onto it, not daring to move. Not daring to breathe as she listens for the sound of his footsteps, not daring to look up in case he's standing right beside her and the last thing she sees is the knife glinting above her . . .

When she's sure he's not coming closer, at least for now, she inches her way on her stomach towards the drystone wall. She rolls behind its cover and lies there, heart thudding in her chest as the minutes pass. Where is he? If he's somehow doubled back, got between her and the car park . . .

As the rain stills momentarily and the cloud breaks, she dares to raise her head above the wall. At first, she can't see him anywhere, and a shiver of panic arches up her spine. But then she spots him – further away than she'd thought, thank God. Jamie's hunched against the cairn, holding something to his face.

She'd hurt him badly, then. Badly enough for him not to come after her, at least for a while. At least until he's figured out a way to take her unawares. Anna shakes her head. Not going to happen, Jamie. Not this time.

Her instinct is to make for the car park, as fast as she can, while he's still caught off balance, but she daren't risk it, not yet. Her leg is screaming at her and if she tries to move too quickly, it's going to give out on her completely and then she'll have no chance against him, none at all. And if he decides to make his move and come after her while she lies here, what then?

Anna thinks of what he'd done to Morven. What he'd have done to her, if she hadn't seen a chance to get away and grabbed it with both hands. And the answer comes quick and clear and certain – if he comes after her again, she'll do whatever it takes to survive.

49

2.30 P.M.

Jamie Gordon's House

Fergie's voice is fading in and out as Mahler runs back to the car. 'Chopper ... doesn't think he'll get there, visibility's too poor. Boss, you need to wait for back-up – Brora and Golspie cops are at an incident in Lairg, but Braveheart's got Dornoch on their way to you, and—'

'Jesus bloody Christ!' Mahler tosses the phone onto the passenger seat and throws the car into reverse. The nearest firearms unit is in Inverness, traffic are in Dingwall and the only back-up he can expect is thirty minutes away. Christ Almighty, why hadn't he called her earlier? Why hadn't *she* called him earlier?

Down the hillside, hurtling towards the town on the rutted single-track road, stones and cotton grass churning under his wheels. Touching the brakes at the roundabout and racing back towards the road to Badbea as the weather finally breaks and fat aggressive raindrops spatter the windscreen.

All the pieces are coming together now, showing him the shape he's been searching for. Showing him what Gordon had done, how almost faultlessly clever the man had been. If Donnie Stewart had been less easily influenced, if Gordon had been spotted leaving his hotel on the night of Morven's murder . . . and then there was Anna.

Anna must have been a complication he hadn't bargained for. But Gordon had thought on his feet, adapted his original plan. And exhausted, jet-lagged Anna had been the perfect alibi, hadn't she? All it would have taken is a little recreational something slipped in her drink, something to make her hazy, confused enough not to notice him resetting the clock in his car. And the next morning, a dull-witted detective inspector without the brains to see what was in front of his nose had done the rest.

Anger and a slow burn of shame mocking his stupidity, his slowness as he clears the village, following the main road north. Thanks to him, they'd been chasing Connor Ryan when they should have been on Gordon's trail. Thanks to him, Donnie Stewart—

Mahler cuts off the train of thought, makes himself refocus. Time enough for recriminations later. Right now he needs every bit of concentration he can muster.

He glances at the satnav. Passing Navidale now, the broad sweep of the A9 beginning to veer away from the sea, the woodland turning into Caithness scrub as the road winds north. The slow creep of fear, crawling up his spine as he realises just how much of a start Gordon's got on him. And what a perfect spot he's chosen for another murder.

Badbea.

Badbea, the ruined Clearance village perched on the edge of the cliff. Desolate enough on a brilliant summer's day, but on a day like this . . .

The sign for the turn-off is so small he nearly misses it.

Mahler pulls off the road and kills the engine. Gordon's 4×4 is in the furthest corner of the deserted car park. It's facing the road, the driver's door half-open, but there's no one inside.

320

Mahler tries for a signal on his mobile, but there's nothing. He goes over to the car, touches the bonnet – cool, but not entirely cold. Still a chance, then.

The 4×4's boot is open, a snag of thin, dark fabric caught on a spur of exposed metal where the carpet's been rucked up. In the corner, a rolled-up towel, sticky-bright with blood, placed as though to protect the boot's interior. So he'd hurt her, then. But not fatally. Not yet.

Mahler scans the sky, but there's no sign of the coastguard chopper. Gordon's chosen his time and place well, confident no one would brave Badbea in weather like this. Confident he'd have all the time he needs to deal with the last obstacle in his path. But if he finds out Anna's sent that message . . .

The weather is closing in, making it hard to see more than a few metres ahead. Time to move, before visibility deteriorates any further. Mahler sets off following the path, but realises it's too risky – the wind and rain are muffling his footsteps, but it's not enough. He steps off the gravel into a rut of peat-darkened water, cursing as the freezing liquid oozes over his shoes, and heads for the clifftop at a punishing half-crouch, ducking low whenever the thinning undergrowth threatens to reveal his position.

The rain is heavier now, driving needle-sharp against his face. He almost trips over the remains of a fence flattened by the wind, running roughly parallel to the path. Using it as a guide, he follows the land as it slopes down past the ruined buildings, towards some sort of memorial cairn. He's almost there when a figure rears up out of the greyness in front of him.

If Gordon had been ready for him, Mahler wouldn't have had a chance. But Gordon clearly hadn't been expecting him to be there, and his split second of indecision gives Mahler the time to react. He dodges sideways, reaching for Gordon to try and get him in an armlock, but Gordon recovers quickly. His fist lashes out, catching Mahler on the side of his jaw – it's a glancing blow, not a full-on punch, but it's Mahler's turn to be taken by surprise. While he's still scrambling to stay on his feet, Gordon swings at him again. This time, something slams into his side and connects with a rib. Something hard. Something heavy.

Mahler pitches forward onto his knees, gasping for breath, but there's a rustle of movement behind him. Winded, he rolls sideways moments before whatever Gordon's using as a weapon smashes down again. But he doesn't roll far enough – the blow misses his head but slams into his upper arm. Pain explodes along the bone and into his shoulder, white-hot, agonising. Mahler grits his teeth, fights to stay conscious as the world starts to grey out around him.

When his vision clears, Gordon is bending over him, holding a wheel wrench. Anna's managed to damage him, that much is obvious – he's swaying slightly, and his face is a mess. One eye is swollen closed, the cheekbone underneath a battered, bleeding ruin. In spite of everything, Mahler raises a faint smile. Gordon's still on his feet, though. And he's still gripping that bloody wheel wrench.

'So she managed to get a message to you after all – I did wonder. And here you are, her white knight come to save her.' Gordon squats down beside him, smiling, as though he's chatting to an old friend. 'Really, this is the best you could do? I think she was expecting better.'

Was. Mahler tries not to let the implications of that take hold. 'Of course not. My back-up—'

'Isn't going to get here in time, is it?' Gordon stands up, brushes off his jeans. 'That's if it's coming at all – crap time to choose to throw away the rule book, Inspector! I hope it won't reflect too badly on you when they hold the public enquiry.'

'Where is she? Where's Anna?'

'Temporarily misplaced. But don't worry, I'll find her later.' Gordon glances down at Mahler, who's fumbling for his phone with his good hand, and shakes his head. 'Seriously?'

He plants his foot on Mahler's arm. The pain screams up towards his shoulder, bursting like a signal flare along his nerve endings. 'Stop trying to be a bloody hero. Anna won't thank you for it – and it's not like anyone's going to know, are they?'

A fuzziness creeping into his brain. He squints up at Gordon, who's flickering in and out of sight. Think. Focus. *Talk*. 'There are three people dead already. Isn't that enough for you?'

'You think I wanted this?' Gordon reaches inside his jacket. And pulls out the hunting knife. Small. Serrated. Deadly. 'I made a mistake. One mistake, twenty bloody years ago—'

'You killed Janis Miller. Call that a mistake?'

'I . . . I only meant to frighten her. It just . . . it happened. And I moved on. What else could I do? I worked hard, made a good life – you've heard about my charity work, right? I gave back. What happened with Janis was all over and done with, until—'

'Until Morven threatened to rake it all up again. And you killed her for it.'

Gordon's face hardens. 'Trying to keep me talking until the cavalry arrives? I think we both know that isn't going to happen.' He looks round at the clifftop, gives a satisfied nod. 'Wind's getting up nicely, isn't it?' He holds up the knife so Mahler gets a good look at it, and smiles. 'On your feet. Time to take a walk.'

The pressure on Mahler's arm disappears. Gordon moves aside, just enough to let him stagger to his feet, and grips his other arm above the elbow. 'Move.'

Mahler lets himself be pushed along the path, past the memorial cairn. How much further to the cliff edge? The rain is easing a little, but not enough to make out anything beyond the ruined tumbles of stones.

'The children were tethered here like cattle,' Gordon says in his ear. 'Wind plucking at them from morning till night, even in the summer months. Can you imagine living like that? Knowing the slightest mis-step, a moment's inattention—'

Now. Mahler pushes his good elbow back and up, driving it towards Gordon's solar plexus. His aim's not perfect – Gordon's grip on his upper arm absorbs a lot of the momentum and the angle isn't great – but he connects with the man's upper abdomen with enough force to wind him. Gordon grunts, doubles over, and the knife slips from his fingers to clatter on the path.

Mahler scrambles over to kick it out of his reach, but Gordon's up again and coming for him, eyes and mouth wide, near-feral, hands preparing to lunge—

Movement by his side. A filthy, white-faced figure launching itself at Gordon's back, bringing something down on his shoulders, his head. Stepping back to watch as he crumples forward into a pool of peat-stained water. Frowning, assessing. Raising its arm again—

'Anna! Are you okay?'

No reaction. Mahler calls her name again. Finally, she turns to look at him.

'Inspector?' She walks towards him, slowly, like a sleepwalker. She's limping badly and there's blood running down her face, but she's still gripping the fence post and her eyes are wide, stunned. 'He killed Morven.'

'I know.' The pain is huge, now, a stalking beast with fangs and claws. He grits his teeth and makes himself focus on her face. 'Anna, did he hurt you?'

'He killed that other man, too. The kitchen porter at Bunchrew. And he told me he wasn't a monster. How . . . how could he say that, after everything he'd done?'

'I don't know. Look, I need you to put that down now. Can you do that for me?'

'I . . .' she looks down at her hands, as though she's trying to work out what to do. Then she slowly lowers the bloodied fence post. 'What about him?'

Mahler uses the memorial cairn to haul himself upright and drags himself over to Gordon. 'Let me see.'

He bends over the man. He's unconscious, and the wounds on his head are bleeding heavily, but he's still breathing and his pulse is steady enough. Mahler tries his mobile again – still no signal, but the weather's easing. And if June hasn't heard from him or the Dornoch police yet, she'll have half the Division heading towards Badbea by now.

'He's not in any danger. There are more police on their way, and they'll radio for an ambulance when they get here. How about you? Any nausea, blurred vision—'

'Only when I look at him.' A momentary darkness in her face. 'Christ, I wish I'd hit him harder. I wish—' Her voice altered, fragmenting. She turns away, scrubs at her eyes. 'Sorry, sorry. God, this isn't me! I don't—'

'Anna, it's okay. It's just the shock, that's all. Are you cold?'

'Of course I'm cold, it's bloody freezing.' The hint of a smile, through blue lips, but the darkness is leaving her eyes. 'Can you make it back to the car park if I help you, Inspector?'

He shakes his head. The pain is tearing at him, rending him with poison claws. Staying conscious is the best he can hope for right now. 'We're best to stay here until help arrives. And Anna? You can probably call me Lukas.'

Silence. A faint uncertain sun softening the clouds. And Anna Murray smiling at him. Mahler reaches out and puts his good arm round her shoulders. Feels the fall of her wet hair against his neck, the touch of her damp, shivering skin as she leans her body into his. And this, he thinks, he can allow himself.

Not to name this raw, unfocused thing, not to give it substance – that absolution isn't his to claim, not yet. But in this moment, Anna is here with him. She's hurt and exhausted, but she's alive.

And in all the ways that matter, she has saved him.

50

MONDAY, 11 AUGUST

Burnett Road Police Station

The incident room is being dismantled. Whiteboards are being wiped down, phones disconnected, files packed away in boxes to await the procurator fiscal's final approval to prosecute. Considering the weight of evidence they'd recovered from his laptop and Gordon's Helmsdale house, together with Anna Murray's testimony, Mahler's fairly confident the fiscal's not going to have much of a problem with that.

He stands in the doorway to his office, watching the last set of photographs being taken down. Fewer ghosts, now, for him to deal with. Apart from Kevin Ramsay, who Mahler suspects has booked a seat in his nightmares for some time to come.

'We will get him, you know.' Karen walks over to the corner still set aside for the investigation. 'Braveheart's not going to let this one go cold.'

'I know.' Andy Black's attempt to build a case around Eddie Scrimgeour had imploded when Scrimgeour's ex had confessed to starting the rumour about an affair with Gemma. June's chewing-out of Black had been legendary, according to those passing her office at the time, and since then she's been seen prowling the incident room at all hours to make sure he's got the message.

But the investigation's being scaled down, all the same – just Andy, Karen and a few spare uniforms as needed. And with no new leads, Mahler wonders how long it'll be before Chae Hunt decides to redeploy Karen as well.

'You won't let it go either. You're too good a copper.'

Karen shrugs. 'It's the job, Lukas. It's what we do. We're thrawn buggers, aren't we? Don't like bastards like Gordon getting one over on us.' A grin. 'Though from what I hear, Anna Murray's got an eye for a chain of evidence herself. That file she'd put together on her sister—'

'Almost got her killed.' And had earned him his own bollocking from June when she'd heard about it. Though God knows what she imagines he could have done about it. 'But when you turned up that info on Janis Miller – that was good work, Karen. If you hadn't found that—'

A shrug. 'We were bloody lucky Gordon was mentioned at all – no one expected him to be at the party, and the glandular fever gave him the perfect alibi anyway. But I still don't get how he managed to make Anna Murray think he dropped her back at Bunchrew at ten, not eleven.'

Mahler shakes his head. 'He didn't, not really. Anna told us she thought it was closer to eleven, but she was pretty hazy about the whole evening and there was no-one on reception at Bunchrew to back up her version. For what it's worth, I think Gordon also reset the clock in his car before they drove back to Bunchrew, just in case she glanced at it. After that, Gordon needed to make us believe that he'd gone back to his hotel just after ten – which he did, of course. Only as soon as he got up to his room, he hopped out the window, down from the flat-roofed shed and doubled back to his car.'

Gordon had taken a massive risk leaving Anna Murray in his car alone, but what else could he have done? And Mahler's guessing he'd brought along a little chemical insurance to keep Anna suitably drowsy on the way back to Bunchrew.

'Crafty bugger. How long do you think he'll get?'

'Life, no question.' Which effectively means twelve years or less for the punishment part of his sentence. Though Mahler suspects the psychiatric reports will mean Gordon's likely to do his time at the State Hospital, the official name for the high-security psychiatric institution at Carstairs.

'So he bloody should.' Fergie looks up from the files he's sorting. 'He's had twenty years of life that poor lassie in Glasgow never had.'

'Janis Miller? Gordon said he hadn't planned to kill her.'

Fergie stares at him. 'You believe that?'

'It's what his lawyers will try to push. And he's certainly doing a good impression of a disordered mental state right now. But for the record . . . no, I don't believe that. I think James Gordon planned everything he ever did. And anything unexpected that cropped up, he just incorporated into his blueprint.'

'Like Donnie Stewart?'

'He was one of two things Gordon hadn't bargained for. The first one was Anna Murray – when Gordon called at Bunchrew, he'd intended one final attempt to make Morven drop the Janis Miller investigation.'

'He'd already made plans to kill her, though. He'd got everything prepared.'

Mahler nods. 'Including his alibi. But when he ran into Anna Murray, he thought on his feet and realised she could give him an even better one, if he held his nerve. Donnie Stewart, though – he was a real complication. In the beginning, Gordon thought he could handle Stewart by buying him off. When that started falling apart, Gordon started to panic. And he silenced Stewart the only way he could.'

'Bastard, eh?' Karen shakes her head. 'To think my sister's daft on those rubbish books of his.' A pause. 'So, Anna Murray . . . how's she doing now?'

'Pretty well, I'm told. She's remarkably strong-minded.'

A longer silence this time. Less . . . silent. Mahler looks up to see Fergie and Karen staring at him.

'You haven't seen her? Or spoken to her?'

'Not since Badbea, no.' Which is not entirely true. He has visited her in hospital, watched her in fretful, restless sleep. Apologised. Rewound the day to make it end with her unbroken, whole. Made promises he knows he will not keep. Can't allow himself to keep. 'But Maxine's doing an excellent job with the whole family. She keeps me informed.'

'Well yes, but . . . Anna Murray will be going back to the States soon, won't she?'

'I assume so, yes. Though she'll be back for the trial, obviously.'

'Obviously.' Another pause, as though they're waiting for him to add something. When he doesn't, Karen pushes her chair back and stands up. 'Right, then, I'm off to the Eastgate – Mina's found a new way of being a pain in the arse and it's my turn to warn her off.'

'I'll probably regret asking, but what's she up to now? And why does it need a DS to deal with it?'

Karen pulls a face. 'Braveheart reckons it's good for me to keep in touch with what's happening on the streets right now. And what's happening this week is that Mina's taken to loitering outside Markies, singing "Flower of Scotland" and pretending she's a "Yes" campaigner. You wouldn't believe the complaints we've been getting.'

'From which side?'

'Trust me, this one's neck and neck.' She starts for the exit, then turns back. 'By the way, word is Andy Black's thinking of moving on. Got a cousin in Florida, going to run a bar together or something.'

'Presumably not a gastro-pub, given his junk-food addiction.' Mahler allows himself a vision of Black somewhere in the Everglades, serving pitchers of beer to bandana-wearing, pool-playing patrons called Earl or Billy-Bob. And reflects that after all, his day has taken a turn for the better. 'Let me know who's organising the collection for his leaving do, won't you? And give Mina my best.'

51

MONDAY, 8 SEPTEMBER

Five a.m. A reasonable hour to be waking up on a duty day, when Mahler likes to be at his desk, properly caffeinated and halfway through his daily admin before the team files in for their seven-thirty briefing. Not so reasonable on a rest day after a week-long stint liaising with the drugs team on raids at half a dozen addresses throughout the city. Not reasonable at all when he'd finally fallen asleep at two-thirty with Maxine's latest case update imprinted on his mind.

He gives it until half-past before acknowledging defeat. He gets up and crosses to the window, opening the curtains to look out. The pre-dawn sky is already bright, sunlight touching the morning river with silver. The view had been one of the main reasons he'd bought this place – after years of living with a postage-stamp of tired city grass in what was laughingly called a garden flat in Hammersmith, the chance of waking up to sunrise over the Islands had been too good to pass up. Even though the attraction of waking up to any sort of sunrise is rapidly starting to pall, Mahler still reckons it was worth the money.

He could clear out the garage. Startle Marco and Duncan by actually taking up the offer of a day out on their boat. Drop in to see his mother at the recovery centre and then head over to the west coast, walk the Torridon hills. Or make a trip back to his grandfather's old place in Rogart, see if the 'for sale' sign's still outside . . . at five in the morning, he thinks, all these things are possibilities.

And for a while, he goes through the motions. Throws on garage-clearing-cum-hillwalking clothes. Watches the first episode of *Happy Valley* on catch-up because Fergie, Karen and half of Burnett Road seem to be enraptured by it – and, to his surprise, finds himself watching the second one as well. Until the clock in his head starts counting down. An hour until check-in opens. Forty-five minutes. Thirty . . .

When he gets to the terminal at twelve-fifteen, Anna Murray is waiting in the queue for security. Her hair is longer, less formal, and she's wearing some sort of draped scarf Karen would probably tell him is a pashmina in shades of sea-blue and midnight, over a white shirt.

And there is a moment when she hasn't seen him, when he could still choose to turn and leave quietly. But then the queue does a slow shuffle forwards, and she looks up. And perhaps there never was a moment when he could have left, after all.

'Lukas?' She ducks under the security tape, crosses over to him. 'I wasn't expecting . . . are you okay? How's your arm?'

'I was passing. And I thought you might like something to read on the flight.' He holds out the *100 Best Referendum Cartoons* he'd picked up in Waterstones. 'Unless you've already got it?'

She stares down at the cover image – a woad-painted Alex Salmond menacing Alistair Darling with an enormous thistle – and bursts out laughing. 'Thank you. I promise I'll treasure it.'

'Will you be back? Before the trial, I mean?'

She nods. 'If I can get more time off work. My parents . . . they'll need me to be there for them as much as I can over the next few months. And at some point, I'll have to make up my mind about what to do with Morven's flat – I mean, technically it's mine, but that just feels too weird right now.'

'I thought you'd decided to keep it?' The flat suits her, in a way he can't imagine it ever suiting Morven. 'It's clearly what she wanted.'

'I suppose so. But—' she breaks off to listen as the first call for her flight comes through. 'I'm probably not in the best place to make major decisions at the moment – though Glyn Hadley seems to think I ought to roll with it. Did I tell you he'd offered me representation if I wanted to talk to the production company Jamie had been in contact with? Just as a consultant, of course.'

'How would you feel about that?'

A shrug. 'At first I thought, no way. Anything he was connected with . . . but it's still a story that needs to be told, isn't it? He was right about that. And maybe if I do it, I can . . . I don't know, wipe his fingerprints off it. Make it about the people of the Clearances, not about him.'

'That would mean spending some time over here, wouldn't it?'

'Yes, probably.'

Silence. Which he could fill, perhaps. Reshape. But the words he has for her should come from someone different. Someone untainted. 'You shouldn't rush into anything. Take time to readjust to your surroundings again.'

She shrugs. 'I don't even know if I'll still have a job when I get back. Though *Monstrous Regiment* has been reissued – maybe it'll hit the bestseller lists, who knows? Might even outsell his.' A brittle anger in the look she gives him. 'You know what his signed copies are going for on eBay? Nothing sells like a triple bloody murderer, right?'

'I'm sorry. But we will get a conviction. And he will be locked up for a very long time, I promise.'

'That'll have to do, won't it? At least we won't have to put up with seeing his face next to Morven's every time some reporter does a piece on her. You know the worst thing, Lukas? The thing she'd have hated most of all? He turned her into a victim. And my sister was a lot of things, but she was never that.'

He searches for the right response to that. But decides maybe there isn't one.

'So, the eighteenth.' Anna points at the newspaper headlines on the stand at WH Smith, announcing the latest Yes/No opinion poll. 'Made up your mind yet?'

Mahler shakes his head. 'I don't know. I'd like to say I'm open to persuasion, but . . . I'm not good at taking a leap in the dark.'

'Me neither. But maybe sometimes it's the right thing to do.'

The second boarding call for her flight. The silence deepening between them. Forming a brief shape, and fading with her smile.

'Well, I'd better—'

'Of course.' A parting handshake? No, that would be faintly ridiculous. He settles for a smile and a hand raised in farewell. 'Safe journey, Anna.'

A nod. And a smile that doesn't quite make it all the way to her eyes. 'Take care, Lukas. Say goodbye to Fergie for me.'

She ducks back under the tape and runs to join the end of the security line. Not looking back, and why would she? He watches her disappear through the screens, and goes back to the car. Thinks about driving up to Rogart after all, but twenty minutes later finds himself heading along Ness Bank on autopilot towards his flat.

As though to mock him, when he turns into the driveway, Fergie's malodorous Audi is lurking in the car park. As usual, the other cars have given it a wide berth, as though its rusting paintwork and sagging suspension might be catching.

He pulls in at a respectable distance and walks over. Fergie's pushed his seat back and is dozing with his mouth open, the vibrato behind his snores making the disco-ball air freshener dance with every exhalation.

Mahler raps on the window. Fergie makes the sort of sound Mahler usually associates with documentaries about endangered rhinos, and sits up.

'I know I'm going to regret asking, but what the hell are you doing here?'

'Just passing. Flight get away all right, then? That's where you went, isn't it?'

'It was on my way. And yes, the flight left on time.'

Fergie produces a disappointed sigh. 'Ach, boss. You could at least— Oh, here, I'm stuck again. Hold on.' He unclips his seat belt, rams his shoulder into the driver's door until it gives up and lets him escape. 'Need to get the WD40 out again tonight, eh?'

Fergie glances at him. Clears his throat. And gives him the kind of sideways glance that usually comes with a health warning. 'You know Karen's passed her promotion?'

Mahler hadn't. 'Good for her.'

'Aye.' Another throat-clear. 'She's having a wee do tonight to celebrate – nothing big, just a couple of drinks and a bite to eat at Spoons.'

'That sounds . . . unmissable.' Like bubonic plague. Or some yet-to-be-discovered mutant flesh-boiling malady. 'But I'm not sure I can cope with that much excitement.'

There's a slow-gathering pain creeping under his ribs. Muscle strain, he tells himself – he's out of condition since Badbea, his arm still not back to full mobility despite the physio. But he will manage this, somehow. More running, perhaps. Maybe tomorrow, maybe tonight. Maybe every night until the image of her walking through departures has faded, locked in one of the dusty rooms in his mind.

Fergie shakes his head. 'Look, I know it's not your thing, boss. But it's like that course you wanted me to do last month, the challenging attitudes one – you never know, you might even enjoy it.'

'The one you faked an emergency call from Zofia halfway

335

through to get out of? On a scale of one to ten, how likely do you think that is?'

'Fair enough. But it wouldn't hurt to show your face, would it? You could always leave before the karaoke. And the kebabs.'

'Trust me, Fergie, I will.'

52

FRIDAY, 19 SEPTEMBER

HMP Porterfield

Liam Gerrity is in hell. Not because he's coming off the gear – he's still on remand, so he doesn't get hassled too much by the substance misuse do-gooders. And anyway Liam knows people who . . . know people. People who don't want Liam Gerrity to start rattling, who'll make sure he's sorted, even banged up in fucking teuchter town. Because he's seen and heard things. Done things, sometimes. But mainly he's kept his eyes open and his mouth closed and he reckons they appreciate that.

But today . . . ever since he woke up to the chainsaw snores of his cellmate, a specky little runt from the Western Isles whose poison-gas trainers he's convinced are a fucking health hazard, Liam's been dealing with a bad case of the twitches. And the more he tries to tell himself it's nothing, the worse it gets.

Part of it's the Referendum crap, he knows that. Yesterday, the place had been buzzing – a smell of something in the air, maybe excitement, maybe just something different for them to think about, who knows? Something that wasn't about what bastard was eyeing you up to see if you're worth taking on. Even if a couple of bams were swaggering about with their King Billy ink on display, making cracks that would have earned them a sore face if he'd come across them anywhere but here.

But this morning, Porterfield is like a morgue. Not just his wing, the whole fucking place. Like someone died. Like Scotland had been knocked out of the World Cup and the European Cup, both on the same day. By the Faroe Islands. Well, Christ, they should be used to that feeling, shouldn't they?

Liam thinks about heading to the gym – no classes for him, no work to attend, not on remand. Nothing to do and all day to do it in, if he wants to, and at least out of the cell he's spared sheep-shagger boy's amazing toxic trainers. But on the way there, he starts twitching again, the full hairs standing up on the back of his neck thing, and he knows someone's watching.

One of the new guys, he thinks. Last week's special delivery from the castle had brought a new load of chancers to the wing – not just teuchters, this time. Couple of Eastern Europeans, a lad from Methil, and another guy he's only glimpsed a couple of times. First-timer, probably, keeping his head down and trying not to be noticed. Still, there's something about the guy that bothers him. The sooner he hears back from that DI about transferring down to Perth, the better.

The feeling of being watched is suddenly worse, like hundreds of little beasties crawling up and down his spine. Fuck it, time to go. Liam turns to head back along the corridor . . . And an arm snakes out to wrap around his neck, almost jerking him off his feet. He claws at the arm, trying to rip it free, but his other arm is wrenched upwards and he's slammed against the wall. He feels the rough stone surface opening a gash along his cheek, the sudden wetness trickling down his face. And *oh Christ, he can't breathe he can't breathe—*

More pressure on his throat. Lights dancing in front of his eyes, red sparks shooting through the black. And in the last fragmented second before everything disappears, a murmur in his ear of the words that form his personal welcome to hell.

'Mr Hollander says hello.'

ACKNOWLEDGEMENTS

So many people to thank here – firstly, *Good Housekeeping* for their First Novel competition, of course! My agent at LBA Books, Luigi Bonomi, and the brilliant Alison Bonomi who saw something in *Shadow Man* and who together with Francesca Pathak and Bethan Jones at Orion helped bring it fully into being. For technical help and advice on police matters, I'm hugely grateful to Paul Harrison, my dear friend Jenny Smedley, and Murray Aitken of the former Northern Constabulary – sorry for bugging you for what must have felt like forever on endless queries! Needless to say, any gaffes are my own and I apologise in advance for any which have slipped through.

Further grateful thanks are due to the management at Bunchrew House hotel (which is a lovely place and not at all the sort of place where grisly goings-on really happen!) for their kindness in allowing me to use their setting. Book Frisbee friends – you know who you are – thank you all so much for your unfailing support and general 'good eggedness'.

Special mentions to my lovely daughter Nicola Nagler, who always said I could do this, and my brother Roy MacPhail, who good-humouredly let me mine his life in San Diego for background and sense of place. Thanks also to my indefatigable friend, Anne Nicolson-Craig, whose kindness, optimism and hospitality are the stuff of legend.

And finally, Val McDermid and Louise Welsh, whose crime-writing course at Moniack Mhor quite literally changed my life, and whose continuing support and encouragement has meant more than I can say.